THE MELISSA RING

BOOK 1 OF GRAY'S FORREST

◁ ROBERT WAYNE BEE ▷

RowaBe
PUBLISHING

The Melissa Ring by Robert Wayne Bee

Copyright © 2014 by Rowabe Publishing

Rowabe Publishing, LLC
P.O. Box 5405
Evansville, IN 47716-5405
www.rowabe.com

ISBN 978-0-578-14884-7

This book is a work of fiction. Names, characters, places, events either are products of the author's imagination or are used fictitiously. Any resemblance to actual persons, living or dead, or actual events is entirely coincidental.

All Scripture is from the King James Version.

Tom Sheppard's VICTOR sermons are taken from material originally published in *40 Days* and *buzzwords & bee-attitudes* both written and published by Robert Wayne Bee.

Cover artist: Ryan Maglinger

For my best friend, Jeff Reine

Let your light so shine before men, that they may see your good works, and glorify your Father which is in heaven.

Matthew 5:16

CHAPTER ONE

Chapter One

As Paul rode his motorcycle across the Audubon Memorial Bridge, he found himself humming "Back Home Again in Indiana." He chuckled as he realized his mistake. While Paul was indeed returning to River City, River City was no longer in the state of Indiana; the southern part of the state had seceded to form the new state of Wabash during his five-year absence. Paul did not know how long it would take him to get used to that; but he did not know how long it would take to get used to River City being his home again either.

At the foot of the bridge, Paul passed the new sign, which read, "Welcome to Wabash, 100th State of the Union." Under that sign was a smaller white sign, which read, "Entering Adams County." Paul had not expected that one and wondered why they had changed the county name. One hundred yards past that was a more familiar sign, which read, "Welcome to River City." Paul eased the motorcycle onto the South Street exit ramp, navigated the sharp, two hundred seventy-degree turn, and then merged into the westbound traffic of South Street. This would take him directly to the Forrest.

The Forrest was not an actual forest but the old downtown and southwest section of River City. There were numerous theories about how the Forrest got its name. Some people believed it was because it bordered a large wooded area along the Wabash and Ohio Rivers, which it did. Others believed it was because so many of the streets in the Forrest were named after either trees or numbers, which was also true. Actually, the Forrest was a derogatory term for Forrest Township, which was named after Colonel Robert Forrest, a Revolutionary War hero.

When Paul reached Pine Avenue, he turned right and drove four blocks to the Pine Avenue Parking Garage. Paul entered the garage, passed the empty attendant's booth, wondered when it was last occupied, and turned right. The ground floor of the parking garage was full; it usually was. Even as deserted as the Forrest had become in recent years, there was still enough traffic to fill the bottom floors of the parking garage. The top floors occasionally filled; the basement floors never filled. There were reasons for that. First was demand. There was simply not enough demand for parking in the Forrest. Second was knowledge. Few people knew the basement floors even existed. Third was fear. Few, who knew about those floors, were brave enough to go down there. Some people even thought they were haunted.

Paul descended to the basement level, where there were a few cars. As he passed through the subbasement, he noticed one car parked next to the stairwell. He continued to the second subbasement, the bottommost floor, where there was only a pickup truck and a sports car. His paternal grandparents had parked his truck exactly where he had asked them; his maternal grandfather had purchased the new sports car on Paul's behalf and had it parked next to the truck against Paul's explicit wishes. Paul parked the bike he had spent the last five years on, next to the pickup and climbed off it.

Paul loosened the chinstrap and removed his helmet. The cold air of the parking garage was invigorating as it made contact with the light perspiration on his head. Paul had been riding for almost eight hours; and he was eager to stretch his legs and feel fresh air on his face even if it was cold. After he secured the helmet to the back of the motorcycle, he removed his saddlebag, which contained his possessions of the last five years. It was difficult to grasp that one stage of his life was now complete, as another one was just beginning.

He opened the driver's side door of the truck and tossed the saddlebag over onto the passenger side of the bench. Over the visor, as he knew there would be, there was an envelope with his name on it. Paul closed the truck door, opened the envelope, pocketed the keys that fell out, and extracted a note.

Dear Paul,

Welcome home! Pop and I know you can do this. Call us when you get settled in, sooner if you need something.

Love, Nan

PS: Your Dad would be so proud of you!

Paul reread the letter, smiled and almost cried before replacing it in the envelope. He folded the envelope and tucked it into the pocket of his jacket as he walked past a door, marked "Restricted Area--Authorized Personnel Only" and towards the stairwell.

As Paul climbed three flights of stairs to the ground level of the parking garage, he questioned his decision to avoid using the tunnels. It was certainly a quicker, more direct route to his destination; it would be much warmer than walking outside in the cold wind; and unless some vandal had broken down one of the access doors while he was away, the tunnels would be deserted. But, was that not contrary to his mission, what Nan and Pop had challenged him to do, what his entire family and a fair number of friends in their own ways had groomed him to do? If he ever intended to help the citizens of the Forrest and River City, he would have to walk amongst them.

When Paul emerged from the parking garage, he was rudely greeted by a cold gale from the north and the imposing facade of the Canterbury, which loomed in front of and over him. He turned left walking along Pine Avenue for a half block. Although he had just been on a motorcycle for almost nine hours, Paul had not felt cold until he exited the parking garage. The frigid wind hit his back; and Paul adjusted the scarf, which Nan had given him over five years ago, raising it higher on the back of his neck. Then, while painfully remembering a jaywalking citation he received from the River City Police Department on his first day of college several years ago, he turned right, crossing Pine Avenue legally at the intersection.

He was now walking west along 3rd Street with the Canterbury on his right. It had been his home during college; and it would be his home again. As he approached Oak Avenue, Paul was able to see more and more of the Imperial Hotel. Like the Canterbury, the Imperial Hotel towered physically over Oak Avenue; and like the Canterbury, it also towered over him emotionally. The Imperial Hotel was where he had worked as a front desk clerk during college; and he would be working there again, but this time, in a much different capacity. Turning right on Oak Avenue and lost in his reveries of yesterday, Paul collided with another pedestrian.

CHAPTER ONE

Chapter Two

Marcy Green was very late. Her alarm clock had failed to go off at the correct time. She had spilled an entire cup of coffee, the extent of her breakfast, on her blouse and skirt and had to change clothes hurriedly. The Canterbury's elevator had seemed to take forever. Worst of all, she had just missed her bus. Without enough money for a cab and with her own car still broken down, she had no other choice but to walk. Her interview was at 11:00; and it was already 10:35; but she had nineteen blocks to walk in heels. She would never make it in time; and she really needed this job. That was when she was knocked to her feet by a pedestrian coming around the corner while looking up at the buildings.

"I'm sorry. I wasn't looking where I was going. Let me help you back up."

Marcy was back on her feet again more from the strength and determination of her new benefactor than from her own. She stood there, defeated and blubbering semi-coherently about the trials of her day, as he scrambled to gather the contents of her purse for her, all while offering a sympathetic ear.

"There! I believe I successfully herded all your belongings back into your purse. Are you okay?"

As she reclaimed her purse, she made her first real eye contact with him. He was tall and handsome; and his eyes were a most hypnotizing blue.

"I said are you okay?"

"What? Oh! Thank you; yes, I'm beautiful. I mean I'm okay; you're beautiful. I mean…"

Marcy took a deep breath and a moment to compose herself, as the man hid a chuckle.

"I'm late for a job interview; and I really need to go."

"Let me drive you there; it's the least I could do."

Marcy hesitated for a moment before replying meekly.

"Okay."

"My name's Paul, Paul Gray."

Paul extended his hand; and Marcy took it.

"Marcy, Marcy Green."

"It's very nice to meet you Marcy Green. I'm parked at the Pine Avenue Parking Garage."

Paul pointed behind himself with his thumb, while offering his left arm.

Marcy grabbed his bicep as they walked east along 3rd Street.

"Where is your job interview?"

"Crookston Tower. Crookston Enterprises is looking for an administrative assistant."

"Well, I hope you get the job."

"Thanks."

"Step inside out of the wind. I'm parked in the basement. I'll bring my car up, so you don't have to walk."

Marcy watched as Paul ran down one flight of stairs and listened as he quickly descended two more levels and opened the stairwell door. Now, there in the silence of the parking garage, while she was waiting for him to retrieve his car, she realized how calm she was around him, a man she had never met. She could hear a car approaching in the distance; and she wondered what type of car he drove.

He was wearing jeans and a leather jacket, so she hoped he was not riding a motorcycle or driving an old pickup truck. However, she was not in a position to be so demanding; she would have to take whatever was offered. To her surprise, a red sports car pulled up next to her. Paul jumped out of the car and rushed around to the passenger door, opening it for her. She thanked him as she sat down in the car. Paul rushed back around to the driver side and took his seat behind the wheel.

Crookston Tower would normally be thirty-two blocks away; but many years ago, the Crookston family had a grand vision of building a huge tower in the middle of the Forrest and having all roads lead to it. They purchased and cleared four city blocks and built Crookston Tower; then they purchased even more land to construct two diagonal boulevards through the city. Many long-time residents of River City, who hated the confusion these diagonal roads caused, referred to the two boulevards as Crookston's Scar.

Crookston Circle, a roundabout, encircled Crookston Tower, with four streets leading away from it. Center Avenue to the north and south, Main Street to the west and east, Independence Boulevard to the southwest and northeast, and Freedom Boulevard to the northwest and southeast. As a result, Crookston Tower was only nineteen blocks away.

"Is the River City Diner still there?"

The question took Marcy by surprise. She was lost in a beautiful daydream, where Paul was her handsome boyfriend and he was taking her on a date in this beautiful car.

"I'm sorry. What?"

"I asked you if the River City Diner is still there."

"Oh! Yeah! It is; I haven't eaten there in a really long time though, so I can't vouch for whether it's still any good or not."

"I ate there almost every day when I was in college and working at the Imperial Hotel."

"I take it that you're not from around here."

"No. I was born and raised in Georgia, moved to Puerto Rico when I was fourteen, came to River City for college and stayed here six years; but I've been traveling around the country for the last five. Today is actually my first day back in River City."

"Well, welcome back to River City, Paul Gray."

"Thank you. It looks like we're here, Crookston Tower, and by the look of the clock, with several minutes to spare."

Paul parked the sports car along the curb, turned on his emergency flashers and ran around the car to the passenger side to open the door for her. She smiled coyly and took his hand as she exited the car.

"Thanks. I'm glad I ran into you; you've been a real lifesaver."

"My pleasure! And, good to meet you, Marcy. Perhaps, I'll see you around."

"Perhaps."

Her response was barely audible above the noise of the traffic.

"I better go before a cop gives me a ticket. Good luck on your job interview."

"Thanks."

This was even softer, more mouthed than voiced.

The red sports car was out of sight; and she wondered if she would ever see him again. Her earlier anxiety had returned to fill his absence. She turned to face the revolving door, which served as the tower's main entrance, and accidentally ran into it instead.

Chapter Three

The River City Diner was still there, just as Marcy had said it was. After taking her to Crookston Tower for her job interview, Paul had driven the sports car back to the space next to his pickup truck and retraced his steps to the intersection of 3rd Street and Oak Avenue; but this time, he was careful not to upend one of his fellow Riverites. Now, walking north on Oak Avenue with a strong wind hitting him in the face, Paul finally spotted the door to the restaurant. The other spaces were all empty; the diner was now the Canterbury's sole first floor tenant. The city was not the thriving metropolis he remembered. Reality was crashing down on him as the gravity of his mission now became much heavier. River City, particularly the Forrest, was quickly becoming a ghost town. Even the Imperial Hotel, although it was still open, looked tired and defeated. Paul wondered if he would be able to affect any meaningful, lasting and positive change.

Entering the diner was a badly needed salve as it provided a stark difference to the outside world just when he needed it most. It was cloudy outside; but it was brightly lit inside. It was cold outside; but it was warm inside. Outside sounded like a dying city; inside sounded like life. Best of all, it smelled like home; it even felt like home. Paul removed his jacket and scarf; hanged them on the coat tree, which none of the other diner patrons seemed to be using or to have ever used; and slid into a window-side booth near the diner's south wall. As Paul settled in, a young waitress, barely out of high school, approached his table.

"Welcome to the River City Diner. My name is Ashleigh; and I'll be your server."

She handed him a menu and placed a small glass of water next to him.

"I'll give you few minutes to look over the menu."

"Thank you."

Paul took a sip of water as he glanced at the menu. He wondered why diners even had them, since every diner seemed to serve the very same thing--comfort food. Still, he looked over his options a second time as he took another sip of water. Although he felt genuinely comfortable and even at home for the first time in a very long time, he also had the strangest feeling that he was being intently watched. He surveyed the other diners but found nothing unusual.

"Are you ready to order?"

Ashleigh had appeared at his table startling him slightly.

"Oh! Yes. I'll start with a cup of chili and a garden salad."

"Would you like shredded cheddar cheese on the chili?"

"Please!"

"And what dressing would you like on your salad?"

"Italian."

"And to drink?"

"More water and…uh…a strawberry milkshake."

"Would you like to go ahead and order your meal now?"

"Yes. I'll have the mushroom and Swiss burger."

"How would you like that cooked?"

"Medium."

"And your side?"

"Onion rings, please."

"A cup of chili with shredded cheese, a garden salad with Italian dressing, a mushroom and Swiss burger cooked medium with onion rings, and a strawberry milkshake. Will that be all?"

"For now."

"I'll have that chili right out."

"Thank you, Ashleigh."

As Paul waited for his food, he looked out the window at the traffic on Oak Avenue. He noticed the faces of the pedestrians; their facial expressions were as bleak as the city they inhabited. The city was not the only thing that was dying; the people were losing hope that things would ever get better. Ashleigh brought Paul the chili and a taller glass of water. The cup containing the chili sat on a saucer, which also contained a generous amount of individually wrapped crackers.

"Excuse me, ma'am. Do you have any hot sauce?"

"Our chili's already very spicy. Are you sure?"

Paul silently laughed at a private joke.

"Oh, I'm positive."

Ashleigh quickly returned with a bottle of hot sauce; and Paul generously added it to the chili as the waitress's eyes widened in disbelief. Paul slowly savored the first spoonful. It was wonderful and meaty; and of course, it was hot both in temperature and in seasoning, comfort food at its finest.

For the first time since he entered, Paul turned his attention towards the television hanging in the opposite corner of the diner. The volume was turned down low; and he was sitting too far away to hear it; but it was a local kid's show, called *Zumbo's Hour O' Fun*, so Paul and the few patrons, who were facing the television, were not that interested to know what was being said anyway. One clown, who Paul assumed was Zumbo, had green hair and was dressed in a black jumpsuit with pink, orange and green dots.

He was pushing another clown, who had blue hair and was dressed in blue and yellow, out a window. Paul turned away in disgust; he absolutely hated clowns. However, Paul was not just averting his eyes because of the programming; he was also conspicuously searching the diner. While he had eaten his chili and watched the television, he had had that feeling of being watched again; but again, he could not determine who was watching him.

"So, how was the chili?"

Ashleigh had startled Paul. He had not even noticed that she had exchanged his empty chili bowl for a salad and refilled his water.

"I'm sorry. Yes, the chili was great; thank you. I was just watching that ridiculous show on the television. I can't believe it can stay on the air as violent as it is."

"Oh, that! Zumbo's a local celebrity and has been for a few years now. He owns a chain of fast food restaurants, a chain of toy stores, and a couple of local factories. He even opened an amusement park and hotel on the east side of the city just last year."

"Really?"

Ashleigh nodded but looked around to see who was within earshot before bending over the table and whispering something to Paul in confidence.

"If I were you, I wouldn't buy any of his products or services."

Paul's disdain for clowns turned to a curious fear as he read the troubled expression on Ashleigh's face. He wondered what she knew about Zumbo and if she would ever tell it.

"The news will be on in a few minutes and we'll turn the sound up so you can hear it."

With that, Ashleigh promptly walked away from the table as if nothing had happened and Paul soon turned his attention to the salad. The salad was very basic: a bed of iceberg lettuce with chopped onions, sliced cucumbers and cherry tomatoes; the Italian dressing was on the side in a small soufflé cup. The salad was fresh; but Paul was secretly hoping for something more, possibly some meslun and broccoli flowerets. He poured half of the dressing onto the mixture of vegetables and lightly tossed the salad with his fork before eating it. As he ate, he ruminated on clowns—very evil clowns.

When Paul finished eating the salad, Ashleigh returned and replaced the dirty plate with one containing a cheeseburger and onion rings and a tall glass containing a strawberry shake. Everything was sinfully delicious. The cheeseburger was flame-broiled—medium—exactly the way he had ordered it. It was topped with an unusually thick slice of Swiss cheese, which was only lightly melted over the meat so as not to compromise the natural texture and flavor of the cheese. It was also topped with freshly sautéed, sliced mushrooms, not mushrooms from a jar. Paul could also detect an assortment of spices on the burger—cayenne pepper and garlic salt.

The onion rings were thick and crunchy; Asian breadcrumbs had been used instead of the traditional batter. They were served with a dipping sauce of ketchup, mayonnaise and horseradish—too much horseradish in Paul's opinion. He chose to finish eating the rings plain. The strawberry shake was heavenly though; according to the menu, it was a blended concoction of vanilla ice cream, whole milk and strawberries and topped with whipped cream, strawberry syrup and a whole strawberry.

As Paul finished eating his lunch, he finally discovered who had been watching him. The man was quite adept in the art of surveillance having so far been able to quickly avert his gaze before Paul could make him; but this time, Paul had appraised the room with his peripheral vision. Later, when it was not so obvious, Paul studied the man with great interest. He was very short; but he was not quite a dwarf. His complexion was very pale but he was not quite an albino. He was dressed in black—black suit, black shirt, black tie, black leather shoes, black pea coat, dark sunglasses, which was odd for a blustery fall day, and a black fedora.

The man caught Paul watching him and attempted to detour any suspicion by smiling. It was not an expression native to his face; and the overall effect was more unsettling than comforting. His gums, as well as his lips, were blood red, the only true color that could be found on him; and his pointed teeth seemed to be much smaller than they should be. The man was quite distinctive in presence; and Paul was particularly good with faces; but while he was confident that he did not know this man, he had a disconcerting feeling that the man knew exactly who he was. Paul stood up and crossed the diner quickly, which took the mysterious little man by surprise.

"Do we know each other?"

The man was less skilled at handling confrontation; and his anxiety became obvious.

"Why have you been staring at me?"

A few diners were starting to watch the commotion, as the strange man simply ignored Paul's questions, looking instead towards the table, at which Paul had been sitting. At once, he smiled broadly, causing Paul and the other diners to turn their heads to see what the man was watching. There was nothing at the table; it was empty. The man had used the diversion to push Paul out of the way and rush out the door.

"Is everything okay?"

It was Ashleigh. The waitress's presence was a signal to the diners that the incident was over; and they returned their attentions back to their lunches.

"Yeah. I think so. I caught that man staring at me; he's been staring since I entered the diner."

"Well, you are quite handsome."

Ashleigh blushed and smiled meekly at the same time; but Paul simply ignored the compliment. He was more interested in the stranger's identity.

"Do you know who he is?"

"He's not a regular. I've never seen him before. Do you want me to call the police for you?"

"No. It was probably just my imagination."

"Well, perhaps, I should call them anyway. He left without paying for his coffee."

"Put it on my bill and bring me a cup as well. Do you have any pie too? Pecan perhaps?"

"Ed just took a fresh one out of the oven. Whipped cream?"

"Please!"

Paul slowly returned to his table; and Ashleigh brought his pie and coffee.

"Did you need cream or sugar for your coffee?"

"No, I take it black."

"If you need anything else just let me know."

Paul smiled at her as he nodded his approval. As Ashleigh had said, the pie was indeed warm, but not too hot, slightly gooey and delicious. Pecan pie was his favorite; and it always reminded him of Nan, whose particular talent was baking. Her pies were the best; but this one was very good too. The coffee was hot and strong. Eating regularly at this diner and at Nan's would soon pack on the weight, so Paul made a mental note to start exercising immediately.

Paul had finished the pie and was nursing his coffee as he looked out the window towards the Imperial Hotel. There, standing near the hotel's main door, was the strange man from the diner; he was still watching Paul intently. Paul craned his neck to see him better and noticed the man quickly averting his gaze away from the diner and towards the hotel. Whatever the man saw through the hotel window flustered him and he hurried away. Ashleigh turned up the volume of the diner's television, so the patrons could hear the news, which was just beginning.

It's Channel 42 News at Noon brought to you with limited commercial interruptions by Fifth National Bank. Good afternoon, I'm Brad Newton.

Canada is now part of the United States! The House of Representatives voted unanimously Saturday night to accept the Senate bill recommending statehood. Instead of joining as one large state though, each province and territory of the former nation will enter the union as separate states, with the metropolitan areas of Toronto and Montreal each becoming their own state as well, increasing the number of states in the union to one hundred sixteen. The President will sign the bill into law during a special East Room ceremony on Monday.

The spirit of international joining continued yesterday, as King William V formally received the President of Burundi at Buckingham Palace. Burundi was one of two remaining unaligned nations, the other being Ethiopia. Burundi now becomes the one hundred eleventh nation to join the Commonwealth of Nations, a group originally founded as former British colonies. The organization, headquartered in London, now exists as an economic union of the world's democracies.

Civil war continues in Ethiopia as Muslim rebels captured the city of Bahir Dar this weekend after a month long siege. In August, forty-six percent of Ethiopians voted to join the United States of Africa, forty percent voted to join the Organization of Islamic States, nineteen percent voted to join the Commonwealth of Nations, while less than one percent voted to join the Russian Federation of Nations. Ethiopian Muslims have been protesting the validity of that vote. The International Red Cross estimates there have been twenty-thousand causalities in the Battle of Bahir Dar alone. Most of the casualties have been civilians.

The Jabberwock, a serial killer, who themes his murders to Lewis Carroll's Alice in Wonderland, has claimed the life of his fourth victim. Leonardo Pedina was found hanged in his Adams County jail cell Sunday night. His mouth had been covered with a nametag, which read "The Mouse." Pedina, also known as Topo Pedina, was connected to the L'Ombra crime organization and was awaiting trial on charges of racketeering and money laundering. If you have information on this or any of the crimes associated with the Jabberwock, you are asked to call the FBI.

Brenda Henderson was in River City this weekend campaigning for her husband, Senator Charles Henderson; but she took the opportunity to launch her own "Sour Seventeen" campaign against the fast food industry. WRCI reporter, Tricia Robertson has the details.

Her husband may be running for President; but Brenda Henderson has her own agenda—to promote healthy eating habits. Henderson unveiled a list of seventeen fast food franchises at a political rally Saturday night and challenged the restaurants on the list, which she dubbed the Sour Seventeen, to overhaul their menus, eliminating items, which are high in sodium, fat, and sugar and replacing them with healthier options. A spokesperson for Henderson explained that she selected River City as the location to issue her challenge, because it was recently ranked as the fattest city in the United States.

It is worth noting that River City is also the international headquarters of three chains on the list including Zumbo's Big Top Burgers, which Henderson specifically called out as being the worst of the worst. We contacted Zumbo's and the other restaurants for a response; but nobody agreed to grant us an interview. You can find a transcript of Brenda Henderson's speech and the list of restaurants at our website. From Roberts Arena, and for WRCI news, I'm Tricia Robertson.

Thank you for that report, Tricia.

The FAA needs your help to find a missing flight attendant. Global Airlines Flight 6676 landed safely this morning at 4:15 at River City International Airport; but Lisa Sanger, the flight's sole attendant was not aboard. Federal authorities have found no evidence of foul play and have questioned the passengers and crew; however, nobody remembers seeing her after takeoff. If you have any information concerning the fate or current whereabouts of Lisa Sanger, you are encouraged to call the FAA.

A twelve-year-old boy remains in a coma following a fall out of his second story bedroom window last week. Dougie Bishop of Nilesville, who enjoyed sitting on the roof at night to watch the stars, lost his footing Monday night when exiting through his window. Dougie Bishop is the son of Zoara Christian Church Assistant Pastor Aaron Bishop. During yesterday's services, Reverend Bishop called on his flock to join him in prayer for his son's recovery.

NASA reports all systems go for Thursday's launch of the Spaceship Olympus. It will take the Olympus seven months just to reach Mars. Once there, the crew of twenty-eight astronauts will spend one year living on the red planet, conducting experiments and starting construction on the Mars Space Station before returning home.

Marine biologists at UCLA have announced a major breakthrough in decoding dolphin communication. Dr. Merrick Tummler and his team have found what Tummler has called the Rosetta Stone allowing him to have very basic conversations with dolphins in their language. Last year, Tummler was awarded the Gylnedderkoppen Medal in Biology for an invention that replicates the sounds of the dolphin language. Tummler explained in a press conference Friday afternoon that last year he had discovered how to make the sounds and now he has discovered which sounds to make.

Developers have broken ground in South Illinois on what will be the world's first true arcology. When finished, Honeycomb City will house, educate, employ, and entertain six million residents. A representative from Skep Development, the engineering firm behind the design, construction and eventual operation of the mammoth complex, explained that everything a person could ever need or want will be readily available making it possible to live from cradle to grave inside the city without ever needing to leave. Construction is expected to take five years.

While residents of the future city will not need to leave, they will certainly have the ability to do so. Earlier this year, construction started on the high-speed rail lines, which will connect Honeycomb City to Chicago, Indianapolis, River City, Nashville, Memphis, Dallas, Minneapolis and St. Louis.

Western Indiana University is now officially Wabash University River City. The one hundred seventy-one year old institution had been allowed to retain the older name for the last two years despite the now geographical inaccuracy; but Chancellor Luther Grimsley, who is the second great grandson of university founder, Hubert Grimsley, said it was time for a change. Grimsley had long scoffed at the popular idea to rename the university after his family explaining that it needed to honor the region and not just one person or small group of people. Chancellor Grimsley also unveiled the university's new motto, "It wurks for you," which plays off the university's new acronym.

Captain Andrew Thomas, originally of River City, will assume command of the nation's newest and largest aircraft carrier, the U.S.S. Grover Cleveland. The Ford-class aircraft carrier, whose homeport will be Naval Air Station North Island in San Diego, has a displacement of one hundred twenty thousand tons and almost ten thousand crewmembers. During the commissioning ceremony, Captain Thomas gave the ship her motto: "A Stream of Light," which refers to President Cleveland's dedication of the Statue of Liberty in 1886.

Over eight years behind schedule, construction on the Millennium Mall in Nilesville is finally nearing an end. The project, which has been plagued with delays, stoppages, and setbacks, will be completed sometime next week. The mall will have a soft opening on November 1 with a grand opening on Black Friday weekend. Millennium Mall will be the second largest mall in the country behind the Mall of America in Bloomington, Minnesota.

After a yearlong engagement, Brendan Kenton, the Chairman and CEO of Kenton Energies, married the former Sarah Carpenter Saturday in a regal ceremony at the Zoara Christian Church; a lavish VIP-only reception followed at the tony Freundshaft Haus. Two years ago, Mr. Kenton was pronounced River City's Most Eligible Bachelor. The couple is expected to honeymoon in Italy.

After the break, we will look at this week's weather and check sports.

The anchorman's image dissolved into a commercial for Fifth National Bank. Paul hated commercials; and over the years, he had developed the ability to ignore them automatically. His unique skill kept him from even noticing the next commercial, which was for Zumbo's Big Top Burgers and their appropriately named Zumbo Burger, which was not at all approved by one Mrs. Brenda Henderson of Iowa.

Instead, Paul took the opportunity to ruminate over the events that had already transpired that day, his arrival in River City, his encounter with Marcy Green, and his interaction with the strange little man in the diner. Despite that man's departure from the diner, Paul still felt like someone was watching him. He conspicuously surveyed the diner and looked outside the window; but this time, he found neither the man nor anyone else watching him.

His unconscious effort to block out the commercials lasted much longer than necessary though. He also missed the weather report calling for sunny skies but colder temperatures and the results of several recent sporting events, including the losing streak of the Hornets and the shutout of the Sea Bees. Neither of these would have interested him much anyway

Local sportscasters always put a good spin on it; and the local teams certainly had a dedicated fan base; but all five of River City's professional sports teams were abysmal. There was the River City Hornets, which played professional football; the River City Snow Bees also known as the Bees, which played professional hockey; the River City Stingers, which played professional basketball; the River City Yellow Jackets also known as simply the Jackets, which played professional baseball; and the Nilesville Bumblebees, which played professional soccer. Nobody knew why but there seemed to be two unwritten rules: local teams must play poorly and name themselves after stinging insects. It is worth noting that the mascot at Western Indiana University, now the Wabash University River City, is the Fighting Rooster; and they have great teams with winning records.

Paul was not the only one in the diner, who was disinterested in the commercials, the semi-helpful weather reports and the news about failing local sports teams. At this point, the other diners started moving their attention to other matters, which for many of them meant finishing their meals, settling their bills and vacating the diner. The diner employees were coming to life too; a busboy cleared Paul's table of the accumulated dirty dishes leaving only the cup of coffee. Unlike the others, Paul regained interest, watching the last portion of the news.

Pop diva, Donna Aster, has canceled the remainder of her tour, which included an upcoming show at Roberts Arena. When asked by reporters, the singer gave no explanation; but a spokesperson for Miss Aster stated exhaustion and personal problems as contributing factors to the decision. If you had tickets to the show, you can obtain a refund in person at the Roberts Arena box office.

Despite admonitions from physicians and consumer protection groups, gamers are already lining up for next week's release of Hall of Doors. Critics claim that the virtual reality aspects of the game can lead to psychosis, blindness and permanent brain damage. Those cautions have not stopped eager fans though from lining up in the cold and rain to purchase a copy of the game, which is based on the 1980's cult classic television show of the same name. A sequel to the game is already in development.

And finally, this afternoon, local author, Gus Morton, will be at the

downtown Margins Bookstore signing copies of his new science fiction novel, Termination Shock; our own Tirole Triplets will be broadcasting their show, Good Afternoon, Tri-State, from Margins and interviewing Morton on his life and career.

That is all for Channel 42 News at Noon. Stay tuned for Good Afternoon, Tri-State. For everyone here at WRCI, I'm Brad Newton. Have a pleasant day.

Chapter Four

John Dorman consulted his notebook with great interest. It was almost time. He would need to be in place to verify his theory. John quickly gathered his coat and keys and rushed out his apartment door and down the hallway. Halfway between his apartment and the elevator though, he paused for a quick calculation. The Canterbury's elevators were old and slow; and he did not have time to wait for them. He turned around and sprinted towards the staircase instead.

He was not as young as he used to be; and forty-one flights of stairs were a lot for any age; but if he hurried, he would still beat the elevators and make it in time. It was very important to be in the right place at the right time today. Descending so many flights of stairs was winding him; but adrenaline and the excitement of the moment were recharging him almost as quickly. Reaching the first floor, he proceeded down the hallway and then across the lobby to the Oak Street Door, where he exited the Canterbury.

The cold wind immediately slapped his bare face; and John regretted not bringing a hat or scarf. There was certainly no time to retrieve them now; and he only needed to cross the street to the Imperial Hotel where he would be out of the elements to verify his hypothesis. Traffic was light, as it always was in the Forrest, so John took a chance by illegally crossing in the middle of the intersection. A few moments later, not only was he across the street and inside the Imperial Hotel; but he had commandeered a table in the hotel's lobby near the window where he could see everything.

John removed his coat and checked his watch. It must be his lucky day; he had actually made it with a couple minutes to spare. John decided to use these extra moments to catch his breath and compose himself before everything happened. He extricated his notebook from his coat pocket and turned it to the appropriate page, checking and rechecking his notes. He consulted his watch again. 10:35. It was time!

John craned his neck to see the intersection of Oak Avenue and 3rd Street. The subject of his interest should be appearing any minute. John also noticed a female running down the sidewalk in front of the Canterbury towards 3rd Street. She was distracted; and it was obvious that she was not looking where she was going. Predictably, she collided with another pedestrian at the corner.

It took a moment for John to realize what had just happened. The pedestrian into whom she bumped was the man John had been waiting all this time to see—Paul Gray. This could change everything. At this angle, he could not see much; but he was confident that it was Paul. He did not know the woman, although he recognized her as a fellow tenant of the Canterbury. John furiously made some new notes in his notebook making sure to document everything including the time.

After a few minutes, John watched Paul and the woman walk back in the direction Paul had just been moments earlier. No, this could not be happening; Paul was going in the wrong direction. It was not supposed to happen this way; it has never happened this way; there would be serious repercussions. After the staircase descent, he knew he did not have the energy to follow them, not starting from this distance. He would have to wait patiently; and hope that it was only a brief delay.

Fourteen minutes later, Paul returned, as if nothing had happened, and entered the diner; John almost missed it. With the one exception, everything else seemed to be going exactly as expected. John made more notes in his notebook and wondered what Paul had done and where he had gone during those fourteen minutes. He also wondered about the identity of the woman and what ripples she might have created in this timeline.

John surveyed the diner looking for any other unexpected differences; unfortunately, he found one. Across the diner from where Paul was sitting was a short, pale man. He recognized him immediately; it was one of Sam Hayne's family members. John thought the man's name was John, just like his own. What was he doing up here? Dorman checked his notebook. No, this man was not supposed to be here—not here, not now.

He was not the only one to spot him. Paul had spotted him too. John Hayne was watching Paul Gray; and Paul Gray was watching John Hayne. This was going to get very awkward very quickly. Fortunately, neither of these men knew that John Dorman was watching both of them intently and taking notes. Dorman watched Paul approach Hayne; and then he watched Hayne rush out of the diner. John Hayne crossed Oak Avenue illegally just as John Dorman had done earlier and took a position in front of the window where Dorman was sitting. Hayne was still looking towards the diner at Paul; and Dorman was quite literally looking over Hayne's shoulder.

Hayne happened to turn around and for one very long minute, he locked eyes with Dorman. Dorman could tell that Hayne recognized him too and was wondering why he was here, as much as Dorman had earlier. Confused, John Hayne quickly walked away.

Two unexpected interactions happening so close together! Dorman silently concluded that this timeline had been drastically altered but to what extent, at this time, he did not know. He would need some time to investigate both the identity of the woman and the nature of Sam Hayne's involvement with Paul Gray, before he would proceed further. John Dorman gathered his belongings, donned his coat and left the hotel lobby.

CHAPTER FOUR

Chapter Five

"Let me warm that coffee up for you."

A kindly looking older woman refilled Paul's coffee cup before he could either accept or deny the favor. She also took a damp rag and wiped down the table. What happened next pleasantly surprised Paul. The woman motioned to Ashleigh, and without instruction, the younger waitress retrieved the coffee pot and rag as the older waitress sat down at the table opposite Paul.

"My name's Georgia Hopper. My husband, Ed, and I own and manage this little place."

When Georgia mentioned her husband's name, she nodded towards the kitchen. Paul followed the direction of the nod over the counter and through a service window until he came eye to eye with a burly older man, who nodded a quick but warm and welcoming greeting before returning to his duties.

"Nice to meet you Mrs.—"

"No Mrs.; just Georgia," she quickly interrupted.

She had the same pleasantly disarming nature as her husband, a skill obviously well suited for their choice of business. Although he had only just met them, Paul already felt like he knew them and loved them.

"Very nice to meet you Georgia; I'm Paul Gray."

"Ashleigh told me you had some trouble with one of the other customers."

"Oh…no trouble. I just caught someone staring at me; and it made me a little uncomfortable."

Georgia laughed loud and long. The laughter was sincere and infectious. Paul was chuckling without realizing exactly why.

"Sweetie, if stares make you uncomfortable, get ready for a lifetime of misery, because a strapping young buck like yourself is going to receive more than your share of stares."

Georgia continued laughing; but Paul blushed.

"None of us recognize the guy; and he probably won't ever return; but if he does, we'll keep a close eye on him; and let you know what we learn."

Paul was unsure of how to respond to this.

"Uh…thanks."

The conversation abruptly went quiet but Georgia stayed at the table eyeing Paul intently. She grabbed his right hand with both of hers. For a moment, he wondered whether the strange little man from earlier was controlling her in some way. It lasted only a minute; but it seemed like an eternity. As quickly as the conversation died, it came back to life.

"You're okay, Paul. Better than okay, you're…special. Yes, we're going to get along just fine, you and me."

Paul looked confused over her sudden pronouncement.

"That? Oh, that's just a thing I do with the regulars; it helps me get a sense of them, whether I can trust them or not. Ashleigh thinks I'm psychic; Ed thinks I'm crazy; I think it protects me from people who have evil in their hearts."

Paul was regaining his good-natured composure.

"So, what did you learn?"

"Honestly?"

"Honestly."

Georgia took a moment to collect her thoughts. When she resumed speaking, her tone was very different. It was no longer folksy and hospitable but ominous and prophetic. Pauses, pregnant with gravity, separated her statements.

"You're not originally from around here; but you've been here before.

"You've recently returned after a long quest of self-discovery.

"You're here with a great purpose, a purpose chosen for you, although one you now have truly accepted as your own, a purpose so great though you don't think you quite have the ability to fulfill it.

"You have an impossibly high code of ethics for yourself; and you push yourself to excellence in everything you do.

"You care deeply about others and feel the need to help whoever, whenever and however needed, even if it requires a tremendous sacrifice on your part; however, you don't let many people inside.

"You're wealthy, extremely wealthy; but you don't want anyone to know just how wealthy, because you don't want to be defined by that wealth.

"Best of all, you're loyal, trustworthy and honest. I like that.

"You'll be a regular here, once a day at least I imagine; but you won't have a usual order; you crave variety; and you'll be a camper lingering over bottomless coffee cups, perhaps even doing some of your work here instead of in an office somewhere."

Paul said nothing. Georgia did not ask whether she was right. Paul's expression betrayed that fact. Georgia stood up but paused before leaving the table. She gently placed a hand on his shoulder.

"Don't question your abilities, Paul. You'll succeed at this great purpose of yours. It'll take a very long time though; and yes, there'll be challenges; but in the end, you'll succeed. I may have just met you; but I already have great faith in you, many people around here do; they just don't realize it yet. You'll make life a lot better for all of us."

With that, Georgia walked away from the table and through a swinging door that led assumedly to the kitchen. Paul was not sure what had just happened; but he was rather glad it had. Of course, Georgia had been right about everything including his doubts and fears about not only his future but about the future of the city also. He had felt at home when first entering the diner; but now he felt more, not simply a place to call home, but a people to call family.

Paul looked out the diner window as he sipped his refilled cup of coffee. Georgia had certainly given him a lot to process on a day that had already had several interesting encounters to contemplate.

There was a boy standing outside the window looking around nervously; Paul guessed he was about eleven years old. A deep sense of duty overwhelmed Paul. Georgia had emerged from the kitchen and was now behind the diner's counter. She too had noticed the boy now pacing the sidewalk. Paul's eyes met hers; and a knowing glance was exchanged between them as he grabbed his jacket and darted out the door.

"I'll be right back in, Georgia."

"Oh, I know you will."

Paul did not hear her reply or her laughter. He was already standing outside the diner. He also did not hear her whisper to herself.

"I was right. This is your purpose, Paul."

Paul cautiously approached the young boy and then crouched down next to him so they would be eye to eye; he did not want to scare him anymore than he already was.

"Are you lost, buddy?"

The boy did not say anything. It was obvious that his family and teachers had trained him to avoid talking to strangers.

CHAPTER FIVE

"My name is Paul. I'm eating lunch in this diner; and I noticed you were looking for something or someone. I have a cell phone if you need to call your parents. I know you're probably old enough to make your own decisions; but if you need to use my phone or you need my help in some other way, will you come inside and find me?"

The boy nodded. Paul stood up and then walked back in the diner and to his table keeping a watchful eye over the boy the entire time. Georgia was watching him too and slowly approached Paul's table.

"Is he lost?"

"Yes…and a little scared, although he's trying to act brave. I offered to call someone for him or help him if he needed it; but I didn't want to force myself on him."

Georgia dropped her voice to a whisper.

"Well, whatever you said to him worked; he's coming inside."

Georgia moved away as the boy slowly walked to Paul's table.

"Paul, can I use your phone to call my Mom?"

"Yes, you may."

Paul retrieved his cell phone from his pocket and handed it to the boy.

"Do you know her phone number?"

The boy eagerly nodded as he dialed.

"Mom!"

"I'm in a restaurant."

"Yeah, I'm okay."

"I don't know."

"Paul, let me use his phone to call you."

The boy quickly handed the phone back to Paul.

"Hello, this is Paul Gray."

"Mr. Gray, I'm his mother. Where is he?"

"The River City Diner on Oak Avenue between 3rd and 4th Streets; it's on the first floor of the Canterbury across from the Imperial Hotel."

As Paul gave directions to the boy's mother, he noticed Marcy enter the diner and sit down at an empty table.

"I know exactly where that is; and I'm only a few blocks away. I'll be there in few minutes. Is he okay?"

"He's fine; and I'll stay here with him until you get here."

"Thank you so much, Mr. Gray."

"You're welcome; it's my pleasure to help."

With his problem solved, the boy's countenance immediately changed; and he immediately accepted Paul as an old friend.

"My name's Tommy."

"Tommy, it's very nice to meet you. It's really cold outside. Would you like a cup of hot chocolate to warm you up, while you wait for your mom?"

Paul motioned to Ashleigh.

"Yah, but I don't have any money."

"It's my treat, Tommy."

His eyes lit up like a Christmas tree.

CHAPTER FIVE

"Ashleigh, my friend, Tommy, here would like a cup of hot chocolate."

Ashleigh quickly returned with a cup of hot chocolate.

"Tommy, would you like some whipped cream on that?"

He nodded and so she shook the can a couple times before spraying a generous amount in the cup. Tommy quickly took to the beverage when she finished.

"Careful! It's hot. Don't burn yourself."

Paul looked over towards Marcy; she was crying. His next task was already waiting for him. His first day was getting busy. A young woman hurried into the diner; and immediately spotted Tommy.

"Mom!"

"Oh, Tommy, you had me so worried."

She hugged him for several minutes choking back tears.

"And you must be Paul."

Paul stood up to greet her.

"Guilty."

The woman started to offer her hand but changed her mind and hugged Paul instead. Tommy returned to drinking the hot chocolate, which was mostly gone now.

"I'm Beverly Citrino; and you've already met Tommy."

Paul gestured towards an empty chair; and he and Beverly sat down.

"We're from Nilesville and don't usually come into the city, the big city I mean; but my husband's favorite science fiction author is Gus Morton; and he's signing copies of his new book at Margins today."

"Yes, I noticed that on the news."

"Tommy's school is on fall break this week, so I thought it would be a good time to get a signed copy for my husband for Christmas. As we left the bookstore, I noticed that Tommy and I had gotten separated. I've been retracing my steps ever since and searching frantically for the last half hour. Thanks again for being such a Good Samaritan; I hate to imagine what could have happened to him."

"I'm just glad I was able to help."

"How much do I owe you for the hot chocolate?"

"It's my treat. Did you want anything?"

"No, thank you. We're heading back to Nilesville now; Tommy wants to eat at his favorite restaurant before we go home."

"What's your favorite restaurant, Tommy?"

"Zumbo's!"

Paul withheld a grimace.

"He really likes their Fun Meals."

Beverly Citrino's expression matched Paul's sentiment. At least kids liked the place.

"Thank Mr. Gray for the hot chocolate, Tommy."

"Thank you, Paul."

"You're welcome."

Beverly hugged Paul one last time as she and her son exited the diner; Paul handed Tommy's cup and saucer over the counter to Ashleigh. He took his own cup and jacket and sat down at Marcy's table.

Chapter Six

Marcy's feet were getting tired. She had walked back from Crookston Towers in heels, because it was too cold to take off her shoes. She still did not have enough money for a taxi; but while she did have enough money for a bus ride, having just missed the bus, the next one would be a rather long wait. It was barely afternoon; and the day had already been a series of horrible moments, except of course for meeting Paul Gray. Meeting him was the high point of her day; but Marcy doubted she would ever see him again. She just wanted to get back to her apartment as quickly as possible and go back to bed.

She was only a block from the Canterbury when her heart skipped a beat. Paul was outside the diner talking to a young boy. He was still around; she would get to see him again after all. Paul reentered the diner; and a moment later, the boy followed him. Marcy wondered who the boy was. She tried to compose herself as she approached the diner. She knew that men did not find women, who cried over their many perils and acted like a damsel in distress, as appealing as they once did centuries ago.

Marcy entered the diner, noticed Paul was talking on the phone and sitting at a table with the boy, and took a seat at a table, where she could watch Paul with her peripheral vision. A pretty, young waitress was bringing something in a cup to the boy. Marcy guessed it was hot chocolate, because the waitress was putting whipped cream on top of it. Paul seemed to have a bond with both the waitress and the boy. Marcy imagined that the waitress was Paul's girlfriend and the boy was his son. Paul was probably a deadbeat dad, who was finally returning to accept his responsibilities. How could she have allowed herself to fall for a guy like that? No, he would not interact with the child so well if he were a deadbeat dad. Marcy succumbed to her own produced drama and began to cry again. The waitress approached her table.

"Welcome to the River City Diner. My name is Ashleigh; and I'll be your server."

She handed Marcy a menu and placed a small glass of water next to her.

"I'll give you few minutes to look over the menu unless you already know what you want to order."

"Just a glass of water for now."

"Let me know when you're ready to order."

"Is that guy over there your boyfriend?"

Ashleigh had already started walking away from the table when Marcy asked the question. The sheer bluntness of it, from a stranger no less, had taken her by surprise. She turned to face Marcy.

"Excuse me."

"That guy over there, is he your boyfriend?"

"No. He's just a customer."

Ashleigh braced herself for a further inquisition, which never came. She took the opportunity to leave the table. A woman entered the diner, noticed the boy and dashed towards the table where he and Paul were sitting. She hugged the boy and then hugged Paul before sitting down at the table herself. Paul seemed to have a bond with her also. Perhaps, she was the boy's mother, not the waitress. Marcy could not keep herself from feeling jealous over a man she barely even knew. Paul and his company had been talking for several minutes; Marcy had considered leaving. The woman eventually stood up, hugged Paul once more and left with the boy.

Paul cleared his table giving the boy's empty cup to the younger waitress. He picked up his own cup and jacket, crossed the diner, hung his jacket on the coat tree near the door and sat down at Marcy's table. She managed to suppress a selfish smile.

"How did the interview go? Did you get the job?"

"No. The receptionist told me they had already filled the position. They didn't even call me to cancel the interview. I hurried this morning for nothing."

"I'm very sorry."

"Who was the kid?"

"Oh. His name is Tommy. He had gotten separated from his mother. I let him use my cell phone to call her and stayed with him until she got here."

There was a long awkward silence, which Paul eventually broke.

"Do you want to talk about it?"

"About what? The kid?"

"No. About what's bothering you."

"Nothing's bothering me."

"So, you normally give strangers the third degree. Oh, not just me either. I overheard your conversation with Ashleigh a few minutes ago."

As Paul said this, he made eye contact with Ashleigh. She smiled, glad that Paul was the one dealing with this woman. Marcy felt small and stupid and said nothing refusing to even look Paul in the eye. He motioned for Ashleigh, which made Marcy feel worse.

"Ashleigh, my friend, Marcy, here hasn't had anything to eat all day; and she's been having a very bad day in general. She didn't get a job she was wanting. I wonder if you could bring her some comfort food to give her some energy and cheer her up a little."

Marcy refused to say anything or even look up at either Paul or Ashleigh. Paul took the initiative and ordered for her.

"Whenever I'm feeling down, especially when it's gloomy outside like it is now, I always eat a grilled cheese sandwich and a bowl of tomato soup. It makes me feel so much better."

Ashleigh nodded in agreement. She was only too happy to be a part of a solution instead of perceived as a problem. Marcy shrugged in indifference.

"Would you like me to bring you a soda with that, Marcy?"

"Diet?"

"Sure."

"Ashleigh?"

"Yes, Marcy."

"I'm sorry that I snapped at you earlier."

"Oh, that's okay."

Ashleigh gave Marcy a warm side hug before leaving the table to place the order with the kitchen.

"I'm not sure I have enough money in my purse to pay for this."

"Don't worry; it's my treat."

"Thanks. How did you know that I haven't had anything to eat all day?"

"You told me earlier, when I was helping you gather your belongings on the sidewalk. Plus, I didn't think you had enough time to walk back from Crookston Tower and get something to eat too. Now tell me what else is wrong; and I'll see what I can do to help you."

Ashleigh brought the diet soda and placed it in front of Marcy.

"I have no job. My car is broke down, so it makes it difficult to find a job; but without a job, I don't have enough money to get it fixed. I have no boyfriend. I'm also way behind on my rent, so I'll probably be homeless soon. The only good thing is without a job I don't have to worry about my broken alarm clock anymore."

"When were you last employed?"

"Almost three months ago. I was a secretary at Stile Manufacturing, which was acquired by Crookston Enterprises. I was one of the many employees, who were terminated, after the acquisition period. With the bad economy, I haven't been able to find anything else; and when I noticed the opening at Crookston Enterprises—"

"You thought you would have a better chance at the job given what had happened at Stile?"

"Yeah. Something like that."

"What's wrong with the car?"

"I think they said it was the transmission; I don't remember, perhaps I just don't want to remember, because remembering involves an amount that I can't afford."

"How old is the car?"

"It's a fifteen-year-old Seldon."

"Where is your apartment?"

Marcy pointed up.

"You live in the Canterbury?"

Marcy nodded meekly. Ashleigh had brought the grilled cheese sandwich and tomato soup. The platter also contained a generous serving of potato chips and a large dill pickle wedge. It was apparent that Marcy was famished the way she started in on the plate of food. Paul sat there quietly; the wheels in his head were spinning. He retrieved a notebook and pen from his pocket and made some quick notes in it while Marcy finished eating. Ashleigh later approached the table.

"Have you left room for dessert?"

Marcy looked at Paul wondering how to respond.

"They have delicious pie. I had a piece of pecan earlier."

"Do you have coconut cream?"

"We sure do."

"And Ashleigh, can I go ahead and settle my bill and get a coffee to go. I'll be leaving soon."

Ashleigh cheerfully nodded and walked back to the counter to fill the final order. Marcy looked despondent; her encounter with Paul was ending again. She wondered if there would be a next time. There was a pronounced silence between Paul and Marcy as Paul finished making notes in his notebook and composed his thoughts. Ashleigh brought the coconut pie, the coffee in a plastic cup, and the bill. Paul glanced at the bill to confirm that Marcy, Tommy and the strange man's orders had all been added to it; then he placed his credit card on the bill for Ashleigh to process.

"As for your broken alarm clock…"

Paul reached into his wallet and pulled out five twenties, handing them to Marcy.

"When you leave here, go over to Bocks Mart and purchase a new alarm clock. If you've been unemployed for three months, I'm guessing there are few other things besides just an alarm clock that you need for your apartment, so use the extra money to get what you need.

"As for your rent, since you live in the Canterbury, I am now your new landlord and I am waiving whatever rent you now owe plus the next year's rent to help you catch up on your other bills."

Paul motioned for Georgia.

"Georgia, Marcy here starts her new job tomorrow; and I don't want her skipping breakfast like she did today. Would you make sure she eats a good breakfast and put her bill on my tab? Ashleigh already has my credit card number."

"It would be my pleasure."

Georgia gave Paul a knowing glance and broad smile and walked back to the counter.

Marcy loudly whispered, "I don't have a job."

"Yes, you do. I was just getting to that part. As for employment, you need a job; and I need a personal assistant, so now you work for me. I'll pay you whatever you were making at Stile Manufacturing plus ten percent. That is, if you want the job."

Marcy was dumbfounded but found the presence of mind to nod.

"Good. Welcome aboard, Marcy! You do have a cell phone, don't you, because I will be calling you several times a day?"

Paul and Marcy traded cell phone numbers.

"As for your car…"

Paul pulled a page from his notebook and handed it to Marcy.

"I personally know Wayne Carter over at Wayne Carter Seldon in Cricksburg; he's an old friend of the family. The top number is his direct line. Tell him you know me. He's an honest man; you can trust him. I'll call him tonight and let him know you'll be calling. He can help you purchase a new car and he'll tow your old car and salvage it for you."

"I can't afford a new car, not even with a job."

"As my personal assistant, you need a car, because there'll be a lot of errands involved in the job; plus, you're representing me now, so I need you to project the right image; a new car will help. I'm sending you to Wayne, because I know he won't overcharge you. The bottom number is for Adam Miller; he's a vice president at Fifth National Bank; he'll help you with financing."

"Is he your friend too?"

"Extended family actually…but I'm also his boss."

"You own Fifth National Bank."

"It's a public company, so I don't own it; but I am the majority shareholder and chairman of the board; and Adam and I are direct descendents of the founder."

Marcy's jaw dropped.

"Given that you will be using your car so much for your job, I'll give you a decent car allowance in addition to your salary. You should strongly consider purchasing a minivan, because you might occasionally be chauffeuring people around or transporting items around town for me."

It was all quite overwhelming; and Marcy simply nodded in agreement.

"As for the Canterbury's elevator, which you mentioned earlier as a reason for running late, that will be one of your very first tasks tomorrow. Find out who maintains the elevator and schedule a service call.

"I think that addresses all of the problems you mentioned except not having a boyfriend. I'm sorry but I cannot help you with that one."

Ashleigh returned Paul's credit card and handed him the receipt to sign. Paul added a thirty-five percent tip to the bill, signed it and returned the receipt. Both Marcy and Ashleigh noticed Paul's very generous tip.

"Thank you very much."

"Thank you; you're a great waitress; you'll probably be seeing me on a daily basis."

Ashleigh walked back to the counter; she was beaming.

"And I will you see you tomorrow morning. Remember to purchase an alarm clock. And get a good night's sleep; you have a very busy day tomorrow."

Paul started to stand up.

"Wait!"

He sat back down.

"Where's your office? When am I supposed to be there? What's the name of the company?"

"Oh, I'm sorry. The name of the company is Foster Gray Holdings. I'll be setting up my office in the penthouse of the Canterbury. Come up tomorrow morning at 9:00."

"What do you do exactly?"

"I…help people."

Marcy's expression said she did not understand that brief explanation, so Paul expounded.

"This afternoon, I helped a lost boy find his mother; and I gave you a job because you needed one. Sometimes, I'll help individuals in personal ways as I helped you and Tommy; but eventually, I want to help this city…this entire region…prosper again; and that means tackling some very ambitious projects that will help dozens, hundreds, or even thousands of people all at once."

Marcy was not any clearer on the matter of Paul's job description; but she nodded as if she were. Paul stood up and grabbed his jacket and scarf from the coat tree.

"Thanks for the job, for everything really."

"You're welcome; you'll be earning every cent of it very soon."

"Where are you going?"

"I'll be on patrol…making my rounds…finding people who need my help."

Marcy immediately felt bad for falling back into her habit of aggressive nosiness especially after Paul had just given her a job and solved most of her immediate problems, all of her problems except not having a boyfriend. What did he mean that he could not help her with that? Was he married?

"I'll see you tomorrow at 9:00."

Paul grabbed the coffee in the plastic cup, waved farewell to Ashleigh, Georgia, and Ed and exited the diner. Marcy was amazed at how self-confident Paul seemed to be regardless what happened. He had been so gentle with the lost boy, fatherly even. He had been such a good listener to her; and dependable too, taking charge of her problems as if they were his own. She daydreamed about working for Paul and eventually marrying him.

Chapter Seven

As Paul stepped out into the cold, fall air, he felt very proud of the steps he had taken in the diner. On his first day back, he had already helped a couple people; and now he even had an assistant to help him with the bigger picture. He was officially on the job and making measurable progress however small it may seem. He walked north on Oak Avenue, past St. Anthony's Catholic Church. While he walked, he made a note in his notebook to attend mass on Sunday and to check on Father Andrews afterwards. He continued walking north past stores and restaurants and sadly past more than a few empty storefronts; but now, empowered by his little successes, Paul could see not only their present emptiness but also their future possibilities.

Five blocks north of the diner, Paul found his first stop. Next to a brand new blood bank was Dan's Hardware. Paul remembered the place from his college days and wondered whether it was even still there or not. The building was old both inside and out; no attempt had ever been made over the years to modernize it; but it was a small locally owned hardware store, not a big chain, Paul respected that.

The store on the other side of Dan's Hardware would be his second stop; and that was Margins Bookstore. While Dan's Hardware had done nothing to update their building, Margins had done everything to update theirs. It was still historic on the outside; but the inside was very modern and well lit, yet cozy and inviting, perfect for shopping for books. Margins was not a small, local company; but they were not a large chain either. Moreover, they did something no other bookstore, large or small, seemed to do anymore; they carried stationery and office supplies.

Chapter Eight

Paul entered Dan's Hardware and was immediately greeted by a tall, older man, who, although it was cloudy outside, squinted when the door opened. The man was nearly bald but had a well-groomed van dyke; a pair of reading glasses hung from his neck. He wore a beige cardigan, a light blue shirt and a red tie. The man resembled a college professor more than a hardware salesman. Other than him, the store was deserted and poorly lit.

"Can I help you find something?"

Paul did not like aggressive salespersons; and the tone in his voice was less friendly than it had been at the diner.

"I'm just looking for a few tools I need."

"Well, you've come to the right place; we have tools, all kinds of tools. Which tools did you need exactly? Do you have a list?"

Paul did have a list; he had made it last night. He had intended to browse the store first, and then consult the list only as a quick reminder before leaving. Hoping it would quiet the man, humor him even, Paul extracted the list from his pocket. Paul simply held his list as a talisman, preferring instead to look at the tools on the shelves instead of a list. The man however was looking over Paul's shoulder, craning his head and succumbing to the use of his reading glasses all to read the list clearly. He would scurry away, find a few objects on the list and place them on the counter only to return.

"Do you have a shopping cart or basket I could use?"

The man was totally lost in the world of Paul's list and had not heard what Paul had said.

"What's that?"

"Do you have a shopping cart…or a basket?"

"Oh, no! We don't need them here."

Paul was not quite sure what that meant. The man had finally managed to wrest the list from Paul's grip and was busy moving about the aisles and grabbing items off the shelves.

"Young man, don't you have any of these tools already."

"Yes, I had some tools; but I gave them to a man, who really needed them, so I now have to start from scratch."

"Well then, I must say that this is a very thorough, well-made list; I'm very impressed. Brand names and specifics. There's no need to guess what you intended. And, it covers all the basic and most intermediate tools, one would need, with no redundancy or frivolous items. I can see that you're a man, who actually knows what he's doing. Unfortunately, most of my customers are spouses, who are sent here to purchase an item but know nothing about hardware."

Paul immediately felt guilty for being so gruff with him earlier. Apparently, this man had very good reason to act the way he did.

"You get a lot of wife business, do you?"

"Yes and a surprisingly large number of hapless husbands too."

As the man was filling the list, Paul remembered his grandfather's general advice regarding tools. Purchase your own tools; don't borrow someone else's. Purchase quality American-made tools; don't buy tools made in China. Don't waste money on power tools, when hand tools work just as well.

Paul's grandfather was particularly stubborn about the third rule, always noting that Jesus was a carpenter, who only used hand tools. Occasionally Paul would jokingly remind him that he used and liked his power drill, to which his grandfather would always retort that Jesus would have used a power drill too if he had had one. Power drills were the only exception to the rule. Paul wondered what Pop would think about allowing a sales clerk to shop for you.

"Sir--"

"It's Dan."

"Dan, you obviously know this store much better than I do and you have the list of everything I need. If I gave you my credit card and address could you finish filling the order for me and deliver it tomorrow."

The man's eyes lit up. He seemed to genuinely enjoy serving customers even if he came across a bit strong at first.

"It would be my pleasure."

Dan made an imprint of Paul's credit card. He also wrote down Paul's name, address and telephone number.

"You want this order delivered to the Canterbury then?"

"Please. The penthouse floor. There's an empty room directly across from the elevator; just put it all in there; and I'll get it."

"Very good, Mr. Gray."

"If you're Dan; I'm Paul."

At that comment, Dan laughed. It was a hearty and sincere laugh; but there was something unusual about it. Paul imagined that Dan did not have much reason to laugh often and just forgot how to do it when it was needed. Despite his first impressions, he was actually starting to like the man.

"And Dan, can you make sure the delivery person receives a gratuity...

above whatever delivery charge there may be of course…say thirty-five percent."

"Tipping is not expected; but of course, it is appreciated; and that's very generous of you. I'll make sure that Tom receives it when he returns from the delivery. Will there be anything else?"

"Yes, one more thing. If I need anything more can I just call you and have it delivered too."

Dan handed Paul a business card.

"Please do; and I'll set up an account for you."

"Put my company name, Foster Gray Holdings, on the account and make sure that my assistant, Marcy Green, can charge to the account too."

Dan nodded eagerly and wrote all of the information down.

"Thank you, Dan; it's been a pleasure doing business with you."

"No, thank you; the pleasure has been all mine."

Paul shook Dan's hand and was startled by how strong Dan's grip was and how ice-cold his hand was. Paul then exited the hardware store. He was hit by a bracing wind, which was much warmer than Dan's skin had been. His visit to Dan's Hardware had been a strange but ultimately not unpleasant experience. Paul entered the bookstore next door.

"Here comes another fan right now."

"What?"

Paul was rudely pulled into a line containing two other people. At the head of the line was a table, where a middle-aged man was signing books. Paul had little time to survey his surroundings as a professional video camera was pointed at him. A bright light was shining in his face and a microphone was shoved in front of his mouth.

"What's your favorite Gus Mortor novel?"

THE MELISSA RING - GRAY'S FORREST

"I'm just here to purchase office supplies."

"There you have it; a fan, who likes all of Morton's books. We have to sign off; but Gus Morton will still be here signing books for another hour, so come on down."

"From Margins Bookstore, I'm Timothy Tirole."

"I'm Thomas Tirole."

"I'm Tamara Tirole; and we're the Triplet City Triplets."

"Until tomorrow, for Channel 42…"

"Good Afternoon, Tri-State!"

It was difficult to discern which triplet was which; they spoke rather fast and regularly finished each other's sentences and thoughts. Sometimes, they even spoke in eerie unison. The whole encounter was disorienting and Paul began to see the trio as a smarmy three-headed monster. While distracted by them, the line in front of Paul had since disappeared.

"Who should I make it out to?"

Paul turned around to face the table.

"What?"

"Who do I sign the book for?"

"Oh…uh…Paul…I guess."

The man wrote something on the title page of the book, closed it and handed it to Paul.

"Enjoy."

"Thank you."

As Paul walked away from Gus Morton and the triplets, who were now packing up their equipment to leave, and towards the customer service desk, he glanced at the book's newly penned inscription. It read, "To Paul, Keep reaching for the stars. Gus Morton." Paul rolled his eyes and wondered how good the novel could possibly be if the author had to shanghai customers into purchasing a copy.

The girl behind the customer service desk did not impress Paul very much. She was talking on a cell phone; and based on her side of the conversation, it was a personal call. She was also chewing noisily on a large wad of gum. Her long blond hair completely covered her nametag. Although there was nobody in front of him, Paul patiently waited for her assistance not wanting to interrupt her conversation.

"Somebody wants something."

Still holding the phone to her ear, the girl looked blankly at Paul; and when he did not speak immediately, she snapped at him.

"What?"

"May I set up a business account?"

The girl shoved a blank application towards Paul and resumed her conversation. There was no ballpoint pen on the counter; and she had not offered him one, so Paul took out his own pen and filled out the application while standing at the counter. As he completed it, he could not help but think how much easier Dan Tuley had made the process. When he finished, the girl stamped it and put it in some bin under the counter, which Paul could not see.

He had originally intended to give someone at Margins a list of office supplies to fill and deliver. He had also intended to order business cards and stationery. However, after his encounter with customer service, he decided to leave these tasks for Marcy to do tomorrow. Paul found an available cashier near the front and paid for the book he had not even wanted. The cashier was as helpful and friendly as the girl at the customer service counter had been. Paul left the bookstore unimpressed.

Again, Paul exited into a cold, northern wind. He had just completed everything that he had hoped to accomplish on his first day back in town and then some; and he was pleased with the progress. It had been a long day; he was tired; and now he just wanted to retire for the day and rest up for an even busier day tomorrow. Paul walked south on Oak Avenue back towards the Canterbury.

One block later, as Paul passed some vacant storefronts, he noticed a group of young men up ahead. Two of the men were wearing the same black and yellow leather jacket depicting the stylized head of a rat wearing a bandana. The Spanish words, Las Ratas, in bright yellow appeared above the logo. The other man was short, frail and wearing thick glasses; he looked terrified. Books were strewn on the sidewalk near him.

The taller gang member had pinned his victim to the wall with his left arm across his throat while punching him hard in the gut with his right fist. The shorter gang member was brandishing a switchblade and doing the talking, although Paul was far enough away to not hear exactly what was being said. The gang members were so fascinated by their recent catch that they did not even notice Paul approaching.

"Leave him alone."

Paul's voice boomed with authority and the two rats froze for a second. The larger had let go of their victim, who now slumped to the ground. However, they quickly regained their courage and faced their challenger assuming a menacing stance.

"And what if we don't?"

The shorter was swinging his switchblade in Paul's direction as he approached. The larger had produced his own switchblade. Paul said nothing and showed no emotion.

"I asked you a question. What…if…we…don't?"

The shorter took a step closer to Paul to punctuate each word spoken. Paul remained silent and stoic.

"Vicente, let's teach him a lesson in respect."

Lightning moves slower than what happened next. The rats had no time to react to it. Paul landed two kicks and four strikes, disarming both gang members and rendering the larger rat unconscious. Paul pocketed their blades. The shorter was staggering and disoriented. Paul raised him to his feet and pinned him to the wall in the same manner they had pinned their victim.

"I said, 'Leave him alone.' Do you understand?"

The shorter was silent from the shock. Paul placed pressure on his windpipe and the man's face started turning a dangerous shade of red.

"Do you understand?"

"Yes."

"What's your name?"

"Ignacio...Ignacio Torres."

"And sleeping beauty over there, what's his name?"

"Vicente Flores."

Vicente stirred and Paul dragged Ignacio over to a place where he could keep his arm on Ignacio's windpipe while putting a similar pressure with his boot on Vicente's. Both members were incapacitated and fighting for each breath. Paul turned his attention over to their victim.

"Come here."

The young man, who had regained some composure during the melee, did as he was told.

"What's your name?"

"Robert Papier"

"Robert, Ignacio and Vicente here want to apologize for treating you so badly."

Neither man said anything, so Paul briefly cut off their air.

"Isn't that right, guys?"

They did their best to agree while choking. Paul noticed that a rather large, dark circle had formed on Ignacio's pants between his legs as well as a puddle on the sidewalk under him.

"Ignacio…Vicente…I don't want to see you or anyone else wearing these jackets in this area again. When you wake up, go tell the rest of your gang that."

With that, Paul exerted enough pressure to render both men unconscious. He released his arm on Ignacio, who fell in a heap on the sidewalk. Paul checked for pulses to make sure they were okay.

"Robert, help me remove their jackets."

Without question, Robert helped Paul remove the gang jackets. When they woke up, the men would be very cold as they were only wearing A-shirts underneath. Paul frisked both men's pants for any other weapons but found nothing. Paul next helped Robert gather his books; he retrieved his own shopping bag from Margins, which he had dropped during the fight.

"Are they going to be okay?"

"Yes, they'll wake up in about fifteen minutes; but they'll feel like a train has hit them. Are you okay?"

"Yeah, I'm fine."

"Which direction were you going?"

Robert pointed south down Oak Avenue.

"I'm a student at WIU…I mean WURC…I had just finished my last class of the day and I was heading back to my apartment at the Canterbury."

"Well, I'm Paul Gray. It's nice to meet you. I'm your new landlord. I'll walk back with you."

Paul offered his hand to Robert, who shook it although weakly.

"Why did you take their jackets?"

"To dispirit them and their fellow gang members."

They walked in silence for a moment.

"What martial art was that?"

"Kajukenbo. I'm a seventh degree black belt."

Paul did not mind the inquisition; but he much preferred to develop a friendship with Robert instead.

"What are you studying…at WURC?"

Paul smiled. He was having as much trouble using the correct name as some of the students.

"Computer programming. I'm hoping to design surveillance systems someday."

"Really!"

"Listen, you've put a target on your back. Las Ratas will be coming for you now. And me too probably."

"I'm counting on it."

"You are?"

"Yeah, what can you tell me about them?"

"Well, there are probably a dozen of them; their leader's name is Carlos Rivera; and they live in the tunnels."

"The tunnels under the Canterbury?"

"Yeah, I guess; that's all I know."

"That's a lot; and it will help."

They walked the rest of the way in silence.

When they were outside the Canterbury's doors, Paul stopped.

"Robert, there's a project that I could really use your help on. Tomorrow, my assistant will be setting up my new office up in the penthouse; her name is Marcy Green; and I'll leave the specifics of the project I have in mind with her."

"Okay. Whatever."

Paul removed his notebook, scribbled his name and number and removed the page, handing it to Robert.

"If you encounter those guys again or you need anything, call me."

Robert nodded.

"And would you take these jackets up to the penthouse. There's an empty room across from the elevator. Just throw them in there. I'm not going in just yet."

"Sure."

Paul handed the jackets to Robert and continued walking down the street.

"Paul."

Paul stopped and turned back around.

"Thanks for helping me back there."

"You're welcome, Robert."

Robert entered the Canterbury with his books and the gang jackets, while

Paul continued walking south on Oak Avenue.

He walked to his truck, which was parked in the second subbasement of the Pine Avenue Parking Garage, and retrieved his bags; then he walked back to the Imperial Hotel. When he entered the hotel's lobby, it was like going back in time to a happier and simpler era. The hotel had not changed that much in the five years he had been gone; in fact, sadly, it had not changed at all. The hotel looked tired and past its prime

Paul crossed the deserted lobby and approached the front desk, where there was only one clerk working. The clerk's nametag had a capital letter I with a crown, the hotel's logo, in the top left corner. The top line in stylized red letters read "Imperial Hotel, River City." The next line in bold black letters read "Robert Topper." The bottom line in smaller black letters read "Front Desk." Paul wondered if this was the day for Roberts and Toms, as he had met several of each today.

"Welcome to the Imperial! How may I help you?"

"I know it's a little early; but I have a reservation for tonight and wondered if I could go ahead and check in now. My name is Gray…Paul Gray."

Robert Topper tapped the keys on his computer and consulted the information on the screen.

"Yes, Mr. Gray, your room is ready…in fact, someone has already registered for you."

Paul wondered how anyone knew where he would be; he had told nobody his specific plans; and few people even knew he was returning to River City today.

"Who registered for me?"

Robert looked at his screen again.

"Well, this is very confusing. He signed his name 'Paul Gray'…and that was also the name on the credit card, which he used to pay for the room. It was an older gentlemen…he was with a very kind-looking lady if that helps. They registered for you early this morning, then went up to the room for a few minutes but returned the key and left. I hope there's no problem."

Paul finally realized what had happened. Most people, including Paul himself, were not accustomed to calling his grandfather by his real name; everyone just called him Pop, even if they were not related to him in any way. Most people did not even know what his real name was.

"Robert, I'm sorry; I didn't realize that they knew I would be here tonight. That was my grandparents; I was named after him, hence the confusion with the names."

Both Paul and Robert breathed sighs of relief as Robert handed Paul the key to his room.

"And Robert, please put the charges on my card instead."

Paul handed Robert his credit card and signed the room folio.

"Mr. Gray, there was another man asking for you earlier today too, after your grandparents left. I told him you had not arrived yet; but I didn't give him your room number. I hope that was okay."

Paul was confident that nobody else would know that he was here.

"Did he leave his name?"

"No; but he did say that he'd return later today."

"If he does return, send him up to my room…but call me and let me know he's coming."

"As you wish. Have you stayed with us before, Mr. Gray?"

Paul mused over how much to say.

"Yes, I've been here before; but it was several years ago."

"Well, if you do have any questions, please dial 0 for the front desk. Enjoy your stay with us."

"I will."

Paul grabbed his bags and made his way to his room, which was on the third floor. It was a standard room overlooking Oak Avenue; Paul did not want a suite. It would set the wrong tone for what was to come. There was an envelope on the corner of bed with his name on it. Paul immediately recognized the handwriting.

> *Dear Paul,*
>
> *I knew you would choose to stay at the Imperial on your first night back instead of your new apartment.*
>
> *After being on the road for so long, I thought you might need some toiletries and sundries. I also brought you some fresh clothes; and I had your black suit cleaned and pressed. Wear the red tie with it tomorrow. Pop and I are so glad that you're back.*
>
> *Love, Nan*
>
> *PS: Why haven't you called us yet?*

With that, Paul laughed heartily. Nan knew him better than he knew himself. He peeked in the bathroom to find new toiletries on the sink counter just as she had said. He looked in the closet and drawers and found the fresh clothes. His black suit was hanging prominently in the closet; a red power tie draped around the neck of the hanger. He agreed that the red tie was a perfect choice. Paul took his cell phone and called a number he knew by heart; after a couple of rings, the party answered.

"Hello."

"Hello, Pop."

The old man's voice perked up when he realized who was calling.

"Paul! Are you back in town yet?"

"Yeah, I arrived late this morning."

"Wait just a minute, Paul."

Pop Gray started talking to someone else in the room; although he held the receiver next to his chest, Paul could hear every word of the conversation.

"It's Paul! He's back in town."

"Is he okay?"

The woman in the room with Pop was very excited about Paul's call and tried talking to him, raising her voice to compensate for not speaking directly into the receiver.

"Hello, Paul! It's Nan. We've missed you."

"Flora, he can't hear you. Go pick up in the kitchen."

Paul had to laugh and cry just a little. It was so wonderful hearing their voices again and being so close to them again. He loved his grandparents dearly; and he had missed them, while he was on the road; and he knew that they loved and missed him too.

"Nan will pick up in the kitchen in a minute. Did you have a safe ride?"

"Yeah, I didn't have any problems; and the weather was great until I entered West Kentucky, then the wind really picked up."

"The weather around here just turned a few days ago. It was terrible hot last week."

"Hello, Paul!"

"Hello, Nan."

"How do you like your hotel room?"

"More importantly how did you know I would be staying here tonight?"

"Oh, a grandmother just knows these things."

CHAPTER EIGHT

They all shared a laugh.

"Did you find the clothes I left for you, the suit and tie?"

"Yes, thank you, Nan. And you're right; that red tie looks great; I'll be wearing it tomorrow."

"And did you find your truck okay? Did we park it in the right place?"

"Yes, you parked it exactly where I wanted it."

Paul flinched for moment as he thought about Pop and Nan being in the second subbasement of the Pine Avenue Parking Garage so close to the tunnels under River City. He had not anticipated any danger when he asked them to do it; but now that he knew about Las Ratas, he shuddered to think about what might have happened.

"I know how much you like to write; and I didn't know if you'd have time to pick up some stationery yet, so I purchased some and put them in the desk drawer, just a few basics, there's more in your apartment."

Paul looked in the desk drawer and found letterhead, blank cards, envelopes, some new notebooks and journals, pens, and even some stamps. Nan had truly thought of everything. His failed trip to Margins Bookstore had been largely unnecessary.

"I just found them. Thank you so much, Nan. I'll probably start using them tonight before I turn in."

Paul really enjoyed writing; and he was both a voracious letter-writer and diarist. He had inherited this trait from Nan, who encouraged him regularly, by gifting him choice stationery items, leather bound journals and fancy fountain pens for example. One Christmas, Nan even gave him a rather expensive wax seal kit, which he cherished and had used frequently before his road trip. Circumstances required him to leave it behind in River City, so he assumed it would be up in his penthouse apartment somewhere.

Nan always reminded him that the art of letter writing, however lost it might be in today's society, was the hallmark of a real man. Never use the fax machine or computer, when you could send a handwritten note or letter instead. It shows you have a timeless character. Paul silently committed himself to gathering his supplies and resuming the habit immediately.

"What have you been doing since you got back in town?"

"Oh, I helped a lady get to her job interview on time, had lunch at the River City Diner, helped a little boy find his mother, bought some tools at a local hardware store, and purchased a signed copy of a science fiction novel that I didn't really want."

Paul left out the parts about the strange man in the diner and Las Ratas. He did not want to worry his grandparents just yet.

"Not back a day; and you're already on the job; aren't you. Does anyone know you're back yet?"

"Nobody who would remember me…not yet."

There was moment of silence as Nan tried to wrangle the conversation to a better topic.

"Well, I tried to make your penthouse apartment as homey as possible for you. Pop and I moved all your stuff up there this weekend; everything you sent back home is up there too; and I added a few things I thought you might need. I hope you like it."

"I'm sure I will Nan; you didn't need to do that. That was on my list of things to do tomorrow."

"I know; but we wanted to do it. Pop had all the files for the business put in that large room on the south side of the penthouse. Is that where you wanted them?"

"Yes, that's where the new offices will be."

"Make sure you hire some people to help you; the job is too big to do by yourself."

"I've already hired an assistant…Marcy Green…the lady I helped get to her job interview…she didn't get that job, so I hired her. And I have some other prospects in mind for other positions."

"Good. Pop and I will be expecting you for Sunday dinner; I'm making a pecan pie…you're favorite. Will you be coming for church too?"

"As soon as early mass at St. Anthony's is over, I'll drive down there and join you for worship service at Covenant Baptist."

Paul Gray had an unusual spiritual life; he was bi-religious. His father had been a Southern Baptist; and his mother was and still is Roman Catholic. Paul and his sister, Linda, were raised in both faiths; but when Paul's father died, Paul and his family moved to Puerto Rico to live with his mother's family, where Paul only practiced the Roman Catholic half of his faith.

When Paul moved to River City to attend college at, what was then, Western Indiana University, he developed a unique religious routine. He would attend early mass at St. Anthony's in River City and then drive across the river to Cricksburg and attend worship services at Covenant Baptist with his grandparents.

When Paul was on his five-year trek, he had tried his best to maintain both faiths. Based on his location, sometimes he was only able to attend Catholic churches and sometimes only Baptist. Sometimes both and sometimes neither. And, a few times, he briefly attended churches of other denominations for various reasons.

People were always curious about Paul's religion. They wondered how he was able to practice more than one at the same time. To Paul, it was very natural; however, he never encouraged others to be bi-religious, explaining that he was the product of many backgrounds. Being bi-religious was a matter of chance not choice.

"After that, I'm all yours for dinner and the rest of the day. Do you have any chores that you need me to do for you while I'm down there?"

"Not on Sunday, we don't. You should know that. Sunday is for God, family, and friends."

"And football. The Hornets are playing Sunday."

Since Nan had picked up in the kitchen, Pop had been listening to, but not participating in, the conversation. However, he never missed a chance to insert his favorite pastime into the dialogue whenever he could. Pop Gray worked very hard; as a farmer, he had his entire life, so he had few hobbies. Watching football and woodworking were really the only two; but he was passionate about both. Since he was back in the conversation, he took the opportunity to discuss his other hobby.

"Did I hear you say that you purchased some tools?"

Paul rolled his eyes and wondered how it had taken so long for Pop to hop on this subject.

"Well, I needed to replace what I gave away."

Paul explained to Pop in detail what had happened at Dan's Hardware; and Pop took a moment to mull it over in his mind.

"American tools?"

"Yes, Pop."

"Hand tools only?"

"Well, there may have been a few power tools on the list."

"Hmmph! Just as I thought. You kids today are always looking for a shortcut."

There was a brief silence and Pop's voice softened.

"Well, I want to inspect these tools before you do any work for me. And I want to visit this hardware store and meet this Dan fella, before I give any of this my blessing."

It had been five years; but for a moment, it did not even seem like a day had passed. It is amazing how a simple phone call about nothing at all could be

CHAPTER EIGHT

so important to you.

"Nan…Pop…I really need to settle in now. Today has been a very big day; and tomorrow promises to be an even bigger one. Thanks so much for everything."

Goodbyes were exchanged all around with assurances of meeting on Sunday, and then Paul disconnected the call.

With his grandparents contacted, Paul's next task was to grab a shower and wash the day off him. He got the water as hot as he could stand it and then stood under the spray letting the water massage him, first his face, then the top of his head, then the back of his neck and finally his shoulders. After his shower, he found some fresh clothes in the drawers, a pair of boxers, a t-shirt, and a pair of sleep pants; and he put them on. He had just finished dressing when his room phone started ringing.

"Hello."

"Mr. Gray, it's Robert at the front desk. The man, who was asking about you earlier, has returned; and he's standing here in the lobby. He says his name is John Hayne. Did you still want me to send him up?"

Paul took a moment to decide. Somehow, the name Hayne sounded familiar; but Paul did not know where he had heard it.

"No, Robert, tell him I'll be down in a minute."

"As you wish."

Paul was unshod and not exactly dressed to receive company; but that did not bother him very much at the moment. He was more concerned about finding out who John Hayne was. He grabbed his phone, wallet, and room key and made his way down to the lobby. Now, later in the day, there was some light traffic through the hotel; however, there was only one person sitting in the lobby. He had found a chair closest to the elevator so he could see Paul when he stepped onto the ground floor. It was the strange man from the diner.

John stood as Paul approached.

"So, your name is John Hayne? That's more than I was able to get out of you earlier today."

"Paul, may we talk privately up in—"

"No, we will talk publicly down here in the lobby."

Paul walked past him and found a seat, where he could establish eye contact with Robert if necessary. John hesitated but reluctantly followed him to the table. Paul motioned towards a chair opposite of him; and John sat down. For several minutes, neither man said anything.

"Well, you wanted to talk, so talk."

"It's difficult to know how to start."

"It wouldn't have been any easier up in my room. Start with this. Is John Hayne your real name or a lie you told the front desk clerk?"

"John Hayne is my real name."

"You see. We're making real progress. Now, why were you staring at me at the diner earlier today?"

"I wanted to ensure that you were who I thought you were."

"And who did you think I was?"

"Paul Gray."

"Well, I am Paul Gray; but you knew that already. So how do you know me and more importantly what do you need with me?"

"We're…related."

"Related how?"

"Your paternal grandfather's mother was Mary Hayne; she was my cousin. That makes us first cousins twice removed."

Paul thought he remembered Pop and Nan telling him about the Hayne's a long time ago. According to Nan, the entire Hayne family was crazy.

"That still doesn't answer my other question. What do you want with me?"

"My cousin, Sam Hayne, who is also my employer, has requested the pleasure of your company for tea tomorrow afternoon."

With this, John retrieved an enveloped invitation from his coat pocket and handed it to Paul. Paul opened the envelope and read the contents. As John had said, it was an invitation for tea in Scarsdale, West Kentucky.

"Scarsdale? Are you the Hayne's that own the amusement park?"

John merely nodded.

"Why does Sam Hayne want to meet me?"

"Paul, are you not in River City to claim an inheritance from one Silas Foster?"

"Yeah…what of it?"

"Then has it ever occurred to you that you might have inheritances from other sides of your family as well?"

Paul was well aware of this fact. Although the estate of Silas Foster would make up the lion's share of Paul's vast wealth, over time, he had received inheritances from other family lines with the expectation of more to come in the future. Paul simply was not aware of the Haynes, their exact relationship to him, and that they had anything for him.

"The Haynes would like to bestow something on me."

"That and Cousin Sam would like to discuss a business proposal with you. I'll let him give you the details at tea."

John was only a messenger; it was obvious that he did not wish to discuss business any further than he already had. Paul assumed that discussing business and bestowing gifts were part of Sam Hayne's job.

"Tell Cousin Sam that I accept his invitation to tea."

Having completed his mission, John smiled. It was a creepy smile.

"I shall collect you at three-thirty tomorrow then."

"I can drive myself."

"The matter of your transportation is non-negotiable."

"Whatever."

"Will you be here tomorrow or at the Canterbury?"

"The Canterbury."

"Until then."

John Hayne tipped his hat and left quickly. Paul realized that Nan was right. The Hayne's were crazy. He sat there in the lobby for a moment, then stood up, took a five out of his wallet and handed it to Robert on his way to the elevator.

"Thank you for your help, Robert."

"My pleasure, Mr. Gray."

When Paul returned to his room, he worked on his correspondence, on which he had recently gotten quite remiss. He ordered a large pizza with pepperoni, sausage, mushrooms and black olives and a two-liter of cola from Second City Pizza and Wings, which was one of Brenda Henderson's Sour Seventeen restaurants to avoid. After dinner, he made a few phone calls, started a new journal and made an action list of tasks for tomorrow. He had accomplished much on his first day back in River City; and he was pleased with his progress.

Chapter Nine

Marcy's Friday was going much better than her Thursday had gone. A handsome stranger had magically erased all of her problems, which she had found so unsolvable yesterday. Her new alarm clock worked perfectly; and she actually found time to kill this morning. After three months of unemployment, she had a brand new job. She was not exactly sure what the job entailed yet, but it was a job; and it paid better than her job at Stile Manufacturing had. Perhaps the best part was that her new boss was Paul, that handsome stranger who had entered her life yesterday. Paul had also waved her financial problems away. Yes, today was certainly much better than yesterday.

Marcy had risen, dressed and even eaten a good breakfast in the diner; and it was only 6:00, three hours before she needed to report for her first day of work. She had asked Georgia about Paul and discovered that he had already been in, eaten breakfast and left. Marcy had nothing else to do to occupy her free time this morning, so she decided to go to the penthouse early. Paul was already up; perhaps he was already working too. The elevators, which were so slow yesterday, moved swiftly today; and when the doors opened, she was standing, for the first time, in the penthouse hallway.

The Canterbury was one of the tallest buildings in the Forrest. Its ground floor contained a large windowless lobby, windowless, because there was a ring of storefronts surrounding it on all sides. These storefronts opened out to the street; and the only one with a tenant was the River City Diner, which faced Oak Avenue. There were doors from the lobby to Oak Avenue on the west and Pine Avenue on the east; on the north and south ends were small hallways leading to stairwells. An elevator shaft, which had been open in the buildings earlier days but was now closed, stood as the only architectural feature in a rather bleak room filled with furniture, which was in bad need of replacement.

Below the ground floor was a basement, which was used for storage, laundry facilities and utilities. There were at least two subbasements below that; but residents of the Canterbury wisely avoided those areas. Most people knew they were dangerous; some even thought they were haunted.

The second floor of the Canterbury was deserted. It was designed for office spaces but the last tenets had vacated years before Paul Gray had ever lived in the building as a college student and employee of the Imperial Hotel across the street. These second floor spaces were accessed by a hallway, which overlooked the lobby on the other side. A person of vision could imagine how grand and bustling the building had once been; but now, a shadow of its former self, it was merely a ghost town. Floors three through forty-four were the residential floors with forty units on each floor. The Canterbury had 1680 apartments but little more than sixty percent occupancy.

The penthouse was a big unknown; few residents ever wandered up there. In that sense, Marcy was a pioneer. The penthouse hallway was dimly lit with emergency lights near the stairwells on opposite ends of the hallway. She could not make out anything except a light coming from under the door ahead of her. Cautiously she opened the door. The room looked like a meeting room turned storage room. There was stuff in piles all along the wall. In the center of the room though was a man lifting weights. It was Paul. He was shirtless and wearing only a pair of shorts and sneakers.

Seeing him in this state of semi-undress verified Marcy's earlier assessment of him. Paul was not merely a handsome man; he was a Greek god. He was well built without looking like a testosterone-pumped freak. His naturally bronze skin was accented with the perfect amount of body hair. Paul was perhaps the most beautiful man that Marcy had ever seen; and she just wanted to stand in the doorway and watch him forever.

"Hello."

Paul lowered the dumbbell and sat up on the bench.

"Marcy! You're early…very early."

Paul swiped at his face and chest with a nearby towel and modestly threw on a t-shirt.

"Have you had breakfast yet?"

"Yeah, Georgia said you had already been in, so when I finished eating, I came up thinking I could help you in some way."

"You might want to take these next few hours and enjoy them; after 9:00, there won't be many breaks."

"I have nothing else to do."

"Very well, I've already eaten breakfast and had my morning workout, so I'm heading back to my room at the Imperial to take a shower. From there, I'll be at mass at St. Anthony's; and I want to briefly check on Father Andrews afterwards before my appointment with the general manager of the Imperial Hotel. After that meeting, I'll change clothes, check out of my room, and come back here to start work. Follow me."

Paul led her out into the penthouse hallway, where Paul found some light switches. The previously dark penthouse hallway was now flooded with bright light.

"The door at the end of the hall is where our offices will be."

Paul unlocked the door and turned on the lights inside. Marcy followed him. Like the earlier room, this room, actually a suite of rooms, appeared to now be used for storage. Office furniture and boxes were scattered everywhere with no purpose.

"As you can see, this place doesn't even look like an office yet. For the next few days, we'll mostly be in organization mode. Marcy, if I were you, I would go back to your apartment and change clothes. You look very nice; but given today's agenda, you might be more comfortable in jeans. I'm sorry; I really should have told you."

Paul handed Marcy a set of keys.

"I'll be back at 9:00; and I'll show you around the penthouse and then catch you up on what's happened before we jump into the fray of establishing the office. Until then, you're welcome to look around up here or claim a desk and start setting up your space."

Paul dried off his right hand and offered it to Marcy, who shook it.

"Welcome aboard!"

With that, Paul abruptly left, heading for the stairwell and not the elevator. Marcy looked around what was about to become her future office. She concluded that as the only employee of Foster Gray Holdings, she was, at least for the time, the de facto receptionist. She found the closest desk and office chair and dragged them to a place near the door. She looked in the drawers; they were all empty. Marcy sat down at the desk in the deserted room, which looked more like someone's basement, and started to cry. When she imagined her new life as Paul's assistant, she had not imagined this. After a few moments of wallowing in self-pity, she stood up and walked around the desk.

"You should be ashamed of yourself, Marcella, acting like some silly schoolgirl. What did you think was going to happen? Did you think he was going to propose? He doesn't want or need a girlfriend; but he clearly needs a personal assistant, a job by your education and experience, for which you are well qualified. Paul either is or is about to become a very powerful and influential man in this city. It's time you start acting like the assistant to such a man and stop playing the ingénue. He didn't hire you just to solve your problems. He hired you to help him solve his. So get downstairs and change clothes; you only have a few hours before he returns; and you have a lot to accomplish in that time."

Chapter Ten

After mass, Paul remained seated admiring the interior of the church he so loved. He had been in many churches in his lifetime, both Catholic and Protestant; but none was more majestic in their architecture than St. Anthony's. Just sitting in the church made it easy to believe in a large and powerful God. A balding middle-aged priest walked towards him and took a seat in the pew in front of him.

"I thought I saw you in the congregation. How are you, Paul?"

"Great."

"Well you certainly look great."

Paul was wearing the black suit, white shirt and red tie that Nan had prepared for him. It was difficult for Paul to hide his good looks; but dressed like he was, he looked like a fashion model.

"And you haven't aged a day since I last saw you."

"Paul, it's a sin to lie to a priest."

They shared a hearty laugh.

"Can I assume that you are back in town to—?"

Paul quickly interrupted him holding a finger to his lips.

"Yes, but that's a secret for now."

Father Andrews mimed the actions of first zipping his lips closed, then praying with his hands folded then pointing to the ceiling.

"I won't tell. I can't tell. Seal of the confessional!"

"Actually, that is why I'm here. I could use your help."

"Name it."

"Before I start, I would like the support of other religious leaders here in the Forrest. They could be valuable sources of information to me. Telling me who needs my help the most and what exactly I'm up against."

"Paul, what you're up against is a group of very corrupt people. No, scratch that; they're not corrupt; they're evil. Are you absolutely sure you want to do this?"

"Father Andrews, I don't want to; I have to. You know that. There are many people counting on me; they just don't realize it yet. It's why I need all of the religious leaders. I need all the prayers I can get if I'm going to succeed at this task of mine."

Paul looked at the priest with expectancy.

"Oh, sure! Why not? My life isn't exciting enough."

The priest paused a moment before continuing in a different tone.

"And you're right, Paul; something needs to be done very soon. Shame on me for not doing something about it myself."

Paul offered a hand on the priest's shoulder to console him.

"I'm living in the penthouse at the Canterbury; I'm setting up my office up there too."

Paul tore out a sheet from his notebook and handed it to the priest.

"This is my cell number and the cell number of my assistant, Marcy Green. Call us if you need anything."

"Yeah, I know Marcy; she attends St. Anthony's regularly."

"Oh, that reminds me. What can you tell me about a local street gang called—"

"Las Ratas, the rats, it's a fitting name."

"You've heard of them then?"

"Oh yes, I get the pleasure of washing their tags off of the church on a regular basis. Have you already run into them so soon?"

"I stopped two of them from beating a kid up a few blocks from here. I took their jackets as a souvenir."

"Then you'll be seeing them again."

Paul stood up.

"Well, I just wanted to let you know I'm back in town. You'll be seeing a lot more of me now. And Marcy or I will contact you about starting that group."

Father Andrews held his thumb up in approval as Paul exited St. Anthony's and made his way to the Imperial Hotel, which was cattycorner to the church.

Paul navigated himself to the elevator through a now crowded lobby of departing guests. On the second floor, he found the hotel's office, introduced himself to the receptionist, and took a seat in the small, waiting area near her desk. Paul had made a point of being early for the appointment. However, while he had been notified of Paul's arrival, Gilbert Gillenwater, the hotel's general manager, did not start the interview until twenty minutes after the agreed time. Paul wondered whether he was being made to wait unnecessarily or if the man actually was that busy.

When he did finally call Paul back, Gilbert made him wait standing up, while he leisurely perused Paul's resume with his feet on the desk; he noisily wallowed a toothpick around his mouth as he read. Gilbert

Gillenwater was not an attractive man. He was morbidly obese; his skin and what little hair he had left were oily; and he was sloppily dressed in clothes that looked old and dirty. Although there was a large desk between them, Paul could easily smell body odor and alcohol. His desk and office were as tidy as he was.

"You don't look Puerto Rican."

"Excuse me."

"I said you don't look Puerto Rican. The owner of this hotel is from Puerto Rico. You're supposed to be his grandson; but you don't look Puerto Rican."

"My mother is Puerto Rican; but my father was from Cricksburg."

"He was white?"

"Yes."

"Besides your grandfather owning this hotel, why should I hire you?"

"I've been working in hotels since I was fifteen years old, six of those years at this very hotel; and during that time, I have done every job that can be done in a hotel. I have a Master's degree in Hotel Management. I'm a certified lifeguard, a classically trained chef; and I can fix anything that's broken. I'm punctual, very organized, and have excellent people skills. And oh yeah…I'm fluent in forty-two languages."

Gilbert Gillenwater rolled his eyes in disgust.

"Well, your grandfather thinks you're something special; but I don't see it. Still, I'm required by him to give you a job with a title, so you're the hotel's brand new Director of the Lost & Found Department. You can organize the hotel's subbasements; that should keep you out of my hair for a good long while. In fact, I don't have any office space up here to spare, so you can just make yourself an office down there with the other rats, where you belong."

Gilbert Gillenwater stood up and brought his face closer to Paul. The smell was unbearable and Paul badly wanted to vomit.

"Listen, boy; don't ever interfere with my management of this hotel; and I'll try to remember to put in a good word for you with Grandpa. Do we understand each other?"

"Yes."

"Yes what?"

"Yes, sir."

"That's better. Now get lost; I don't want to see you again."

Paul left the office and found his way back to his room, where he changed into more casual clothes. It took all of his willpower not to deal with Gilbert Gillenwater both harshly and immediately.

"Be patient, Paul, be patient. Do this the right way," he kept reminding himself while changing clothes.

Chapter Eleven

Paul stepped off the elevator and into the penthouse hallway. He opened the door to his apartment enough to throw his last bag inside without entering. He then walked down the hallway towards the office of Foster Gray Holdings Inc. Besides the lights, there was no indication that Marcy was even still here. He hoped he had not scared her away.

He opened the door and was greeted by an unexpected sight—a reception area. Behind the desk, there was a folding screen blocking the view of the rest of the office. There was a manila pad and pen on the desk. To the left and right of the door there were small sitting areas, with chairs, end tables and lamps. There were even some potted plants.

"Paul, you're back; how was your meeting with Mr. Gillenwater?"

Paul was very impressed that Marcy knew who the general manager of the Imperial Hotel was.

"I believe it was constructive."

"Good."

Paul was still looking around the reception area in amazement.

"Marcy, you've done a great job organizing so much in so little time."

"Don't worry; there's still a lot to do."

Marcy led Paul around the screen. The rest of the space was untouched; but still Marcy had managed to create an oasis of order in an otherwise desert of chaos and confusion. Paul noticed that Marcy had heeded his advice and had changed clothes. She was dressed comfortably in blue jeans; but they were very nice jeans and she was wearing a dressy green blouse. The look was still professional much like you would expect from a casual Friday dress code.

"Did you have a chance to look around the rest of the penthouse or would you like me to give you a guided tour."

"I did look around more to scavenge for items than to explore; but a tour would certainly help me visualize the plans you have for the place."

"Very well then."

He led her out of the office and into the hallway stopping at various points for explanation.

"I want to use the entire penthouse floor for the business. You've already seen our offices; but did you know there were four more floors?"

"While I was looking around for supplies, I did notice that. This place is so much larger than I thought. I wasn't expecting that."

The penthouse of the Canterbury was very unusual indeed. It was actually a group of buildings on top of the main building connected by a central hallway. The office of Gray Foster Holdings was the building on the south end of that hallway.

"The door on the other end of the hallway leads to my apartment.

"The room across from the elevator, where you caught me exercising this morning is being used for a storage room but I would like to make it a banquet room where the company could hold receptions."

Marcy nodded and made notes on a manila pad. Paul pointed to two smaller rooms on the opposite side of the hallway.

"These are rather small rooms, which I would like to start using as conference rooms.

"The other four suites of rooms, occupying the corners of the Canterbury, are similar in size and design to my apartment and Foster Gray Holdings' offices; but I don't have any plans for them at the moment. Possibly we'll outgrow the one area and need to expand."

"What are your plans for the rest of the building, the lower floors?"

"Obviously I want to fill the vacant stores on the first and second floors. And, the lobby and hallways on each floor could probably use a makeover. Eventually I would even like to see how we could use the lower levels."

Marcy continued to nod and scribble.

"Oh and don't forget to have the elevator inspected."

"I've already called and made an appointment for Monday."

Paul was startled by Marcy's sudden efficiency.

"I ordered some tools and cleaning supplies from Dan's Hardware; they're supposed to deliver them sometime today."

"They've already been delivered. He put them in the…what are we calling that room across from the elevator? I checked the delivery against the copy of the list you gave him. Everything's there."

"Great. I noticed that you found some office supplies; I set up an account at Margins yesterday after I left the diner, so you can order anything else you might need."

"I've already compiled a list."

Marcy started to hand Paul a list; but he reached into his pocket and produced a list of his own, handing that to her instead.

"I too made a list a couple of days ago; combine the lists and send it in."

Marcy perused Paul's list and made some notes.

"I don't mean to alarm you, Marcy; but are you aware of any gang activity in the Canterbury's subbasements?"

"I've seen a gang in the neighborhood wearing black and yellow jackets; in fact I saw a couple of those jackets in the...Paul, we really need to give that room across from the elevator a name."

"Okay, from now on, it's called the Sunset Room, since it faces the sunset."

"Great name! I saw a couple of those jackets in the Sunset Room earlier today."

"Yeah, I took them away from a couple of gang members yesterday afternoon."

Marcy's jaw dropped but she quickly regained her composure and continued.

"Okay. Well, I've heard they're living in the basement; but that's just a rumor."

"They were assaulting a young man, who lives here in the Canterbury. I told him to come up here sometime; and you would give him the specifics of a project that I could use his help on."

Paul handed Marcy another paper. She scanned it and made some notes on her legal pad.

"What can you tell me about that Hayne amusement park in West Kentucky?"

"Hayne's Family Scream Park in Scarsdale?"

Paul nodded.

"Some friends and I went there last year; it's a really nice place...if you like haunted houses...it's certainly better than Zumboland. I hate that clown... his show...his cereal...his hamburgers...his amusement park."

"He makes cereal."

"Yes, and it tastes awful."

"Well, I have an appointment to meet Sam Hayne this afternoon for tea. He's sending a car for me at 3:30."

"Tea? What century is he living in? He sounds like a loon."

"Be careful; I'm related to that loon."

"Seriously?"

"So I'm told."

"Good luck then."

Paul was noticing how quickly he and Marcy were developing a rhythm; he thought to himself that he had picked the right person to be his assistant.

"Marcy, I met with Father Andrews after mass. We are starting a group of religious leaders in Forrest Township. I think that will be an excellent way to assess the community's needs. When you get a chance, try to compile a list of churches in the Forrest, so I can contact them. Make that a priority."

Marcy nodded while making notes.

"As I already said, I met with the general manager of the Imperial Hotel."

"You said it was a constructive meeting; but was it really?"

Paul nodded and shook his head.

"He thinks he has hired me as the Lost & Found Director, because my grandfather owns the hotel."

"What the real story?"

"Oh, my grandfather did own the hotel; but he purchased it five years ago as a graduation gift to me; he's only been holding on to it for the last five years, while I was on the road. I own the hotel; but Mr. Gillenwater doesn't know that yet. Last week, I had my grandfather call him and pressure him into giving me a meaningless job. I have a secret connection at the hotel, who has kept me informed on Mr. Gillenwater's activities while I've been on the road. Now that I'm back I want room to build a case against him before I terminate him."

"Wow. What am I supposed to do?"

"About the Imperial…nothing. I just wanted you to know, because I will be spending a little time there while you hold the fort down here. Until I reveal myself, only you and my secret connection will know who I really am. To Gilbert Gillenwater and the rest of the staff, I'm just a slacker grandson, who has an insignificant though important sounding job because his grandfather owns the hotel."

"Got it."

"That catches you up on what I've been up to for the last twenty-four hours. Do you have any questions?"

"Yes, what exactly is my job description here? Do you want me to manage your schedule?"

"Managing my schedule, yes; but also managing my contacts. I'll want to handle some of my own correspondence; but for the most part, you'll handle most of the communications in and out of the company. And, as you may have already surmised, you will be doing most of the heavy lifting on these various projects of mine. I'll meet with you each morning; but then, most days, I'll be out there in the field."

Paul made a gesture to the nearest window indicating that the field was actually the Forrest.

"Besides all that, you're also in charge of everything up here on the penthouse. As I hire more people, you'll function as a chief of staff."

Marcy's eyes widened and she gasped slightly as she made further notes on her legal pad.

"Too much?"

She hesitated, answering after only a brief moment.

"No, I can handle it."

"Great. Now let's try to make this place look more like an office before I have to have tea with my loony cousin."

They both laughed.

Chapter Twelve

"So tell me, Paul; what are your goals for the Forrest district?"

Paul and Marcy had worked hard organizing the Canterbury's penthouse floor and establishing the offices of Foster Gray Holdings and had taken a break for lunch at the diner. Now, lingering over coffee before returning to the penthouse, Marcy had taken the opportunity to ask Paul some more pointed questions. Despite the awkward silence it produced, Paul sipped his coffee and carefully considered his response to her first question before answering.

"Marcy, I walked through the Forrest yesterday…well…a small part of it anyway. I saw a city, which is dying from more than one disease. Crime, pollution, unemployment, urban blight, poor public transportation and a multitude of other huge problems have conspired against this city. However, these problems are not a natural progression of events; a small group of very powerful yet very evil people has intentionally manufactured them. They don't care about this city; they want nothing more than to control the populous for their own selfish gain."

Marcy nodded in agreement to everything Paul said.

"But I don't just see this city how it was and is but how it can be. I see a city, which has enormous potential; and with some very hard work on everyone's part, there's no reason that it cannot be the best city in this country by any measurable standard. I'm willing to put all of my time and resources and to enlist the help of everyone I already know and will meet into making that happen."

The passion in Paul's words brought tears to Marcy's eyes.

"You told me yesterday that you're from Georgia by way of Puerto Rico. So why would you want to help us?"

Again, Paul thought long before giving his response.

"While I only lived here while attending college, my dad was from across the river in Cricksburg. His parents still live and work on a large farm there. My paternal grandmother's father though was a very wealthy and powerful man here in River City; but he was also very evil. He died a few months before I received my master's degree; and the terms of his will made me his sole beneficiary."

"Why didn't your grandmother inherit at least a part of his estate," Marcy interrupted.

"As I said, Silas Foster—"

"The Foster of Foster Gray Holdings?"

Paul nodded before continuing.

"Silas Foster was a very evil man. He didn't care who he hurt, including his own family. His will specifically stated that his estate would only pass to his closest male descendant. Well, he had six children, all boys except my grandmother, who was the youngest child; but his sons all died at early ages before they could even produce an heir. My grandmother herself had only one child, my father, who died in Somalia when I was only fourteen years old. And I only have one sibling, a younger sister, so I was not only the closest but the only male heir, when Silas Foster died."

"Why didn't your grandmother and sister contest the will?"

"Well, first, they don't really need the money, none of us do. We're all very wealthy in one way or another. My grandmother benefited from another inheritance on her mother's side and then married my grandfather, who was and still is a wealthy farmer and businessman in Cricksburg. My sister, like myself, has benefited from a collection of trust funds her entire life; and she too married a very wealthy man in San Juan.

"But the main reason, I suppose, is the responsibility that comes with the inheritance. We're very ashamed of Silas Foster, how he made his money, how he treated the citizens of River City, and how he contributed to the city's current state. However, with Nan's age and my sister, Linda, having her entire life based in San Juan, I was really the only one in the family, who has the time and life circumstances to assume the responsibility."

"You said he died just before you earned your Master's degree. If it's so important to you and your family to right Silas Foster's lifetime of wrongs, why then did you wait so long and go on a road trip for the last five years."

"Per the conditions of my great-grandfather's will, I was not able to receive the entire inheritance until my thirtieth birthday, which is not for another three months. My grandparents have been trustees of the estate during this time. My grandfather suggested that I take some time…see the country… find myself. He and I both knew that when I returned to River City, there would be little time for such things as I would be very busy.

"I took his advice, climbed on my dad's old motorcycle, and just hit the road. For a while, I used my dad's old diary as a guide. He had made a list of things he wanted to do, places he wanted to visit, books he wanted read; and I did all of those things that he never did and now, never will have a chance to do. I even did some of the things and went some of the places, which he was able to see and do before he died. By doing this, I felt like I was finally able to connect with him man-to-man instead of simply as my father.

"Then, I made my own list and completed everything on that. And, for a while towards the end, I just went wherever the wind took me without any real plan before returning here yesterday. I've lived several lifetimes of adventure in those five years; and it was enough. I can now complete my mission here in River City without regrets or the temptation to leave."

Paul's story fascinated Marcy in so many ways.

"You told me earlier today to compile a list of area churches for you; and while we were working in the penthouse, you mentioned dealing with the religious issues of the community first. Why are you starting with religion, when there are far more pressing problems in the community like crime?"

"River City, particularly the Forrest district, has decayed for so long, because some rich and powerful men have placed their interests ahead of God's interests; and unfortunately innocent people have suffered greatly for those misguided priorities. If this city is to be reborn, I must ensure that the community's religious issues are addressed first and that I am the man that God wants me to be. Do you still have your legal pad?"

Marcy nodded as she produced it and a pen.

"Make one column for community goals and one for my personal goals. I'll need your help completing the goals in the first column and I'll need you to hold me accountable for the goals in the second column.

"Personal goal: attend church services every week; and that means both churches. Now that I'm back, I need to get back in that habit."

On her earlier query during lunch, Paul had explained his unique religious background. While she remained very curious about it, she asked no further questions.

"Personal goal: resume a daily private devotion that includes intense Bible study and prayer. This is another habit, which I lost on the road. Before I meet with you every day, Marcy, I will have exercised, showered, dressed, eaten breakfast and had this devotion. Hold me to that; and don't let me slide on it, even a little bit."

Marcy nodded as she wrote.

"Personal goal: tithe to both churches. This is possibly a disadvantage to being bi-religious; but I cannot, in good conscience, give to one and not the other or split my one tithe between them or some other accounting acrobatics. No, I'll give ten percent of my income to St. Anthony's and ten percent to Covenant Baptist; and I'll give another one percent to a different area church each week."

Although Paul did not see it, Marcy's eyes widened.

"Personal goal: volunteer my time at area churches. I plan to mention this at the meeting; but I'll make myself available to all the churches represented and perform any handiwork they need completed. From the churches I've already seen, this is a real need. Marcy, I'll need you to coordinate my schedule so I can help all of them in an efficient manner.

"Community goal: found the Forrest Council of Churches. I've already mentioned this and have charged you with contacting all churches in the area; but I want you to add some people to that list: my pastor at Covenant Baptist Church, the Bishop of River City, the abbot at St. John's, and the pastors of any area mega-churches, even if they're not physically located in the Forrest. There's also a large Mormon church directly across the Wabash River in Nilesville; it's so close you can see it from the upper floors of both the Imperial Hotel and the Canterbury; make sure you contact them too. Don't forget other religions besides Christianity; during my college years, I recall a Jewish synagogue being on the far east side of the Forrest. And finally, contact Integrity Medical Center, River City College, the River City Fire and Police Departments, the Adams County Jail and Wabash University River City; they probably all have chaplains; invite them as well.

"Community goal: build a non-denominational chapel, open to all and all the time, somewhere in the Forrest district. As I was walking through the city yesterday, I saw the need for a quiet place people could go if necessary. Perhaps, there is a small, empty church, which can be used for this purpose."

"Good luck keeping something like that free from vandalism."

Paul continued without acknowledging Marcy's snarky comment.

"Community goal: hire an executive chaplain and faith community liaison. This person will help us accomplish the other community goals on this list freeing you and me to concentrate on other tasks. He can operate out of the community chapel."

Paul had reached the end of his mental list; and in his silence, Marcy had the opportunity to catch up the transcription. She had placed her pen on the legal pad and was now massaging her wrist.

"And Marcy, we need some type of war room up in the penthouse, a table and chairs, some local maps on the walls, this list posted somewhere conspicuous…a place where we can make action plans."

Marcy dumbly nodded while looking over Paul's shoulder at a strange man who had entered the diner. Paul turned around and followed her gaze to discover John Hayne standing quietly behind him. It was a bit unsettling. Paul checked his watch; it was almost three-thirty. He and Marcy had been at the diner much longer than he realized. Paul stood to make the necessary introductions.

"Marcy, this is my cousin, John Hayne."

"First cousin, twice removed," John corrected.

"Yes, whatever. John, this is my personal assistant, Marcy Green."

John tipped his hat and produced one of his creepy smiles.

"Marcy, can you continue without me for a while."

Marcy nodded silently; she was almost in a state of shock from the strange man's appearance, expression and actions. Only Paul seemed to have any composure.

"Georgia, are we good on the bill."

Georgia nodded but then noticed the man standing next to Paul and joined Marcy in her state of shock.

"Well, they have everything under control here; it looks like I'm all yours."

"This way please."

With that, John Hayne escorted Paul Gray out of the diner and towards a black hearse parked outside. He opened the door to the back seat of the hearse; and Paul climbed inside. John Hayne drove the hearse away as Marcy and Georgia watched in morbid curiosity from inside the diner.

Chapter Thirteen

The drive to Scarsdale was uneventful, partly because most of the route was already familiar territory to Paul, who had traveled it regularly to see his grandparents during his college days and partly because John Hayne was not a very talkative person. Sitting in the back of a hearse with a silent driver was quite unsettling.

Once they entered Scarsdale, West Kentucky, the scenery changed dramatically. Either the Hayne's owned the entire town or the entire town was coat tailing on the various successful yet macabre businesses owned by Sam Hayne and his family. The town was not simply the location of a horror-themed amusement park; the town itself was a horror-themed amusement park. Street names were themed, Dracula Drive, Werewolf Way, Franken Street. The whole effect was at once cheesy and creepy. Everywhere there were signs pointing to various points of interest, each with a spooky theme, but the main attraction was obviously Hayne's Family Scream Park.

In the middle of town was a grand house, a castle really; and it looked like it had been transported directly from Transylvania. Paul correctly guessed that this was the home of Sam Hayne. John Hayne parked the hearse near the front door and assisted his passenger's exit. Paul was then directed towards a dimly lit parlor near the front of the house where he sat at a small round table and waited patiently for his host. He did not have to wait long.

Sam Hayne made quite the entrance. While John was short and pudgy, Sam was tall, thin and gangly. What hair showed from under his top hat was unkempt. He was dressed as a dandy; but a rather color-blind dandy, as nothing he wore matched anything else. His expressions were grossly exaggerated and he did not speak as much as he projected, as if he were on stage acting in a play.

"Dear Cousin Paul! I'm absolutely thrilled to finally make your acquaintance."

Paul stood in respect for his host.

"No! No! No! Please sit back down."

Sam clapped his hands.

"John, please offer our honored guest some refreshments."

John entered the room pushing a small and rickety tea tray. He placed a saucer and cup in front of Paul; and then poured him some tea. He offered Paul some cream and sugar to which Paul politely refused. As Paul sipped the hot beverage, John repeated his actions with Sam. Paul immediately regretted passing on the cream and sugar; the tea tasted like swamp water.

John produced a tray of cucumber sandwiches; and Paul took one. He also produced a tray of something resembling Battenberg cake; and Paul took one of those as well. The cucumber sandwiches tasted terrible; the mayonnaise was spoiled; and the Battenberg cake, if that is what it was, was hard as a rock.

"I hope you find the refreshments enjoyable."

"Yes, they're quite good."

Paul had a mother, two grandmothers, a sister and a roomful of aunts, who would have descended on him like a pack of wolverines if he had answered otherwise, even if it was the truth.

"I understand that you have recently returned from a long trip."

Until he knew what Sam's intentions were, Paul was uncomfortable giving verbose responses.

"I have."

"Splendid! I also understand that you will soon be claiming your inheritance from the late Silas Foster."

"I will."

If Paul's brief answers upset Sam, he did not let it show.

"Again, splendid. May I assume that you will be using your ample resources then to affect many positive changes in River City?"

"You may."

"Splendid. I was very well acquainted with your great-grandfather and his rather questionable business practices. No offense; but we…considered him a vile, little man."

"No offense taken; we felt the same way."

"Splendid. I also understand that you have an assistant, one Marcella Green I believe."

Paul was not aware of Marcy's full name; and this question seemed much more invasive than the others had.

"Yes."

"May I inquire how that came to be?"

"She needed a job; I needed an assistant."

Paul was growing fatigued with Sam's questions.

"I understand that you have already taken possession of the Canterbury. May I inquire as to one of your tenants…a John Dorman?"

Sam's expression had changed dramatically, as he anticipated the answer to this particular question; he was now gravely serious, gone were the eccentric actions that had so defined him earlier. He looked hungry now somehow. The question puzzled John; but he was able to answer it honestly.

"I have not had the opportunity to meet many of the residents, so I'm not familiar with the name."

Sam hesitated while contemplating John's response but quickly reverted to his earlier demeanor.

"Splendid! May I impose to ask some favors of you?"

Paul simply nodded.

"I merely ask that we have these teas on a regular basis. I am most intrigued by the details of this grand plan of yours—this plan to revitalize the dying River City. I would enjoy the opportunity to hear regular progress reports on your success."

Paul again merely nodded his approval.

"Splendid! I would also ask that you share whatever information you may happen to discover about Mr. Dorman…when you do finally meet him of course…any detail whatsoever."

"May I ask why?"

For the first time since he met him, Paul thought Sam's expression had turned sinister.

"We find him…fascinating."

As quickly as his expression had changed though, it changed back.

"Before you return home, I would like to offer you a small gift."

"It's not necessary."

"Neither is it debatable. John, retrieve the box."

John returned with a small box and placed it on the table in front of Paul.

"Well, go ahead; open it!"

The excitement on both Sam's and John's face was palpable. Paul opened the box to discover a small, gold signet ring. The emblem on the ring was that of a bee.

"Put it on; it goes on the middle finger of the right hand."

Paul honored the request and was surprised that the ring fit so perfectly.

"What is it?"

"Just a bauble I had lying around the house. I thought it would be the perfect gift for you. I'll have some other little gifts for you from time to time, as you pay your visits. Now, if you'll excuse me, I do have some business to attend to; I'm sure your schedule is equally occupied."

Paul ignored his host's bluntness, as he was ready to leave too. Both men stood up; and Paul offered his hand to Sam.

Sam looked at it with shock and disgust; but he corrected himself quickly.

"I'm sorry. I don't shake hands."

Sam raised his hands in the air and made some air kisses while barely touching Paul's cheeks.

"I bid you farewell, Cousin Paul."

As John and Paul exited the building, Sam called back to him.

"Paul, if you ever need anything to achieve those goals of yours, don't hesitate to call upon me; I'm at your service. I can assure you that I'm not without resources or influence."

"Thank you, Sam."

Paul took his seat in the back of the hearse, as John drove him back to the Canterbury. John could not hear him; but Paul murmured something under his breath.

"Well, that was weird."

Chapter Fourteen

Paul exited the Canterbury's elevator as Marcy was waiting to enter it. She looked embarrassed at his presence.

"I'm sorry, Paul; I didn't know when you would be returning. It's almost 5:30; and I hadn't heard from you; and I didn't know what my hours were; but I was at a good stopping point, so I just decided to--."

Paul let go of the elevator door, which he had been holding for Marcy's convenience. The doors closed and a noise behind them indicated that the car had departed.

"Relax, Marcy. I don't want to work in an office environment that is so suffocating. I know you started at 9:00 today...actually a lot earlier...and you're probably ready to leave...but let's establish your hours...the office's hours...as 8:00 to 4:00. Sometimes you'll need to come in earlier, more your prerogative than mine; and sometimes you might be running late for whatever reason. At the other end, sometimes you'll be able to leave early; and other times, you'll be working rather late. It will all depend on what is happening at the time. As long as the work is completed and I can reach you by cell phone if necessary, I really don't care when you come and go. Understand? Are you okay now?"

While he had been talking, Marcy was having a minor anxiety attack; but after he finished, she took several deep breaths and regained her composure before nodding.

"Good. Was there anything that happened while I was gone that needs my attention before Monday."

"No. How was the tea with your cousin?"

"You were right; he's a real loon; however, I need to meet with him on a regular basis, so remind me to schedule that."

"Is there anything else? Did you want to continue working?"

"No, let's quit for the day…for the weekend actually; but Marcy, we need to organize some type of reception and soon. I need to meet all of the Canterbury's tenants in a relaxed setting; I don't want to be an invisible landlord. Also, find out everything you can about John Dorman; he's one of those tenants; however, be discrete about it."

Marcy nodded and made a mental note because her pen and legal pad were not handy. Paul walked towards his apartment as Marcy again pressed the elevator call button.

"I'll see you Monday morning at 8:00, Marcy."

"Good night, Paul."

"Good night."

The elevator doors opened again and Marcy started to enter as Paul called after her.

"By the way, what's Marcy short for?"

"Marcella."

"How many people would know that or use it?"

"Besides my mother? As few as necessary. Why do you ask?"

"Just wondering. Good night, Marcy."

Paul entered his apartment as the elevator doors closed.

Paul's new home, the penthouse apartment, which was originally occupied by his great-grandfather, was palatial. It had been built specifically for

Silas Foster; and until now, he had been its only occupant. During its five-year vacancy, when Paul Gray was riding across the country on his father's motorcycle, it had been temporarily commandeered by that pack of wolverines, which were Paul's female relations.

Unbeknownst to Paul, they had appointed themselves his interior decorators, removing anything outdated or strongly associated with Silas Foster and replacing it with furnishings appropriate for a young and wealthy twenty-first century male. They had done a great job; the place did not seem feminine at all; in fact, they had captured Paul's very masculine tastes and style perfectly.

Besides the bags he had with him on the road and the items Nan had placed in his hotel room, all of his belongings were already here including items he had sent back home from the road. Nan had even filled the kitchen with more than enough food, so there was very little he needed to do to settle in. He found appropriate places for the few personal belongings he had brought from the hotel; most of it was dirty laundry. As this was the first time he had ever been in this part of the Canterbury, he gave himself a tour.

Beyond the large foyer, there was a great room; and past that, separated by a custom-made breakfast bar, there was an enormous kitchen, Paul's favorite room in any house. On the right side of the great room was a door leading to an office; and on the left side were double doors leading to a dining room. Entry to the kitchen was through the dining room; and from there, there were doors again to the left and right, the left one led to a large pantry; and the right one on the far end of the kitchen led to the laundry room.

Much to Paul's dismay, there was no staircase; Paul always preferred to take the stairs. Silas Foster had installed an elevator instead; and its first floor station was located in the foyer. The second floor contained a theater and a huge game room with all manner of amusements and diversions.

The third floor was the master suite; besides a bedroom and a bathroom with a whirlpool, it contained a large walk-in closet, dressing area, exercise room, study and a wraparound balcony, which overlooked River City. Although this was his residence now, and he lived here by himself, he was hesitant to claim this room as his own; but he noticed that his family had placed his clothes in the closet and toiletries in the bathroom, so he conceded that this was, in fact, his room now. He was particularly excited about the well-furnished exercise room; he would not need to use the weights located down the hall in the Sunset Room.

The fourth floor contained six bedrooms, each with a private bath. The fifth floor was empty and unfinished. Paul wondered why it had even been built; and for what purpose Silas Foster may have used it. Perhaps his family simply did not know what to do with it, when they were redecorating. The sixth and top floor contained an easterly facing sunroom, an indoor pool and a winter garden. There was also a door to an outside patio. Paul did not go outside; it was too cold this late in the day and year; but he could see that the ledge was lined with gargoyles.

It was getting late; and Paul was ready to retire for the night; however, he still had one more very important job to do. The problem was that he needed to do it in the middle of the night, so Paul took a catnap on the couch of the great room; and woke himself up around midnight.

Chapter Fifteen

Paul scavenged around in the kitchen to find a bowl, a spoon, a box of corn flakes and a quart of milk. This was just the energy he would need for the upcoming task. After he ate, he went to his closet to find the necessary clothes: a black turtleneck sweater, a pair of black trousers, a pair of black socks, and a black knit cap; and then, he changed into them. He removed his driver's license from his wallet, placed it in his right back pocket, and put his wallet on a shelf in the dressing room. He removed the key to his penthouse apartment from his key ring, placed it in his right front pocket, and put his key ring on the shelf. He silenced his phone and placed it in his front left pocket. Finally, he searched his bathroom, hoping that Nan had stocked it thoroughly; and after a few minutes, he found the item, which he was seeking—a couple of cotton balls, which he pocketed. Although he was not wearing any shoes, he was now ready—well, almost.

He turned out the lights in his apartment and closed the door. The penthouse hallway was dimly lit; but bright enough to make his way to the Sunset room where the tools he ordered from Dan's Hardware were still located. After he turned on the lights, he immediately found the necessary item—a pair of night vision goggles. He turned off the lights, closed the door, donned the goggles, and made his way towards the stairwell.

Paul quickly descended the staircase to the second sub-basement. Paul opened the door carefully and closed it just as carefully behind himself hoping that it did not creak; it did not. He crouched behind some boxes near the stairwell door; and turned on the thermal vision feature of the goggles. Then he stood up and looked around. His thermal vision made it easy to count the sleeping figures; there were fifteen.

Paul quietly made his way back up to the basement level where he located the distribution board for the entire building. It took him some time but he finally located the pertinent circuit breakers. He then removed his cell phone and called the Imperial Hotel.

"Thank you for calling the Imperial Hotel! This is Peter. How may I assist you?"

"Peter, this is Paul Gray; I'm the new Lost & Found Director; and my grandfather owns the hotel."

"Yes, Mr. Gray, I just read the memo regarding your position. Welcome to the Imperial Hotel."

"Thank you, Peter, and just call me Paul. Do you have someone working in security or engineering this evening?"

"Tony is working security; and Dakota is down in engineering."

"Great! Put me on hold; contact both of them; and give them the following instructions. Tell Tony to put a doorstop on the door in the second subbasement, which leads to the tunnels; also tell him to block the path from that door to the staircase as quickly as possible with whatever he can find. Next, tell Dakota to shut off all power to the subbasements. When they finish, come back on the line and let me know."

"Is there a problem, Mr. Gray, I mean Paul."

"I have some squatters over here at the Canterbury; and I need to relocate them. There are fifteen of them; and they'll probably be running through and out the hotel very soon. You should be prepared to call the police just in case."

"Okay. I'll notify Tony and Dakota immediately."

As Paul was waiting for Peter, he found some doorstops on the floor and pocketed them. It did not take long for Peter to come back on the line.

"Paul, they've done as you requested."

"Great. Thank you and thank Tony and Dakota for me. I look forward to

THE MELISSA RING – GRAY'S FORREST

meeting all of you in person, possibly next week. Good bye, Peter."

"Good night and good luck, Paul."

Paul disconnected the phone call and switched off the lights to the subbasement, second subbasement and tunnels. He was counting on two things that the gang was heavy sleepers and that they did not have any light sources immediately available. First, the gang probably relied on two things: that most people were too scared to come down to the second subbasement and those who did would immediately turn on a light rousing the gang from their sleep. Secondly, when he fought the two members on his first day in River City, he noticed that they were not wearing any expensive clothes or jewelry; he doubted whether they would even have basics like a flashlight or cell phone.

He made his way back to the second subbasement and crept around wedging doorstops in the doors leading to the stairwells and tunnels and moving heavy boxes and items to places where they would not expect them. He was careful not to make any noise. As he moved around the Canterbury's second subbasement and around the sleeping gang members, he noticed a box full of old baseballs; and immediately seized on a secondary plan to put them to good use.

Paul carried the box of baseballs to a strategic location behind some larger boxes, placed the cotton balls in his ears and opened a sound effect application he had downloaded earlier to his cell phone. The application came with several sound effects but there was only one in which he was interested—a police siren. He turned the volume on the phone as loud as he could, performed a mental countdown and pressed the play button.

What happened next was both horrifying and hilarious; sheer pandemonium had erupted in the Canterbury's second subbasement; Paul's plan was working perfectly. The first gang members to wake quickly and successfully found the light switches; but when they realized there was no power, panic reigned as they were unable to get their bearings in this now unfamiliar landscape. None of them was able to find their way to a door— any door.

While pitch darkness was confusing enough, Paul's siren was disorienting in its own way. Added to that were the simultaneous screams and yells

CHAPTER FIFTEEN

from fifteen terrified gang members and Paul's own vocal contributions. Fortunately, there were four vacant floors between the second subbasement and the closest occupied room. Above, nobody heard a thing; but below, the din made it impossible to communicate effectively.

Paul implemented the baseballs next. With the benefit of his night vision goggles, he was able to see whenever one of the gang members wandered too close to him or one of the doors. Moreover, he was able to hit them easily with one of the balls; and the resulting contact managed to induce a temporary shock and an unintended change of direction. Mostly though, contact was between gang members; thinking they were fighting an unseen army, the members of Las Ratas had taken to hitting each other without question, sometimes accidentally and sometimes intentionally. One of the gang members ran full force into a support post and knocked himself unconscious.

This bizarre battle lasted almost twenty minutes; and Paul could tell that all fifteen men had lost their will to fight. He turned off the siren, removed the cotton balls from his ears and made his way to the door leading to the tunnel to the Imperial Hotel, and opened it. He called out to the gang members.

"I finally found the way out; everybody follow me."

Now without any competing noise, the wounded gang members were able to make their way towards and through the door. They did not even realize that it was a strange voice leading them. Paul counted the number of men, who passed by him on their exit from the battleground—there were fourteen. Paul closed the door and jammed it hard so the gang members could not retreat and then turned on the thermal vision feature. Where was the fifteenth man? Had he managed to escape?

After a cursory search, Paul found him laying on the ground unconscious near a support beam. Paul quickly removed the jam leading to the staircase, which he had descended earlier then returned to the man laying on the floor. Paul put his hands underneath the man's shoulders and dragged him over to the stairwell door. The man did not seem too large, so Paul picked him up and carried him two floors to the main basement where there were still working lights.

The man was still unconscious; but Paul could see a large goose egg on the man's forehead; a black eye was taking shape; his lip was bleeding; and his nose appeared to be broken. The man stirred a little and grabbed his left side. Paul wondered if his rib was broken or if there was internal bleeding.

"Are you okay?"

The man stirred a little more; and Paul took his hand. Neither Paul nor the wounded man noticed that at that very moment, Paul's newly acquired ring was starting to glow brightly and that energy was passing between Paul and the injured gang member. Paul used his cell phone to call for an ambulance; and then he called Peter and told him to restore power to the subbasements of the hotel. He found the breakers to the lower levels, which he had turned off earlier, and turned them back on.

The ambulance arrived quickly; and Paul briefed them on the incident while they examined the man, who was now conscious and able to communicate with them.

"Mr. Gray, he appears to be okay; but it would be prudent for the hospital to examine him, possibly x-ray his head and ribs."

Paul nodded in agreement.

"I want to ride along."

Chapter Sixteen

r. Gray!"

A doctor roused Paul from his nap in a waiting room chair.

"Is he okay?"

"He's in perfect condition, not a scratch on him."

"That's impossible, doctor. I not only saw his injuries; I saw him get injured."

"See for yourself."

The doctor led Paul to a small room in the emergency department of Integrity Medical, where a young Hispanic male sat on the edge of a bed. Paul recognized him as the same man he had carried out of the second subbasement of the Canterbury; but at the same time, he was not the same man. There was no bump on his forehead, no black eye, no broken nose, not even a cut lip--no evidence of last night's melee.

"He's not even complaining of a headache. He might very well be the healthiest person in this entire hospital; he's certainly the luckiest considering what all happened. Get him out of here; I need the bed for people who are really sick."

The doctor left the room and there was a long awkward silence between the two remaining men. Paul broke it by offering his hand.

"I'm Paul Gray. I own the Canterbury where your group was squatting."

The young man took Paul's hand. Again, Paul's ring glowed; and again, neither man noticed it.

"I'm Clemente Morales."

"Well Clemente, let's get you out of this place."

"Sir, I don't have any money to pay the hospital bill."

"I've already taken care of it, Clemente. Come on."

Like a lost puppy dog, Clemente Morales followed Paul Gray out of the hospital and to a truck parked in the parking lot. While the hospital staff had been running a battery of tests on Clemente during the night, Paul had walked back to the Canterbury in his sock feet to retrieve his shoes, coat, wallet, keys, and most importantly his truck. Now, sitting in the cab, Paul asked Clemente for directions.

"Where can I take you, Clemente?"

The young man looked at him blankly.

"Where's your home?"

"Las Ratas is my home."

"I meant 'Where's your family?'"

"Las Ratas is my family."

Paul was getting nowhere.

"You're not returning to that gang, Clemente. Is there anywhere else I can take you?"

Again, Clemente returned a vacant expression.

"How old are you?"

"Nineteen"

He was not even a minor. This would be very difficult.

"How long have you been a member of Las Ratas?"

Clemente Morales considered the question; he was slowly calculating the answer in his mind.

"Ten years."

"You were nine years old, when you joined the gang?"

Clemente nodded silently.

"Where are your parents?"

"They're dead."

"Both of them?"

"My father was killed when I was two years old. My mother had been sick for a very long time almost since I was born; and she died when I was six. I was scared and didn't want to live in an orphanage so I ran away."

"You have no other family, no older siblings, no grandparents, no aunts and uncles."

Clemente shook his head.

"Where did you go when you ran away?"

"I wanted to get as far away as possible, so I hid in boxcars."

"You rode around the country on a train for three years before joining Las Ratas?"

Clemente nodded his head.

"Where were you born, Clemente?"

"East L.A."

"Have you ever been to a school or church or held a job?"

Clemente shook his head.

"Where are your possessions? Do you have any possessions?"

Clemente shook his head.

"Just the clothes on your back?"

Clemente nodded his head. The clothes on his back were nothing to mention. Despite the cold weather, he was wearing a dark blue t-shirt, a pair of jeans, a pair of white crew socks, an old pair of gym shoes, and of course, a Las Ratas jacket. Everything was dirty and threadbare.

"Are you hungry, Clemente?"

Clemente nodded more eagerly this time.

It was now clear to Paul what needed to be done today. He started the truck and drove it back to the lowest level of the Pine Avenue Parking Garage then the two men made their way on foot to the River City Diner cutting through Canterbury's lobby.

Ashleigh greeted them with glasses of water and menus and gave them time to make their selections; Paul had sensed her well-hidden hesitation. Had he not been there with him, the diner probably would have turned Clemente away based on his appearance. Paul already knew what he wanted to eat; but he watched with interest as Clemente, who had a puzzled look on his face, studied the menu.

"Clemente, can you read?"

Paul had tried to whisper so Clemente would not feel embarrassed.

"Yes, I can read; I just don't know how to order in a fancy restaurant."

Clemente blushed a little at his confession as Ashleigh returned to their table.

"Ashleigh, I would like country fried steak, scrambled eggs, hash browns and a side order of pancakes, and a tall glass of orange juice to drink. Oh, and a cup of coffee."

Before Ashleigh could ask Clemente for his order, Paul interceded.

"How does that sound to you, Clemente?"

He nodded; and as he nodded, his eyes were dancing with excitement at the prospect of such a large meal.

"Make it two, Ashleigh."

Paul always thought he had a healthy appetite until he watched Clemente eat. Paul could never remember going to bed hungry in his entire life, even when he was on the road; he doubted whether Clemente had ever went to bed full. Like Paul, he ate every bite on his plate; but unlike Paul, he asked Ashleigh for a couple biscuits so he could sop up the remaining crumbs, gravy, grease, and syrup. When he finished, his plate almost sparkled.

There was much to do, so Paul did not linger at the diner, as he would have liked to. He settled the bill and led Clemente out the diner and into the Canterbury's lobby where he pressed the elevator's call button. He did not offer to tell Clemente what he had planned; and Clemente did not ask. Paul assumed that he was used to just going along with the group.

Paul led Clemente to his apartment.

"Do you live here?"

"Yes."

"By yourself?"

"Yes; but for a while, I don't know how long; you'll be living here too."

Clemente's expression betrayed an overwhelming sense of awe.

"I'll show you around later; right now, we have some work to do."

Paul called for the elevator; and when they entered the car, Paul pressed the button for the third floor.

"You have an elevator in your apartment."

Paul simply nodded; he was not used to it yet either.

"The third floor is my room."

Clemente followed him out of the elevator and through the master suite to the wardrobe where Paul found a sweatshirt, a pair of sweatpants, a pair of white crew socks and a pair of boxers. Paul then moved to his bathroom and located the sundries Nan had placed in his hotel room. He rummaged through them and found what he was looking for, a bar of soap, a small container of shampoo, a can of deodorant, a new toothbrush, a small tube of toothpaste. Paul was not sure whether his family had stocked the extra bathrooms with linens, so he grabbed a bath towel, hand towel and washcloth. He handed all of these things to Clemente and then led him to a bedroom on the fourth floor.

"This will be your room. Go in the bathroom, take a shower and change into those clothes."

He had not made it back to the elevator yet, when he heard Clemente call for him. Paul ran back to Clemente's room and bolted into the bathroom without knocking. Clemente was standing naked in the shower stall staring at the controls; his old clothes were lying in a pile on the floor near the door.

"I don't know how to turn the shower on."

"I'm sorry, Clemente; I should have showed you; I just assumed you knew."

Paul reached around him and turned the shower on getting his own arm wet in the process; and then he quickly showed Clemente how to adjust the temperature and turn the water off. He also showed him where to put his wet towels. Paul gathered Clemente's old clothes and left quickly, closing

CHAPTER SIXTEEN

the door to the bathroom and bedroom behind him.

Paul went outside on the sixth floor patio and after checking the pockets, placed Clemente's old clothes, except the gang jacket and shoes, in a metal waste can. The shoes, he placed on the foyer floor; and the jacket, he threw into the Sunset Room with the other two. Paul was building quite the trophy collection.

He returned to his apartment, found a matchbook in the kitchen and an extra jacket in his closet and then went to his office where he sat at the desk for the very first time. While Clemente showered, Paul made some notes in his notebook and checked some addresses on his cell phone; but most importantly, he prayed, not just for Clemente but for himself; he hoped he was doing the right thing. He recalled seeing Clemente's naked body standing in the shower stall and how much more evident the years of caked-on dirt were on him. He wondered if Clemente had ever had a proper shower in his life.

"Mr. Gray?"

Clemente, who now looked and smelled much better, was wandering around the great room looking for his host.

"In here, Clemente."

Clemente entered the office.

"And Clemente, call me Paul."

Paul handed him the extra jacket and showed him where he had placed his old shoes; and Clemente put them on, then Paul led Clemente outside to the patio.

"Clemente, I placed your old clothes in this waste can. They were filthy and worn; and I think they are an unnecessary reminder of the past."

Paul produced the matchbook he had found in the kitchen.

"I think it would be emotionally beneficial, if you—"

Clemente needed no further instruction or justification; he took the matchbook out of Paul's hand, lit a match and threw it onto the pile of clothes. Despite the cold weather, both men stood quietly and watched the fire totally consume the clothes and burn out, and then Clemente retreated to the elevator and waited for Paul who followed only seconds later.

"I apologize that I did not have some shoes to lend you; but we'll be purchasing some new clothes for you today; and as soon as you have new shoes, I want you to throw those old shoes away. Understand?"

Clemente nodded his head. The two men returned to the foyer via the elevator, where Paul grabbed his own jacket, then they made their way out of the apartment, halfway down the penthouse hallway and then down the elevator to the Canterbury's lobby.

"There's a place to purchase men's clothes just a few blocks from here on Cedar Avenue, so we'll just walk."

Paul led him out the Pine Avenue exit, then north a half block to 4th Street, where they turned right. They walked two blocks until they reached Cedar Avenue, where they turned left and walked another one and half blocks. Paul pointed to a store across the street—Taylor's Haberdashery.

"That's where we will be purchasing your clothes later today, Clemente; but first, we have one more job to do."

The two men walked further down Cedar to a store almost directly across the street from Taylor's. Paul and Clemente entered the Avalon Salon and Spa and, considering the business's location, were met with a surprisingly posh and tranquil environment. Paul motioned to some empty chairs and told Clemente to have a seat while he spoke with the receptionist.

"Welcome to Avalon! Did you have an appointment?"

"No, we don't. I was hoping you accepted walk-ins."

"We do. What services do you require?"

"It's not for me. It's for my friend, Clemente, over there."

Paul pointed towards Clemente and the receptionist studied him intently. Clemente, not knowing how to respond to this attention, waved to them like a small child. The gesture would have appeared comical if not for the charming naiveté, in which it had been delivered.

"Obviously, he needs a haircut and a shave…probably a manicure. What do you suggest?"

"Definitely the Frog Prince package."

"Exactly what does the Frog Prince package involve?"

Paul chuckled as he asked the question

"Bring us your ugly old frog; and we'll use every spell in our book…plus a few that aren't in the book…to change him back into a handsome prince."

The receptionist sounded like she was reading a script for a commercial marketed heavily towards desperate wives.

She and Paul both laughed loud and long.

"Well, it sounds like what he needs. Start working your magic."

"Uh uh! Not yet! Magic comes with a price."

"Well, I don't have any gold balls handy, so will magic accept a plastic card instead."

"Gladly!"

The receptionist took Paul's credit card and processed the bill for Paul to sign. He added a twenty-five percent gratuity.

"And would you make sure all of the good little witches involved receive a share of the tip."

The receptionist grinned at Paul but spoke to Clemente.

"Hop on back here, frog boy; when we get done with you, every princess in the land will want to dance with you."

Clemente followed the receptionist through a door; and Paul took his seat in the lobby. Five hours later, Clemente emerged; and the transformation was remarkable. If it were not for the clothes he had loaned him earlier, Paul would not have even recognized him. Gone were the shoulder-length hair, the bushy eyebrows, the facial hair, and the un-manicured fingernails. In their place was indeed a handsome prince.

Paul and Clemente walked out of Avalon.

"Clemente, I don't know about you; but I'm getting a little hungry."

Clemente nodded enthusiastically.

"Well, while you were getting all your salon and spa treatments, I scoped the block; and I could only find one restaurant."

Paul walked to a hot dog cart further up the block.

"Two all the way."

The vendor placed two wieners in buns and then topped them with mustard, chili and onions. Paul paid for them, handed one of them to Clemente, and quickly ate the other.

"I don't know about you; but I could go for another one easily."

Clemente nodded.

"Two more all the way and a couple of Cokes."

Paul and the vendor once again made their exchange; and then Paul and Clemente wolfed down their second hot dogs. As they stood on the sidewalk, drinking their Cokes, Clemente described his experience at Avalon in detail.

"They even gave me a massage."

"Well, did you enjoy it?"

Clemente's eyes lit up as he nodded.

"Then, that's all that matters. If you're finished, let's get you some new clothes, frog boy."

"I'm a prince now," responded Clemente sheepishly.

Taylor's Haberdashery was as out of place in the Forrest as Avalon Salon and Spa was. One would believe they were instead in a shop on Savile Row in London. The place reeked with refined masculinity. An older gentleman approached them. Short one British accent, he could have been the valet of an English nobleman.

"Did we bring our money today?"

The clerk sounded patronizing; but Paul ignored his question.

"My friend here needs a new wardrobe."

The salesclerk surveyed Clemente haughtily.

"That much is obvious."

He crossed his arms and offered Paul both a sneer and a moment of mocking laughter.

The man's attitude infuriated Paul. He immediately thought of Gilbert Gillenwater.

"Clemente, why don't you look around the store and see if there is anything you like."

When Clemente had moved out of earshot, Paul readdressed the clerk.

"My name is Paul Gray; and among many other businesses and properties in this city, I just happen to own this building. That young man over there, the one you don't think so highly of, has had a harder life in his nineteen years than you and I put together. The clothes I took off him earlier today weren't even fit to launder; right now, he's wearing some old clothes I lent him. He needs a fresh start: suits for a job interview, casual clothes, work clothes, everything."

Paul once again produced his credit card. The salesclerk noticed that it was a platinum card.

"Just so you know. I'm paying for everything. And, if I especially like the clothes, which we purchase today, and I enjoy the remainder of our visit to your store, I will return and purchase some clothes for my own wardrobe and refer this store to my friends. If I'm not satisfied though, I may strongly consider putting a rave in this place when the lease runs out. Now do you want to help my friend purchase a wardrobe or should we find another store?"

The clerk, now humbled, walked towards Clemente and assisted him in building a wardrobe. They spent a couple of hours in the store and purchased a whole closet full of clothes for Clemente. The clerk's attitude had really turned around; and he even made a great effort to explain to Clemente both how to wear and care for the clothes. Before leaving the store, the three men selected clothes for Clemente to wear the next few days and arranged for delivery of the remainder on Monday. With their arms filled with boxes and bags, Paul and Clemente made their way back to the Canterbury.

Much like the feeling he had had in the diner on his first day in town, when John Hayne had been spying on him, Paul sensed someone was now following Clemente and him. It had started shortly after they had left the haberdashery. Occasionally, Paul would turn around; but he was never able to locate the tail. The feeling was growing as they approached the Pine Avenue entrance of the Canterbury; and Paul was wondering if one of the members of Las Ratas was seeking revenge.

"Clemente, I don't want to frighten you; but we have had someone trailing us almost since we left Taylor's. If they follow us inside, I want you to run around to the diner and have Georgia call the police. Do you understand?"

Whether it was curiosity or street instinct, Clemente ignored Paul's instructions and turned around to face their pursuer.

"Paul, I'm not sure, you can fight him all by yourself."

Paul turned around to discover a friendly little beagle standing on the sidewalk behind them, looking back and forth expectedly between the two men. Paul knelt down and scratched the dog behind the ears.

"What's your name, buddy? I don't see a collar. Don't you belong to someone?"

Like his father and paternal grandparents before him, Paul was a natural empath. It worked with people to some degree; but Paul's real talent was communicating with animals, especially horses, cats…and of course dogs. Paul had never met an animal that he did not like and did not like him back, so he took a moment to connect deeply with the beagle.

"Do you want to come home with us?"

The dog barked and Paul stood up.

"Well, come on then!"

Paul, Clemente and the beagle entered the Canterbury, summoned the elevator, and then rode it to the penthouse.

"Do you take in all strays?"

Clemente's question in the elevator caught Paul by surprise. It was painfully sincere and not even slightly sarcastic. When the elevator arrived at the penthouse and they exited it, Paul stopped the party outside his apartment door to address Clemente's question.

"Clemente, listen to me very carefully. Neither of you are strays. A stray is a person or animal that wanders around because it doesn't have a home. Both you and this dog have a home now…with me."

"But why? Why would you do all of this for me? I don't understand. I've been on the streets for thirteen years; and nobody's even tried to help me before."

"Clemente, I can't explain why the masses that walked by you, didn't stop to help. I can only tell you that God has abundantly blessed my life; and to show my appreciation and love for Him, I allow myself to be an instrument He can use to bless others like you."

Paul took his key and unlocked the door. When the door opened, the beagle immediately ran into the apartment investigating and sniffing every inch of the first floor.

"Take your clothes up to your room; and then come back down. It's getting late; and I'm not sure I have enough time to cook for you, as I would like to; plus, I'm in the mood for some Chinese. If that's okay with you, I'll call in an order for delivery."

Clemente took his packages up to his room; and eager to have a new floor to explore, the beagle quickly followed him. Paul used his phone to locate a nearby Chinese restaurant that delivered, called them and placed an order.

The deliveryman from Forbidden City arrived at the same time Clemente and the beagle returned to the great room. Paul paid the young Asian man, gave him a generous tip, and placed the food on the breakfast bar along with some plates he found in a cabinet a few minutes earlier. He also filled two tall glasses with ice water.

"I wasn't sure what you liked from a Chinese menu, so I ordered a little of everything. I thought we could sample all of them."

Paul opened each of the cartons, placing a tablespoon in each, and declaring its contents for Clemente's benefit. As each carton was opened, the wonderful and unique aromas of Chinese cuisine gradually pervaded the room.

"Crab Rangoon…beef lo mein…General Tso's chicken…Kung Pao shrimp…be careful, Clemente; that one's probably very hot…sweet and sour pork…Yeung Chow fried rice…and of course, some fortune cookies for later."

Paul looked at the beagle, which was standing inches away licking his chops.

"I'm sorry, buddy; I don't have any dog food; but when we finish eating,

I'll find something for you. Clemente, I would really like to pray before we eat."

Paul bowed his head, while Clemente silently watched him.

"Dear heavenly Father, thank You for this food that you've graciously provided. I thank You for bringing Clemente into my home. Please use me to bless him as only You can. May Your will be done as he starts rebuilding his life. And, thank you for sending me this cute little dog too. I ask these things in the name of my Lord and Savior, Jesus Christ. Amen."

Both men filled their plates; and then Paul handed Clemente a fork.

"There's a sweet, little lady in San Francisco, who I dearly love and consider my Chinese grandmother; during the brief time I lived in her house, she taught me how to use chopsticks. She told me that I either could eat with them or be hit with them; I wisely chose to learn to eat with them. Although she's thousands of miles away, she will somehow know if I eat this food without chopsticks. She would then hunt me down like an animal and beat me to within an inch of my life. However, I don't expect you to follow suit."

Both men chuckled.

"I'm not used to eating in that big dining room; it just seems so formal. Let's just sit here in the great room next to the coffee table."

Paul took a seat in a chair facing the entryway; and Clemente found a spot on the couch nearby. Clemente had taken a few bites using the fork, which Paul had given him; but he studied Paul's technique with the chopsticks. He walked back to the breakfast bar and retrieved the other pair of chopsticks and the carton of beef lo mein, sitting that on the coffee table in front of him. It only took him a few attempts; but soon, he was eating with the chopsticks as if he had always known how to do so.

"Look at you using chopsticks like a pro."

"No, look at the dog."

Clemente directed Paul's attention to the beagle, which had grown rather impatient with so much food available and had seized the first opportunity to help himself to some of it. He quickly devoured the contents of the carton sitting on the coffee table and had stuck his snout far down into it to consume every last morsel. In the process, the carton had become stuck; and for the next few minutes, he vigorously shook his head to free himself. At last, the carton fell to the ground, and the beagle barked and growled at it, then licked it. One stray noodle sat on the dog's nose; he employed his tongue and a great deal of contorting to remove and ultimately devour it. Paul and Clemente laughed heartily at the dog's silly antics.

"As much as he likes the beef lo mein, you should call him Noodles."

"Do you like that name, buddy?"

The beagle barked in response.

"Noodles it is then."

When Paul and Clemente had eaten their fill, Paul retrieved the two fortune cookies and handed one to Clemente. Paul opened his cookie and read the fortune.

"Don't offer your hand to the man, who lingers on your threshold."

"What does that mean?"

"I don't know. At the bottom, it has the number, 4213; perhaps, that's my lucky number. What does yours say?"

Clemente opened his fortune cookie.

"One journey ended yesterday, while another starts tomorrow. There aren't any numbers"

There was an art to writing fortunes. Either they imparted sound advice that could apply to almost anyone and any situation or they made vague predictions, which were malleable enough in hindsight to be interpreted any way the reader wished. Apart from their entertainment value, Paul did not place much faith in their messages.

Paul, Clemente and Noodles had consumed almost all of the food; so before he got too lazy, Paul cleared away the remnants as Clemente sat on the couch petting a half-asleep beagle in his lap. When Paul returned to his chair, Clemente asked him several questions about his faith, which lasted long into the night until sleep finally overtook him. Paul found a blanket and covered Clemente and Noodles before retiring to his room for the night.

Chapter Seventeen

Despite having stayed up rather late with Clemente discussing religion, Paul woke early, naturally, and surprisingly refreshed. Although he had not realized it at the time or even now, he had just spent his first night in his new bed. He was more eager to initiate his brand new exercise room and resume the ambitious regimen he had had in college. After exercising, Paul showered, shaved, and dressed for church: dark gray suit, white shirt and a navy blue tie. Since he had made a special trip earlier in the week to St. Anthony's to meet Father Andrews, Paul decided to forego the earlier and closer service and just attend Covenant Baptist Church in Cricksburg. He would resume his two-church schedule next Sunday.

Paul took the elevator to the first floor and noticed Clemente and Noodles were no longer there. For one brief moment, Paul feared that Clemente had decided to return to his former life and take the beagle with him. Reason however won and Paul surmised that at some point, he got up to sleep in his bed and took Noodles with him. The blanket, which had covered them, had been folded neatly and placed on the edge of the couch.

Even more than the exercise room, Paul was excited about breaking in his new kitchen. As a teenager in Puerto Rico at his grandfather's hotel, he had already started working in the kitchen doing whatever he could; and when he moved here to River City for college and worked at the Imperial, he would occasionally fill in when the kitchen was short staffed. During the summers, Paul had managed to obtain a culinary arts degree on the side. He had even picked up some kitchen tricks and recipes from different people during his five-year cross-country odyssey.

As he cooked breakfast, he wondered to himself about how he would raise the topic of church with Clemente. He did not want to force it on him; but he did not want to not give him the opportunity either. These wonderings immediately became a moot point when Clemente emerged from the elevator and entered the kitchen with Noodles close behind. Clemente was dressed in one of the suits, which they had purchased at Taylor's yesterday. It was a navy blue suit; with it, he wore a baby blue shirt, a yellow power tie, which he had tied perfectly, and a pair of black Oxfords. Clemente had not buttoned the jacket; and Paul noticed that he had opted for a pair of blue suspenders over a belt. Clemente's makeover was now complete; and he looked fantastic.

"What smells so good?"

"French toast and bacon! Did you sleep well?"

"Very. I hope you don't mind. Noodles slept in bed with me."

Clemente paused for a minute, thinking he may have broken a rule and then added some justification.

"I didn't want him to feel scared and lonely during the night."

Paul suppressed a laugh.

"It's okay, Clemente."

Paul turned his attention to the dog that was directly underfoot.

"And I didn't forget you this time either."

Paul knelt down and fed a few strips of bacon to Noodles.

"Paul, before we eat breakfast, could I say the prayer."

Paul was pleasantly surprised but he tried hard not to show it.

"Sure, Clemente."

Paul bowed his head and listened intently to Clemente's prayer.

"God, it's Clemente…Clemente Morales…I just wanted to thank You for sending Paul to help me. After all of the things I've done, I know I don't deserve it; but he's taken really good care of me. He bought me these nice clothes...and he cooked this breakfast...and it smells and looks really good. And, thank You for sending Noodles too. I didn't tell Paul this; but Noodles wasn't the only one, who was a little scared and lonely last night. I just wanted you to know these things. And, God, if it's not too much to ask, could You send someone to take care of the rest of the guys, because I know they're probably scared too. I guess that's all."

Clemente had stopped praying, so Paul concluded the prayer for him.

"Amen."

Paul choked back tears as he said that one small word. Again, the two men refrained from using the dining room, preferring to sit at the breakfast bar this time instead. They ate their breakfast in relative silence. They were not mad; both men just had a lot on their minds. When breakfast was over, Paul washed the dishes as Clemente sat on the couch with Noodles.

"Clemente, I want you to do me a favor."

Clemente rose to face Paul; and Paul handed him a twenty-dollar bill.

"I want you to go downstairs to the diner and order two large coffees to go. Give the waitress this twenty and tell her to keep the change. If her nametag says 'Ashleigh,' tell her that you were the guy, who was eating breakfast with Paul Gray yesterday morning. I'll meet you in the lobby."

Clemente nodded that he understood and left the apartment. Paul took a moment to gain his composure. Clemente's prayer had really affected him. While Paul really did want some coffee to drink as they drove to church, he had also sent Clemente to the diner to send a gentle message to Ashleigh not to judge others so quickly. Clemente's prayer had reminded Paul though, that he was no better. He had seen the members of Las Ratas as pests that needed to be removed not as people, who were hurting. With God's help, he needed to correct his own thinking.

Paul opened the door and looked back at Noodles, who was watching him keenly.

"And what are you waiting for? Aren't you coming?"

Noodles did not wait for further coaxing; he immediately ran out the door and towards the elevator. Paul had timed things perfectly. As he and Noodles exited the elevator on the first floor, Clemente was returning with two cups of coffee from the diner. The expression on his face was priceless.

"Paul, you won't believe what just happened."

"What?"

Clemente handed Paul one of the cups and then related his story excitedly.

"I did exactly as you said…and it was Ashleigh…but she didn't recognize me, until I told her who I was…and then she told me that I cleaned up really good…and she smiled at me…I think she winked…she wants me to come back and see her…she said so!"

"Take it easy, Romeo."

Paul laughed to himself but stopped as a thought crossed his mind. He wondered if that was the first time that Clemente was the object of someone's flirtations or seen as a desirable mate. The two men and dog exited the Canterbury on Pine Avenue, crossed the street to the parking garage and then descended to the second subbasement, where Paul's truck was parked.

"Noodles is coming with us to church?"

"Most of the way!"

Paul drove to a place with which he was intimately familiar but a place he had not seen since he had left for his five-year road trip. As he pulled into the driveway, he noticed that his grandparent's farm had not changed one bit. It was still the wonderful place he remembered. Paul parked the truck and the occupants exited. He led Noodles to the front porch and sat down on the steps. Clemente followed and then stood nearby.

"Noodles, Clemente and I are going to go to church over there."

With one hand, Paul scratched the dog's head; and with the other, he pointed to a path.

"We'll be back very soon, probably a couple of hours; and when we return, you'll get to meet Pop and Nan. They love dogs even more than I do; and if I know Nan, you'll probably get a couple pieces of the best fried chicken that you'll ever eat. Now, you be a good boy and sit here on the porch until we return. Okay?"

The dog barked twice and then licked his chops. Paul wondered if he had understood the word, chicken. He stood up, and then slowly led Clemente towards then down the path to the church. One time, he stole a glance behind him; Noodles had obediently remained on the porch. Paul had promised the dog that he would return in a couple hours; but bizarre, unforeseen events would cause him to unintentionally break that promise. Paul would not see the dog again, until much later that afternoon.

Not only were Pop and Nan Gray two of the founders of the Covenant Baptist Church in Cricksburg, West Kentucky, they had also donated the property on which the church was located. For its forty-one years of existence, Pop had been a deacon and a trustee of the church; Nan had been the church clerk and pianist; and they both taught Sunday School. The church had grown a lot in that time from the small country church to one with three hundred regular members.

When Paul and Clemente reached the church, Paul realized that the service times had changed since he was last here. Worship service had already started and they were late. When Paul opened the doors, he could hear the congregation singing "Blessed Assurance." He waited in the church lobby for a moment. Being here once again was bringing back a flood of very pleasant memories; he had missed this place so much. He steeled himself, took a breath and opened the door to the sanctuary; Clemente followed close behind.

A few people including the pastor and the music director noticed Paul and Clemente as they entered the sanctuary and found a couple of empty seats near the front. Most importantly, Nan saw them from the piano; she missed a note; but quickly recovered. The song was one of Paul's favorites; he knew it by heart and sang along with the congregation. Clemente stood next to him quietly and reverently. When the song ended, the congregation sat down; and the pastor walked to the pulpit to give his sermon. It would be a sermon, the members of that church would not soon forget.

"Today's sermon is the first of six, entitled 'God's Formula for Success;' and the main text for this series will be the seventeenth chapter of First Samuel.

There is an old story of a poor farmer who complained to his pastor about his recent misfortunes.

"Pastor, I don't know what I'm going to do. It has been a very bad year. This year's crop was the worst ever. My tractor is broke and I cannot afford to fix or replace it. And the-"

The pastor quickly interrupted. "Do you have a rooster?"

"Well, yes, I do; but I-"

"Bring the rooster in the house and see me next week."

The poor farmer did exactly what the pastor suggested; and the following week, the farmer had more complaints.

"Pastor, I did exactly what you told me to do. I brought the rooster in the house; but my life is worse than it was. The rooster makes so much noise; and there are feathers everywhere. And my wife said-"

Again, the pastor quickly interrupted. "Do you have a goat?"

"Well, yes, I do; but I-"

"Bring the goat in the house and see me next week."

The poor farmer did exactly what the pastor suggested; and the following week, the farmer had even more complaints.

"Pastor, I did exactly what you told me to do. I brought the goat in the house; but my life is even worse than it was. The goat chases the rooster around the house; and it is eating all of our food. It has even chewed holes in all of my shirts and the sheets on the bed. I don't

know why you-"

The pastor interrupted once again. "Do you have a donkey?"

"Well, yes, I do; but I-"

"Bring the donkey in the house and see me next week."

The poor farmer did exactly what the pastor suggested; and the following week, the farmer had more complaints than ever.

"Pastor, I did exactly what you told me to do. I brought the donkey in the house; but my life is the worse yet. The donkey has broken our furniture. There is nowhere to sit. Moreover, the smell is unbearable. I don't know how much more I can take. "

"Take the rooster, goat and donkey out of the house and see me next week."

The poor farmer did exactly what the pastor suggested; and the following week, the farmer was in wonderful spirits.

"Oh Pastor, life is so much better than it was before. The noise and smell are much better; and we can finally eat and get some sleep. Thank you so much for your help."

The pastor had done nothing but help the farmer correctly view the situation.

"Cricksburg, West Kentucky, is still rural enough that most you can identify with the farmer in the story. You probably grew up on or near a farm; some of you may even be farmers."

With this, Pastor Tom Sheppard quietly acknowledged a few men in the congregation by extending an open hand in their direction. Each of these men was a known farmer in the congregation; and one of the men was Pop Gray.

"But you don't have to be a farmer to identify with this story. At times, we all see our lives with its problems through our human eyes instead of

CHAPTER SEVENTEEN

through God's heavenly eyes. Stand with me as we read together from God's word—First Samuel, seventeenth chapter, verses one through fifty-one, starting with verse 1."

The congregation stood. Paul shared his Bible with Clemente, as the pastor read the passage.

1 Now the Philistines gathered together their armies to battle, and were gathered together at Shochoh, which belongeth to Judah, and pitched between Shochoh and Azekah, in Ephesdammim.
2 And Saul and the men of Israel were gathered together, and pitched by the valley of Elah, and set the battle in array against the Philistines.
3 And the Philistines stood on a mountain on the one side, and Israel stood on a mountain on the other side: and there was a valley between them.
4 And there went out a champion out of the camp of the Philistines, named Goliath, of Gath, whose height was six cubits and a span.
5 And he had an helmet of brass upon his head, and he was armed with a coat of mail; and the weight of the coat was five thousand shekels of brass.
6 And he had greaves of brass upon his legs, and a target of brass between his shoulders.
7 And the staff of his spear was like a weaver's beam; and his spear's head weighted six hundred shekels of iron: and one bearing a shield went before him.
8 And he stood and cried unto the armies of Israel, and said unto them, Why are ye come out to set your battle in array? Am not I a Philistine, and ye servants to Saul? Choose you a man for you, and let him come down to me.
9 If he be able to fight with me, and to kill me, then will we be your servants: but if I prevail against him, and kill him, then shall ye be our servants, and serve us.
10 And the Philistine said, I defy the armies of Israel this day; give me a man, that we may fight together.
11 When Saul and all Israel heard those words of the Philistine, they were dismayed, and greatly afraid.
12 Now David was the son of that Ephrathite of Bethlehemjudah, whose name was Jesse; and he had eight sons: and the man went among men for an old man in the days of Saul.

13 And the three eldest sons of Jesse went and followed Saul to the battle: and the names of his three sons that went to the battle were Eliab the first born, and next unto him Abinadab, and the third Shammah.

14 And David was the youngest: and the three eldest followed Saul.

15 But David went and returned from Saul to feed his father's sheep at Bethlehem.

16 And the Philistine drew near morning and evening, and presented himself forty days.

17 And Jesse said unto David his son, Take now for thy brethren an ephah of this parched corn, and these ten loaves, and run to the camp to thy brethren;

18 And carry these ten cheeses unto the captain of their thousand, and look how thy brethren fare, and take their pledge.

19 Now Saul, and they, and all the men of Israel, were in the valley of Elah, fighting with the Philistines.

20 And David rose up early in the morning, and left the sheep with a keeper, and took, and went, as Jesse had commanded him; and he came to the trench as the host was going forth to the fight, and shouted for the battle.

21 For Israel and the Philistines had put the battle in array, army against army.

22 And David left his carriage in the hand of the keeper of the carriage, and ran into the army, and came and saluted his brethren.

23 And as he talked with them, behold, there came up the champion, the Philistine of Gath, Goliath by name, out of the armies of the Philistines, and spake according to the same words: and David heard them.

24 And all the men of Israel, when they saw the man, fled from him, and were sore afraid.

25 And the men of Israel said, Have ye seen this man that is come up? Surely to defy Israel is he come up: and it shall be, that the man who killeth him, the king will enrich him with great riches, and will give him his daughter, and make his father's house free in Israel.

26 And David spake to the men that stood by him, saying, What shall be done to the man that killeth this Philistine, and taketh away the reproach from Israel? For who is this uncircumcised Philistine, that he should defy the armies of the living God?

27 And the people answered him after this manner, saying, So shall it be done to the man that killeth him.

28 And Eliab his eldest brother heard when he spake unto the men; and Eliab's anger was kindled against David, and he said, Why camest thou down hither? And with whom hast thou left those few sheep in the wilderness? I know thy pride, and the naughtiness of thine heart; for thou art come down that thou mightest see the battle.
29 And David said, What have I now done? Is there not a cause?
30 And he turned from him toward another, and spake after the same manner: and the people answered him again after the former manner.
31 And when the words were heard which David spake, they rehearsed them before Saul: and he sent for him.
32 And David said to Saul, Let no man's heart fail because of him; thy servant will go and fight with this Philistine.
33 And Saul said to David, Thou art not able to go against this Philistine to fight with him: for thou art but a youth, and he a man of war from his youth.
34 And David said unto Saul, Thy servant kept his father's sheep, and there came a lion, and a bear, and took a lamb out of the flock:
35 And I went out after him, and smote him, and delivered it out of his mouth: and when he arose against me, I caught him by his beard, and smote him, and slew him.
36 Thy servant slew both the lion and the bear: and this uncircumcised Philistine shall be as one of them, seeing he hath defied the armies of the living God.
37 David said moreover, The Lord that delivered me out of the paw of the lion, and out of the paw of the bear, he will deliver me out of the hand of this Philistine. And Saul said unto David, Go, and the Lord be with thee.
38 And Saul armed David with his armour, and he put an helmet of brass upon his head; also he armed him with a coat of mail.
39 And David girded his sword upon his armour, and he assayed to go; for he had not proved it. And David said unto Saul, I cannot go with these; for I have not proved them. And David put them off him.
40 And he took his staff in his hand, and chose him five smooth stones out of the brook, and put them in a shepherd's bag which he had, even in a scrip; and his sling was in his hand: and he drew near to the Philistine.
41 And the Philistine came on and drew near unto David; and the man that bare the shield went before him.
42 And when the Philistine looked about, and saw David, he

disdained him: for he was but a youth, and ruddy, and of a fair countenance.

43 And the Philistine said unto David, Am I a dog, that thou comest to me with staves? And the Philistine cursed David by his gods.

44 And the Philistine said to David, Come to me, and I will give thy flesh unto the fowls of the air, and to the beasts of the field.

45 Then said David to the Philistine, Thou comest to me with a sword, and with a spear, and with a shield: but I come to thee in the name of the Lord of hosts, the God of the armies of Israel, whom thou has defied.

46 This day will the Lord deliver thee into mine hand; and I will smite thee, and take thine head from thee; and I will give the carcases of the host of the Philistines this day unto the fowls of the air, and to the wild beasts of the earth; that all the earth may know that there is a God in Israel.

47 And all this assembly shall know that the Lord saveth not with sword and spear: for the battle is the Lord's, and he will give you into our hands.

48 And it came to pass, when the Philistine arose, and came and drew nigh to meet David, that David hasted, and ran toward the army to meet the Philistine.

49 And David put his hand in his bag, and took thence a stone, and slang it, and smote the Philistine in his forehead, that the stone sunk into his forehead; and he fell upon his face to the earth.

50 So David prevailed over the Philistine with a sling and with a stone, and smote the Philistine, and slew him; but there was no sword in the hand of David.

51 Therefore David ran, and stood upon the Philistine, and took his sword, and drew it out of the sheath thereof, and slew him, and cut off his head therewith. And when the Philistines saw their champion was dead, they fled.

"Let us pray."

Paul and the congregation of Covenant Baptist Church bowed their heads and closed their eyes as their pastor led them in prayer. Clemente, however, stood quietly and watched everything intently.

"God, we ask that You open our eyes this morning, so that we may see our lives as You see them. Help us to face our Goliaths with courage, so we may overcome them for Your glory. Show us what You would have us do. We ask these things in the precious name of Your Son, Jesus. Amen"

Without instruction, the congregation sat down.

"If the title of this whole series of sermons is 'God's Formula for Success,' then the title of today's sermon is 'View the Situation Correctly.'

"The farmer in our story did not view his situation correctly. He saw only the problems, when God wanted him to see the many blessings He had given him. He had a vision problem.

"You may recall back in the book of Numbers that the children of Israel did not view their situation correctly when they were camped outside the Promised Land. Moses had sent twelve spies; and when they returned ten of those twelve spies reported that the land was filled with giants. Only Joshua and Caleb gave a positive report of the many blessings, which existed there. The ten spies had a vision problem

"Here in First Samuel, King Saul and the Israelite army are not viewing their situation correctly either. They see a mighty army and one very large, very intimidating giant—Goliath. They have a vision problem.

"But one man is viewing the situation correctly—David. David doesn't see a giant. No! Let me read the last part of verse twenty-six again. '*For who is this uncircumcised Philistine, that he should defy the armies of the living God?*' David sees a heathen who dares to defy God. David does not have a vision problem.

"I ask you this morning. Are you viewing the situation of your life correctly? Do you have a vision problem?

It was not time for an altar call, Tom Sheppard had prepared a much longer sermon; however, he never had the chance to finish it. As he asked that final question, he received an answer from the congregation.

"My friend, Paul, doesn't have a vision problem!"

The conservative congregation collectively gasped. They were not accustomed to the pastor's sermons being interrupted like this. Clemente

Morales stood and walked towards the pulpit. He stood next to Pastor Tom, faced the congregation and spoke from his heart.

"My name is Clemente Morales; and until Friday night, I was a gang member living homeless on the streets of River City; but Paul Gray…"

Clemente made eye contact with Paul; and Paul noticed that Clemente's eyes were welling up with tears; however, he composed himself and continued talking.

"…Paul Gray took me away from all that. He fed me, gave me these nice clothes and let me stay with him in his apartment. I was nothing but a rat just like our gang name; but Paul saw something more in me."

Clemente turned to face Tom Sheppard, who was still standing quietly next to him.

"Pastor, Paul doesn't have a vision problem. A lot of people walked by me on the streets; but they only saw a rat; they never stopped to help me. Only Paul did."

Clemente started telling the congregation his life story in painfully intimate detail. He told them about the death of his parents. He told them about riding around the country in a boxcar. He told them about his life with Las Ratas and all of the bad things he did as a member, things like vandalism, theft and assault. He told them about the last forty-eight hours and the events that occurred in the second subbasement of the Canterbury.

At times, he had to take a few minutes to compose himself as the tears overtook him. He cried. From his seat in the pew, Paul cried. From her seat near the piano, Nan cried; but then Nan was tenderhearted and cried often. Pop cried. There was not a dry eye in the sanctuary; the entire congregation cried, even the pastor cried.

"Paul told me to burn the clothes I was wearing; and I did; but what Paul doesn't know is I kept one thing—the shoelaces."

Clemente raised his right pant leg. Just above the knee, he had tied a dirty shoelace around his thigh. The congregation craned their necks to see it.

"These shoelaces represent my past. The gentle pressure I feel with each step I take has reminded me of a different world, one filled with pain. I don't want to go back there. I can't."

When he finished relating his life story, Clemente fell on his knees and pleaded with the members of the congregation.

"I don't want to go back there; but I don't know any other way. The street is the only life I've ever known. I need your help. I'll do anything. Please don't let me go back there. Please see me as more than a rat."

With this, Clemente fell prostrate sobbing loudly into the dais's carpeted floor; there was no more story for him to tell; all that remained now was raw emotion. Nan sat down on the floor next to him; she placed a sympathetic hand on the back of Clemente's head. Pop sat down on the floor next to them. Another man, who Paul did not recognize, joined them, as did the pastor and his wife. Paul was in a stupor from the events, which had just occurred and the words, which Pastor Tom and Clemente had spoken. Nan broke his trance by summoning him to join them, which Paul did. Several silent minutes passed in the church; parishioners were praying silently in the pews. Eventually, the pastor rose and addressed the congregation.

"In His mysterious yet perfect way, God has brought this young man to us. You've heard his story; and you've heard his heartfelt plea. What say you?"

Pastor Tom did not finish his sermon. He did not extend an alter call. He did not even close the service in prayer. All of these things he would have done during a typical Sunday morning service; but this had been anything but a typical Sunday morning service. Instead, the small group sitting on the floor stood and formed a receiving line facing the congregation. One at a time, the members of Covenant Baptist Church filed past them, first past Nan, then Pop, Paul, Clemente, Pastor Tom, his wife Edith, and finally the other man, who Paul later discovered was the youth pastor, Tim Alexopoulos.

Hugs and handshakes were exchanged, as were words of encouragement and sincere offers of assistance. Clemente could not believe the number of hugs he had received nor the outpouring of love he was now feeling; for the very first time in his life, Clemente felt at home. Eventually, the congregation had dispersed leaving just the seven people in line.

"Pastor Tom, is that what heaven will feel like?"

The innocence of Clemente's question startled him.

"Yes, Clemente, I suppose it will."

"Am I a Christian now?"

"Do you want to be, Clemente?"

Clemente nodded his head.

"Paul told me that he helps people, because God has blessed his life; and he wants to show his appreciation and love for God in return by allowing himself to be an instrument for God to use to bless others. Well, God has blessed me too by sending me Paul and bringing me to this church. I want to show my appreciation and be used as an instrument as well."

Pastor Tom led Clemente to the closest pew, where they sat down. The other five gathered around them and joined hands. Pastor Tom presented the plan of salvation to Clemente; and there in a now nearly empty church, Clemente Morales accepted Jesus Christ as his Lord and Savior.

The Bible tells that Moses' face glowed when he left the Lord's presence and descended Mt. Sinai with the Ten Commandments. Paul wondered now whether it was simply his imagination; but he thought Clemente's face was glowing. Regardless, the Holy Spirit's presence was undeniably present; the others there felt it too; and they would speak of that day for many years to come.

Nan checked her watch; it was already almost four o'clock. It was Pop and Nan's custom to entertain the pastor and his wife after church; but she did not have Sunday dinner even started yet. She had expected five; but now there was also Clemente and Pastor Tim. Nan was worrying about how she would prepare dinner for so many so quickly. As it happened, her worries were for nothing. As the small group departed the church and walked the path back to Pop and Nan's house, they discovered the rest of the congregation already there.

Kids were playing with Noodles on the porch; but when the beagle noticed Paul and Clemente, he charged toward them and bathed both of them in doggie kisses, which smelled surprisingly like fried chicken. A group of teenage boys had shucked their coats and ties and started a game of football. When Paul and his party entered Pop and Nan's house, they discovered a house full of people and food.

One lady, who had assumed control of the event, emerged from Nan's kitchen to explain to the newcomers what was happening.

"Flora, I hope you don't mind that we commandeered your kitchen; but it was getting late; and I thought you probably needed help with dinner, so we all brought dinner to you. Each of us brought a few dishes we already had from home; and then we had some of the men go to Aunt Virgie's and Crescent City to purchase several buckets of chicken. We probably cleaned them out."

With this, the lady laughed; and in appreciation, Nan hugged her. Paul wondered whether Brenda Henderson would ever endorse this makeshift dinner, because Aunt Virgie's Front Porch Chicken and Crescent City Chicken were on her list of naughty restaurants. Paul concluded that the members of Covenant Baptist Church probably did not care very much about Brenda Henderson and her opinions about their diet. Pastor Tom called for silence.

"I can see that some of you have already eaten or are still eating; but I ask you to stop for just a moment while I say grace."

Everyone stopped and bowed their heads as Pastor Tom gave a brief prayer, which combined the prayer of dismissal, which he would have given earlier with a prayer blessing the food, making sure to give thanks for the many members who had made this dinner happen. When the prayer was over, the pastor called for the congregation's silence one final time.

"I have two quick announcements. First, because of the very unusual nature of today's service and lateness of the hour, I'm sure that everyone will understand if I cancel the evening service. Please spread the word and make sure everyone knows."

There were nods and hushed words of agreement throughout the crowd. Paul consulted his watch and noticed that there were only a couple of hours before the evening service was scheduled to start. The people in Pop and Nan's house quieted themselves to hear the pastor's second announcement as he took a moment to compose himself.

"After ya'll left the church, Paul, Pop, Flora, Tim, Edith and myself had the wonderful privilege of witnessing Clemente Morales surrender his life to Christ; he has expressed the desire to follow his Lord in baptism and join our church."

The crowd erupted in cheers and expressions of joy; and Clemente was subjected to another round of hugs from everyone in attendance. Interspersed between the hugs were offers of plates of food. Clemente had never eaten so much in his entire life; and this would be the first time he would ever refuse the offer of more food. As Clemente feasted on chicken and the loving attention from his new church family, Paul found Pop and Nan in a corner and gave both of them a long, warm hug.

"I've really missed you guys."

"And we've really missed you too, Paul"

Nan was starting to cry again.

"Listen. I'm so sorry. I didn't know all of this would happen when I brought him."

"Hush your mouth, Paul Gray."

Nan's countenance quickly turned dark.

"You didn't bring him here; God did; and don't you dare go apologizing for things that God does. Do you understand me?"

"Yes ma'am."

As quickly as it had darkened, Nan's countenance brightened again; and she hugged Paul tightly.

CHAPTER SEVENTEEN

"I understand what you meant though, Paul."

Nan had to pause a moment and wipe her eyes before continuing.

"I'm just so glad you're back home."

"Pop, can I speak with you in your workshop?"

Pop nodded; and the two men went outside. As they passed by Pastor Tom, Paul firmly grabbed the minister's hand. Paul's eyes quietly besought what his mouth could not say in such a large crowd. Pastor Tom understood and followed the men to Pop Gray's workshop.

Paul summoned every last ounce of courage he could muster before making his confession to the two men.

"I'm not the saint that Clemente has made me out to be."

Paul paused for a moment before continuing.

"When I first encountered Clemente and his gang, I viewed them as nothing more than an unwanted nuisance. I didn't want to hurt them, mind you; I just wanted to scare them away, so the residents would feel safe. It wasn't until later, when I discovered Clemente unconscious on the floor, that I started seeing him as a human being, who badly needed my help. I'm just not worthy of the admiration Clemente has heaped on me today."

"Yes, you are."

It was Clemente; he had followed the three men to the workshop and had heard everything Paul had said.

"Clemente, I didn't know you were standing there. I'm so sorry."

"Don't be."

Clemente's face was almost angelic; and he hugged Paul tightly.

"Friday night, before our encounter, as I was falling asleep, I prayed that

God would send someone—anyone—to take me away from my horrible life with the gang. I don't regret one moment of what happened next, because it was probably the only way it could've happened. In that dark basement, you may not have seen me as something more than a rat; but God did; and very soon, you did see me as much more. Didn't you?"

"It's odd, Clemente; I now see you as the little brother I never had."

"Paul, it's not odd; it's God," interjected Pastor Tom.

All four men quietly agreed.

"Clemente, have you given any thought as to what your future holds? What would you like to do with your life now? I've received dozens of sincere job offers from church members this afternoon on your behalf."

"Tom, Flora and I have already discussed this; he can come and live with us and work on the farm until he gets on his feet. We'll take care of him."

"Pastor Tom…Pop…thank you for the very generous offers and thank you for everything you've already done for me. Everyone here has accepted me with open arms; and that is something I will never forget. I'll probably need your help a lot in the future as I continue to grow; but I think that right now God wants me elsewhere."

Clemente turned to face Paul.

"Paul, I can never hope to repay your kindness. Can I live and work by your side? You told me that you wanted to bring badly needed changes to River City. Well, I want to help you with that."

"Clemente, it will be very dangerous."

"I know that much better than you do."

The three other men looked at Clemente expecting further explanation.

"Paul, you don't know what you're up against. Carlos has been meeting with the leader of L'Ombra; they're very bad people. They control the government, big business, big labor, big crime and even the local media.

Carlos wants to join L'Ombra; and they'll admit him too, if he can just organize the gangs in the Forrest."

"What's the name of this leader?"

"Claude Zumbini."

Pastor Tom and Pop Gray gasped as Paul sought clarification.

"Do you mean the man who plays Zumbo the Clown on television and owns the amusement park?"

"That's him. If you want to take back River City, you'll have to take it back from him, because he controls it through L'Ombra."

"Who are the other members of this organization?"

"Nobody knows that. It's rumored though that Zumbini forces the members to get a special tattoo on their right forearm to prove their allegiance to him."

"What does this tattoo look like?"

All three men wanted to ask; but Pastor Tom had beaten them to it.

"A winged demon."

Everyone took a moment to accept the spiritual gravity of the situation.

"Okay, Clemente, we'll discuss the specifics later; but you can live and work with me. I would actually consider it an honor."

"Paul, I'm begging you to help the other guys too. Without our help, I hate to think what could happen to them. especially if Carlos manages to join L'Ombra."

"Okay, tomorrow morning, I'll call the River City Police Department."

"No, you can't call the police; Zumbini owns them. Why do you think crime is so rampant in the Forrest; Zumbini wants it that way. We have to do this ourselves."

Paul considered this further request. He had only taken on two gang members on the street by himself; and he had had the advantage of surprise and darkness during his second encounter; two things he probably could not count on a third time.

"Clemente, to take on fourteen men in a safe way, I would need more than just your help; I would need a small army…and supplies."

"Did someone call for an army?"

A dozen men from the congregation stood outside the door to Pop's workshop. One burly man with a beard spoke for the entire group; he introduced himself to Paul.

"Name's Burgess Smith; but everyone around these parts just calls me 'Tiny.' If you're needin' volunteers for this battle of yours, you've got twelve right here; and if you need more, we can probably wrestle up another dozen or so. As for supplies, I own an army surplus store; and you can have whatever you need. That kid's story there really touched me; and I can't stand knowin' there are other boys trapped in that life."

Paul was not sure if he was more shocked by the man's inappropriate nickname or his extreme tenderheartedness. Sensing the solemnity of the moment, Tiny tried to lighten the mood.

"We have to get 'em out of there, Paul…and besides that, I really hate clowns."

Everyone shared a laugh; but it was uneasy laughter. Every man now knew the stakes.

Chapter Eighteen

"Y ou wanted to see me, Pastor."

"Yes, Aaron, come in and have a seat."

Stanley Lucas' office at Zoara Christian Church was opulent. Few members of the church had ever been in this room; and if they had, they would wonder how much of their offerings were going towards ministering to others.

Evening services were over; and the church was now long deserted save for the senior and assistant pastors.

"Aaron, how is your son, Dougie?"

"There has been no change; he's still in a coma. The doctors don't know if or when he'll come out of it."

"I want you to take some time off and spend it with your family."

"Thank you for that kind offer; but keeping busy with my work here at the church would help me to keep my mind occupied. Sitting in that hospital next to his bed makes me feel so helpless."

"I understand; but I really must insist that you take the time off. Perhaps you can help the church in another way. A young lady by the name of…"

Stanley Lucas donned his reading glasses and consulted his notes to remember the lady's name before continuing.

"Ah, here it is. Marcy Green called here Friday afternoon on behalf of her boss..."

Again, Stanley Lucas consulted his notes.

"One Paul Gray. It appears that Mr. Gray is attempting to form some type of council of churches down in the Forrest."

"But Zoara isn't even located in the Forrest."

"Yes, I know that; but we're a large and wealthy church; and those poor churches are probably looking for a handout. I want you to attend their meeting on my behalf. It's tomorrow night at the Canterbury, not far from the hospital, where your son is. Listen sympathetically; but don't promise any financial assistance. After the meeting, you can fill me in. Okay?"

"Well, if that will help."

"Oh, it will, because I'm very busy here; and I can't break away. Now run along and spend some time with your family."

Aaron Bishop left Stanley Lucas' office; and Stanley watched him leave the church through the numerous security cameras scattered throughout the church's campus. Now, by himself, he called a familiar number on his cell phone.

"Claude, it's Stanley."

"Yes, I've taken care of it. Aaron Bishop will be attending their little meeting; he'll keep me informed; and I'll keep you informed."

"Don't worry. Whatever this Paul Gray is planning, we'll sabotage it."

"No, he still doesn't suspect the connection between us. He's too distracted with his son's unfortunate accident."

"I'll handle things on my end; you just make sure I acquire St. George's when it comes available."

Stanley Lucas closed his phone, disconnecting the call. He took off his suit coat and sat back down at his desk. He loosened his tie and rolled up his shirtsleeves. His right forearm bore a tattoo of a winged demon.

Chapter Nineteen

When Clemente exited the elevator and walked into the great room, Paul was in his office having his devotion.

"Paul, are you here?"

"In here, Clemente."

Clemente entered Paul's office; he was dressed in a black Henley shirt, blue jeans and a brand new pair of sneakers. Paul was wearing a navy blue dress shirt, a Kelly green tie, khakis, and brown Oxfords.

"Do I look okay for my first day of work?"

"You look fine. Are you ready for some breakfast?"

"Always."

The two men left the apartment and made their way to the diner. When they arrived, they found Georgia behind the counter crying but trying to hide it from the customers. Paul and Clemente sat down in a booth near the window; and Georgia approached them bravely forcing a smile.

"What can I get for you, Paul?"

"Well, you can start by sitting down here and telling me what's wrong."

Georgia put up no argument. She placed two menus in the middle of the table, sat down next to Clemente facing Paul, and handed him an envelope, which Paul opened and read. The letter was from the bank holding the diner's business loan; and they were notifying the Hoppers that the diner would be seized if the loan was not paid in full by the end of the year, which was a little less than three months away.

"Paul, what am I going to do?"

"Don't worry about this, Georgia; we'll think of something; you and Ed are not losing this diner. Do you understand me?"

Georgia nodded while sobbing in a handkerchief.

"Can I borrow this letter for a couple days, while I look into this for you?"

Georgia nodded again while composing herself.

"Now…what can I get you boys for breakfast?"

"I think I'll have two eggs, sunny side up, bacon, hash browns and toast."

"And to drink?"

"Large orange juice…and of course, coffee"

With this, Paul turned his coffee cup right side up on the saucer.

Paul and Georgia looked towards Clemente, who was still studying the menu, unsure of how to order.

"And for you?"

"I'll just have what he's having."

Georgia took their menus.

"I'll be right back with that coffee."

Paul motioned to Clemente to turn his coffee cup right side up, which he did.

After giving the order to the kitchen, Georgia returned with a coffee pot and filled their cups.

"Georgia, this is Clemente Morales; he'll be working for me now; and you'll probably be seeing a lot of him in the future."

"I hope so."

Georgia gave Clemente a quick side-hug and started crying again.

"Georgia, remember what I told you; you are not losing this diner; I won't let that happen."

The waitress sniffled once, gave Clemente one final and firm squeeze putting her head on his shoulder; and then gave Paul a quick side-hug before retreating to the kitchen.

"Paul, I was thinking."

"What about?"

"Claude Zumbini has L'Ombra to help him take over every aspect of this city; shouldn't we start a similar organization to help you stop him."

Paul was quiet for several minutes.

"Clemente, Zumbini is a very dangerous man; you know that. This is my fight; it's my job to stop him; I can't expect others to take that same huge risk."

"But—"

"Clemente, I don't want anybody else to get hurt. There will be other ways that you can help me."

Without invitation, Ashleigh sat down next to Clemente.

"I'm sorry, Paul; I couldn't help overhearing; plus, the whole neighborhood is already buzzing about what you did to that gang this weekend. Clemente is right. There does need to be some way for citizens to help you get rid of that annoying clown. After all, we live here too; we have an interest in what happens. If you form such a group, I'll sign up immediately."

Ashleigh lowered her voice and leaned across the table so only Paul and Clemente could hear her.

"Besides, I hear things here in the diner—things that might help you."

Ashleigh leaned back and smiled, then gave Paul a knowing wink, then placed her hand on Clemente's hand and squeezed it slightly. She stood and started to walk away but turned around and whispered something in Paul's ear, which Clemente was just able to hear.

"Empire Federal—the bank that sent that letter to Georgia and Ed—is owned by Claude Zumbini."

Having said her peace, Ashleigh returned to waiting tables.

Chapter Twenty

After they finished eating breakfast, Paul and Clemente made their way to the office of Foster Gray Holdings. Marcy was already there sitting at the receptionist desk. She stood and greeted them as they entered.

"Good morning, Paul."

"Good morning, Marcy. How was your weekend?"

"Very busy! I called Wayne Carter like you told me to. You were right; he's a very nice man. He drove up here himself, picked me up, took me down to his dealership; and I…"

Marcy could hardly contain her excitement.

"…drove back here in my brand new Seldon minivan!"

"That's great, Marcy!"

"He's even towed away my old car too."

Marcy could not resist the urge to hug Paul; and when Marcy finally let go, she noticed Clemente standing quietly between Paul and the door. Paul noticed the awkwardness and made the necessary introductions.

"Clemente, this is Marcy Green, my personal assistant. Marcy, this is Clemente Morales; he'll be working with us."

Clemente offered his hand; and Marcy shook it; but the color had completely drained from her face.

"Did you say your name was Clemente Morales?"

Clemente nodded.

"Marcy, is there a problem?"

She was clearly having difficulty regaining her composure.

"No, Paul…I'll be okay. Uh…did you…did you have your devotion this morning? You wanted me to hold you accountable."

"Exercised, showered, dressed, had my devotion, ate breakfast, and ready to start this day, just as I pledged. Thanks for checking, Marcy."

She nodded and smiled. Thinking he was required to follow suit, Clemente offered his own report.

"I showered and dressed and ate breakfast too; but I didn't exercise; and I didn't have a devotion either."

Paul laughed; but Marcy was still startled by Clemente's presence. Clemente felt he needed to further explain himself.

"I started reading the Bible that Miss Edith gave me last night before I fell asleep; and I'll probably read more tonight."

Clemente looked for assurance that he had given the right answer.

"Clemente, I should have explained that I had asked Marcy to hold me accountable for having a daily personal devotion; don't worry; you're not under a similar obligation."

Marcy still had a faint scowl of concern on her face; but she had recovered enough to give Paul her own report.

"Paul, you asked for a war room; and I assumed that you wanted our morning meetings held there."

"Until you get a chance to organize one, we can just have our meetings right here."

"Oh, I already organized it."

Marcy led Paul and Clemente to a room, not far from the reception area. The room was modestly appointed but very efficient. Marcy had managed to gather a table and some chairs from the office furniture scattered throughout the penthouse. The walls were decorated with various maps; and there were large bulletin boards and a white board on one wall near the head of the table. On one bulletin board, Marcy had pinned some index cards; each card contained one of Paul's community goals. Clemente looked around the room with great interest.

"Marcy, I'm very impressed; you've done an amazing job and in such a small amount of time."

Marcy blushed.

"Thank you, Paul. You should really sit at the head of the table."

Paul did. Marcy and Clemente sat on either side of him, with Marcy sitting closest to the door.

"Paul, I want to apologize for my behavior just now; it's just that when you introduced Clemente, it really startled me."

"How so?"

"Friday after work, when I returned to my apartment, I wrote down the things you wanted me to do so I wouldn't forget. You remember, don't you, Paul; you told me outside the elevator."

"I remember."

"One of those things was to schedule your next visit with your cousin in Scarsdale…Sam Hayne. Remember that too?"

"Yes, Marcy, I remember."

"Well, instead of just writing it down to do at a later date, I decided to call him right then to coordinate a regular time."

"And what did he say?"

"I had just introduced myself by name only and hadn't had a chance to even explain how I was connected to you or why I was calling him. It was like he already knew. He told me that he would call me very soon to schedule another visit. He kept calling me Marcella and using the word 'splendid' every chance he got. It was both creepy and annoying."

"So, what does that have to do with Clemente?"

"Yeah, what does that have to do with me?"

"He said that he wanted Clemente Morales…he mentioned him by first and last name…and me to come with you on all future visits. In fact, he absolutely insisted on it. I told him that I didn't know a Clemente Morales; but he said that I would very soon."

"You say you called him late Friday afternoon."

Marcy nodded, while Paul considered this information. With Clemente's help, Paul then recounted the events of the weekend, starting with Marcy leaving for the day on Friday until he and Clemente entered the office this morning. They did not leave out a single detail, especially concerning Claude Zumbini, L'Ombra and tattoos of winged demons.

"If you hadn't even met Clemente until early Saturday morning, how did Sam Hayne know that he would be working here Friday evening?"

"How indeed."

The three paused to consider this new and curious development.

"Clemente, I'm sorry; I hope I didn't offend you; I was just a little freaked out. Welcome to Foster Gray Holdings! I look forward to working with you."

"No need to apologize and no offense taken. I would have been freaked out too; in fact, I'm freaked out anyway."

"Now guys, let's not allow our imaginations to run amok. My cousin may be—"

Clemente looked shocked and sought confirmation for what he had just heard.

"This guy is your cousin."

"Yes, Clemente he's a distant cousin. And he may dress and act oddly, drive a hearse, and live in a scary looking castle; but I don't—"

"He drives a hearse."

Marcy nodded her head in confirmation.

"Focus, people."

The group collectively calmed down before Paul continued.

"I don't think he means us any harm. In fact, he may be trying to help us in a clandestine way."

Paul took the opportunity to describe his encounter with Sam Hayne in detail.

"He expressed his sentiment towards my late great-grandfather; and he was very interested in what I would be doing with the inheritance; he even offered to help. There was the question about John Dorman though. I can't figure it. What were you able to learn about him, Marcy?"

"His name is John Dorman; and he lives here at the Canterbury in Apartment 4213. That's all I could find."

"Paul, 4213 was the number on your fortune cookie."

"So, it was; but Clemente, that's merely a coincidence. We won't allow ourselves to become hysterical and entrapped in silly superstitions. Marcy, when Sam Hayne calls back to schedule, graciously accept the invitation on all of our behalves."

Marcy nodded and made a note on her legal pad.

"Did you have anything else?"

"Robert Papier stopped by and picked up the project specifics."

"Good."

"Your meeting with area ministers is today at two o'clock."

"Today!"

"I'm sorry, Paul; but I wanted to save you some time, so I called around just to determine interest level; and…well…they were all very interested. Many of them wanted to meet with you Friday night."

"Wow! Okay! Then two o'clock it is; but I'm counting on you, Marcy, to pull this all together in time. Will we have a room ready?"

"I'll have the Sunset Room ready by that time."

"Good; and I'll want both of you there too."

Marcy and Clemente looked at him quizzically.

"Marcy, you already have established a rapport with most of them over the phone; plus we'll need minutes of the meeting. I hope you can take shorthand."

Marcy nodded.

"Good. And, Clemente, you are quickly becoming the poster child for why there needs to be change here in the Forrest. I may call on you to share your experiences or to give some special insight."

Clemente nodded.

"What else, Marcy?"

"Well, there was one significant holdout. Rev. Vickers with St. George Episcopal said his church would be shuttering very soon, so there wasn't any point in his attending the meeting. He wished us luck though."

"I'll visit the good reverend this morning and see if I can't persuade him to change his mind, perhaps give him something that will renew his faith."

"I was studying the local map to locate the churches; and I found one that is now empty. You wanted to start a community chapel; and I thought this building might work."

Marcy handed a piece of paper with an address and property specifics on it to Paul, who glanced at it and handed it back to her.

"I assume you've prepared a preliminary agenda for the meeting based on the faith-related community goals I mentioned Friday."

Marcy nodded.

"Good. Place that information on the agenda."

Marcy consulted her legal pad.

"I'm only now starting to plan the reception for Canterbury residents; I thought we could have it in one of the empty rooms on the second floor. That would make it visible from the lobby; but out of the traffic too."

"Sounds great. Keep me updated. Anything else?"

"Just this. It arrived for you in Saturday's mail."

Marcy handed Paul a hand-addressed envelope. The stationery was tastefully expensive; and the handwriting was exquisite. There was no return address. Paul removed the contents—a handwritten note, which he quickly read and placed back in the envelope. Marcy and Clemente were anxious to know what was contained in the envelope; but they wisely remained silent. Paul turned his attention to Marcy.

"Marcy, for the moment, among your other responsibilities, you'll need to be the company bookkeeper too, so contact Adam at Fifth National;

CHAPTER TWENTY

and make sure you're added to the business account. I called him on Friday and have already authorized this. And, you should probably set up another account just for payroll. Make sure you and Clemente fill out all the necessary employment and tax papers. We'll also need company credit cards for all three of us; Adam should be able to fast track that for you."

"Did you order business stationary from Margins?"

"Yes, they said it would be ready and delivered here on Friday."

"Good. How about office phones?"

"They're supposed to be installed later this morning."

"When they are and you have a phone number, order business cards for all three of us. And, Clemente needs a desk; help him get set up. And make sure he can charge at Margins and especially Don's Hardware."

Marcy nodded as Paul now turned his attention to Clemente.

"Clemente, for a while, your job description will be flexible. Some days, you'll accompany me out in the city. Some days, I will give you a special project to work on by yourself. Some days, you'll be helping Marcy here in the office. For the moment, I think it best for you to remain close to the office until we complete some formalities."

Marcy had left the room when Paul addressed Clemente but quickly returned with a legal pad and pen for Clemente. She continued taking her own notes as Paul spoke; and Clemente quickly mimicked her.

"Until I can officially hire you and give you a paycheck and company credit card, you'll need some money."

Paul removed four hundred dollars in twenty-dollar bills from his wallet and handed them to Clemente, who carefully placed the money in his own newly purchased wallet. Paul also handed him a key ring with two keys on it.

"One key is for the office and one key is for the apartment. And, Clemente, you need a cell phone as soon as possible, both Marcy and I need to be able to contact you immediately, so make that a priority. I want you to have one today. You'll also need to get a driver's license as soon as possible; and when you get that, I'll help you purchase a car."

Clemente's eyes lit up.

"While I don't require it for your job here, you'll want to get a GED too."

"Aw, man!"

The light in Clemente's eye dimmed a little bit.

"Don't forget that you have clothes being delivered this morning from Taylor's; you'll need to sign for them and put them in your closet. And, sometime this week, I want you to go to Don's Hardware. Tell him you're working for me now and that you need some basic tools for maintenance jobs."

Clemente nodded.

"I also want you to make some Found posters and post them throughout the neighborhood."

"Oh, come on, Paul; I thought we could keep Noodles."

"And we will, Clemente, if nobody claims him. He doesn't have a collar, so he probably is a stray. However, if he does belong to some nice family, they're probably worried sick about him right now. Make sure you put my cell phone number on the poster. Okay?"

"Okay."

His voice betrayed his frustration for Paul's request, although he knew it was the right thing to do.

"Clemente, we will have these meetings every morning. It is a chance for all of us to compare notes; Marcy and I have taken our turns. Is there anything you would like to add, any questions you have or comments you would like to make before we adjourn?"

CHAPTER TWENTY

Clemente was not prepared for this as Marcy and Paul had been; but he took a few minutes to consider it.

"I guess that I only three questions right now."

"Okay what is question number one?"

"Are you going to purchase the diner?"

Paul related the situation to Marcy in greater detail and handed her the letter from Georgia's bank.

"When you talk to Adam, ask him what we can do about this. Okay?"

Marcy nodded.

"Clemente, I won't let that diner close; I promised Georgia as much; and somehow, I will honor that promise. However, I don't want to simply throw money at problems unless absolutely necessary, especially when I think there are other and much better solutions to not just solve the immediate problem but the long-range problems too. Does that answer your question?"

"I think so."

"Then, what's question number two?"

"How are we going to fight the gang tonight?"

Marcy looked startled, so Paul explained that some people from the church would be helping him remove the remaining gang members later tonight. He then addressed Clemente's question.

"I'm not sure. I'm still working on a battle plan for that; but I promise that we won't hurt them. Let me add that fighting, like money, is not always the correct solution either. Do you understand?"

"Yeah."

"Then what's that third and final question?"

"You heard what Ashleigh said in the diner. Why can't we start a group to match L'Ombra?"

Again, Paul briefed Marcy regarding an earlier conversation, and then paused for several minutes to formulate his response to Clemente's question. He fidgeted with the envelope, which Marcy had given him at the beginning of the meeting; and finally handed it to Clemente, who opened it and read the letter.

"It would seem that there others in agreement with you, Clemente."

"But how did he know? I only had the idea last night after we returned home. Marcy said this letter arrived by mail earlier that day."

Paul motioned for Clemente to hand the letter to Marcy; raising his eyebrows and shrugging his shoulders was Paul's only response to the question.

> *Dearest Cousin Paul,*
>
> *I thoroughly enjoyed our tea, yesterday afternoon; and insist that we do it again very soon. I will contact your assistant to schedule a day and expect you to bring Ms. Green and Master Morales with you.*
>
> *In the interim, I would strongly encourage you to heed Master Morales' most sound advice concerning forming a group to counter Zumbini and L'Ombra. I should very much like to join your group myself during your next visit to Scarsdale.*
>
> *With the warmest regards,*
>
> *Sam Hayne*

After she read it, Marcy was as shocked as Paul and Clemente.

"Very well then, Clemente this was your idea, so you take the lead on it. I want a progress report tomorrow morning."

Paul could not help but notice that Clemente's chest was a little puffed up from the power, which had been ceded to him.

"If nobody has any further items to discuss, I would say that we have more than enough to keep each of us busy today. I need to make an appearance over at the Imperial, and then I'll visit Reverend Vickers, so Marcy, give him a heads up. I'll be back in time for the meeting with the other ministers."

Paul stood up and then made his way to the Imperial Hotel leaving Marcy and Clemente to their own tasks at Foster Gray Holdings.

The Imperial was much too large a complex to efficiently inspect in one visit. Paul had decided to break it into several manageable sections. Today, he would walk through the Imperial Convention Center, which was connected via a skyway on the hotel's south side. It was a product of the 1980's, when the hotel's owners and some city leaders thought the new complex would spur growth in the Forrest, which it did but only for a couple years. Now, the convention center was as old and tired as the hotel and everything else in the area.

For a Monday in such a large complex, the Imperial Convention Center was mostly deserted. Paul noted the dirty and worn carpet and more than a few burnt light bulbs. During his inspection of the complex, Paul did not see a single employee. There were a few groups using the smaller conference rooms; but only one of the larger banquet rooms, the Mayan Room, was occupied.

The door was open, so Paul peeked in the room and noticed a young man in a business suit arranging chairs theater-style. Paul approached the man and introduced himself offering his hand.

"Hi, I'm Paul Gray, the Lost & Found Director of the Imperial."

The man grasped Paul's hand firmly and shook it.

"I'm Tony Limin; and you've found me…but I wasn't lost."

Paul laughed at the joke made at his expense and although he could not risk full disclosure, he felt the need to puff his resume a little.

"Well, I'm also the owner's grandson."

Tony Limin laughed. The laughter was warm, sincere and infectious, as Paul soon responded in kind.

"Isn't someone from the banquet department helping you set up for your meeting?"

Tony Limin looked at him with amusement.

"You may be the owner's grandson and have a fancy title; but you're obviously new. I've been here on a monthly basis for three years now, probably the best convention customer you have, certainly the most consistent. I've never had banquet staff help me; I'm not even sure you have any. I'm lucky if there are a stack of chairs in the room, usually I have to get them myself."

Paul was shocked. He knew the hotel's reputation was bad; but he did not think it was this bad.

"I must say that you have a great attitude about it; I would be mad."

"Well, it helps that I'm a motivational speaker."

Tony laughed again; it was still sincere; but when Paul joined him this time, his own laughter was nervous.

"May I ask why you keep returning so regularly if you're treated so poorly by us?"

"Because this…Paul Gray…Lost & Found Director…and grandson of the hotel's owner…is where the people are, who need my help the most."

Tony Limin's words hit Paul Gray hard; he had found a kindred spirit.

"Hypothetically speaking, if someone were actually here to turn this hotel around, possibly even this whole neighborhood and that someone wanted to get an honest appraisal of your experience with this hotel and to make amends for the years of shoddy service, which you've received, would you—"

CHAPTER TWENTY

"I would be very interested in helping you…or that someone…whoever it was…hypothetically speaking of course."

Tony Limin laughed as he took a book from a box on the floor. The title of the book was *When Life Gives You Lemons* and it bore a picture of its author. In the picture, Tony was smiling and juggling five lemons. He opened the book to the title page and autographed it; then he turned to the blank page at the very back of the book and wrote down his contact information before handing it to Paul.

Paul helped Tony finish setting up for his meeting, shook his hand with the promise of future contact, then made his way to Tradewinds, the hotel's restaurant.

The restaurant was exactly the way Paul remembered it unfortunately. Nothing had been done to update the place whatsoever; even the menu was the same. It was between breakfast and lunch, so Paul was the only one in the restaurant. He ordered fruit salad, chicken teriyaki over rice and iced tea; the food was good but not great. The waitress promptly brought the bill, when Paul was finished eating; and he took the opportunity to ask her a question.

"Who is the executive chef here now?"

"Chef Armstrong."

"Would that be Zack Armstrong?"

"Yes."

"And can you tell me if Chef Armstrong was the one who prepared the chicken teriyaki."

"They're very short staffed back in the kitchen today; and he's here, so yes, it was probably him."

"Thank you very much; you've been a good waitress."

Paul settled his bill with her and walked back to the kitchen where he saw a hulk of a man working on the kitchen line. He was wearing a white chef apron, red t-shirt with "RCFD" on the back, blue jeans and sneakers. Instead of a traditional chef toque, the man was wearing a blue baseball cap and strawberry blonde hair was peeking out past the rim.

"Whoever made that chicken teriyaki should go back to culinary school."

Activity in the kitchen came to a dead stop; and it was absolutely quiet. The chef slowly turned around to face his accuser.

"Do you have a problem with my chicken teriyaki, friend?"

The scowl on the chef's face was intimidating; and he was balling up his fists in preparation for a fight.

"Yes, I do. I want to know where you learned to cook."

"The same place you did, friend."

The chef charged towards Paul; but Paul stood his ground and showed no fear. The other kitchen staff braced for a fight; but the fight did not come, because instead of fighting him, the chef bear hugged Paul tightly instead— too tightly. Paul feared a broken rib was in his future if Zack Armstrong did not let go soon.

"Paul Gray, I missed you."

"It's good to see you again, Zack."

"Let's talk in my office. Hey Tim, take over for a few."

Zack led Paul to a small room adjacent to the kitchen and closed the door.

"Miss Christie comes back here on a weekly basis; and she's kept me updated on your journey."

Paul laughed.

"Yeah, I knew if I sent the postcards to her, she'd keep everyone else informed—everyone that is, who would still remember me."

CHAPTER TWENTY

"Well, there's not many of us left around here anymore; that's for sure. Can I assume that you're back to—"

"Yes, but keep that to yourself for just a little while longer. I need time to build a case. Can I count on you when everything starts to break?"

"I'm a little offended that you would even ask me that question, Paul; you should know I've always got your back. Just promise me that I can hit ole Fishface once or twice before you kick him out on his keister."

Fishface was Zack Armstrong's derogatory name for Gilbert Gillenwater.

"Well, Zack if you're itching so badly for a fight, I've got one scheduled tonight."

"Oh yeah?"

"I've got some squatters in the lower levels across the street. I chased them out Friday night; but I need to find a more permanent solution."

Zack started getting very excited.

"Dude, was that you? Oh, man! Tony and Dakota were telling me about that Saturday; and I was cracking up. Tony said gang members were falling over themselves to get out of the tunnel. He said they looked really beat up when they finally hobbled out of the hotel."

"Well, one of them could have been badly hurt; he ran straight on into a support post."

Zack winced.

"He's a good kid; he just got caught up in something he couldn't handle. According to him, the whole gang is looking for a way out of that lifestyle with the exception of the leader. So, I'm going to try to give it to them; but I need to catch them first."

Zack had been nodding the entire time, seriously considering Paul's words.

"I'm in. When and where?"

"Penthouse of the Canterbury. Nine o'clock this evening. We'll marshal there and establish a plan of attack."

"Do you need an army?"

"If you have one."

"I'll see what I can do."

"And I'll let you get back to work; I still have a lot to do myself before tonight. Thanks, Zack."

"Hey, don't thank me; thank you. Knowing you were coming back some day to clean house has been the only reason a few of us have bothered to stick around."

Paul left Zack's office and started to leave the kitchen, when Zack called to him.

"And you better visit Miss Christie soon; she's been expecting you, you know."

"Oh, I know; if she asks, tell her you haven't seen me yet."

"Lie to Miss Christie?! Do you think I have a death wish or something?"

Both men laughed; and even some of the other employees in the kitchen joined them.

Chapter Twenty-One

As cold as it was, it was too far to walk to St. George's, so Paul made his way to his truck, which was parked in the second subbasement of the Pine Avenue Parking Garage. Despite the fact, that it was lunch hour, traffic was rather light; and Paul was able to get to the church rather quickly. He parked his truck on the street and made his way to a door labeled "Rectory," hoping that was where he would find Reverend Vickers; his guess was sound. The minister was sitting behind his desk eating his lunch.

"Reverend Vickers, I'm Paul Gray; my assistant, Marcy should have called you to tell you I was coming."

"Yes, she's a very sweet girl; but I already told her that I can't help you. St. George's will be closing its doors very soon."

"May I ask why?"

Reverend Vickers motioned towards a chair across from him; and Paul sat down.

"Our Lord shared fish and loaves with the multitudes; I can only offer you a part of my tuna salad sandwich."

"Thank you, Reverend; that's very kind of you; but I just finished my lunch. I'm sorry I've interrupted yours."

The elderly clergyman took a bite of his sandwich, chewed it slowly, and then responded.

"You haven't interrupted anything. In fact, I very much welcome your company. This church gets so little traffic these days."

"What's the problem?"

"People won't come to an old church with a leaky roof; they want to go to a newer building; and when they leave, they take their money and time with them, so the leak doesn't get fixed; in fact it grows bigger causing even more people to leave. The diocese has offered help in the past to cover shortfalls; but they realize now that they are simply throwing good money after bad. I think that it's time to close the doors."

"What will happen to you and to this building?"

"I'm as much a relic as the church building. Oh, there's a chance that they'll assign me to another parish; but I'm nearing retirement; and parishioners are demanding younger pastors. They don't realize the value of wisdom, which only comes from age."

Paul felt sorry for Reverend Vickers.

"And the church?"

"There are already developers lined up to tear it down and replace it with heaven knows what."

"How could they possibly raze this architectural gem?"

"Did you know it's the oldest church in River City? Yes! It was built in 1834 and has survived numerous wars and depressions; but it just can't compete with urban blight and fancy megachurches and developers eager to destroy anything over fifty years old."

"Once upon a time ago, I was a sexton briefly for an Episcopal church in Portland. I love these old churches, especially the ones that still have bell towers."

Reverend Vickers smiled with pride then started crying. It was so obvious that he had a strong emotional attachment to this wonderful building.

"Do you think you could give me a tour of this old church?"

There was a twinkle in the older man's eye.

"I would like that very much."

Paul considered his time with Reverend Vickers that afternoon to be the highpoint of his day. There was a wonderful treasure trove of local history in the structure; and Vickers was a masterful professor pointing out fascinating details and interweaving stories about the congregation throughout history. For his part, Paul explained his plans for the Forrest to the minister.

"Reverend, would you stay and help me fight to save this city?"

Vickers thought about the question; and as he thought, he became starry-eyed.

"Perhaps…just perhaps…this old church and I have one more good fight left in us."

Paul smiled at Vickers; and the minister returned it.

"So, you'll come to the meeting."

"Yes, I will come."

Chapter Twenty-Two

Fitting for a meeting on faith, Marcy, with Clemente's help, had performed a miracle. The Sunset Room looked amazing; it looked nothing like it did, when Paul had arrived in town last week. There was a podium near the window with dozens of chairs arranged theater-style facing it. Near the door, was a table, which contained baskets of donuts and other assorted baked goods as well as a large coffee urn, some canned sodas and bottled waters. Whether by Marcy's suggestion or his own choice, Clemente had changed into a suit before the meeting.

Paul was not late; but there were already several ministers present when he arrived. Marcy and Clemente had greeted each clergyman; and now, Paul made sure that he too briefly welcomed everyone personally. Some he already knew such as Fathers Fergus Andrews and Marcos Guerroro from St. Anthony's and Pastors Tom Sheppard and Tim Alexopoulos from Covenant Baptist and even Reverend Vickers, whom he had just met. However, most of the dozens of ministers, who had arrived for the meeting, Paul only knew by name or affiliation if that.

One of those ministers, Harvey Joseph Morris, associate pastor of Maranatha Community Church, was something of a local celebrity. Brother Harvey, as he styled himself, was an amateur detective, who had helped local police solve many high profile cases several years ago, when Paul was still attending college; but that was long before the corruption.

"Pardon me; but I remember you…you're Brother Harvey aren't you…you helped the police solve some murders a few years ago. I remember reading about it in the newspaper."

Even a man of the cloth is not immune from a spot of pride every now and then; and Brother Harvey feigned modesty while basking in faded glory.

"Guilty; but I'm afraid that my crime fighting days are behind me."

"Perhaps, someday I could impose on you to share a few stories; I'm sure you have many great ones to tell."

"Perhaps. Yes, I would like that."

When he had greeted everyone individually, Paul walked to the podium to officially start the meeting.

"Good afternoon. My name is Paul Gray; and I want to thank you for coming. Before we start, I think it proper that we have an invocation. I had the wonderful privilege of visiting with Reverend William Vickers earlier today; and I was wondering if he would lead us in prayer."

Reverend Vickers, who had been one of the last to arrive approached the podium and led the group in a brief prayer, before returning to his seat.

"I want to make one thing clear before we discuss anything. I'm not looking to form some ecumenical body and merge everyone into one religion or denomination. I have no intention of changing anyone's beliefs. Rather, as a businessman, I'm looking to affect positive change in this area; and I would very much like the input of local religious leaders."

Paul described his great-grandfather's unethical business practices and how those practices had contributed significantly to the current decay of the city. He also told the group about himself and his faith. He shared the community goals, which he and Marcy had prepared. And, when he had finished telling the group all of these things, he paused.

"I suppose what I'm asking from you is your prayers and advice, because I'm going to need both; and if I should err as my great grandfather before me, I need a group that will hold me publicly accountable.

"I understand there are many of you, who are in need. Money and time would go a long way to solving some of the problems you face. I would like to make an offer of both. I should have mentioned this in my list of community goals; but I only had the idea since visiting Reverend

Vickers earlier today. I would like to organize an event that would bring community awareness to all the houses of worship in the Forrest. On this day, visitors would make their way from church to church; and at each location, there would be an open house, so they could tour the facility and meet the staff, perhaps there could be organ recitals and such. I would like to make it an annual event and call it the Parade of Steeples.

Next, Paul asked Clemente to stand next to him; and he related his story. Clemente added his own plea for their help with the gangs. When they were finished, Bishop Prescott stood and requested the floor. Paul stepped aside and offered him the use of the podium.

"We've heard this gentleman's words; and I think it would be wise to discuss them."

He then turned to Paul.

"Mr. Gray, would you, Ms. Green, and Mr. Morales give us the room for a few moments."

Paul was not exactly sure what response he had been expecting; but this was not it. He and his associates left the room as requested and closed the door behind them. An hour later, they were called back into the room.

Paul approached Bishop Prescott, who was still behind the podium. Marcy and Clemente stood behind and on either side of him. The Bishop started speaking.

"We have been encouraged by your statements and plans today; but it isn't the first time religious leaders have been promised that their interests would be highly regarded. Many times politicians and businessmen say things to make themselves look good, then change their minds later. However, Fergus Andrews, Tom Sheppard and even William Vickers have put in very good words for you, enough for the rest of us to give you the benefit of the doubt. We have unanimously agreed to pray for you, give you the advice and emotional support, which you've requested and even our own influence if necessary regarding every goal you've mentioned; however, we have a few conditions.

"First, we suggest that you change the name of this group from Forrest

Council of Churches to Forrest Council on Faith; this term does not have the ecumenical insinuation, which council of churches has. It also encompasses our Jewish and Buddhist friends, who are present."

Bishop Prescott made both eye contact with and sweeping gestures towards a Jewish rabbi and a Buddhist priest in attendance.

"Second, the council should have some say over who the liaison will be. Either we should be allowed to choose the person ourselves; or we should be allowed a consent or veto of your choice. We would also ask that this person be given total freedom within your organization. If we are to hold you responsible, we should have a person who is able to compile information unfettered.

"Third, we know that Ms. Green is a member of St. Anthony's and Mr. Morales recently joined Covenant Baptist and that you yourself are a member of both churches. We ask that any future hires be affiliated with a house of worship and that their pastor be invited to join this group. Also, we will assist you with your plans to help displaced gang members; but we require that they too affiliate themselves with a house of worship as a condition for both your and our assistance.

"Do you agree to these terms?"

"Fully."

"Good, then there is one final condition. We ask that you put all of this in contract form, which you will sign publicly in a special ceremony. If this group feels that you have broken your promise or that you are working in league with any of the evil men of this city, we will inform the media."

Bishop Prescott then addressed the assembled ministers.

"Then, it is agreed that we shall meet on a weekly basis; every other week starting next Monday at a different member-church without Paul Gray and his associates present; and every other week here at the Canterbury with them in attendance. I think we should dismiss this meeting in prayer with each minister taking a turn. Let's all join hands and form a circle."

Everyone formed a circle and Paul found himself between Father Andrews on his left, and Pastor Tom on his right. Further to his left were Marcy and Bishop Prescott, and further to his right were Clemente, Tim Alexopoulos and Reverend Vickers. Each minister in attendance prayed for Paul and his staff that God would give them wisdom and courage and that through them, God's will would be done in all things.

Everyone's eyes were closed, so nobody noticed Paul's ring glowing brightly—nobody that is except Father Andrews. He noticed with great interest; and when the prayer was over, he lingered near Paul.

Bishop Prescott approached.

"Thank you for your kind hospitality, Paul. I look forward to hearing good news from you."

"Thank you for attending, Your Excellency. I only hope I have good news to give."

Bishop Prescott patted him on the shoulder and departed.

One middle-aged man approached Paul and introduced himself.

"Hi, I'm Pastor Aaron Bishop; I'm the associate pastor of Zoara Christian Church. Our senior pastor asked me to attend on his behalf."

"Thank you for coming, Pastor. I beg your pardon; but I don't know you; however your name sounds so familiar."

"Have you been watching the news? My son is the boy who's in a coma."

"Yes, that's where I've heard your name. I'm sorry for sounding so insensitive. I hope his condition improves very soon. Is there anything I can do?"

"No offense taken and thank you for the regards. I would ask that you pray, because the doctors have done everything they can do; he's in God's hands now."

"Well, we can certainly all do that."

"There is however an unrelated favor I would like to ask of you."

"Name it."

"As I said, I'm here today on behalf of our senior pastor whose schedule is always very busy; but I would like to attend all future meetings in my own right…if that's okay."

"It's okay with me. I'm just thankful so many ministers and churches are willing to offer their advice to help this community."

Aaron Bishop started to say something but changed his mind. Instead, he shook hands with Paul; and Paul's ring glowed again. This time, two people noticed it, Paul, who mentally filed it away, and Father Andrews, who watched with keen interest. Aaron bid farewell and started to leave before being intercepted by Clemente.

"I just noticed your ring. How did you acquire such a magnificent piece of jewelry, Paul?"

Since the meeting had ended, Father Andrews had been fervently attempting to speak with Paul; but when he finally found his chance, his effort was startling, as Paul jumped slightly at the sudden question coming from behind him. Paul turned to face his priest and finally registering the question, which had been asked of him, took notice of his ring for the second time since his cousin had bestowed it upon him. He fidgeted with the ring as he spoke.

"Oh, this? My cousin gave it to me Friday. I'm not really sure why there's a bee on it."

"Well…in heraldry, a bee can symbolize many things…industry…eternal life. You may even have a relic there, Paul."

"My cousin is quite shrewd; I doubt he would part with something of any real value. It's probably just a piece of nineteenth century costume jewelry, which he couldn't sell."

"Perhaps."

Although he sensed the line of questioning could not be prolonged any further, Father Andrews continued to study the ring from afar. Thorough research was required before he asked Paul any further questions regarding the ring.

Paul's intention had been to take a quick nap after his meeting with the ministers, so he would be fresh for tonight's adventure in Canterbury's second subbasement; however, that did not happen. Instead, he, along with Marcy and Clemente, entertained the ministers, who had expressed interest in forming a prayer vigil during tonight's adventure in the lower levels. In all, nine ministers remained from the earlier meeting: Fathers Fergus Andrews and Marcos Guerroro from St. Anthony Catholic Church, Pastors Tom Sheppard and Tim Alexopoulos from Covenant Baptist Church, Reverend William Vickers from St. George's Episcopal Church, Pastor Aaron Bishop from Zoara Christian Church, Brother Harvey Morris from Maranatha Community Church, Reverend Kiango Jackson from Twelfth Street Baptist Church, and Rabbi Benjamin Cohen from Temple Adath Shalom. It had not escaped Paul's attention that while Clemente had spoken to all of the ministers, who had attended the earlier meeting, he had spent much more time with these particular ministers. He knew they were there because of Clemente's persuasiveness.

Other people were now arriving very early to assist in one way or another with what was quickly being referred to as the Canterbury Raid. To Paul's dismay, Pop and Nan were two of those early arrivals.

"What are you two doing here?"

"We've come to help?"

"Nan, this isn't a game; you could get hurt!"

"Don't be silly, Paul! Of course, we're not going down in the basement; but we can help in other ways. Everyone will probably be foregoing a proper dinner to be here, so we can help Marcy order some pizzas before you start."

Paul briefly made eye contact with his assistant, who quietly answered his unspoken question with a sheepish grin. It was clear that the people in Paul's life without instruction or previous introduction had colluded

CHAPTER TWENTY-TWO

behind his back. Nan noticed the exchange and offered a brief statement to diffuse any tension.

"Oh, I spoke with Marcy earlier today; she's such a lovely girl."

Nan waved at Marcy and then quickly found her way back to the original conversation.

"During this raid…is that what we're calling it now…Pop and I are going to join the prayer vigil; you'll need the Lord on your side, Paul, if you have any hope of this ending without someone getting seriously hurt. And after the raid, you need some help talking some sense into those boys; and Pop and I are better at that than anyone here."

Paul aggressively nodded his head in jest at Nan's matter-of-fact statement; and Nan returned with a playful punch to his arm; at the same time, she noticed Edith Sheppard arrive.

"Oh, there's Edith. Excuse us, Paul. I wanted a word with her before it gets too busy."

Nan and Pop left Paul to join a small group of ministers, which included Edith Sheppard and her husband Tom.

Ashleigh also arrived early and immediately infused herself into everything that was happening as if she had always belonged there. Despite their awkward first encounter, she and Marcy had become quick friends. She and Clemente however were becoming more than friends; they were becoming a couple; and that warmed Paul's heart more than anything else had that week. He wondered if she was here because she really wanted to help bring change to the Forrest or because she wanted to spend more time with Clemente. He concluded that it really did not matter; but it was probably for both reasons.

"I was serious about joining your group, Paul."

"I can see that."

"Clemente's already put some stuff together to show you during your next meeting. He showed Marcy and me at lunch today; and we think it's great."

"He's a very capable young man; and I look forward to his presentation; I'm sure I will be equally impressed."

Clemente was grinning from ear to ear; and he discreetly took Ashleigh's hand as he stood next to her.

"I know Georgia and Ed will join too. They really believe in you, Paul, and what you're trying to do. They're just distracted with everything that is happening with the diner."

Paul was starting to feel uneasy with the direction of the conversation. He did not think it was appropriate to discuss the diner's business with Ashleigh, especially since he was not even sure how he would be helping the Hoppers yet. His unease did not last very long as Ashleigh rather abruptly led Clemente to a small group of people on the other side of the room to socialize briefly with them.

There was a sudden commotion in the penthouse hallway; and Paul went to investigate. Tiny Smith had just arrived; and as promised he had brought a small army with him—twenty-three men by Paul's hasty count. Tiny made the necessary introductions; but there were so many of them; and he had done it so quickly; and enunciation was not exactly in Tiny Smith's skill set. Like Tiny, everyone in the group seemed to have stereotypical nicknames like Bubba or Sonny or Cletus. The entire group was dressed and armed for a major hunting expedition.

"We brought LED incapacitators, net guns, tasers, gas pistols with tear gas and sleep gas pellets, tranquilizer guns with RIP cartridges, restraints and stun belts; and of course some gas masks for us. I hope it's enough."

Paul privately wondered whether Tiny and his regiment had parked a fleet of tanks outside the Canterbury too.

"I'm sure it will be. Thank you so much for coming and bringing supplies and reinforcements."

Earlier Marcy, Ashleigh and Nan had ordered thirty-four large pizzas and seventeen two-liters of soda from Second City Pizza; and the food was now arriving. These were placed on the table near the coffee urns and

CHAPTER TWENTY-TWO

remaining pastries. Paul quickly steered Tiny and his party towards the food, hoping it would defuse their collective aggression.

Zack Armstrong brought an army too. Half of them were off-duty employees from the Imperial Hotel; and like Tiny before him, Zack made the introductions; but unlike Tiny, Zack spent more time introducing each person. For Zack, there was much more at stake than ousting some gang from a basement, he was attempting to build a groundswell of support for Paul, when the time finally came to oust an unwanted creature over at the hotel. Beside Zack, Paul only knew one other person from this group, Rick Brisker, the head bartender.

"Remember me, Paul."

"I remember you cheer for the wrong side at Barnyard Bowls."

The two men shook hands while laughing. Paul had attended WURC, back when it was still called Western Indiana University, where the mascot was and still is the Fighting Roosters. Rick had attended the University of Oregon, home of the Oregon Ducks. For many years, there had been a friendly rivalry between the two universities; and an exhibition football game, called the Barnyard Bowl, was played every year on New Year's Day.

"Are you back to—"

Sensing his question, Paul quickly interrupted him and surveyed the other hotel employees wondering how much they already knew. Zack ended Paul's speculation.

"Paul, they already know. You can't keep good news like that secret for long, especially in a hotel like the Imperial. Don't worry though; every man here will help you with the gang today and with the hotel when you're ready to make your move there. We'll keep your secret; and we've got your back. And for every employee standing here, there are four more employees, working across the street at this very moment, who also support what you are doing."

As he spoke, each head in the group was nodding in agreement. With this revelation, Paul felt the need to make a brief speech if for no other reason but clarification.

"It's true. I am the new owner of the Imperial; and big changes are coming there very soon. I think…I hope…you'll really like these changes; but for a little while longer, while I can build a solid case against Gillenwater, I need all of you to continue on as usual, to ignore me and what I'm doing, to look at me as some slacker grandson who doesn't matter. Just be patient. Okay?"

The heads continued to nod; and every hotel employee now felt emboldened that better times were imminent, not simply for the hotel but for the entire community.

"Before we get started, make sure to help yourselves to some pizza. I think there might even be some leftover doughnuts too."

The Imperial employees made their way to the refreshment table and helped themselves to pizza. Zack lingered behind to introduce the other half of his brigade, although they did not need an introduction. Paul already knew the entire Armstrong family; they were his distant cousins. Including Zack, there were thirteen kids in the Armstrong family, twelve boys and one very tough girl. As large as he was, Zack was rather small compared to his brothers, most of whom were firefighters. Each in turn bear hugged Paul and expressed happiness at his return to River City. By the time Paul had personally greeted the entire Armstrong family, he was feeling quite sore. As the Armstrong siblings lined up for pizza, Paul called out to Zack.

"Would you compile a list of hotel employees and indicate which ones are—"

"On your side? Consider it done."

Zack winked as he left Paul and re-joined his siblings. Three of the hotel employees having already finished their pizza and now nursing cups of soda, found an opportunity to re-introduce themselves to Paul.

"You may not remember us; but I'm Tony; and this is Dakota; we helped you with your first raid Friday night."

Paul shook their hands again.

"I remember that; but unfortunately, we were only communicating through Peter; I didn't get to speak with you directly, much less face-to-face."

"When Zack told us what you were doing tonight, we knew we wanted to help more actively this time. This is Dan; he works in security too!"

"It's great to meet you; and thank you for coming. With this many people, we should be able to resolve this quickly and without injury to anyone."

Clemente and Ashleigh interrupted the conversation. There were two police officers standing behind them. It was Ashleigh's turn to make introductions.

"Paul, this is Officers Baldo Havens and Kevin O'Connell. They're probably the only good and honest cops in this entire city."

The older officer, the one introduced as Baldo Havens, spoke for both of them.

"Unfortunately, she's right. Almost the whole department is corrupt now; but it wasn't like that when I first joined the force; 'to serve and protect' actually meant something back then; and it still does to me. Ashleigh tells us that you'll be kicking Zumbini out of his ivory tower soon."

Paul good-naturedly glared at Ashleigh, who, as good-naturedly, averted her eyes. What she lacked in discretion, she more than made up for in enthusiasm.

"Well, officers…baby steps…tonight it's just a gang squatting in the basement…but eventually…yeah…it does look like Zumbini and I are positioning ourselves for an eventual showdown."

"We'll help you when and how we can; but just remember that while Zumbini has the mayor and the chief of police on his payroll, our hands are tied. The powers want the Forrest to wither and die. Officially, if you had called for us in this part of town, we are supposed to ignore the call."

"I understand; and I want you to know that I appreciate whatever help you're able to give me. Whatever you do; don't jeopardize your careers."

Ashleigh and Clemente led the officers into the Sunset Room and offered them some pizza. Sixty-eight people had come to help Paul, certainly more than he could have ever imagined. As everyone that he was expecting had arrived, he decided it was time to start; but as he approached the podium, one of the hotel employees, the dining room manager, Jose Fernandez, stopped him.

"Promise me…promise me…you won't hurt them."

The young man was sobbing heavily and having great difficulty just getting his words out.

"Do you know them?"

Jose nodded.

"Are you related to some of them?"

Jose nodded again; and his sobbing was starting to draw the attention of others.

"I don't want anyone to get hurt, them or us; but for the resident's safety, I need them out of the basement. For their own safety, they need to be off the streets too. First help me catch them, then help me convince them to accept what I can offer them."

Again, Jose nodded while sobbing until finally collapsing into the nearest chair to compose himself before the meeting started. Paul took the podium and called the meeting to order; and for the next four hours, those assembled discussed how they would conduct the raid and what they would do afterwards. While Paul's solo raid only a few days earlier had been long, noisy and hastily planned, tonight's raid would be the exact opposite.

Ten of them, mostly ministers, would stay in the penthouse until the raid had ended; they would pray for the safety of everyone. The remaining fifty-six would form seven groups of eight and converge on the second subbasement from different locations. Each group would be responsible for blocking one exit and incapacitating two gang members.

Team 1, led by Officers Baldo Havens and Kevin O'Connell and including Clemente Morales, entered the second subbasement by the elevator. Team 2, led by Paul Gray, entered from the north stairwell. Team 3, led by Zack Armstrong, entered from the south stairwell. Team 4, led by Father Marcos Guerroro, entered from the northern tunnel connected to St. Anthony's Catholic Church. Team 5, led by Tiny Smith, entered from the eastern tunnel connected to the Pine Avenue Parking Garage. Team 6, led by Dan, one of the Imperial Hotel security guards, entered from the southern tunnel connected to Forrest Library, who, with an earlier phone call by Marcy, was very willing to cooperate to remove the gang from the lower levels, as they were having problems with them too. And, Team 7, led by Tony, the other Imperial Hotel security guard, entered from the western tunnel connected to the Imperial Hotel.

All teams remained in radio contact with each other and an eighth team, consisting of Marcy and Ashleigh, who stood outside the Sunset Room, ready to call for help if something went wrong downstairs. Nothing went wrong though; everything went exactly as planned and without incident; and the entire event lasted less than five minutes. As each team entered the second subbasement from their respective locations, they lobbed two smoke canisters into the room; and since the raiders were all wearing gasmasks and the gang members were not; there were soon fourteen half-conscious bodies on the floor.

Officers Havens and O'Connell confiscated Carlos' gun and a half-dozen switchblades; and then the gang members were escorted to a suite of empty rooms, which was once a small clinic on the Canterbury's second floor. There, they were separated, restrained, and visited by a succession of seven teams of three; each team endeavored to convince the gang member in question to accept Paul's offer of assistance.

Paul, Clemente and Marcy were the final team; and the last gang member they encountered was Carlos Rivera.

"Well, if it isn't Demente Morales. We wondered what happened to you."

Carlos' attempt at wit only amused himself. Marcy placed a steadying hand on Clemente's shoulder, as Carlos felt the need to continue talking.

"Do you think you're one of them now, because you're wearing those fancy clothes? Well, you're nothing—nothing but a rat. You always have been and always will be. You hear me."

Marcy's grip on Clemente's shoulder tightened.

"Carlos, I can help you find a better life—a life off of the streets."

"I don't need your help. We do just fine on our own."

"By 'we,' do you mean Las Ratas, because seven of your fellow gang members have already accepted my offer tonight? That's half—more than half if you count Clemente; and I think four more will change their minds very soon. How long do you think a gang of three will last, Carlos?"

"If I wasn't wearing these restraints, I'd show you how long you would last against me."

Without thought, Paul unlocked Carlos' restraints and waited for the young man to prove himself. Carlos was at once surprised and terrified; and he massaged his wrists while planning his fighting strategy. Marcy was scared by this development; but she tried not to show it. Clemente though was as calm as Paul was. Carlos lunged for Paul and was quickly pinned to the floor.

"First, I took down two of your fellow gang members singlehandedly, when I found them attacking an innocent kid on the street."

Paul freed Carlos, who again calculated his attack. When he rushed Paul, he was again pinned to the floor.

"Next, I took on all fifteen of you singlehandedly, and managed to force all of you out of the Canterbury and to save Clemente from a life in your gang."

Again, Paul freed Carlos, who clumsily attacked Paul with his fists and who was pinned to the floor even quicker than the last two times.

"Then tonight, I led a successful raid into the lower levels to finally remove your gang from this building once and for all; and saved another seven members in the process."

Paul had barely freed him the fourth time, when Carlos' quick movement was countered with an even quicker movement by Paul.

"I've given you four chances just now to fight me one on one; and four times, I've easily pinned you. You fight sloppy, Carlos; that's why you lose quickly."

Paul released Carlos; but this time Carlos sat down on the cot. He was not willing to repeat his earlier mistakes.

"You may have fought two of us; but none of us moved from this building. You may have chased us out; but we quickly returned. What makes you think we won't be right back here tomorrow night?"

Thinking he had outwitted Paul, Carlos laughed heartily; and Paul allowed him his moment before responding.

"Because this time, Carlos, we aren't chasing you out into the streets of River City. If you want to act like a wild animal, then we'll release you as we would an animal. When…or rather if…you return to River City, I don't think you'll have much fight left in you."

This final insult caused Carlos Rivera to attack again; but this time his target was Marcy. Before he could touch her, he was pinned to the floor one last time; but this time, it was Clemente, who responded to the threat.

Chapter Twenty-Three

Paul awoke to doggie kisses; Noodles was standing on Paul's chest licking his face. This was odd, because since the dog had been staying with them, he usually slept in Clemente's room. There was a piece of folded paper between the dog's neck and the leash. Paul removed and unfolded the paper. It was a copy of the "Found" poster, which Paul had asked Clemente to make. There was a picture of Noodles and Paul's cell phone number. On the back of the poster, there was a message scrawled in crayon. Paul read aloud to the dog.

"I want to live with Paul and Clemente forever, because they're awesome!"

Paul looked seriously into the beagle's eyes.

"Did you put him up to this?"

Noodles simply wagged his tail; he did seem rather content with his current living arrangements.

Paul exercised, showered, shaved and dressed; then went to his office to have a personal devotion. Clemente was nowhere in the apartment; Paul assumed he was at the diner eating breakfast and spending time with Ashleigh. As Paul made his own way to the diner, he discovered other "Found" posters along the way, both in the Canterbury lobby and near the diner's door.

Clemente was not at the diner though; and neither were Marcy or Ashleigh. Georgia waited on Paul, who had recently fallen into a usual breakfast order of scrambled eggs, bacon, hash browns, toast, orange juice and coffee. Paul quietly ate his breakfast alone and in peace then proceeded to Foster Gray Holdings to see what was happening there; and what was happening there was indeed a pleasant surprise.

Ashleigh was seated at the receptionist desk. The telephone rang; and strangely, Ashleigh answered it.

"Good morning! Foster Gray Holdings….No, I'm sorry Mr. Gray is not in at the moment; he's a very busy man; he's probably somewhere keeping the world safe from creepy clowns….No, I'm sorry Mr. Morales is not in either; he's a very busy man too; he's probably helping Mr. Gray with those clowns….Would you like to speak to Ms. Green? She's Mr. Gray's executive assistant; and she's very efficient….I see; well, thank you for calling Foster Gray Holdings."

Ashleigh was the perfect ham; and Paul gave her a round of applause after her performance.

"Good morning, Mr. Gray!"

"Good morning, Ashleigh. I see we have new phones."

"Yes, they were installed yesterday morning."

Ashleigh handed Paul a slip of paper with the telephone number; and Paul programmed it into his smart phone.

"Everyone is here, if you're ready to start."

"I'm ready."

Ashleigh did not lead Paul to the war room; she was taking him on a special tour. The first stop was Marcy's new office. She stood to greet Paul when he and Ashleigh stopped outside her door.

"I needed an office, Paul, one, which is separate from the receptionist desk."

"I agree; and it looks great, Marcy."

Ashleigh and Marcy then led Paul to Clemente's office. Clemente was sitting with his feet on the desk acting as if he were barking orders in the phone.

"I want that report by tomorrow afternoon. Understand? I might even put in a good word for you with Paul….Yeah, we're partners. Hey, I have to go; I'm needed in a very important meeting. We'll do lunch sometime. Later."

Again, Paul gave a round of applause; but this time Ashleigh and Marcy joined him. Clemente took a bow.

"Well, we do have an important meeting if everyone's ready."

They made their way to the war room and took the same seats as yesterday; but Ashleigh, being new, sat next to Clemente. She had brought coffee and donuts, which were already sitting in the middle of the table. Marcy, sensing Paul's puzzlement over Ashleigh's attendance, explained.

"If it's okay with you, I could really use some help at the reception desk and performing basic clerical duties, when I'm tackling your more challenging projects; and Ashleigh wanted some extra money anyway. I thought she could work here a few hours a week. Plus, she has a report of her own to give you…and I think she wants to hear Clemente give his report."

Marcy snickered as Clemente and Ashleigh blushed.

"It's okay with me; in fact, it's great with me. You forgot to mention how well Ashleigh already fits into our little group. Welcome aboard, Ashleigh! Marcy, I trust you'll handle all the details."

Marcy and Ashleigh exchanged smiles.

"And Marcy if you're feeling that buried with work, just let me know."

"Well, I intended to mention this during my report; but we could use five more people around here, Paul. There's already that much work."

"Okay, but let's discuss that further during your report. Before we get too sidetracked, I wanted to start today's meeting by telling each you…Marcy, Clemente and you too Ashleigh…that yesterday's meeting with the Forrest Council on Faith and the raid in the lower levels was very successful; I'm very pleased with the progress made; and it's largely because of your efforts.

Great job; and thank you…all of you. And, for my part, I only have two brief points. Marcy, Aaron Bishop approached me and asked that he permanently attend all future meetings; I told him that was okay."

"Yes, I know; I had overheard his conversation with you; but he told me the same thing later in person. I've already made the necessary changes."

"Good. Secondly, it would seem that events at the Imperial are moving much quicker than I had originally planned; and I'm not able to work in total anonymity as I had hoped. It's time to start a committee of hotel employees, who can help me expedite my little coup. I've already asked Zack to compile a list of hotel employees, who might be willing and able to help us. They were good about helping the Canterbury with our gang problem; let's make sure the Imperial Hotel is similarly rewarded by returning the favor, but first, we need that list."

Marcy made notes on her legal pad.

"And that's all I had; I plan to work around here today unless I'm needed elsewhere. Clemente, you're up."

Clemente cleared his throat.

"As you requested, I now have a cell phone."

Clemente recovered the phone from his pocket, sent Paul a text message containing his new phone number and then showed the phone to Paul.

"Marcy already has the number."

Paul read the text message and stored the phone number on his own cell phone.

"The rest of my clothes arrived from Taylor's yesterday morning. Marcy told me to check the delivery; and I did; everything was there; and I've already put the clothes away."

"Good job."

"I made 'Found' posters and posted them around the neighborhood."

"Yes, I know. One of them woke me up this morning."

Everyone laughed at Paul's expense including Paul himself.

"I checked into getting a driver's license. Being a new state, Wabash hasn't had time to pass many regulations, so if you're over eighteen years old, pass the vision exam and written test, you get your license."

"No learner's permit? No driving test?"

"Nope!"

"Well, you still need to learn to drive; you didn't attend school, so how could you possibly know—"

Realization set in; and Paul answered his own question.

"Never mind…I really don't want to know the answer to that question…do I?"

Clemente shook his head and looked genuinely embarrassed; it was Marcy's chance to rescue him.

"I'm taking him Friday to the DMV to get his license."

"And then I can buy a car!"

"And then we'll discuss it. Continue with your report."

"I also enrolled in GED classes at WURC. Those start after Christmas; and in late May I should be able to take the test."

"Very good, Clemente!"

"Paul, I don't know what you have planned for the guys today; but I would like to offer a suggestion."

"Please do."

"I would like to take them to Avalon and then Taylor's so they could have the same fresh start I had. I thought after that I would take them to Dan's Hardware. I need to pick up some tools as you had requested; but I thought you might want them to have some tools too. Perhaps, we could all help work on the churches before the Parade of Steeples."

Paul was beaming with pride. Clemente was already surpassing his wildest expectations.

"Clemente, that sounds great. Marcy, has credit been established at each of these places?"

"Yes, I've already taken care of it; plus, like you said, Adam was able to fast track those credit cards; and Clemente already has one, as do I…and here's yours, Paul. Before he leaves, I'll make sure he takes some petty cash too… just in case. Clemente, bring back receipts."

Marcy was very stern when she issued this last request, punctuating each word with a light tap on the table with her fists.

"Clemente, it has been my experience that bookkeepers are the sweetest people in the world until you break that one rule. They'll let you get by with charging the most frivolous items as long as you give them the receipt in a timely manner; but if you lose that receipt or worse, fail to get one, they suddenly become terrifying monsters, who will question even the most logical and most necessary of purchases. Consider yourself warned."

Marcy was both smiling and nodding.

"Seriously though, make sure you take them to get something to eat too."

"I'll take them to Tradewinds for breakfast and charge it to their rooms. For lunch, I'll take them to the diner. And tonight, I thought we could order some pizzas."

Paul nodded his approval as Marcy interjected.

"I've already established credit at the Imperial, which is kinda strange because you own the place and Second City Pizza too; after last night's order, Second City loves us."

Ashleigh interrupted next.

"And you have credit at the diner too. Georgia keeps meaning to tell you that."

"That's great, Ashleigh. Tell Georgia though that for the moment, I only want Marcy, Clemente and myself to have that privilege."

Ashleigh nodded.

"Clemente, this evening while you're having pizza, I'd like to join you and talk to the guys. I want them to know exactly what I expect from them."

Clemente nodded as Marcy asked Paul a question.

"Paul, have you given any thought to permanent living arrangements for them. They can't stay at the Imperial too much longer; that would get very expensive very quickly."

"What does everyone think about turning the northwest suite into a miniature apartment building for them? I walked around it a few days ago; and it's almost as large as my place so there's lots of room, when the group increases in size. We would just need to do some cleaning and furnishing first."

"Paul, that's a great idea!"

"Thank you, Marcy. What do you think of it, Clemente?"

Clemente was silent for several minutes.

"I like it; and I think the guys will too. They'll feel like you have faith in them allowing them to live so close to you."

"I do. So, let's make sure we meet for pizza tonight in their new place even though there's no furniture yet; and Clemente, let's have an old clothes burning ceremony for them at that time too."

Clemente agreed.

CHAPTER TWENTY-THREE

"How are Carlos and the other guys doing? Have we heard?"

"I spoke to Tiny early this morning; and he said they woke up in their new home very upset."

Paul laughed.

"Well, they know what they can do to improve their condition at any time. Did you have anything else to share, Clemente?"

"Just one more thing. As I said before, we need to form a group to counter L'Ombra; and I propose the Order of the Lamp. L'Ombra means shadow in Italian; and what drives away shadows—a lamp. I've already started five lists."

Clemente handed Paul five pages. The first page was titled "Members of the Order of the Lamp" and it already contained nine names:

> *Paul X. Gray, Chief Executive Officer of Foster Gray Holdings*
> *Marcella Green, Executive Assistant at Foster Gray Holdings*
> *Clemente Morales, Personal Assistant to the CEO of Foster Gray Holdings*
> *Ashleigh Lovett, Waitress at River City Diner/Receptionist at Foster Gray Holdings*
> *Paul "Pop" Gray, Owner of Gray Farms*
> *Flora Gray, Owner of Gray Farms*
> *Zachariah Armstrong, Executive Chef of the Imperial Hotel*
> *Edward Hopper, Owner of River City Diner*
> *Georgia Hopper, Owner of River City Diner.*

Towards the bottom was one more name, "Samuel Hayne, Chief Executive Officer of Hayne Family Enterprises" and the parenthetical note of "pending." Next to each name, except for Paul's and Samuel's, there was already an accompanying signature. Paul signed his name and handed the page back to Clemente.

The second page was titled "Lamp Affiliated Groups;" and it contained two names:

Forrest Council on Faith (29 members)
Los Guardianes (8 members)

"Who are Los Guardianes?"

"Since it was disbanded last night, I thought the former members of Las Ratas needed a new name, so I chose Los Guardianes. It means 'the guardians' in Spanish."

"Yes, I know, Clemente; I speak Spanish."

Clemente looked surprised.

"I'm half Latino; my mother's family is from Puerto Rico."

Clemente looked even more surprised.

"I'm sorry. I suppose I should have told you. Make sure you include a membership sheet for each of these groups."

Paul handed the page back to Clemente; and Clemente made a note on his legal pad.

The third page was titled "Lamp Affiliated Companies;" and it contained five names:

> *Foster Gray Holdings*
> *The Canterbury*
> *The Imperial Hotel*
> *Gray Farms*
> *River City Diner*

Towards the bottom of the page was one more name "Hayne Family Enterprises" with the parenthetical note of "pending."

"Add Pine Avenue Parking Garage; it's technically part of the Canterbury; and also add Imperial Convention Center; it's part of the Imperial Hotel. Otherwise, it's good for now; I have a lot more properties, as you'll soon discover, as does Pop; but this is a very good start."

Paul handed the page back to Clemente, who made the necessary corrections.

The fourth page was titled "Known Members of L'Ombra;" and it only contained one name, "Claude 'Zumbo the Clown' Zumbini, Chief Executive Officer of Big Top Enterprises." Towards the bottom was one more name; it had no title; but there was a parenthetical note of "possible." The name was Carlos Rivera.

The fifth and final page was titled "L'Ombra Affiliated Companies;" and it contained five names:

> Big Top Enterprises
> Big Top Foods
> Big Top Toys
> Zumbo's Big Top Burgers
> Zumboland

Paul handed these pages back to Clemente without correction or comment.

"Now that I've seen the implementation of your idea, I admit that I like it much better. It will be a very helpful tool. Put those pages in a binder; and keep it in your office. You'll probably be updating one or more of those pages on a near daily basis. Did you have anything else?"

"No, that's all I have to report."

"Well, you did a great job, Clemente."

"Can I go next? I only have one thing to report; but it's important; and then I need to get back to the diner."

"Sure. Go ahead, Ashleigh."

"You can add a name to that 'Known Members of L'Ombra' page."

"How do you know the person is in L'Ombra?"

"Clemente and Marcy told me about the tattoo yesterday at lunch; and after they left, I waited on a man with that tattoo."

"Did you get his name? Do you know who he is?"

"Yeah; and you do too. It's Gilbert Gillenwater."

Everyone's jaw dropped.

"I'm sorry to leave on that strange note; but Georgia and Ed will be wondering what happened to me."

Paul had been contemplating this surprising revelation; and responded to Ashleigh from a thick daze.

"Thank you, Ashleigh."

As she exited the offices of Foster Gray Holdings and made her way to the River City Diner, Ashleigh mentally switched gears from receptionist to waitress; corporate spy, it would seem, would be a permanent setting of her mind for the near future.

"Well, that certainly casts a disturbing shadow on everything. Paul, you have to do something soon."

"Yes, I do."

Paul stalwartly composed himself. Outwardly, to Marcy and Clemente, it seemed that he had forgotten what Ashleigh had just told them; he was calm and handling business as usual. Inwardly, the wheels in Paul's head were spinning frantically.

"Marcy, I believe you're next. Incidentally, before you ask, I did have my private devotion."

Marcy was having more difficulty collecting her thoughts after hearing the news than Paul had; but Paul's presence had a strange way of setting her at ease.

"Per your request, Adam has added me to the business account; and we now have a payroll account too; plus, we've already completed all necessary employment forms for Clemente, Ashleigh and myself—everyone that is, except you."

"My income comes from other sources. Are you sure it's okay to hire Clemente?"

"I checked. The only employment eligibility requirement in the state of Wabash is proof of either citizenship or legal residency. Clemente was born in East L.A.; and fortunately, his parents applied for a social security card when he was born. I've sent for those records for both our files and Clemente's."

"I was more concerned about his lack of schooling."

"You, as the employer, are allowed to make it a requirement for employment; but the state and federal governments don't care."

"Great! I'm sorry, Clemente. We're talking about you, as if you weren't sitting here with us. I just want to make sure everything is legal."

Clemente raised his hands in the air.

"No offense taken. I'm just thankful you took a chance and hired me."

There was an awkward pause before Marcy continued with her next point.

"After the phones were installed, I called to order business cards; and they will be able to deliver them Friday with the stationery."

"Good."

"I spoke with each of the ministers yesterday about making a list of any work they needed done around their church in preparation for the Parade of Steeples. I'll contact them today and compile that information for you."

Paul merely nodded. He asked no questions nor made any comments, which was out of his character. Marcy paused to give him more than enough opportunity before continuing with her next item.

"I'll start planning the Parade of Steeples today; but it would be easier for me if we could combine it with the reception at the Canterbury."

"I agree; and perhaps, we could also have the contract signing ceremony, which Bishop Prescott and the council demanded, on that same day."

Marcy nodded and made a note on her legal pad before continuing.

"With everything that happened yesterday, I haven't been able to work on any of your faith-related goals for the community…the chapel…the mission. And I forgot to ask Adam about the diner and Georgia's letter from the bank."

Marcy was visibly frustrated with herself, because she had not completed all of the tasks, which Paul had assigned her.

"I'm sorry, Paul; I didn't mean that I couldn't handle it."

"Don't worry about it, Marcy. Actually, my plans for today were to stay here in the office and make some phone calls about those projects to help us out a little. Listen. I knew this day would come, when I would need to hire more people, because of the heavy workload; I just didn't think it would happen during the first week."

Paul chuckled to himself and gave Marcy a moment to settle herself.

"You mentioned earlier that we could use more people around here. What did you have in mind?"

"We need a bookkeeper, a building manager for the Canterbury and probably someone to handle personnel. If you're going to step up efforts over at the Imperial, you probably need someone for that too. Oh, and don't forget that we haven't even started looking for a faith liaison yet."

Paul removed his pocket notebook and a pen and made some quick notes, when he finished, he turned his attention back to Marcy.

"Did you have anything else?"

"Only one thing. Last night, every single hotel employee told me to remind you to visit Miss Christie. Do you know whom they're talking about?"

CHAPTER TWENTY-THREE

This was exactly what Paul needed to hear to lighten the dark mood created by Ashleigh's report. Paul laughed, this time heartily, although Marcy and Clemente were not able to join him.

"Yes, I know who Miss Christie is."

Marcy and Clemente continued to look at each other with puzzled faces. Obviously, Paul was not ready to tell them who this Miss Christie was, because he immediately changed the subject.

"If nobody has anything else to discuss, we have enough to keep us busy; Clemente, you better get over to the Imperial and collect the guys before they get too restless. Call us if you have a problem."

Marcy and Clemente left the war room, while Paul remained seated. He consulted his notebook and then started making the first of many phone calls.

Chapter Twenty-Four

P aul was still busy with the phone later that evening, when Marcy stuck her head in the war room.

"Paul, Clemente and the guys are ready for you; and I just ordered the pizzas. You've been working ten hours without any break."

It was true. Paul was still in the war room and had been since the meeting. Around noon, Marcy had asked if he wanted to grab lunch. Paul had been on the phone at the time and waved her off; but when she returned, she had brought him a burger, fries, and a slice of pecan pie from the diner and a canned soda from a nearby vending machine, all of which he ate while making other phone calls.

"Come on; Ashleigh is already here too."

Paul followed Marcy to the northwest suite. Clemente and Ashleigh were talking to seven young Latinos. After their transformation at Avalon and their outfitting at Taylor's, Paul barely recognized them from his earlier encounters with them. Clemente made the introductions.

"Guys, this is Paul Gray, the man responsible for those clothes you're wearing; it's in your best interests to do everything he tells you. Understand. Paul, this is Pedro Garcia…Andrés Garcia…Diego Martinez…Juan Martinez…Felipe Hernandez…Bartolomé Lopez…and Tomás Gonzalez."

Clemente paused so Paul could shake hands and greet each man personally.

"Clemente, where are their old clothes?"

"Up on the roof in seven separate metal cans."

"Good."

Paul turned his attention back toward the transformed gang members.

"As Clemente said I've paid for those clothes you're wearing. I've paid for the food you've been and will be eating today. I'm paying for those rooms you're sleeping in; and I own this building, where you will soon be living. If you want to continue receiving these nice things and to receive more and better things in the future, you will follow my rules.

"First the 'no's:' No criminal behavior, no associating with gangs or prostitutes, no pornography, no gambling, no drugs, no alcohol, no cursing and no disrespecting Mr. Morales, Ms. Green, Ms. Lovett or anyone else for that matter."

For each of these commandments, Paul accentuated the word "no."

"And now the 'you will's:' If you do not have a high school diploma or the equivalent or if you cannot read, you will let us know immediately, so we can enroll you in the appropriate program.

"If you smoke, you will let us know that too, so we can find you help to quit. You will shower every day, because nobody wants to smell your dirty body. You will engage in a vigorous daily exercise regimen, which I will design for you. You will engage in an equally ambitious reading program, which I will also design for you.

"You will attend church every week. Where you go is up to you; but you will let us know where you go, because we will regularly check to make sure you went.

"Every day, except Sunday, you will work; and I guarantee it will be hard work. One of us, probably Clemente, will give you your daily assignment. And finally, you will let us know if there is anything that is keeping you from doing something that you should or making you do something you shouldn't."

As before, Paul accentuated each "you will."

"I would also highly suggest that you keep a journal. It's not a requirement; and nobody, including myself, will ever read it; but you'll find that it can be very helpful.

"Now, if you follow all of my rules, there will come a day, when I think you are ready; and on that day, I will pull you aside and ask you what your dreams are."

There was a long silence; and Pedro's curiosity could not stand it any longer.

"What happens then?"

Paul answered with a broad smile on his face.

"Then, I make your dreams come true."

Paul led the group to the roof where, as Clemente had said, there were seven metal cans, each with a pile of dirty clothes inside.

"If you think you can follow my rules and if you're ready to eat some pizza, then set your old clothes on fire; and when the flames burn out, head downstairs. However, if you can't follow my rules or if you don't want my help, then pick up your clothes right now and leave; but don't go back to life on the streets here in the Forrest, because if I ever catch you again, there won't be a second chance."

Paul handed each young man a matchbook and waited. One at a time, they lit their matches and then their pile of old clothes. One at a time, the flames totally consumed the piles and eventually went out. One at a time, each man went downstairs except for one man, Tomás. He stood silently by his metal can of what were now simply warm ashes and metal rivets; his eyes were full of tears. Paul stood next to him. Everyone else had left.

"Was that the initiation?"

"Yes, I suppose in a way it was."

"Don't you want us to rob a convenience store or kill someone to prove our loyalty to the gang instead?"

"No Tomás, this is not that type of group."

"Then why would you just give us all of this stuff until you know we deserve it."

"You don't deserve it. That is the point. You just have to be willing to receive it as you are and put an effort towards bettering yourself."

Tomás fell to his knees and wailed loudly. When Paul thought he had cleansed his soul, he pulled him to his feet and led him downstairs.

"Are you ready to start your new life, Tomás?"

Emotionally drained, Tomás simply nodded as he walked alongside Paul.

"Then let's grab some pizza before those guys eat it all!"

Chapter Twenty-Five

Aaron Bishop was being chased by a small group of people through the darkened hallways of Zoara Christian Church. He only recognized two of them, his pastor, Stanley Lucas, and Zumbo the Clown from the local children's show.

Aaron made a quick turn to evade his pursuers and found himself in the hallway outside his son's hospital room at Integrity Medical. The hallway was deserted—no doctors, no nurses, no patients, no people chasing him. There was a faint sound though; it was a child's voice. Aaron could not tell what the child was saying; but he could tell from which room it was coming. Slowly, he entered his son's room to find him sitting up in the bed. His eyes were rolled back in his head.

Dougie Bishop was repeating the same phrase; but it was still too quiet to discern, so Aaron approached the bed and placed his ear next to his son's mouth.

"Trust Paul."

"Paul who, Dougie?"

The boy did not answer the question; he just kept repeating the same command.

"Trust Paul."

The hospital room door suddenly burst open. The group had finally caught up to him and was now blocking his only exit. Aaron was trapped and the group slowly moved closer to him. He frantically opened the window and looked for a balcony or ledge; there was none. He surveyed the distance to the ground. He was on the sixth floor and would never survive the jump; still, it was better than the alternative. As Aaron Bishop jumped from the window, he was engulfed in a bright flash of yellow light.

Aaron did not die. He was standing on a sidewalk outside a deserted warehouse. Time was starting to speed up; hours passed like seconds and days like minutes. Aaron could see the seasons pass; and as he watched the warehouse, it started transforming into a large and beautiful church. It was mauve in color; and there was a large rose window of purple glass over the main door. Aaron could read the sign near the door; it read "Amethyst Cathedral."

"Build it."

The voice was Dougie's; but Aaron could not see him. His son's disembodied instructions kept repeating and kept increasing in urgency as the same group, which had chased him through the church and hospital, were now chasing him down the street in front of the gorgeous purple church. Aaron felt a gloved hand on his shoulder and hot breath on his neck.

"Build it."

"Turn around and face me, Aaron."

He could smell the clown's greasepaint but also the alcohol-sated decay of his breath.

"Build it."

"Turn around, Aaron."

Aaron did not dare turn around; he knew the fear would consume him.

"Build it."

"Turn around, Aaron."

The clown's grip on his shoulder tightened.

"Build it."

"Turn around, Aaron."

Aaron tripped and started falling. He landed on the floor next to his bed; his bedclothes were soaked in sweat. He was breathing heavy; and his heart was pounding in his chest.

It had been the same dream from the night before; but Aaron did not know what it meant.

Chapter Twenty-Six

Paul woke up in the middle of the night and went downstairs to pour himself a glass of cold milk. He had just had a very disturbing dream. In the dream, he was walking down the penthouse hallway of the Canterbury, when his ring started glowing brightly--so brightly, it was blinding.

When it had stopped glowing, he was standing on a sidewalk outside a beautiful purple church. Nearby, there was a man being chased by a small group of people. Paul recognized several people in the group; one was Zumbo the Clown; one was Gilbert Gillenwater; and one was Carlos Rivera. He even recognized the man being chased; it was Pastor Aaron Bishop. They were gaining on him quickly; they looked to do him great harm. And, there was a boy's voice, which he did not recognize calling out to him.

"Save my dad, Paul. Help him build it."

Chapter Twenty-Seven

Four days passed; and Marcy finally managed to exhume herself from the mountain of work under which she was buried.

Clemente had become a foreman of sorts supervising the former gang members as they worked at area churches; he was hard but fair. When he encountered an obstacle, he showed amazing ability to solve the problem himself. Occasionally, he would call Paul; but more often, he would call Pop or even Dan Tuley for guidance. He was even showing great skill at working with the ministers; they liked him as much as they liked Paul.

For their part, Los Guardianes, as Clemente was now calling them, were showing marked progress; they did what they were told, whether by Clemente or Marcy; and they did it efficiently. Their behavior was impeccable too.

Life at the diner continued without further incident; none of the diner's regular customers would suspect that there was an ominous financial specter over the place.

While he met with Marcy and Clemente in the morning, Paul retreated to his office for the remainder of the day and stayed on the phone. He hardly left the penthouse, so Marcy, Ashleigh and occasionally Georgia would bring his meals to him. Afraid of spooking Gillenwater prematurely, Paul had even retreated from his efforts at the hotel.

Sunday morning came; and Paul felt good about his accomplishments; he was ready for a day of rest. He exercised, showered, and dressed; but he debated forgoing his daily devotion. He had been in a nearly constant state of prayer as he had made his phone calls during the week; and he was about to attend services at two different churches. After consideration, he did not want to start the bad habit of skipping, so he spent a few moments in private devotion.

When he left the apartment, there was no sign that Clemente or Noodles were even awake yet, so he left and made his way to the diner for breakfast. The elevator stopped on the eighth floor; and Marcy, who was dressed up, entered the car.

"Diner or church?"

"Both…and in that order."

"Would you care to join me?"

Marcy blushed.

"I would love to."

When the elevator doors opened again, they were on the ground level; and Paul and Marcy exited the car. Six young men dressed in dark suits greeted them. Clemente was not the only former gang member who cleaned up nicely.

"Where's Tomás?"

Pedro spoke for the group.

"He's not Catholic, Mr. Gray."

"Oh, okay. Have you all eaten?"

All six heads nodded.

"Well, Marcy and I are going to eat breakfast at the diner before mass. You're more than welcome to join us, perhaps eat a pastry and drink some coffee."

Paul and Marcy led the group to the diner. Ashleigh was not there; but Georgia was; and she waited on them. At such an early hour on a Sunday, business at the diner was slow. Paul and Marcy sat at a booth; the others formed two groups of three and took the booths on either side. While the guys nursed cups of coffee, Paul and Marcy ate their breakfast of bacon, eggs and toast quickly and in relative silence.

When they finished eating, Paul settled everyone's bill; and they walked to St. Anthony's and attended mass together. Paul thought about how strange this makeshift family of theirs must seem to the other parishioners.

After mass, they walked back to the Canterbury. The group paused outside the entrance and waited for Paul to say something.

"I know each of you have worked very hard this week; and I'm sorry that I've been so busy with other matters that I haven't been able to spend quality time with each of you on the job; but very soon, that will change. Remember; this is Sunday; it's a day of rest. Now, if you'll excuse me, I need to be in Cricksburg."

Paul did not notice that Marcy had not followed him into the elevator. Paul went to his apartment to collect Clemente and Noodles; but they were not there. Instead, there was a note on the breakfast bar:

> *Paul,*
>
> *We've already left. See you at church!*
>
> *Clemente*

Paul left his apartment and took the elevator to the second subbasement. This time, it was empty, just some boxes; there were no gang members living here anymore. Paul took the east tunnel which lead to the Pine Avenue Parking Garage. There, in a row, was his motorcycle, truck, sports car and Marcy's minivan. There were no other vehicles parked on this level. Paul drove his truck to his grandparent's farm and wondered how Clemente would get there without a vehicle. When he arrived, there was an unfamiliar car parked in front of his grandparent's house; and Noodles was sitting on the porch. The dog recognized Paul as he exited his truck, and he bounded for him. Paul responded by scratching the hound behind the ears for a few minutes.

"I have to go to church, Noodles; but I'll be back."

The dog obediently stayed behind.

Unlike last week, Paul entered Covenant Baptist Church on time. He looked for Clemente and found him sitting up front near where they had sat last week. As the organ played a prelude, Paul walked down the center aisle of the church and stopped at the pew in which Clemente was sitting. There were already several others sitting with him. Paul took a seat and scooted over as Pastor Tim followed him into the pew sitting next to him. From left to right, they nearly filled the pew, first Pastor Tim, and then Paul, Tomás, Clemente, Ashleigh, Edith Sheppard, and finally Pop Gray. Pop Gray was saving the end seat for Nan.

Clemente craned in front of Tomás to talk to Paul.

"I hope you don't mind that I brought Ashleigh and Tomás, they don't have churches."

"Not at all, Clemente. I'm just glad they're here."

Paul accentuated this by side-hugging Tomás with his right hand while patting him on the shoulder with his left.

Services started and while Ashleigh and Tomás remained quiet and respectful, Clemente was not a casual observer; he was a very active participant. When the congregation sang, he sang along loudly. When a deacon led the church in corporal prayer, he was mouthing a prayer to himself. When the pastor was preaching, he was following along in the Bible and taking notes in a journal.

"As you will remember in last week's sermon, I gave you the first part of 'God's Formula for Success:' 'View the Situation Correctly.' Unlike the ten spies, who saw only a land inhabited by giants and unlike King Saul and the Israelite army, who saw an unconquerable giant, David viewed the situation correctly and saw a sinful man defying God. This morning, we look at the second part: 'Issue a Proper Solution.'

"We remain in the seventeenth chapter of First Samuel; and we find that King Saul and the Israelites are not issuing a proper solution; in fact, they aren't doing anything. Ignoring Goliath didn't make him go away. Ignoring our own problems, or worse, running from them doesn't make them go away. Not everyone in the Bible solved their problems correctly though. Consider the children of Israel.

"Joseph's brothers hated him and conspired to kill him. Reuben, the oldest brother, could see the problem of killing their brother; but he offered an inadequate solution, which amounted to temporary imprisonment. Judah, the fourth oldest brother, could also see the problem of murder and offered another yet still inadequate solution. The other brothers agreed with his plan though; and they sold Joseph into slavery. David's solution to the giant problem was permanent and in keeping with God's law; both Reuben's and Judah's solutions to the disagreement with their brother were temporary and contradictory to God's law."

As Pastor Tom's sermon continued, Paul thought to himself how he had solved some problems incorrectly. He had chased the gang out of the basement; and as Carlos had stated, they quickly returned. Even now, he wondered if he had solved the problem correctly, because seven gang members were still not willing to receive his help.

Immediately after services, Tiny Smith found Paul.

"Paul, we have a small problem."

"What is it?"

"Four of 'em came up to the house early this mornin'. They've decided to take you up on your offer. I'm actually surprised they lasted out there this long; but I reckon they's getting powerful hungrified and tired of wandering around the woods in their birthday suits in this cold weather. I put 'em up in my bunkhouse before I left. I'll feed 'em, hose 'em off and give 'em some fresh work clothes; and then I'll bring 'em up to you early tomorrow morning."

"Thank you, Tiny; but what's the problem?"

"Well, the other three are missin'."

"Missing?"

"Yeah, my neighbor was tellin' me this mornin' that he noticed three young bucks, nekkider than jaybirds, out by his wife's clothes line tryin' to make theyselves all decent like. And, Cletus was just tellin' me 'fore services that there's food missin' from his general store. They's probably headin' your way, Paul."

Tomás was listening to Tiny Smith's account with interest; and there was a faint look of horror on his face.

"I'm sorry, Tomás; in hindsight, I probably didn't solve this problem correctly; but without official cooperation from law enforcement, we didn't have many choices. We were trying to evict you from the lower levels without hurting you."

Tomás was finally realizing that had he made different decisions that could have been his fate. For the first time in his life, he could appreciate the predicament that his behavior as a gang member caused for others and ultimately for himself.

"Mr. Gray, you did what you had to do."

Paul and his party gradually filed out of the church speaking to fellow members along the way. Although much earlier than last week: the church eventually emptied leaving just the nine of them: Pastor Tom and his wife, Edith, Pastor Tim, Pop and Nan, Clemente, Ashleigh, Tomás and Paul. They made their way down the path leading back to Pop and Nan's house.

There was another surprise waiting for Paul at the house. Fathers Andrews and Guerrero, Marcy and the six other guys from Los Guardianes were sitting in the living room waiting for them. Noodles was sitting in Father Andrews' lap; and the priest was scratching his head. Nan pulled Paul into the kitchen and provided an explanation.

"I asked them all here, Paul. I asked Zack and the Hopper's too; Zack will be along later this afternoon; but the Hopper's declined."

"Why?"

"Why did they decline? I don't know, Paul; they probably had a lot on their mind with the diner."

"No, I meant why did you ask everybody here."

"There are several reasons, I suppose. I didn't like the idea of us down here and them up there; it just seemed snooty not to ask them to join us. And, as I've always told you, Sundays are for God and family and friends; I didn't want you to feel like you were sacrificing one part of your life to have another; and those boys in there need to learn what family means. Besides, I just like having a full house on Sundays; it does my heart good to have so many of my blessings under one roof."

"I'm glad you invited them. Thank you."

Paul kissed Nan gently on the cheek.

Nan had prepared a banquet: coleslaw, fried chicken, mashed potatoes and milk gravy, green beans, corn on the cob, macaroni and cheese, homemade biscuits, sweet tea and blackberry cobbler for dessert. Dinner was delicious as always; everyone seemed to really enjoy Nan's cooking, especially Noodles, who had pieces of chicken sneaked to him by everyone at the table. After dinner, they all retired to the living room to watch the Hornets game with Pop.

The members of Los Guardianes had been anxious and uptight since Paul had taken them to the diner for breakfast earlier that day; however, by dessert, they were loosening up; and by kickoff, they were already feeling like a part of the family; and in a way, they were.

During dinner and the football game, Paul watched Clemente with particular interest. He seemed totally at ease, like this was exactly where he belonged. Paul had also studied Marcy. She looked much different from when Paul first met her; she was more self-confident. Perhaps, Paul thought to himself, he had solved some problems correctly; and some people's lives were better having known him.

Paul's cell phone rang.

"Hello."

He had started to walk outside so his conversation would not disturb the others; but he quickly realized the call involved someone else in the room.

"Yes, I'm the one, who found the beagle."

"Please do."

"Yes."

Pop muted the television; and everyone listened to Paul's side with interest. It was not just Clemente; everyone in Paul's life had quickly become very attached to the dog.

"No, there wasn't a collar."

"No, there wasn't a microchip implant either; I already checked for that too."

"The dog's right here; I'll see."

Paul held the phone away from his mouth and faced the dog. Clemente looked nervous.

"Roscoe…here, Roscoe."

Noodles did nothing but wag his tail.

"I'm sorry; he didn't answer to the name."

"I don't know; hold a moment; and I'll check."

Paul knelt down next to Noodles; lifted the dog's left ear and examined it. Noodles responded by licking Paul's face affectionately.

"No, there are no markings under the left ear."

"Well, I'm sorry I didn't find your dog."

"No bother at all."

"Good luck."

Paul disconnected the call and pocketed his phone, and then he scratched Noodles a few times behind the ears before standing up. Paul noticed everyone in the room was quietly waiting for him to say something.

"Noodles isn't the dog they lost."

Everyone sighed in relief; but Clemente's was the loudest and most heartfelt sigh to be heard.

"Marcy, may I speak with you for a few minutes out on the porch?"

Marcy followed Paul outside. Noodles considered following them; but Pop's lap, where the dog had located himself after the phone call, was very warm; and Pop was scratching the right spot.

"Marcy, I want you to know how much I appreciate what you do."

Marcy smiled as Paul continued.

"I know your job is not easy, especially these last few days as I've been sequestered in my office."

"Paul, I realize you have a lot of big problems to solve all at once."

"You've taken control of things while I haven't been as available as I would like to be; and you've done a wonderful job. They'll be several new faces around the table tomorrow. Perhaps, the extra hands will lighten the burden."

"Oh Paul, you'll probably just go and take on another twelve projects; and we'll be right back where we started."

They both laughed.

"Yes, I probably will. There's still so much to do; and we've only really just started. You'll be managing all of these new employees for me; and you'll be on each of the new committees, which we're forming too, so yes, you'll still be very busy. I just want you to know that even when I'm preoccupied,

I still notice what you do; and I really appreciate it."

"Thank you, Paul; that means a lot."

"But it would be empty praise, if I didn't back it up with something."

Paul handed Marcy an envelope, which she opened. It contained five one hundred dollar bills and an Avalon Gift Certificate.

"I know we're busy; but find some time to enjoy a day at the spa; and then use the money to buy something you want, not something you need."

"Paul, this is too generous."

Paul shook his head in disagreement.

"No, it's not. I always knew that there would be a lot to your job and that I would depend heavily on you; but this last week, I realized just how much so. With what I was doing, you and Clemente picked up my slack and made everything run smoothly. I'm also giving you a raise in salary."

Marcy hugged him and kissed him on the cheek.

"Thank you, Paul."

"Did you handle that special task I gave you?"

"It's in the car."

"Good. Get it and meet me in the living room."

Marcy walked to her car as Paul reentered his grandparent's house. Paul couldn't have timed his announcement any better, because halftime had just started.

"Mute the TV; I want to make an important announcement."

Pop muted the television. As Paul cleared his throat, everyone in the room was wondering what Paul's announcement was.

"As most of you know, this last week has been a hectic one. I've been in my office making phone calls and hiring new people to help us with the many projects I've started; and I haven't been as visible as I would have liked. Fortunately, Marcy and everyone else picked up my slack. I've already given Marcy a raise and bonus."

At the word "raise," Marcy reentered the living room carrying a bag, which she handed to Paul. Paul's speech was interrupted with applause for her. When the applause abated, Paul continued.

"But there is someone else, who needs to be rewarded."

Paul paused for dramatic effect.

"Clemente, would you come here."

Clemente stood next to Paul and faced the group.

"I am so proud of you. As I've found myself unable to handle certain tasks this week, I later discovered that you had already handled them without me even delegating them to you. And, even though you were busy, you helped Marcy with some of her work. But, I've also received compliments about you from Marcy, from the ministers on the council, and even from Dan Tuley. To know that things are so well-handled and that the community responds so positively to you, means a lot to me; and I want to take a moment before the game comes back on to show my appreciation. As you know, your business cards did not arrive with the others; but I have them now."

Paul handed Clemente a box, which Clemente opened. He drew a card and examined it carefully; and when he noticed his name and title, his jaw dropped.

"But this isn't my—"

"It is now. Read the card aloud so everyone knows."

"Foster Gray Holdings, Inc…Clemente Morales…Chief Operations Officer."

CHAPTER TWENTY-SEVEN

Again, there was applause from the room.

"Clemente, you've proven that you're trustworthy. You deserve the title and the raise that goes with it."

"I don't know what to say. Thank you, Paul."

"Marcy tells me that you got your driver's license, Friday; and I know you wanted my help buying a car; but I'm not buying you a car."

It was hard to be too upset after everything Paul had already done for him; but Clemente did feel a tinge of short-lived disappointment.

"I'm buying you a car and a truck instead."

The look on Clemente's face was priceless.

"Are you kidding me?"

"No, I'm not kidding. The truck is yours; but the car is actually a company car for you to use. There will be times when you need to drive in the style expected of an executive; and there will be other times, when you want to be casual and possibly get a little dirty."

Paul threw two key rings to Clemente, who caught them effortlessly.

"They're parked behind Pop's workshop."

Clemente dashed out the door, Ashleigh followed close behind, and unable to withstand it further, Noodles chased after them. Paul lingered to address the members of Los Guardianes.

"I want each of you to know that when you work for me and you work really hard, you're richly rewarded."

Paul caught up with Clemente and Ashleigh behind Pop's workshop. Clemente was beside himself with excitement; he didn't know which vehicle to look at first.

"Before you get too excited, there's more."

"More?"

"Yes; but you have to make a decision. Your room is way too small; and you need to move."

Clemente looked dejected.

"You have three choices. You can come down here and live with Pop and Nan as they offered last week. You can move into the northwest suite with Los Guardianes, when that is remodeled. Or you can move into your own apartment at the Canterbury; I checked; and there's a large apartment available on the forty-second floor."

Clemente was having difficulty hiding his disappointment.

"Well, I love Pop and Nan; but now that I'm starting to gain more responsibility, moving down here seems like the wrong choice."

"I agree."

"And, even though I was once in a gang with them, moving in with Los Guardianes at this point doesn't seem like the right choice either. They might think you've demoted me."

"Again, I agree."

"I guess I'll move into my own apartment. Why can't I continue to live with you?"

"Clemente, you're staying in a guest bedroom; you don't really have much space."

"I have all I need."

"Well, there is a fourth choice. You could move into the fifth floor of my penthouse...after we remodel and redecorate it to your tastes and needs."

"Yes! Yes! Yes! I want to do that one."

"Clemente, I'll allow you to supervise the renovations; but I expect an urbane, well-appointed bachelor pad and not something that belongs in a fraternity house."

Ashleigh interrupted.

"Don't worry, Paul; I'll help him; and I won't let him do anything that isn't tasteful."

Paul grinned.

"One more gift."

"Another one?"

"After receiving a big promotion, it's customary to celebrate at an expensive restaurant."

"Where are we going?"

"Paul meant you're supposed to ask your girlfriend."

Ashleigh accentuated the last word.

"Oh…you're my girlfriend…aren't you, Ashleigh?"

About certain things, Clemente was still rather naïve.

"Yes, Clemente, I'm your girlfriend; was there something you wanted to ask me?"

"Uh…do you want to celebrate my promotion?"

"Where are you taking me?"

"I dunno. Where am I taking her, Paul?"

"The Stratosphere Room. I've already authorized the expense through Marcy, so charge the dinner to your company credit card, just bring back the receipt."

"Paul, the Stratosphere Room is atop Crookston Tower."

"Yes."

"That's not just an expensive restaurant; that's the most expensive restaurant in town."

"I know."

"Well, I don't have anything to wear to a place like that."

"Ashleigh, I've already thought of everything. I foresee a lunch with Marcy in your near future; and after lunch, I foresee Marcy helping you shop for a dress and accessories at Beau Madame. I've already authorized that expense as well."

Ashleigh was in a pleasant state of shock.

"Paul, I don't know what to say. Thank you. Thank you very much."

"You're welcome. I know that you have already contributed a lot to this company too; and I want you to know I really appreciate it."

Ashleigh blushed.

"Don't worry; I'll make sure Romeo here dresses up in his best suit and drives the sports car instead of the truck for the big date."

Everyone laughed.

"Ashleigh, both of your jobs are at the Canterbury. How can we get you to move in? There are plenty of empty apartments; and you would save a lot of money in gas. As landlord, I would even cut you a break on your rent."

"Well, I was wanting to move out of my current apartment…"

"That settles it then. Get with Marcy and handle the details; and when you're ready to move, we'll use the box truck, which I just purchased and we'll get the guys to help. I'll even pay for the pizza!"

"Now Clemente, as Chief Operations Officer, I will expect even more from you."

"I understand."

"Tomorrow, Tiny is bringing four of the guys; Carlos and the other two guys ran away."

"Yeah, I heard."

"I'll need you to get them settled in and take them to Avalon and Taylor's. And on Tuesday, I need you to check on the whole group; but after that, you are going to be busy elsewhere."

Clemente nodded.

"That means you need to make your first decision. Who are you putting in charge of Los Guardianes?"

"Well, Pedro is a natural born leader; but Tomás' heart has changed the most; he's really proved that he's ready to take on more responsibility."

"What's your final decision?"

Clemente took a minute.

"Pedro."

"Ashleigh, would you send Pedro and Tomás out here."

Ashleigh reentered the house; and a few moments later, Pedro and Tomás joined Paul and Clemente on the porch. Paul nodded at Clemente to begin.

"As Chief Operating Officer, I have more responsibilities now. I can no longer supervise you every minute of the day; I need to promote one of you to Capitan of Los Guardianes; and I've selected Pedro."

Pedro silently nodded indicating his acceptance, as Paul took over.

"And Tomás, Clemente has told me that you are showing great potential and are ready for more responsibility too. What would you like to do?"

Tomás was not ready for the question but he attempted to give an answer.

"Before I joined the gang, I worked with my family on a farm in Mexico. I guess I've always been more comfortable outside the big city."

"Would you enjoy working on this farm?"

Tomás eyes lit up; it was the first time, Paul noticed true passion in the young man's face.

"Technically, you would still be a member of Los Guardianes and you will still need to abide by all of the same rules; but what if you moved down here and lived and worked on this farm and worked as a custodian over at the church. After a few months, if you've proven that you can handle it, I'll give you more responsibility down here."

"Thank you. I would like that very much, Mr. Gray."

"One more thing, Tomás. I expect Carlos or Claude Zumbini to try something very soon if not in the area of the Canterbury then down here. Can I trust you to protect my grandparents, this farm and the church as best you can?"

Tomás nodded.

"Paul, they'll both need phones, driver's licenses, keys, charging privileges at Tuley's."

"Agreed. Coordinate with Marcy on that."

Clemente nodded.

"And gentlemen, I'll expect you in our morning meeting tomorrow."

Paul led them all back into the house. He glanced at the television; the football game had just broken for a commercial.

CHAPTER TWENTY-SEVEN

"While they're airing commercials, may I make a few more announcements?"

Pop muted the television.

"First, with Clemente's promotion, Los Guardianes needed a new leader; and Clemente and I have chosen Pedro."

There was polite applause.

"Next, Tomás has expressed a strong desire to work on a farm, so he will be working down here on the farm with Pop and Nan.

"And finally, I have really enjoyed these Sundays with all of my friends and family gathered together in one place. I like it so much; I want to make it a tradition. Everyone already knows that I start my Sundays with breakfast at the diner, then mass at St. Anthony's, then worship service at Covenant Baptist, then Sunday dinner here at Pop and Nan's house. However, so I don't interfere with Pastor Tom's evening services at Covenant Baptist again as I did last week or keep company here too late into the evening, I would like to extend a standing invitation to anyone and everyone to come and hang out with me at my apartment on Sunday evenings. And of course, my entire Sunday schedule is open to anyone who wants to tag along for all or part of it."

Everyone cheered giving approval to this new tradition before turning their attentions back towards the game.

Pastor Tom was the next person to interrupt.

"Paul, could I have a word with you."

Paul and Pastor Tom went outside and sat down on the porch.

"I've watched you chair the council on faith meeting, and then lead the raid in the Canterbury's lower levels, and deal with your employees just now. I want you to know that I'm very impressed. You exemplify how I believe a Christian businessman should act in today's society; specifically, you aren't a slave to your money. You seem to genuinely care for your employees as if they were your family."

"Thank you for the kind words, Pastor. I do care about my employees, because in my opinion, they are family."

"I was wondering if you would ever consider ordination as a deacon of the church or even as a minister."

"I'm flattered, Pastor Tom; really I am; but I can never accept that."

"May I ask why?"

"There are three things, which I can never allow myself to do. I can never be ordained; I can never hold public office, whether elected or appointed; and I can never be married. While you're correct that I have absolutely no hang-ups with money, I would have serious hang-ups with love and power; and my work is too important right now to compromise them with my weaknesses."

"Is that why you are so quick to delegate so much authority to others like Clemente?"

"Yes. I don't mind taking all the responsibility; but I can never allow myself to grow comfortable with the trappings of power, even corporate power."

"And what about Marcy?"

"What about Marcy?"

"Isn't she your girlfriend?"

"She's a good friend and a valuable employee; but I assure you there is nothing romantic between us; there can never be anything romantic between us."

"You speak from experience?"

"Yes."

Paul paused. The past was painful; however, he knew there must be caring people in his life, who fully understood why he made some of the choices

CHAPTER TWENTY-SEVEN

he did.

"After Dad died and my family moved to Puerto Rico, I rebelled against everything, against my family, against the country, against God; and I rebelled by engaging in very reckless sexual behavior. Before I even graduated from high school, I had a scare; there was a strong possibility that I had gotten a girl pregnant. Fortunately for me though, it was a false positive; but it was enough to make me change my ways."

"What did you do?"

"I took an oath of celibacy; and then delved fulltime into my faith, the martial arts and the culinary arts to get my mind off of everything else. But then, I met this girl in college; and we were starting to get close; and I was starting to seriously rethink my oath. It was about this time, when I learned about my inheritance from Great Grandfather Silas. It was bad enough that I was already questioning my oath; but the thought of adding a huge fortune to that scenario slapped some much needed sense into me, before I could make some irreversible mistakes. I've spent the last five years of my life wandering around the country just clearing my head of unnecessary garbage."

"You are a remarkable man. Few could isolate themselves in this way from the very things that would bring about their downfall."

As Pastor Tom reentered the house to join the others, Zack Armstrong drove up in his pickup truck.

"Hey, Zack!"

"Hey, Paul! Sorry I'm late; some people didn't show up for work today."

"I understand."

Before Zack sat down on the porch, Paul stood and gave him a brotherly hug.

"I want you to know that I've thought about your offer; and I accept."

"That's great. You'll be at our morning meeting tomorrow?"

"Yeah. There is one thing though."

"What's that?"

"Clem and I were talking about his binder…the one with the information about the Order of the Lamp and L'Ombra."

"Yes."

"Well, I think there should be another Lamp Affiliated Group…one you haven't mentioned yet."

"I'm listening."

"There are thirteen Armstrong siblings. Each of us loves you and supports what you're trying to do, not just at the Canterbury or the Imperial but in the entire city; but you're only using two of us."

"You think there should be an Armstrong Army.

Zack nodded.

"I'm okay with it; set it up."

"Not so fast. I'm already busy with the kitchen; and this new job you've just offered me will consume what little free time I had left. And, you've given Zared has his own project. I suggest you put Zeph in charge of the new group."

"Done. Anything else?"

"Yeah, I think you should have a weekly meeting for Lamp members. I know you already have a morning meeting; but that's with Foster Gray employees; and that should really be about your business. There are other Lamp members, who aren't employed by you; and they need to hear your plans and voice their concerns."

"Done."

It was dusk, when Pop and Nan came outside and sat on the porch with Paul and Zack. After greeting Zack, Nan immediately came to the point.

"Paul, Pop and I have been meaning to have a word with you all day; but you've been so busy out here on the porch talking to one employee after another. It's Sunday; you shouldn't be working."

"I'm sorry, Nan; but it's been mostly promotions and rewards; there has been no real business discussed."

"Well, we still have a concern."

"Is it Tomás? I'm sorry; I should've checked with you first."

"No, Tomás is great; and we actually look forward to him moving down here. Our problem is with Sam Hayne."

Paul laughed.

"You've obviously been talking to Marcy."

"Yes, and Clemente too! Don't laugh, Paul. They're concerned; and so are we. You know very well that Sam's crazy; that whole family is. Marcy told us that you met with him already."

Zack interrupted partly to rescue Paul and partly to satisfy his own curiosity.

"Aren't we related to them too?"

Nan looked flustered; but she patiently answered Zack's question.

"No, Zack! You and Paul are fourth cousins. Paul and Sam are first cousins twice removed. You and Sam are not directly related; and be thankful for that. I guess the easiest way to describe it is that your second great grand aunt, Mary Gray, is the mother-in-law of Sam Hayne's aunt Mary Gray."

"They're not the same Mary Gray? Because I always thought they were."

"No, they're different people."

"When we were growing up, Grandpa would tell us ghost stories about the Hayne's; my favorite was 'The Legend of Mordecai Hayne.' Is it true?"

"It doesn't matter; either way proves the family is crazy."

"Wait a minute! Who is Mordecai Hayne?"

Paul felt he had been denied important family history, at least entertaining family history; and he wanted to hear the legend even if it was a tall tale told to entertain kids during Halloween.

"They say that he was born a monster, so his family locked him in the cellar; but when he grew up, he escaped and terrorized the entire town, before the family finally caught him."

"What did they do with him?"

"They chopped him up into pieces and then buried those parts in different cemeteries; but they say he still haunts the cemeteries where his body parts are buried, trying to put himself back together again. Wooo!"

Zack acted as if he were telling stories around the campfire; he was just missing a flashlight to uplight his face.

"That's enough of that out of you, Zachariah Armstrong. You're not helping matters."

Zack leaned towards Paul and acted as he was whispering.

"I'll tell you more stories later."

Zack and Paul exchanged knowing winks and laughed; but sensing Nan's frustration, Paul quickly changed to a more somber expression.

"Thanks for your concern; but while I agree that Sam and the whole Hayne family are…odd; I honestly don't think they're dangerous or mean us any harm."

"Just be very careful around them, Paul."

CHAPTER TWENTY-SEVEN

Chapter Twenty-Eight

After his morning routine, Paul went to the diner for breakfast. It was chilly outside; but Georgia greeted him with a warm smile. Paul had only been back in River City for twelve days; but already, Georgia and the other diner employees knew him and his tastes and habits. She had filled a cup with coffee at his favorite booth, before he could even sit down.

"The usual, Paul?"

"Actually, I'm in the mood for biscuits and gravy today."

"How about some scrambled eggs and hash browns to go with that?"

"Please!"

"And of course, a large orange juice too?"

"Oh, you know me too well, Georgia."

Georgia went to the kitchen to place Paul's order leaving Paul alone with his thoughts. This was one of the few times that he could remember eating at the diner alone; and Paul allowed himself to eavesdrop on other conversations. Unfortunately, they were mostly negative comments on the state of affairs in River City, the same laundry list of complaints Paul heard everywhere he went: crime, unemployment, the high cost of living, and of course, urban blight.

Georgia returned with Paul's breakfast.

"Have any of my people been in this morning, Georgia?"

"Yes, as a matter of fact, I think they all have."

Georgia laughed.

"And are my boys behaving themselves when they're in here? Be honest now."

Clemente may have changed the name of the gang from Las Ratas to Los Guardianes; but to everyone in the neighborhood, including Paul himself, they were simply Paul's Boys.

"They're perfect angels, Paul."

"You'll let me know if they're not."

Georgia just winked and smiled.

"Georgia, sit down; I want to talk to you."

Georgia sat down in the booth opposite Paul and gave him her undivided attention.

"As you already know, I'm your landlord."

Georgia nodded.

"I looked at that letter from your bank; and I spoke to my own banker about it. As your landlord, I'm giving you a rent holiday until this matter is resolved one way or the other."

Georgia could not contain her happiness as she cried tears of joy.

"That's not all. I've just hired a building manager for the Canterbury; and with his help, we'll be making some big improvements around here very soon. Plus, we're also starting a marketing campaign to bring attention back to the Forrest in general and to the Canterbury and the River City Diner specifically. Hopefully, as a result, it will increase your sales."

"That will really help us."

"Well, if it doesn't, we go to Plan B."

"What's Plan B?"

"I will purchase your debt outright and offer you a better repayment schedule."

"Oh Paul, that would be wonderful."

Paul lowered his voice.

"Georgia, if we try to do that, there is a distinct possibility that Zumbini will block Empire Federal from selling your debt. For whatever reason, he's very eager to drive all business out of the Forrest, so he might try to foreclose on your business. But don't worry, because there is still Plan C."

"What's Plan C?"

"I will go into business with you and Ed and open another diner here at the Canterbury, which he can't touch."

Georgia was starting to cry again. She got up and moved across the booth sitting next to Paul. She hugged him tightly and whispered in his ear.

"You don't know how much you mean to Ed and me."

"Well, just keep doing what you're doing. Keep serving this great comfort food and keep sharing that award-winning smile of yours with everyone, who walks in the door. Don't worry about the diner, because, I promise you, it isn't going anywhere."

"Oh, I'm not worried anymore, Paul."

"Good."

Georgia hugged Paul one more time and then continued waiting tables.

Paul ate his breakfast, settled his bill and was about to leave the diner, when Georgia stopped him.

"Paul, I want you to meet some of the other diner regulars."

Georgia led him to a table where a young man sat. He had an Ivy League haircut and was dressed in a business suit and trench coat. She did not need to tell Paul that this was a federal agent; the man looked the part.

"Paul, this is Special Agent Rick Baker; he's in charge of finding that Jabberwock serial killer; and he's also one of your tenants. Rick, this is Paul Gray; he's the new owner of the Canterbury."

Paul and Special Agent Baker shook hands. Paul noted that Special Agent Baker had an especially strong grip.

"It's very nice to meet you; I hope you catch that guy. I heard about it on the news; and he sounds dangerous."

"He is; but we're closing in on him. Nice to meet you too, Paul. Sorry; but I have to run."

Baker left the diner as Georgia was leading Paul to another table.

"Paul, this is Officers Baldo Havens and Kevin O'Connell, the two best police officers in the city."

"Yes, I know; Ashleigh has already introduced us. It's very nice to see you again, officers."

Paul shook hands with both officers; and all three of them silently agreed for the sake of the officers' careers to withhold the full extent of their relationship.

As always, the senior officer spoke for both of them.

"We've been noticing those new helpers you've got. You've done some great work there."

"Thank you. I think they're shaping up to be productive members of the community."

CHAPTER TWENTY-EIGHT

Georgia interrupted the conversation to drag Paul to another table.

"Paul, this is Richard Leek and Jude Royal. They practically live here at the diner, when they're not working at the bank."

"Guys, this is Paul, the new landlord."

Jude corrected her.

"Richard is the one, who works at the bank; I'm a systems analyst."

Paul was barely able to shake hands with them; and he did not have the opportunity to exchange pleasant dialogue before Georgia had dragged him to a final table.

"There is one more regular, who I wanted you to meet before both you and he leave. He's also one of your tenants; he's one of the most interesting people I've ever met; and he tells the most interesting stories."

Georgia was leading him to a table on the far side of the room, where a young man with curly blond hair sat with his back to them. Paul guessed the man was probably a little older than he was; but the man's clothes were what stumped Paul. The man was dressed nicely enough; but the clothes were from the wrong era. Paul wondered if the man had raided his grandfather's closet.

"Paul, this is John Dorman. John, this is Paul Gray, the new owner of the Canterbury."

Paul managed to suppress his shock when he heard the name and even to offer his hand to the man in goodwill; however, having no such warning, John Dorman was not as composed. His alarm at Paul's presence was quite evident to both Paul and Georgia and even to some nearby customers. For one brief moment, John simply froze in place staring at Paul's hand in terror as if it were diseased; and then suddenly, he bolted out of the diner.

"That was odd. I wonder what got into him."

"Georgia, I really must go too; they're expecting me for our morning meeting. Thank you for introducing me to my tenants. Oh, and if John

Dorman left without paying his bill, put in on my tab. Okay?"

Georgia nodded dumbly as Paul quickly exited the diner. She was still trying to guess why John Dorman had acted so strangely.

Paul entered the Canterbury's lobby and called for the elevator. When it arrived and the doors opened, Clemente was in the car.

"Paul, I was looking for you."

"You found me."

"Can we talk…privately?"

"Shall we go to the apartment?"

Clemente nodded, so Paul entered the elevator; and Clemente pushed the "P" button. Paul tried to make small talk about the weather and breakfast at the diner; but Clemente remained quiet.

When they arrived back at their apartment, Paul sat down in an overstuffed chair in the great room. Excited they were home so soon, Noodles leapt into Paul's lap.

"What's on your mind, Clemente?"

Clemente started pacing back and forth rehearsing in his mind what he wanted to say and how he wanted to say it.

"Paul, how rich are you?"

"Excuse me!"

Coming from anybody else, Paul might have been offended by so direct a question; but he knew Clemente's intentions were honorable even if his tact needed some work.

"I don't know how else to say it. How rich are you?"

"Before I answer that, Clemente, tell me why you're concerned."

CHAPTER TWENTY-EIGHT

"You're a big tipper."

"Yes, I believe in rewarding good service."

"And you donate a lot of money to the church."

"Yes, I believe that it's not my money; it's God's money."

"And you gave all of us some really expensive gifts yesterday."

"Yes, I love all of you and appreciate what each of you does for me; and I show my love and appreciation by sharing my wealth."

"And you're always talking about buying businesses or properties."

"Clemente, are you worried that I'll run out of money?"

"Well…yeah."

Paul could not help but laugh.

"I am very blessed. Nearly every branch of my family tree has been fruitful; and I've benefited greatly from that fruit. Yes, I'm wealthy—very, very wealthy. As fast as you may think I'm spending it, I'm actually making it even faster; and that's before I receive my inheritance from Silas Foster in a few weeks. My current fortune looks extremely tiny compared to his.

"Plus, five of the people I just hired will be helping us make, invest, and spend the money more efficiently, so the money never runs out. But, even if it did, Clemente, so what. It's just money. It wouldn't change a thing; I would still try to help people; I would just be limited in the ways I could help them.

"Clemente, do you know what Foster Gray Holdings does?"

"Investments?"

"Yes, but investments in what?"

"Buildings?"

"No! People! We invest in people. Now, do you know why I promoted you?"

"No, I really don't."

"Because I think you have a huge heart. I don't want you simply finishing my projects, Clemente; I want you to start your own projects. I'm giving you a special assignment. You'll need a journal, a pen, and twenty-five thousand dollars, which I'll have Adam put in a special account just for your use. I want you to spend every cent of the money with only two conditions. One, you can only spend the money to help other people; and two, you must document your spending in the journal, who you helped, when you helped them, how you helped them, and why you helped them. When you've spent all the money, I want us to finish this discussion. Okay?"

Clemente was silently processing every word Paul said, so there were several minutes before he answered the question.

"Okay."

"Come on; let's go; we have a company to run."

Paul and Clemente crossed the penthouse hallway from their apartment to the offices of Gray Foster Holdings. When they opened the door, Ashleigh was sitting at the reception desk; and Marcy was talking to a middle-aged man dressed in dirty work clothes. There was a strong scent of alcohol on the man's breath.

"Paul, this is George—"

"Bancroft. Yes, Marcy, I already know who it is. What's the problem, George?"

Marcy, Clemente and Ashleigh were shocked at Paul's sudden apathy.

"I'm a little behind on the mortgage. Could you loan me some money? Just until the next crop comes in. I'll pay you back; I promise."

Paul did not reply for several minutes; and the silence was painfully awkward for everyone in the room.

"I'll give you whatever amount of money you need…"

George's expression immediately brightened.

"Oh, thank you, Paul."

"…on one condition."

George's expression darkened just as quickly.

Paul waited for George to ask the obvious question; however, it was clear George did not want to ask it, because he already knew the answer, so Paul continued.

"I'll give you the money, if you stop drinking."

"Paul, I promise I won't take another drink."

"Well, that's not good enough for me. You need to get professional help."

George Bancroft was becoming anxious.

"You can't tell me what to do."

"You're correct; I can't. But you can't make me give you any money either."

George realized his strategy had backfired on him, so he tried another.

"But we're family."

At the word "family," Zack Armstrong emerged from the war room; a crowd of people followed him.

"Zack! Tell Paul to give me a loan…so I can pay my bills."

"I'm not telling Paul to do anything, much less give you any money. In fact, I would strongly advise him against it, because we all know what you would do with that money, don't we."

"But!"

"And how dare you try to play the family card against him. One, you're distantly related at best and two, you let your own wife and son starve while you sit in a tavern all day."

Again, George's strategy had backfired on him; but he was desperate.

"You call yourself a Christian, Paul. A Christian would help his fellow man."

Clemente clenched his teeth and balled his fist. Paul noticed and placed a firm hand on his shoulder.

"George, if you want to judge my faith; that is your prerogative; but it doesn't change anything. I still won't give you the money unless you get professional help for your drinking problem. As an alternative, I will loan your son the money to purchase the farm from you relieving you of the debt."

"But the farm is all I have."

"Take it or leave it."

"Paul Gray, you'll pay dearly for this."

George Bancroft shook his fist in Paul's face and then stormed out the door. Paul finally noticed the audience he had.

"Folks, let's start our morning meeting."

Everyone made his or her way back to the war room; however, Paul held Clemente back for a moment and whispered something in his ear.

"If I had given that man money, he wouldn't have used it to pay the mortgage on his farm. He would have spent every dime of it in the closest tavern and then been even further in debt, making his problems much worse. I had to consider more than just him, when making my decision; I had to also consider his wife, Elizabeth, and his son, Jack. Money is not always the answer to the problem, Clemente."

Clemente nodded, indicating that he understood; and he and Paul took their seats in the war room. Nobody noticed that George Bancroft had sneaked back into the office and was standing near the door to the war room eavesdropping on the meeting.

"Thank you all for coming. There are many new faces around the table this morning. In fact, there are more new faces than old faces; but I will be making introductions in just a moment. First order of business though concerns our receptionist, Ashleigh Lovett."

"Me? I only had one matter to discuss; and it's not that important."

At this point, Ashleigh turned to address the whole group and not just Paul.

"I'm moving into an apartment here at the Canterbury on Saturday."

She was interrupted by modest applause.

"If anyone would like to help me move, I would really appreciate it."

Paul continued where she left off.

"There are nine unknowing volunteers down the hall; but as an incentive for the rest of you, I'll be grilling burgers and brats in place of the customary pizza. However, that wasn't the issue I meant. I need you to do something, Ashleigh."

"Sure."

"The diner has a regular customer, named John Dorman."

"I know. I've waited on him several times."

Marcy and Clemente did not hide their surprise at this revelation very well.

"I need you to find out everything you possibly can about him."

Ashleigh looked confused at first but acquiesced by silently nodding.

"Great."

The gravity in Paul's voice lightened immediately as he changed the topic.

"We now have a Chief Financial Officer. May I introduce Gregory Washington."

Paul gestured towards a young black man, who stood to graciously meet the applause. Gregory Washington was tall and thin and wore thick glasses.

"Greg and I have been close friends for a long time. We studied together at WURC back when it was still Western Indiana University; he was an accounting major; and I was a history major. And, we worked together at the Imperial Hotel for several years, him, as an auditor and eventually the comptroller, and me, as a front desk clerk.

"Naturally, he will be assuming all financial-related responsibilities of Foster Gray Holdings, which I'm sure is a relief for Marcy."

Marcy blushed and nodded.

"Greg, I spoke to Tiny Smith yesterday. He told me about some petty thefts at his neighbor's house and a local store. Plus, Tiny incurred some expenses himself, when he fed, clothed, and housed a few former gang members. Would you make sure that everyone's compensated for their loss and expenditures? Marcy will give you the contact information."

Greg nodded but looked expectedly at Paul.

"Was there something you wanted to add, Greg?"

Now that he had the floor, Greg was finding it difficult to relay his simple message.

"Miss Christie needs to talk to you."

CHAPTER TWENTY-EIGHT

There was modest laughter from those in the room who knew Miss Christie.

"Paul, when I told her about this job; she wanted me to make it a condition that I didn't start until you spoke to her."

"Okay, no more avoiding Miss Christie. I'll talk to her immediately after this meeting."

As the giggles from around the room subsided, Paul paused before making the next introduction.

"We also have a Chief Legal Officer. Allow me to introduce Matthew Bailey."

A stocky man with blond wavy hair stood briefly as the others applauded.

"Matthew is a partner at Avery Law Offices; and he will be splitting his time between here and there, so while I hope all of you will make him feel welcome, let's be respectful of his valuable time."

"May I add something, Paul?"

"Please do."

The attorney took a moment to steel his resolve.

"I was Paul's great grandfather's attorney, when he died; this is a fact of which I'm not especially proud. As some of you may already know, Silas Gray was an evil man. Originally, as executor of his estate, I welcomed the opportunity to finally rid myself of what I considered his toxic wealth; but now, having met Paul and realizing he is nothing like his great grandfather, I instead look forward to seeing the estate put to a socially beneficial use, perhaps even assisting in that objective."

Matthew Bailey wondered to himself whether he should say anything else; and then abruptly retook his seat.

"Thank you, Matthew."

Again, Paul paused briefly before making the next introduction.

"We also have a Chief Marketing Officer. Allow me to introduce Iris Weber."

A petite lady with long blonde hair and dressed in a navy blue business suit stood. The applause after each introduction had been tapering; but it now resounded louder than before. This was due in part to thirteen of the eighteen people in the war room being young males and in part to Iris being very attractive and very single.

"Some of you may remember Iris. She was once the marketing director at the Canterbury. I believe you left shortly after I started working there."

Iris nodded.

"As I told you on the phone, Iris, I'll need you to start immediately on a marketing plan for the Forrest in general and the Canterbury specifically. I want the Canterbury seen as the epicenter of the Forrest. And don't forget to incorporate the diner into the marketing plan."

"I already have some ideas; and I'll have something to show you by end of week."

Paul gave her a silent thumbs-up before proceeding to the next introduction.

"I met this next man during a recent inspection of the hotel and convention center; however, after a few in-depth phone calls last week, I discovered that we share a unique business philosophy; and I feel as though I've known him for a very long time. Like Matthew Bailey, he will be splitting his time between his own company, LiminAid Stand Incorporated, and us. Allow me to introduce our new Chief Personnel Officer, Tony Limin."

A young, energetic man stood to polite applause.

"I look forward to working with each of you as we make River City the best city in the world!"

Marcy interrupted with a question.

"I'm just curious, Tony. What exactly does LiminAid Stand Incorporated do?"

Paul injected a quick introduction, before Tony could respond.

"Tony, this is Marcy Green, my Executive Assistant."

"Marcy, I conduct motivational seminars."

It was Zack's turn to interrupt.

"Hey, you're that dude, who has all of those books, CDs and DVDs!"

Tony nodded and flashed a smile.

"Tony…everybody…this is Zack Armstrong, the current Executive Chef at the Imperial Hotel and now, our new Vice President of Hospitality Operations."

Zack quickly moved the spotlight back on Tony.

"You must be the only person, who actually uses the convention center; that place is a ghost town."

Paul seized the opportunity to regain control of the discussion.

"Zack, while it's not personnel related, Tony will be helping us with that issue too. As a businessman, who regularly uses meeting space, he can provide us with valuable insights, when we revitalize the convention center…but we've digressed a bit. Marcy, because Tony is splitting his time, you'll still be handling some of day-to-day tasks involved with personnel… oh yeah…and make sure LiminAid Stand Incorporated gets its own office here at the Canterbury, perhaps somewhere up here in the penthouse or on the second floor."

Marcy nodded and made notes on her notepad.

"I hastily introduced Zack without explaining that he will be over all of Foster Gray Holdings' hotels and restaurants. Obviously, this includes the Imperial Hotel and the Imperial Convention Center; but more properties will be added soon, as I continue to organize my inheritances and acquisitions. As a chef, he'll also be helping us save the diner."

"Paul, since the raid, I've been quietly forming that 'committee' of hotel employees, which you requested; and I'm almost done. When you're ready, we should be able to mobilize every employee regardless of department or shift. We've only identified eight employees, who might be sympathetic to Gillenwater."

"Good job, Zack."

Paul paused briefly before making the next introduction.

"I met these next two men, when we were in college. Thane Edwards will be our Chief Acquisition Officer, acquiring strategic properties and businesses. His twin brother, Kane Edwards, will be our Chief Investment Officer, managing our investments and liquid assets."

Two handsome young men stood to acknowledge their introduction and the ensuing applause. Although they were identical twins, they were easily discernible. Thane was more formally dressed and quite extroverted; Kane was more casually dressed and introverted.

"Thane, I'll need you to start working on acquiring that church, which we discussed on the phone."

"I've already moved on it, Paul. The current owner is eager to dump it. I'm meeting him this afternoon; we should be able to sign the papers tomorrow."

"Great work, Thane."

The twins high-fived each other drawing laughter from the room. This jocularity provided a counterpoint to the solemnity, which immediately followed.

"It is my great pleasure to introduce a man, who, outside my immediate family, has had the most influence on my life. I was a rebellious teenager after my father was killed. Only by God working through this man, did I finally turn my life around. Allow me to introduce our Executive Chaplain and Faith Community Liaison, Harry Warner. He has not been officially approved by the Forrest Council on Faith yet; but I have spoken with nine members on that council; and they have all assured me that they know Chaplain Warner very well and see no reason why he wouldn't be approved by the full body."

Paul had to goad Chaplain Warner to stand and receive applause.

"Also, because of his title, Chaplain Warner is automatically a member of all committees and has access to all company information, so please give him your full cooperation."

Paul consulted his notes before continuing.

"By the way, Chaplain, the Council is meeting today; but I'm not privy to the place or time."

"I've already been in contact with Father Andrews; and he told me."

"Great!"

"As most of you know, the Canterbury is not the only property I currently own; it's not even the only residential property I own. There are others including the Canterbury's sister building, the York. For this reason, I've hired a Vice President of Property Management Operations. Allow me to introduce Vicky Heath."

An exotic and statuesque brunette with sultry eyes stood. Her mere presence had at once an intoxicating, an inciting and an intimidating effect on almost every male in the room. Paul quickly moved on to the next introduction.

"Again, as most of you know, I am the majority shareholder and chairman of the board of Fifth National Bank. As Foster Gray Holdings moves to fully acquire Fifth National Bank, Adam Miller will assume the position of President and Chief Executive Officer there and Vice President of Banking Operations here."

Adam stood to acknowledge the introduction as Marcy interjected.

"It's good to finally put a face with a voice."

Adam blushed, nodded and quickly sat down as Paul continued his introductions.

"Last week, Foster Gray Holdings fully acquired Armstrong Construction; and Zared Armstrong joins us as Vice President of Construction Operations. Zared, have you been able to prepare a work schedule yet?"

"I'll be inspecting all of the properties today; and then I'll prepare a schedule for you. We have thirteen construction teams available; and I plan to distribute them in the following manner based on the goals you stated over the phone last week.

"Team 1 will work here at Foster Gray Holdings remodeling the entire area from the top floor down.

"Team 2 will work at your penthouse apartment remodeling the fifth floor."

Clemente smiled broadly.

"Team 3 will work on remodeling the Northwest Suite of the penthouse.

"Team 4 will work on remodeling the public areas of the Canterbury starting on the forty-fourth floor and working down.

"Team 5 will work on remodeling the individual apartments of the Canterbury starting with Ashleigh's and then as the units are available to us."

Ashleigh interrupted.

"You'll finish by Friday; won't you?"

"Yes, Ashleigh, we will finish by Friday; you'll be able to move in."

"Team 6 will work on remodeling the second floor of the Canterbury.

CHAPTER TWENTY-EIGHT

"Team 7 will work on remodeling the first floor.

"Team 8 will work on remodeling the lower floors.

"Team 9 will work on remodeling the new location of the River City Diner."

Ashleigh interrupted again.

"Paul, the diner is moving?"

Paul answered her question in a hushed tone with his right index finger over his lips.

"Shhh. It's Plan C to save the diner; and it's still a bit of a secret. The new location is just next door."

"Oh!"

"Continue, Zared."

"Team 10 will work on remodeling those other storefronts on the first floor starting with the new location of the Avalon Spa & Salon and then as the units are committed."

It was Clemente's turn to interrupt.

"Paul, Avalon is moving to the Canterbury?"

"Yes, Frog Boy, now you won't have to hop very far to get those massages you like so much."

Clemente blushed and laughed at the same time.

"I keep telling you I'm a prince now."

"I'm sorry about all of the interruptions, Zared; as you can see, we're very informal here. Please continue."

"Team 11 will work on remodeling St. George's.

"Team 12 will work on remodeling Forrest Chapel, so let me know when it's available to us, because until then, they and Team 13 will work on remodeling the other churches in the Forrest.

"Los Guardianes will serve as a de facto Team 14; and I'll assign them to the churches with the fewest issues or as cleanup behind Team 13.

"We should be able to handle everything except the roof at St. George's; and I'll hire a dependable roofing contractor for that. Also, you mentioned that St. Anthony's and Twelfth Street Baptist have the fewest issues and larger congregations with willing volunteers. I would like to have weekend workdays at those locations instead, where I cobble together two special teams of volunteers from Armstrong Construction wanting overtime to work with volunteers from each church."

"That sounds great. Marcy, help him coordinate with the churches. And can we make a chart of some kind here in the war room, where we measure the construction progress at each location?"

Zared did not respond; but Marcy nodded as she made notes.

"Although Vicky will be managing all of our residential properties, the Canterbury is still our flagship; and thus, demands special treatment. Allow me to introduce Brock Hudson, who is the Canterbury's new Building Manager."

A brawny young man with scruffy blonde hair stood briefly. He looked like he belonged in the Armstrong family. He had a similar effect on the ladies in the room that Iris and Vicky had had on the men.

"Although yesterday was Sunday, I took some time to make a few promotions. Clemente Morales is now our Chief Operations Officer. Pedro Garcia is now the Capitan of Los Guardianes. And very soon, Tomás Gonzalez will be working down in Cricksburg as the Foreman of Gray Farms and the Custodian of Covenant Baptist Church."

As each man's name was called, he stood briefly to polite applause.

"And that concludes the introductions. Marcy, I'm certain today will be busy for you ensuring everyone has a desk, cell phone, etc."

Marcy nodded and smiled.

"I do have some other announcements to make. Covenant Baptist Church has expressed an interest in founding the Forrest Baptist Mission and locating it in the Forrest Chapel when that is available; Pastor Tim will be leading that. Also, today's hirings are not the last; I'm working on a couple of others including a Chief Security Officer and a General Manager for the Imperial Hotel to replace Gilbert Gillenwater."

"Please let it be Jay. Please let it be Jay. Please let it be Jay."

"Yes, Zack, I've offered the position to Jay; and he has tentatively accepted; however, there are some details before it's official."

"Oh, yeah! Good-bye Fishface! Hello Jay!"

Zack made an aside comment to Clemente; but it was loud enough for everyone to hear clearly.

"You'll like Jay; he actually knows how to manage a hotel."

Clemente chuckled at this comment; and the chuckles rippled throughout the room. Paul cleared his throat loudly to reestablish order before continuing.

"I've also been reminded that as our group grows, Foster Gray Holdings must focus exclusively on the business and allow the Order of the Lamp to focus on other ways of confronting Claude Zumbini. So, there will be a meeting of the Order of the Lamp in the Sunset Room on Thursday night. And don't forget starting this Sunday night, anyone who wants to hang out at my apartment is more than welcome."

Paul checked his notes and then tossed his notepad on the table.

"And that's everything I had to discuss. As you can see, I was very busy last week. Clemente, did you have anything to report?"

"We're initiating four new members into Los Guardianes tonight;

everyone's welcome to come by for pizza afterwards and meet the new guys."

"Clemente, have we heard from Carlos and the other two?"

"They are making their way back to River City; and according to the guys, they're very mad."

Paul betrayed no emotion at this news.

"Do you have anything else?"

"One last thing. Can I take those stupid posters down?"

"Yes, Clemente, take the posters down; Noodles is officially one of us now."

Clemente silently cheered drawing laughter from the room.

"But make sure he gets a license and shots."

Clemente nodded.

"Marcy, did you have anything."

"I completed typing the contract with the Forrest Council on Faith and am currently working on organizing the Parade of Steeples and the reception at the Canterbury afterwards. These events are scheduled for Saturday, November 22."

Marcy turned to address everyone in the room.

"We need everyone's help to make this successful."

"Anything else?"

Marcy hesitated.

"Just one other thing. I almost decided not to bring it up."

Again, Marcy hesitated. She retrieved an envelope from her notepad and extracted a letter from it.

> *Dearest Cousin Paul,*
>
> *I apologize for not scheduling our next tea. I am still looking forward to it; but you can probably guess that as Halloween approaches, we are very busy here in Scarsdale. As a small token of my regret, please accept these free passes to the Hayne Family Halloween Scream Festival. I believe you will find enough for all your employees; but please let me know if you require more.*
>
> *When your group arrives, instruct the admission booth attendant to contact me; and wherever I am in the park, I will immediately, officially and personally welcome you to our establishment and the festival. As we have not been formally introduced yet, I am especially looking forward to meeting Ms. Green, Master Morales and now, his new girlfriend, Ms. Lovett.*
>
> *Tell Mr. Zachariah Armstrong that I hope to have enough time to regale him with family stories even more fantastic than the ones he has heard about Cousin Mordecai.*
>
> *With the warmest regards,*
>
> *Sam Hayne*

There was a long and awkward silence, which Zack finally broke.

"It's a little creepy when he calls you out like that. I didn't even think he knew who I was."

Clemente responded.

"You get used to it."

"Since he's mentioned five of us by name, I'm requesting that Marcy, Clemente, Ashleigh, Zack and I make every effort to go. I'm making it optional for everyone else. If you would like to join us, let Marcy know as early as possible, so she can obtain extra tickets if necessary. Pedro, let the guys know they're invited too."

Pedro nodded.

"Is there any further business to discuss before we adjourn?"

Silence was the response.

"Great. I'm sorry this has been such a long meeting, folks; but we did have a lot to discuss. Since we have a much larger group now, if you need to discuss something let Marcy know beforehand so she can put it on the agenda; otherwise, only Clemente, Marcy and I will have an automatic slot on the schedule."

Knowing the meeting was over and the room would soon be emptying, George Bancroft left as quickly as he could. From where he was hiding, he had heard everything; and he hoped there was something valuable in his newly acquired information, something Claude Zumbini would pay handsomely to know.

Chapter Twenty-Nine

U sing the access tunnel, Paul immediately made his way to the Imperial Hotel and then towards the housekeeping department. There were eight guest rooms outside the housekeeping department. Due to their unique location, they were usually the last rooms in the hotel to fill. However, there were some longtime guests, who were savvy enough to actually request these rooms, as they were cleaned by the hotel's longest serving employee.

Paul noticed a laundry cart blocking an open guest room door. He craned over the cart and called out to raise the attention of the housekeeper inside the room.

"I'm looking for Miss Christy."

There was no response.

"Is Miss Christy in here?"

A short, elderly black woman emerged from the bathroom. She was wearing a shawl over her uniform. Her glasses were very thick making her eyes look inhumanly large.

"Who are you?"

"Miss Christy, it's me…Paul…Paul Gray."

The housekeeper looked confused.

"Miss Christy, I sent you postcards every week. Don't you remember me?"

The housekeeper was now standing on the other side of the cart squinting at Paul.

"I know a Paul Gray; but the Paul Gray I know would have come by to see me the day he returned to River City and not eleven days later."

"I've been a little busy, Miss Christy."

They stood there staring at each other. Paul finally made a funny pouty face; and this coaxed a smile out the housekeeper and finally a hearty laugh.

"I can't stay mad at you. Get in here, Paul, and let Miss Christy take a look at you."

Paul moved the cart aside and entered the room. He hugged Miss Christy.

"My, if you're not more handsome now then you ever were."

Paul blushed.

"Let's sit down for a minute. Miss Christie has to rest."

Miss Christy collapsed into one of the chairs near the window; and Paul sat down next to her. Having caught her breath, she made a discovery.

"What's that?"

"What's what?"

"That ring on your hand."

Paul moved his right hand close to Miss Christy so she could examine the ring. It still was not close enough, so she took his hand and moved it to within inches of her eyes. She stared at it for several minutes; and eventually took her index finger, bent with arthritis, and touched the ring carefully as if it were hot.

"Where did you get this?"

"My cousin, Sam Hayne, gave it to me."

Miss Christy let go of Paul's hand and stared at him for several minutes. Paul felt like she was looking into his soul.

"That ring is very powerful, Paul. Use it wisely."

"I didn't know there was anything special about it; and I wouldn't even know how to use it."

"You don't know now; but you'll know soon…very soon. Miss Christy sees these things."

Paul nodded.

"Now, can you give Miss Christy a hand with these rooms? She's not as young as she used to be."

Paul helped Miss Christy finish cleaning the last six rooms. It had been some time since Paul had cleaned a hotel room; but like riding a bike, he had not forgotten how; and he soon discovered he was as quick and efficient as he ever was. As he cleaned, he took special notice of the condition of the rooms. Like the rest of the hotel, they badly needed renovation; the sheets were threadbare; and the furnishings were out of date.

When they were finished cleaning, Paul escorted Miss Christy across the street to her third floor apartment at the Canterbury, bid her farewell, and grabbed a quick lunch at the diner. While he was nursing the last sips of his sweet tea, he called Marcy and Clemente on his cell phone to check on them; then he called Pedro to ask him where Los Guardianes was working and discovered that they had just returned to St. George's from lunch.

Paul finished his tea and made his way to the second subbasement of the Imperial Hotel. Hotel employees referred to this area as china storage; but it was a repository for everything; and had become a junkyard. Old hotel furniture, items recovered from guestrooms, boxed accounting records from decades ago. The entire floor was full of junk; and there was no organization.

Paul found an old office desk and chair and pushed it towards the door leading to the tunnel to the Canterbury. He continued rummaging and found another chair, for any guests his new "office" might have; a desk lamp, which still worked; a dusty ceramic mug, which was probably left by a guest; some ballpoint pens, which still had ink; and a legal pad.

He located a receptacle, plugged in the lamp, and then placed it in the center of the desk. He put the mug on the desk to his right hand side and put the pens in it; and he placed the legal pad in the center. There was only one more thing, which he needed; and it took him several minutes; but he finally found it—a comment box.

He would need to purchase a new padlock before he announced the purpose or even the existence of the box; but he wanted a place where hotel employees could discretely leave him messages or could meet him clandestinely if necessary; and it needed to be where he could come and go rather invisibly. He surveyed his work; and it was not bad for borrowed materials. Paul finished by clearing a better path from the elevator to his desk and to the tunnel door. As an afterthought, he also fashioned a small hiding place near the desk.

Paul checked the time; and it was getting late, much later than he realized. He had hoped to work with Los Guardianes today but committed himself to doing that for the remainder of the week. As he made his way to the tunnel, he heard the elevator doors open; and he froze. A housekeeper exited the elevator car before realizing Paul was there. His presence startled her and she tried to call for the elevator.

"Wait!"

The housekeeper stopped.

"I won't hurt you."

The housekeeper turned around to face him.

"My name is Paul Gray."

The housekeeper stood silently.

CHAPTER TWENTY-NINE

"And your name is?"

"Jane."

The response was meek.

"It's nice to meet you, Jane. I'm the—"

"I know who you are. Miss Christy told me."

"Why did you come down here?"

"I needed a place to hide."

"From whom?"

Jane was becoming nervous.

"Who are you hiding from, Jane?"

"Mr. Gillenwater."

"Why are you hiding from him?"

"He…he assaulted me…as I was cleaning my last room."

"I'm taking you to the police."

"No! I've went to the police before; and they won't do anything. They actually protect him."

"Wait! This has happened before?"

"Yes, many times."

"Then at least, let me take you to the hospital."

"I don't need a hospital. I don't have any injuries."

"How am I supposed to help you then?"

Jane hugged Paul tightly.

"Just get rid of that terrible monster."

Chapter Thirty

"I seriously want to kill him!"

The initiation ceremony for Los Guardianes' four newest members, Mateo Perez, Jacobo Perez, Tadeo Sanchez, and Jimeno Ramirez was over; and the pizza reception was winding down. Most of the employees from Foster Gray Holdings had already left; and the members of Los Guardianes, having had a long and tiring day at St. George's were already retiring for the night. Paul had pulled Clemente and Zack aside to tell them about Jane.

This time, it was Clemente, who had to calm Paul down.

"Paul, if you do that, you'll go to prison."

"Right now, I'm so mad; I don't care. Zack, how close are you? Can we terminate him in the morning?"

"It's close; but there are still departments, where we don't have an ally. Fishface and his people still control accounting, sales & marketing, and human resources; and they can do a lot of irreparable damage from there."

"How much longer do you need?"

"Maybe four weeks."

"I cannot ask Jane or anybody else to work under these conditions that long. In fact, I cannot even ask them to work there another day with him on the premises. What are our options?"

"If we terminate him now before we're ready, he'll get mad and possibly sabotage the hotel or retaliate in some way, or worse, have Zumbini put pressure on us in other ways. What if he forecloses on the diner before we're ready or sends Carlos to torch one of the churches?

"If we keep him around that long though, company morale will plummet; and the employees might lose faith in you, when we do finally dismiss him.

"And with the police department on Zumbini's payroll, Jane's right; we cannot call them; besides, their lawyers might find a way of suing us for bringing false charges."

The three men thought about their dilemma. Clemente finally broke the silence.

"It's a shame we can't send him on vacation until we're ready to fire him."

"Clemente, that's brilliant!"

"It is?"

"Yes! Zack, who is the assistant general manager of the hotel?"

"Ellen Powers."

"Can we trust her?"

"Completely."

"Is Tim ready to step up and take over the kitchen?"

"Yes."

"Good."

Paul made a phone call; the conversation was in Spanish. Clemente understood it; but after Paul hung up, he translated for Zack.

"I just called my grandfather in San Juan. Early tomorrow morning, Gilbert Gillenwater will receive a phone call from my grandfather congratulating him on the good report he received from me. As a reward, he will be treated to a two-week vacation at my grandparent's hotel in Puerto Rico. My grandfather is even sending the company jet to really sell it."

"And when Gillenwater returns, we terminate him immediately."

"Exactly! And, while he's gone, I want you go through the hotel, department by department, building a case against him and taking back the hotel. Start with the departments most sympathetic to what we're doing. If you find an employee, who is loyal to Gillenwater, find a reason to fire them immediately."

"I love this plan, Paul."

Clemente injected an insight.

"This will also test how much Claude Zumbini knows about what we're doing or at least how much he's told Gillenwater. If he suspects something, he probably won't go."

Chapter Thirty-One

Sell it, Paul's grandfather did. Carlos Rodriguez did not just call Gilbert Gillenwater on the phone, he flew in on the private jet himself and hired a limousine to drive him to the hotel arriving before Gillenwater did. Such things, along with a two-week vacation in a Caribbean paradise and the promise of a promotion and raise were enough to fully entrance Gillenwater. If Zumbini had suspicions about Paul, he did not share them with Gillenwater, because he fell for the ruse completely.

Chapter Thirty-Two

Wednesday morning, as Paul was making his way to the diner for breakfast, Clemente intercepted him.

"Can we talk?"

"Of course."

Paul sat down in a chair in the great room; Clemente sat down in a chair nearby; and Noodles jumped in Paul's lap eager for Paul to scratch him behind the ears.

"I met Miss Christy yesterday."

"Oh yeah."

"Yeah…I like her."

"I do too."

"She thinks you're trying to protect us."

"I am."

Clemente was becoming frustrated.

"Paul…everything…and I mean everything…that I have…I owe to you. A few weeks ago, I had nothing; and now I have…everything. I feel like a prince. But I thought we would be partners."

"We are, Clemente."

"What about your ring?"

"My ring?"

"Miss Christy told me it had special powers."

"Well, Miss Christy can be a bit dramatic at times. As far as I know, it's just a ring, Clemente."

"Would you tell me if it wasn't?"

"Yes. And I wish there was a way to convince you of that."

Clemente was becoming less agitated.

"I'm not a kid, Paul; you don't need to protect me. The only way I can ever repay you for what you've done for me is through my loyalty. Paul, I would fight for you; I would die for you."

"I know that, Clemente."

"Do you? If you decided to march into Claude Zumbini's office this morning to fight him, whom would you take with you as your wingman? Me? Zack?"

Paul considered injecting some humor into the conversation to release the tension; but sensing this was important to Clemente, he thought better of it and remained silent.

"Paul, I want to be your wingman. If you feel the need to protect the others, that's fine; but I'm here to fight alongside you."

"I understand, Clemente."

There was a long silence; and Paul wondered whether Clemente had said everything he wanted to say.

"Did you want to go to breakfast, Clemente?"

"Yeah, but I have something else I need to discuss with you first."

Paul sat back in his chair and waited.

"I spent the twenty-five thousand dollars."

"Already?"

Clemente nodded.

"After my conversation with Miss Christy, I walked around the Forrest like you told me. I was looking for people to help. As you said, many of the people I encountered needed help but not money. Some people just needed someone to open a door or carry a package or lend a sympathetic ear."

"That was the point I was trying to make; I'm glad you learned it firsthand."

"There was one guy who needed money though."

"Twenty five thousand dollars worth?"

"Yeah. He's a recent college graduate; and he has a really great idea for a pizzeria. I would like to give the money to him."

"Great!"

"That's not all."

"I would like us to help him with rent too, possibly with one of the first floor storefronts. I would like to have some of our people help him with his accounting, legal and marketing needs. And I would like us to patronize his pizzeria instead of Second City since he's a small businessman and Second City is a large national chain."

"Clemente, I have full faith in you and leave this project in your capable hands. And I can't wait to see how it turns out."

"Thanks. Can we get that breakfast now."

"Yes; and today, you're buying."

"Hey!"

CHAPTER THIRTY-TWO

Chapter Thirty-Three

Thursday night after work, seventy-two people assembled in the Sunset Room for a meeting of the Order of the Lamp.

Twenty-three people joined including every new employee of Foster Gray Holdings, two Los Guardianes members, seven members of the Forrest Council on Faith, as well as Zeph Armstrong, Tiny Smith and Miss Christy. Although they were not present, Officers Havens and O'Connell and Noodles were made honorary members.

Three new groups were formed: the Imperial Resistance, made of employees from the Imperial Hotel and headed by Zack Armstrong, the Armstrong Army, made of the Armstrong siblings and headed by Zeph Armstrong and the Cricksburg Delegation, made of thirteen members and headed by Tiny Smith.

Fifth National Bank and Armstrong Construction were identified as companies owned by Foster Gray Holdings; and LiminAid Stand Incorporated was identified as an Order of the Lamp affiliated company.

Big Top Productions and Empire Federal were identified as companies affiliated with L'Ombra.

After the meeting several of the members, who were not directly employed by Foster Gray Holdings, thanked Paul for having the separate meeting. Gradually, Paul's group was growing larger and stronger, hopefully, when necessary, it would be large enough and strong enough to complete its objective.

Chapter Thirty-Four

Friday morning before work, Paul, Clemente, Marcy and Zack met for breakfast at the diner. They were just finishing and Paul was settling the bill, when Officers Havens and O'Connell pulled up chairs to join their table. Ashleigh noticed and stood behind Clemente's chair. As usual, Officer Havens spoke for the pair.

"Paul, we wanted you to know that Carlos Rivera, Vicente Flores, and Ignacio Torres have all been spotted in this area of the city. Word on the street is they're coming for you."

Paul nodded.

"Thank you, Officer Havens."

"Ashleigh told us about your meeting last night. I hope you understand why we cannot officially join your group. No hard feelings?"

"Of course, I understand…and no hard feelings."

"We admire what you're doing; but I'm not sure you have a chance at succeeding."

Officer Havens looked around the room to see who could hear him and then continued talking in hushed tones.

"Zumbini has a chokehold on this city. That tattoo you've been talking about and looking for…the winged demon…Kevin and I have seen it on the arms of several of our fellow officers; and there's a rumor that some very powerful men in this city have it too. Paul, be careful; these men don't play games."

Their information conveyed and their warning issued, Officers Havens and O'Connell left the diner. Ashleigh returned the chairs to the tables where they belonged; and then the five of them just looked at each other. Each of them was contemplating what they had just heard.

Chapter Thirty-Five

Team 5 finished remodeling Ashleigh's new apartment Friday afternoon; and Saturday morning, several dozen people showed up to help her move. The move was completely finished by mid-afternoon. As promised, Paul and Zack grilled burgers and brats.

Chapter Thirty-Six

Sunday morning, Paul woke, exercised, showered, dressed and had a brief private devotion before meeting Marcy and ten of the members of Los Guardianes for breakfast at the River City Diner and mass at St. Anthony's Catholic Church. Brock Hudson sneaked in after service had started and sat next to Marcy.

After mass, Paul made his way to Cricksburg, West Kentucky, and the Covenant Baptist Church. He parked his truck in front of his grandparent's house, where several cars were already parked, and scratched Noodles on the head, before walking the footpath to the church. Like his group at St. Anthony's, his group at Covenant Baptist had also grown. Chaplain Warner and Zack had joined Pastor Tim, Tomás, Clemente, Ashleigh and Pop Gray in their usual pew; Edith Sheppard sat in the pew behind them along with Tiny Smith and his family. Paul took a seat between Chaplain Warner and Zack.

"We were raised Southern Baptist, we all just stopped attending church when we became adults. I've been intending to get back; but there was always some excuse."

Zack paused to compose himself.

"Thanks Paul."

Zack gave Paul a brotherly side hug.

"My siblings will probably start attending here too. I'll make sure of it."

Paul thought to himself. He had never extended an invitation to Zack to attend Covenant Baptist Church; and except for the members of Los Guardianes, he had not even required Zack or anyone else to attend any church at all. There was that clause in the contract between Paul and the Forrest Council on Faith; but that had not been signed yet and would not be for several weeks. Paul wondered if the soft approach of simply leading by example was more effective than issuing commands. It must be, because he knew other employees at Foster Gray Holdings were attending other churches, some for the first time, some for the first time in a long time.

Tiny Smith interrupted Paul's thoughts.

"Hey, Paul, you didn't need to pay me for feeding those guys; I was honored just to help you out; but…I do appreciate it."

"And I appreciate everything you've done, Tiny"

The organ started playing a prelude; and the congregation silenced themselves in preparation for worship. Paul and Tiny quickly finished their conversation in whispers.

"Paul, if you ever need anything…"

"All I ask is that you look after things down here…the church…my grandparent's farm; and if something happens, call me."

"I would do that even if you didn't ask me. This area down here is a clown-free zone; and I intend to keep it that way."

The services started and after corporal, choral and special music, prayers and readings, Pastor Tom approached the pulpit.

"Before I begin my sermon, I wanted to acknowledge a former pastor of this church, who is with us today. Harry Warner would you stand."

Pastor Tom gestured towards Chaplain Warner, who reluctantly stood.

"Many of you will remember that his pastorate of this church immediately preceded my own. He is now the chaplain of Paul Gray's company, Foster Gray Holdings; and after the service, I know you will want to welcome him back to this congregation and keep him in your prayers as he continues to serve the Lord and the community in a new and exciting way."

Chaplain Warner sat down.

"We continue to study 'God's Formula for Success.' The first week we learned to 'View the Situation Correctly;' and last week we learned to 'Issue a Proper Solution;' this week, we learn the third point: 'Challenge the Critics.'

"You may have heard of the British author, Rudyard Kipling. You have certainly heard of his amazing adventure stories such as *The Jungle Book* and 'Gunga Din.' Having already had one article published by the *San Francisco Examiner*, Kipling submitted another for consideration. The editor rejected the submission and told Kipling, 'I'm sorry, Mr. Kipling; but you just don't know how to use the English language. This isn't a kindergarten for amateur writers.'

"That statement was made in 1889 at the beginning of Kipling's literary career; nineteen years later, he was awarded the Nobel Prize for Literature. Critics are usually wrong. Rudyard Kipling didn't listen to the critics; and he succeeded.

"In the fourteenth chapter of the gospel of Matthew, we read how our Lord walked on water; but that passage also tells us that for a short time, so did Peter! While Peter looked forward to Jesus, he did the impossible; but when he looked at the circumstances around him and especially when he listened to the critics in the boat behind him, he began to sink. Critics are usually wrong. Peter listened to the critics; and he failed.

"We consider our main text for this study of 'God's Formula for Success,' the story of David and Goliath, and we see that King Saul, the Israelite army and even David's own brothers are critics. They are telling him that he cannot conquer Goliath. However, David did not allow their criticism to change his mind; and he didn't allow Goliath's appearance to deter him. He remained focused on the objective.

"I ask you these four questions. Are there critics in your life? Are you allowing them to influence you? Are you a critic in someone else's life? Do you need to become a cheerleader instead?"

Chapter Thirty-Seven

After the service, Paul's Covenant group merged with Paul's St. Anthony group around Nan's kitchen table. Nan had baked a ham; and it was as delicious as last week's fried chicken had been. After Sunday dinner, everyone reassembled in the living room to watch the Hornets game. Paul lingered to help Nan with the dishes.

"Now, Paul, go in there with the others; I'll be in shortly."

"But Nan, if I don't help you do these dishes, I won't get any other quality time with you at all. I love everyone in there; but I miss the days when it was just you and Pop and I."

Nan laughed as she started washing and Paul grabbed a towel to dry. Noodles stayed underfoot in case there was a scrap of food that needed his attention.

"It does seem like your time is a much rarer commodity these days; but you're doing good work, Paul. Just look at those boys in there; you've made fine upstanding men out of them."

Paul blushed as he started drying the first dish.

"I love having a full house on Sundays; but there is a part of me that misses those old days too."

"Where is Paul? Where is he hiding?"

A vaguely familiar voice bellowed from the living room; and a growing commotion was building in its wake. Paul threw his towel on the counter and ran to the living room to investigate. Nan and Noodles followed close behind him. George Bancroft was standing inside the door holding a nearly empty bottle of whiskey.

"George, leave right now or I'm calling the police."

"I'm not leaving…until I've said my peace."

George was slurring his words.

"Then say your peace and leave."

George took a sip of whiskey; and Nan rebuked him.

"George Bancroft, you take that liquor out of my house right now."

"Old woman, it's a free country…and I'll drink what I please…where I please…and when I please…and none of you can stop me."

George took another sip from his bottle, as Paul started making his way toward him. Clemente, Zack, Brock, and the members of Los Guardianes formed a line behind him.

"That's it. You're leaving now. Nan, call the police."

"But I haven't said what I came to say."

"Sorry; but you just lost your chance."

Paul pushed George out of the house and onto the porch.

"I just thought you should know…that I had a little talk with Zumbini."

George smiled. He was thinking himself very clever. Paul and his backup showed no emotion.

"Yeah, after you refused to give me the money I needed…I listened to your little meeting…and then I went to Zumbini…and he paid to learn your secrets."

"How much did you get, George?"

"A hundred dollars!"

"And you've already drank every dollar of it; haven't you? So what are you going to do for more money now?"

George look puzzled. He realized he might not be as clever as he originally thought. In desperation, George took a swing at Paul; but Paul easily blocked it. He swung his whiskey bottle at Paul; and in so doing, he lost his balance and fell backwards down the porch steps landing on the whiskey bottle. The bottle broke and a large shard cut into his lower left abdomen.

"Nan, call the ambulance instead. George has hurt himself. And call his family."

Edith Sheppard, who was also a nurse, rushed out of the house and attended to George's injury until the ambulance arrived.

Despite the gravity of his injury, George took time to continue taunting Paul.

"You'll never win. Zumbini is a much better man than you'll ever be. And I'm going to help him beat you."

"If he's a much better man, then he shouldn't need your help."

"Don't listen to him, Paul. Don't let this critic get inside your head. Heed Pastor Sheppard's sermon."

These words came from Chaplain Warner, who was now standing behind Paul. He placed a reassuring hand on Paul's shoulder as he continued his words of encouragement.

"He's just a drunken old fool."

The ambulance arrived, as did the police and George's wife and son. After giving a statement to the police, Paul went to Elizabeth and Jack.

"Elizabeth, I'm very sorry. It was an accident. He just fell off the porch."

"Paul, you don't have to apologize. You did nothing wrong. Jack and I know what he is."

"Don't worry. I'll pay his hospital bill; and if there is anything else I can do, please call me."

Elizabeth Bancroft smiled meekly and nodded as her son hugged her reassuringly.

The paramedics stated that George Bancroft's injuries were not as serious as they looked, certainly not life threatening; but he still required stitches and some recovery time in the hospital. Edith Sheppard concurred with their assessment. George Bancroft was taken to the hospital. His wife and son followed behind them.

"Did you want to press charges against him, Mr. Gray?"

"No, that family has enough problems without a frivolous lawsuit."

The officer nodded and handed Paul a copy of his report before leaving. Thinking they might be needed at the hospital, the Sheppard's also left.

Chaplain Warner addressed the crowd on the Gray's front porch.

"Although he meant Paul harm today and still harbors ill will towards him, I think we should all pause for a moment and pray for George Bancroft. He is certainly a lost soul in need of divine guidance."

There were nods of agreement as Chaplain Warner said a brief but earnest and heartfelt prayer for George Bancroft. When the prayer was over, Chaplain Warner addressed the crowd once more.

"Don't let critics like George Bancroft discourage you…any of you. We have a great battle before us; and we cannot afford the luxury of negative thinking."

Again, Chaplain Warner's words were met with nods.

Chapter Thirty-Eight

Later that afternoon, Paul led a caravan back to the Canterbury and his apartment. There was already a group of people sitting in the Sunset Room waiting for them; after the two groups combined inside Paul's apartment, even more arrived to join them. Every employee of Foster Gray Holdings, every member of Los Guardianes, every member of the newly formed Imperial Resistance, and every Armstrong sibling were present. Ultimately, sixty-nine people came just to hang out at Paul's apartment on a Sunday evening; and Paul could not have been prouder or more ecstatic; this was his reward for all of the hard work. Paul made his way to the kitchen and donned his apron.

"So, what would everyone like to nosh on?"

"Dude, what are you doing?"

"Zack, I have a fully stocked kitchen and a room full of hungry guests; and I'm dying to cook for them. I just need to know what they're in the mood for."

"No, I meant what are you doing in the kitchen by yourself?"

Zack searched the crowd.

"Tim…Kenny…Rick…let's help Paul out!"

Soon, employees from the Imperial Hotel's food and beverage department joined Paul in his kitchen ready to help him as needed. Again, Paul smiled and addressed his assembled guests.

"Now I have a fully manned kitchen too, so I ask you again, what would you like to eat?"

At first, there was an awkward silence; but then someone hollered out.

"Rumaki!"

Several people giggled; others looked puzzled not knowing what that was.

"Okay! I can make rumaki; but let's enlarge that from one dish to a broader theme; that theme being pseudo Polynesian or rather food that we associate with Hawaii even though it probably didn't originate there. Now, while my kitchen team and I are working on that, we'll need some music to get us in the mood. I know Alex and the members of Tsunami are here and can help out with that; but I'm betting there are some other closet musicians here, who could be coaxed to join this Polynesian-inspired jam session."

Paul turned his attention to Clemente.

"Clemente, up on the second floor, I have an electric keyboard, an electric drum pad and a couple of guitars. Would you bring them down please?"

Clemente nodded and headed towards the elevator. Paul then turned his attention to Pedro.

"Pedro, we need more chairs. There are some in the dining room; and there are more down the hall in the Sunset Room. Would you and some of the guys bring them in here please?"

Pedro nodded, herded the members of Los Guardianes together, and then led them out the door and down the penthouse hallway, while Paul conspired with his new kitchen team.

"I'm thinking that we put together a pu pu platter: rumaki, egg rolls, crab Rangoon—"

Both Zack and Tim interrupted with suggestions of their own.

"Beef teriyaki. Huli huli chicken."

"Coconut shrimp."

Then Paul and Zack had the same idea at the same time.

"Spam musabi!"

They both laughed at each other.

"Okay, let's do all of that; but now, we need something sweet to go with the savory."

"Pineapple upside down cake?"

The idea had come from Tim; but Paul quickly improved upon it.

"That's great; however, let's do pineapple upside down bars instead; it's quicker, easier and most importantly, it's bite sized. Everything tonight must be a finger food."

Everyone in the kitchen nodded in agreement.

Kenny, who had so far been silent, timidly offered a suggestion.

"How about haupia? No, that's a bad idea; it takes too long to gel; forget I said it."

Paul and Zack looked at each other as their thoughts synchronized.

"We could freeze it instead—"

"—and then check to ensure it doesn't crystallize."

Again, they laughed at how inventive they were and how well they worked together.

Rick interrupted with a question.

"What do you want me to do? Mai tais? Zombies?"

CHAPTER THIRTY-EIGHT

"No, Rick, it's Sunday; and I know many people here are non-drinkers, so I want you to invent some virgin cocktails to go along with the tropical theme."

Rick was the chief bartender at the Imperial Hotel. Bartending and, by extension, alcohol had been his whole life and career. Paul's edict was a serious setback to his craft; but he accepted the challenge with gusto.

As the members of Paul's kitchen team began their preparations, Paul noticed that Pedro and the guys had brought more than enough chairs; and they had started assembling them in a way that the guests could watch the activity in the kitchen. Paul also noticed that some of his guests had left while he was in conference with his kitchen mates.

"Where did everyone go?"

Ashleigh offered an explanation.

"You asked for music. Alex, Tsunami and some of the others left to get their instruments. They'll return in a few minutes."

Clemente returned to the great room with the instruments from the second floor, which Paul had requested. He then produced a harmonica from his pocket, sat down in a chair near the breakfast bar and started playing.

"Hey, I didn't know you could play a harmonica."

Clemente stopped and blushed at Paul's comment.

"A hobo taught me, when I was riding the rails. He gave me my first one; but I lost it before arriving in River City. I promised myself that if I ever had money, my first purchase would be a new harmonica. I bought this one Tuesday."

"Well, keep playing."

Paul's request was joined by goading from Ashleigh and several others. Clemente apologized for not knowing any Hawaiian songs before resuming. As he played, the other guests returned with their instruments. Alex Ragman noticed Clemente playing the harmonica.

"Hey, look; we have a new band member."

The members of Tsunami laughed while cheering Clemente on.

"Oh no! I'm not good enough to play with you."

Alex retorted.

"You have an instrument in your hand, so you're in the band."

Tsunami was the house band, who played in the Imperial Hotel's lounge; by contract, they were restricted to covering current popular music and from playing original music. Alex Ragman was a pianist and vocalist, who usually played in the Imperial Hotel's lounge on the days Tsunami did not play; by contract, he was restricted to covering jazz standards. Although they knew each other, this would be the first time they would actually perform together. Plus, they now had Clemente and a handful of other amateur musicians cobbled into their larger ensemble.

The musicians, including a reluctant Clemente, tuned their instruments and quietly discussed their upcoming playlist as the guys in the kitchen continued cooking. There were some scattered conversations among the guests until someone suggested that Paul should explain what he and the others were doing. Paul had never considered himself a culinary performer before; but as everyone, including Paul himself, soon discovered, he was a natural at it. With frequent comedic interjections from Zack and Rick, the kitchen was setting a high entertainment bar for the musicians to follow.

As each dish was prepared, Ashleigh and Rutger, who waited tables over at Tradewinds, alternated passing the food through the crowd. When the kitchen's show was over and all the food was served, everyone turned their chairs around to face the band, who played every Hawaiian song they knew and then some. Without practice or preparation, they actually sounded great together. There were some mistakes of course; but those few occasions were almost as entertaining. Emboldened by the relaxed atmosphere, everyone took a turn as vocalist including Paul, who had a rich baritone voice. It seemed that everyone had enjoyed the evening. When the lateness of the hour prompted people to start leaving, Paul made a brief announcement.

"I want to thank everyone for coming. This evening has been pure bliss for me; and as I said, I want to make it a weekly tradition, so if you're free next Sunday evening, come by and make sure you bring your instruments with you. Be careful going home, guys."

As people started moving towards the door, Alex approached Paul; the members of Tsunami gathered behind him.

"I speak for all of us, when I say that this has been the most fun we've had in a very long time. Playing at the Imperial had actually become drudgery for all of us. However, this evening, here in your apartment, has given us real hope that things will be better soon. Thank you."

Paul offered his hand; but Alex gave him a heartfelt hug instead; each member of the band repeated this action. In fact, every guest repeated it along with comments about how this is the best place they have ever worked or how they feel more connected to their co-workers.

"Dude, tonight was a blast. I'm already looking forward to next week."

Zack Armstrong gave Paul one of his famous bear hugs; he gave one to Clemente too on his way out.

Matthew Bailey was one of the last guests to leave; he had been quiet most of the evening.

"Paul, I'm not a chef or a musician; but I can do this."

Matthew handed him two sheets from a large sketchpad. One was a drawing of Paul at work in his kitchen; the other was a drawing of Clemente playing the harmonica.

"Matthew, these are beautiful."

Clemente looked over Paul's shoulder and agreed.

"Thank you. When my caseload becomes too much, I draw to relieve the stress. This…this has been such an enjoyable evening; and you'll never fully know how much it's meant to me."

Paul felt tears welling up in his eyes.

Matthew started to shake Paul's hand but followed suit and hugged him instead.

After the last guest departed, Paul started cleaning the great room and kitchen. Clemente attempted to help him; but Paul politely rebuffed, explaining how the act of cleaning in solitude helped him to meditate both on the events of the past week and the challenges of the upcoming one. Reluctantly, Clemente conceded; and he and Noodles disappeared into the elevator, making their way to Clemente's bedroom on the fourth floor.

As Paul cleaned, he ruminated on the events of the last three weeks and considered how fortunate he was. He had a clear and noble purpose—to restore River City to its former glory; and in a short time, he had already made some terrific friends, who were willing to help him with that purpose.

Paul had just finished cleaning; and he was ready to retire for the night, when there came a knock at the door. Despite the lateness of the hour, he opened the door; and there standing in his threshold was John Dorman.

"Mr. Gray, I'm here to apologize for my elusive and aloof behavior. May I come in?"

Paul extended a silent invitation to enter by opening the door wider for John Dorman to pass.

"I regret that we started on the wrong foot. I'm John Dorman."

John Dorman, who had been holding his hands behind his back since entering Paul's apartment, now offered his right hand to Paul, who out of force of habit and without trepidation took it. The pain was instant and excruciating; and it permeated his entire body.

Two blinding lights filled the room; one was yellow and originated from Paul's ring; the other was clear and originated from John's ring, which Paul only noticed a split second before their hands touched. Despite closing his

CHAPTER THIRTY-EIGHT

eyes as tight as possible, those two lights were still clearly visible to him.

There was a deafening roar, which sounded like a very loud vacuum cleaner. Paul could not locate its origin; but it seemed to come from inside his own head. He tried to let go of John Dorman's hand or at least cover one ear with his free hand to protect himself from the noise; but he was paralyzed. He was unable to call out for help; and the noise was making it progressively difficult for him to even think.

Paul had a strong metallic taste in his mouth and the nauseating stench of burnt sugar in his nostrils. He desperately needed to vomit to relieve some of this unbearable pain; but he could not. Paul felt his heart and lungs stop working; and he knew he would soon be dead.

He summoned what remaining strength he had to concentrate on the people he loved: his mother; his grandparents; his sister, brother-in-law, niece and nephew; all of his uncles, aunts and cousins back in Puerto Rico, the many friends he made during his life, especially during his recent road trip; Clemente; and all of his friends, both old and new, here in River City. Paul treasured each of these people much more than his financial wealth; and they were what he wanted to think about with his dying breath.

What seemed like an eternity to Paul only lasted a few minutes. The final thing he consciously noted was of urinating on himself. Both lights subsided; and Paul Gray fell dead on the great room floor.

Chapter Thirty-Nine

P aul woke on a beach. The sun was warm and behind him; and he guessed it was early morning. The surf lapped at Paul's bare feet; it was soothingly warm.

The roar of the ocean was hypnotic; and the aroma of nearby tropical flowers and fruits were intoxicating. Paul noticed that he was bare-chested and wearing only navy blue board shorts with a floral print.

Paul noticed a man walking toward him. It was John Dorman. He was barefoot and dressed in a red aloha shirt, which was unbuttoned, yellow board shorts, a puka shell necklace, a panama hat, and sunglasses. Despite what just happened in Paul's apartment, Paul did not feel any anger towards him; in fact, Paul felt totally at peace. John sat down on the beach next to Paul and silently stared into the oceanic horizon for several minutes.

"You have questions."

"Am I dead?"

"Yes."

"Is this heaven?"

"No."

Paul's countenance darkened slightly; and he started to ask a follow-up question; however sensing it, John preemptively answered it.

"No, it's not Hell either…or Purgatory."

"What is it then?"

"It's a pocket universe, which I created so we could talk privately and at leisure. I specifically designed it to set you at ease."

"Are you God?"

"No."

Again, Paul's countenance darkened.

"Are you Satan?"

"No, and I'm not an angel or demon either."

"What are you then?"

"I'm human."

"Humans can't create universes, pocket or otherwise."

"True."

John paused for several minutes. He was not evading Paul's question; in fact, he intended to answer every question Paul had. It was just that this particular question did not have a convenient answer.

"There isn't a term for what I am, because there are so few people, who are aware of people like me and what we can do. I like to call myself a traveler, because I travel to alternate universes."

Paul did not understand the answer; but at this time, he did not wish to pursue that line of questioning further.

"Why have you been so evasive?"

"Again, I apologize for my earlier behavior; but it was necessary. I had to confirm that you were the person for whom I was seeking."

"You've been looking for me?"

"Yes."

"Why?"

"I need your help to vanquish a great evil."

"Before you killed me, I was already battling a great evil."

"Yes, we share a common enemy."

Paul raised his eyebrows.

"Claude Zumbini is your great evil?"

John nodded.

"Then why did you kill me? I can't help you if I'm dead. Can I?"

"You are dead; but you are not permanently dead."

"How are you going to—"

John interrupted him by shaking his head.

"I'm going to—"

John interrupted him again but nodded this time.

"But how?"

John remained quiet. This was one question, which Paul needed to answer for himself.

"My ring? The one my cousin Sam gave me?"

John nodded but grinned too. Paul looked at his hand; along with the clothes he was wearing in the apartment, his ring was missing. John opened his fist revealing the ring. He gave it to Paul and told him to don it. When Paul placed the ring on his finger this time, he sensed great power.

"You required this special existential state, which I created, so you could commune with your ring and realize its powers. Now, tell me how you've used the ring."

"But I haven't used the ring; I don't know how."

"No, let the ring give you the answer you seek."

For what seemed like hours, Paul meditated on the ring. John was right; this relaxed setting was quite conducive to this exercise; Paul was finally able to establish a telepathic connection with the ring. He reported his discoveries to John.

"The first time that I used the ring was when I first encountered Clemente. He had been badly injured during a melee in the basement of my building. I took his hand. He desired a cure for his injuries, so I used the ring to heal him."

"Go on."

"The second time that I used the ring was when I actually met Clemente later that day in the hospital. We shook hands. He desired a genuine friend, so I became one to him.

"The third time that I used the ring was during the benediction following my first meeting with the Forrest Council on Faith. We joined hands in prayer. The ministers collectively desired my help to rebuild our broken community, so I recommitted myself to helping them.

"The fourth time that I used the ring was when I met Pastor Bishop following that prayer. We shook hands. He desires a confidant and someone to help him build a church; and I want to help him accomplish that very much. I have been having a recurring dream concerning this, as he must be too. I've been using the ring to establish that shared dream so we may communicate.

"The last time that I used the ring was earlier in my apartment when I shook your hand. You desired my presence in this place, so I came. You also desire my friendship and an alliance in defeating Claude Zumbini."

"Now that you know these things, tell me how you use the ring?"

"When I touch a person's hand with the hand bearing the ring, I become aware of what that person desires from me and capable of fulfilling it."

"Yes, but remember that you are not a slave to the ring; while you may know the person's desire, you are not obligated to act on it. Tell me what other powers your ring has."

Paul meditated on this.

"The ring protects me from injury and disease; but it also protects my wealth from depletion; and it helps me to communicate with others."

Paul looked puzzled.

"What is it, Paul?"

"It doesn't make sense. I'm already multi-lingual and communicate well with others; and I'm already very wealthy; and I'm already strong and healthy. Plus, I would have been willing to help all of these people without the ring."

"Paul, has it occurred to you that the ring sought you. It does not give you traits you did not already have; instead, it amplifies the traits you already possess. Plus, the ring has other powers, which you'll discover over time."

Both men silently considered this as they stared into the tide.

"How do we defeat Claude Zumbini?"

John smiled.

"Claude Zumbini is an inter-dimensional demon; and he must be vanquished before he develops quantum sentience."

"What is quantum sentience?"

"The awareness of one's existence in alternative realities and the ability to communicate with and ultimately control those other existences."

"That would be bad?"

"Very."

"So, what do you want me to do?"

"You must defeat your Claude Zumbini and not simply by besting him and rebuilding River City; you must acquire his fortune, dismantle his evil organization, and nearly kill him before bringing his body here."

"Is that all?"

Paul's words dripped with unnecessary sarcasm.

"What will you be doing while I'm doing all of that?"

"Why locating the other ring bearers of course. Did you think you were the only one with a ring?"

Paul looked stupefied. John showed him his hand; and there on the middle finger of his right hand was a transparent ring, which Paul had barely noticed earlier in his apartment. If Paul were not looking for it, he would not have seen it.

"What does your ring do?"

"Among other powers, it makes inter-dimensional travel easier and it helps me locate the other Claude Zumbini's and thus the other ring bearers."

"How many have you found?"

"Only one so far...you."

"How many are there?"

"Including you and me, there are forty-three. The rings are spectral; you have the yellow ring; and I have the crystal ring."

Several hours passed with Paul and John sitting on the beach staring towards the horizon.

"John, what is your home world like?"

"It's similar to yours; but there are some noticeable differences. There are only fifty states. Route 66 was decommissioned almost twenty-five years ago. Boulder Dam is named Hoover Dam. Little things like that."

"What town are you from?"

"Evansville, Indiana."

"I've never heard of it. Where's it located?"

"The southwest tip of the state."

"Where River City is located?"

John nodded.

"And Wabash never seceded from the rest of the state?"

"Never."

Paul took a moment to consider this.

"Do I exist in your world?"

John simply shook his head.

"Does Claude Zumbini?"

"Not anymore. I killed him."

Paul and John sat in silence for what seemed liked hours.

"Sam Hayne is looking for you."

CHAPTER THIRTY-NINE

"I know."

John sighed.

"I should probably meet with him."

"What happens now?"

"Stay here and rest for a few weeks. You need time to ponder everything that has happened."

"But I need to—"

"Time passes differently here, Paul. Relatively, when you return, only three days will have passed; and you'll probably be unconscious for another day or two; and very weak for several days after that. You must realize that inter-dimensional traveling is exhausting your first time. Allow the ring to heal you; it will speed the recovery time up."

"If I'm dead for three days, what about my body, when my friends and family find me, they will have me embalmed and buried. There might even be an autopsy."

"This isn't my first rodeo, Paul; your body is safely ensconced in a hidden room in my apartment. I'm keeping vigil over it as we speak. When you've returned to your world, I'll ensure your body is placed in your apartment before you wake up."

"Now that you've found me where do you go next?"

"My travels do not work that way. They're concurrent not consecutive. When I arrive in a new world, I remain in that world until my body dies."

"So, at this very moment, you exist in more than one world."

"Tens of thousands of them actually."

"And you're in constant contact with each of them?"

"Yes."

"Wow!"

"It loses its novelty quickly."

"What about the John Dorman of my world? What does he do next?"

"Well, I've surveyed and recorded your world and found you, so my primary objectives have already been accomplished."

"What about secondary objectives?"

"I'll work at the library across the street from the Canterbury and live out the remainder of my life I suppose."

"What about being my friend and helping me and my other friends restore River City, not as some inter-dimensional traveler but as a citizen? Plus, even with this ring, I could use some help defeating my Claude Zumbini."

"After everything that has happened, you still see me as a prospective friend?"

"I see everyone as a prospective friend."

Paul infected John with a warm smile.

"I visit these worlds; I interact responsibly to complete my mission; but I never allow myself to live in any them."

"Perhaps, you should start."

John smiled and patted Paul on the shoulder.

"You've got a deal; but we need to keep certain information like the ring private, perhaps we could form a special group affiliated with your Order of the Lamp to discuss the more fantastic topics…Sam Hayne…Miss Christie…Clemente Morales…possibly Pastor Bishop and few others…and of course you and me."

"I think that would be a great idea."

For several days, at least they seemed like days to Paul, he rested on the beach, while John worked on building the prison, which would eventually contain and simultaneously execute forty-two Claude Zumbini's gathered from across space and time. Late in the afternoons though, John would always join Paul on the beach; and the two men would sit silently starring off into the sunset.

One morning, refreshed more than he had ever been in his life, Paul found John working on the prison.

"I think I'm ready to go home now."

Chapter Forty

Paul lay asleep in his bed. Marcy was sitting in a chair near the bed taking turns watching over him and watching the television. The show she was watching was a game show called *Answer the Door*.

It was a brainless show, which involved contestants answering questions and then opening doors to reveal prizes; but sometimes, there were bad things behind the doors. The host was smarmy; and there were a lot of doorbell and buzzer sounds and bright flashing lights.

The show that followed that was a sitcom, entitled *With Friends like These*. It was about a young man, who moves into a large house, which was once owned by an eccentric puppeteer. His puppets, as well as his furniture and other belongings came with the house; and after moving in, the young man discovers that the puppets are alive. Each episode, they get the young man into problematic situations; and hilarity ensues; or at least that is what is supposed to happen.

Since she started working at Foster Gray Holdings, Marcy had little time to watch these shows, which she considered lowbrow entertainment; but it kept her mind off worrying about Paul, who, for the moment, was sleeping soundly.

Chapter Forty-One

Paul woke up. He looked around; he was in his bedroom; and although he thought he had heard voices while sleeping, there was nobody there now. He staggered out of bed and almost fell but regained his footing. Paul noticed that he was completely naked; he also noticed that the ring was missing.

He made his way to the bathroom and shaved off four days of facial hair then got in the shower. The hot water was therapeutic. While he stood under the water, he wondered if what had just happened had all been just a dream.

After showering and drying off, Paul returned to his bedroom to find some clothes to wear. He entered his bedroom at the same time as Marcy, who was noticeably shocked.

"Paul…you're naked…I mean…you're awake…I mean…you're naked too…but you're awake…and that's great…not that you're naked…that you're awake…but you look great naked too…oh dear I'm babbling…are you okay?"

"Marcy!"

"Yes."

"Calm down."

Marcy took a few deep breaths and composed herself.

"Okay, I feel better."

"Good. Now, can I get dressed?"

"Sure."

Marcy did not catch the hint to leave, so Paul just started getting dressed with her still in the room. When Paul started putting on his clothes, Marcy started babbling incoherently again; but Paul paid no attention to her. When he was dressed, she restated her original question.

"Are you okay?"

"Yes, Marcy, I'm fine."

"Where were you? We were all worried sick."

"That's a difficult question to answer. What day is it?"

"Friday."

"And the time?"

"Eleven o'clock. Oh, by the way, I have something for you."

Marcy went to the sitting room outside Paul's bedroom and retrieved a small box. It had a handwritten note, which read, "Give to Paul immediately after he wakes." Paul opened the box; and inside he found his ring. He put it on and placed the box on a table.

"That's a beautiful ring, Paul."

"Thank you. It's the one that Sam Hayne gave me."

"I suppose I never noticed it before. Let me see."

Marcy took Paul's hand; and the ring started glowing immediately. Paul could sense Marcy's wish. She loved Paul. She was sexually attracted to him. She wanted him; and the ring was starting to facilitate that wish. Not only could Paul sense Marcy's wish; she could sense his awareness of it.

Paul had never viewed Marcy as a potential mate; but the ring was quickly changing his mind. He was becoming strongly attracted to her. Marcy was flushing; and Paul was becoming aroused. They were starting to lean into each other to share a first kiss, when Paul remembered John's words. He was not a slave to the ring; he alone chose whether to act. He summoned his last ounce of willpower to reject the ring's power before it was too late; and immediately, the ring stopped glowing. Marcy let go of Paul's hand and collapsed into a chair sobbing.

"I'm so ashamed."

"Of what?"

Marcy did not answer the question. She would not even look Paul in the face.

"You have romantic feelings for me. That's normal. That's human."

Marcy looked up at him; there was a flash of anger in her eyes.

"But you don't have romantic feelings for me. And you pulled away even when you realized how I felt."

"Marcy, look at me."

Marcy did so reluctantly.

"I'll explain everything later in greater detail; but I just discovered what this ring does. It's a magical ring; and it allows me to know what others want from me and gives me the ability to fulfill those wishes. If I had not resisted, the ring would have made me the man of your dreams. Is that what you really want? For me to be forced to love you against my wishes? Wouldn't you prefer a genuine love? Because that's what you deserve."

Marcy remained silent.

"I'm flattered that you have feelings for me; and I really care about you. You are one of my dearest friends here in River City; and I've trusted you with the day-to-day operations of my business; but I just don't—"

"Love me."

Paul shook his head.

Marcy looked despondent. Paul leaned towards her and gave her a kiss. It was tender and sweet and innocent and served as a period on any romantic relationship between them. Whether it was the ring or not, Marcy finally realized her true relationship with Paul; and she accepted it; and most importantly, she was at peace with it.

"Are you okay now?"

Marcy nodded and Paul offered her a warm hug.

"For the moment, let's keep the news of my awakening quiet. Can you assemble Ashleigh, Zack and Miss Christy in the great room? I need to talk privately with Clemente; and then we'll meet you there."

Marcy nodded and hurried out of the room. Paul called Clemente on his cell phone.

"Paul?"

"Yes, Clemente, it's me; I'm okay; and I'll explain everything in a moment. But first, where are you?"

"In my office."

"Good. Can anyone hear your side of the conversation?"

"No."

"Good. Come back to the apartment and don't let anyone else know I'm awake yet."

Paul and Clemente arrived in the great room at the same time, Paul from the private elevator and Clemente from the front door.

"In my office."

CHAPTER FORTY-ONE

Paul and Clemente entered Paul's office; and Paul closed the door.

"Clemente, do you remember our conversation last Wednesday. After talking to Miss Christy, you thought I didn't trust you and was keeping you out of the loop."

"Yes; but I was overly emotional that day. I'm sorry."

"Don't be sorry. Remember that I told you if I had a way of convincing you that I trust you, I would use it?"

Clemente nodded.

"Now, I have a way."

Clemente raised his eyebrows.

"Concerning that conversation, I want you to take a moment and think very carefully and then clearly state what you want."

Clemente took a few moments and then spoke very directly.

"I want us not to be just friends but to be the closest of brothers. I don't want you to treat me like a child, who needs protecting; I want you to treat me like a full partner. I don't want you to keep secrets from me. And I want you to know how loyal I am to you."

"And Clemente, I want these things too. Now, take my hand."

Clemente took Paul's hand; and Paul's ring started glowing brightly. It lasted only a few minutes; but in those minutes, Clemente learned everything there was to know about Paul from his earliest memories to the most recent events; and he did not just learn it he experienced it. He experienced the sadness of Paul learning about the death of his father and the happiness of Paul learning he would be an uncle. He experienced Paul's college days, his five-year road trip and the recent events on the existential beach with John Dorman, all in the greatest of detail. However, it worked both ways; Paul learned everything about Clemente too.

When the ring stopped glowing, Paul let go of Clemente's hand; and both men sat down. Clemente had tears in his eyes.

"Thank you, Paul. That really meant a lot to me."

"To me as well."

Paul allowed Clemente to compose himself before they exited the office and joined the others.

Marcy, Ashleigh, Zack and Miss Christy were sitting in the great room; and Paul spent several minutes explaining what had happened to him.

When Paul finished, Marcy, with the occasional help from Ashleigh and Zack reported what had happened since Sunday night. Paul listened politely; he already knew what she would tell him, because he had just learned it from Clemente during their psychic connection.

Monday, when Paul had not arrived for the morning staff meeting, they tried to call him on his cell phone; and when he did not answer, they searched for him. They covered every inch of the Canterbury, the Pine Avenue Parking Garage, the Imperial Hotel, the Imperial Convention Center, and St. Anthony's Catholic Church. Los Guardianes extensively searched the tunnels. Tiny Smith led a search party to search the area in and around Gray's Farm and Covenant Baptist Church.

Marcy, Ashleigh and Iris called every member of the Order of the Lamp and the Council on Faith; and then they called Dan Tuley and every other person they knew. They even called Paul's family in Puerto Rico. Clemente was convinced that Claude Zumbini had sent Carlos to kidnap Paul in retaliation for Gilbert Gillenwater's abrupt retreat to Puerto Rico; and he wanted to confront him. It took a lot of convincing from Zack, Marcy and Ashleigh to change his mind.

Late Monday afternoon, Marcy received a package at the office. Inside was Paul's cell phone and the clothes, which he had been wearing Sunday night; they had been laundered and neatly folded. There was also a note.

Paul is safe and will be returned in three days.

The note was not signed and had been typed on a typewriter. The package itself bore no return address; it had been placed on the reception desk, when Ashleigh had stepped away.

Around midnight on Wednesday, Clemente received a strange text on his cell phone.

Paul is back. You'll find him in the Sunset Room.

Clemente rushed to the Sunset Room and found Paul lying naked on the floor. There was a note near his body. As the note in the package, which had contained Paul's clothes and cell phone, this note was not signed; it too had been typed on a typewriter.

Paul is okay and will regain consciousness in the next day or two.

Clemente or Marcy, and sometimes both, had stayed by Paul's bed since his return.

After Marcy related the story, there were several minutes of silence, which Paul broke with his business-as-usual attitude.

"I missed the Council meeting Monday…I missed the Order meeting last night too…and every morning staff meeting."

"Chaplain Warner explained your absence at the Council meeting and gave them a good report on our progress. Clemente chaired the Order meeting; and I chaired the morning staff meetings. We handled everything, Paul."

"Thank you, Marcy. Is there anything that needs my attention before Monday morning?"

Marcy shook her head.

"How are things going at the hotel, Zack?"

"We're encountering fewer employees loyal to Gillenwater than I thought; and a few, who are so anxious to be rid of him they're helping us in ways we wouldn't have expected. I think we'll actually be ready for Ole Fishface to return in a couple weeks."

"Good. How is progress on our construction projects? Has your brother said?"

"Yes, all thirteen construction teams are at or ahead of schedule."

"Great."

"How are things at the diner, Ashleigh?"

"We're hanging in there. Ed and Georgia wanted me to give you their regards, when you woke."

"Thank you."

"How are Nan and Pop? Has anyone spoken to them?"

Clemente answered him.

"I called them Monday to tell them you were missing; and they were the first ones I called Thursday morning, when you returned."

"Thank you, Clemente. How are the guys? Are they okay?"

Tears were starting to well up in Clemente's eyes again.

"Paul, when we thought Carlos might have kidnapped you, the guys wanted to find him and lynch him. They may not say very much; but they are all unwaveringly loyal to you."

"I know."

Zack interjected.

"Paul, everyone really missed you. You are more loved than you will ever know."

Paul smiled.

"How much does everyone know about my disappearance and reappearance?"

Marcy responded.

"Everyone knows you disappeared of course; but when I received the package with your clothes and the note stating you would return in three days, I thought Sam Hayne and his special brand of weirdness were somehow involved. So, I decided to back off the search for you and guard all further information. I only confided in Clemente and Ashleigh."

"Hey!"

"Sorry, Zack."

"It's okay…I guess…just remember to keep me in the loop next time."

"What did you tell everyone when I reappeared?"

"We told everyone that you had returned from a meeting with Sam Hayne and that you were exhausted and would be resting until Sunday. We didn't want to cancel Sunday's plans, because we knew how much they meant to you; and besides, the note said you would be awake by then."

Clemente interjected.

"We didn't tell them about your clothes or the notes."

"Good work, guys. With things starting to get a little weird around here, I need the knowledge of those weird things contained to a very select group. John and I have already discussed this. He suggested himself, Sam Hayne, Miss Christy, Clemente, possibly Pastor Bishop, himself and me for such a group. I'm including Marcy, Ashleigh and Zack because of their close relationship to me and because of their mention in Sam Hayne's correspondence. Do we need anyone else though?"

"If these weird things demand several or substantial expenditures or perhaps even windfalls, it may become difficult to explain without Greg's cooperation. And depending on the scope of future weird events, we could use someone like Iris, who is gifted in public relations, to spin them."

"Great idea, Marcy! That's why you're my chief of staff."

Both Paul and Marcy laughed.

"Anyone else?"

Paul paused for responses.

"Miss Christy, you've been very quiet. What have you to say? Do we need to include anyone else?"

The elderly woman was quiet for several minutes.

"Paul, when we spoke last week, I was worried you were needlessly bearing these problems on your own."

"Yes, I know. Clemente told me as much."

Clemente blushed.

"And I'm glad to see that the two of you have become closer as a result. However, I've also learned that you've built several circles of emotional support around you including this new one to deal specifically with the use of your ring. You are not as isolated as I had feared. I see no reason at this time, why you need to include anyone else."

"Then we'll meet with Sam Hayne tonight at the Hayne Family Halloween Scream Festival."

Marcy interjected.

"Paul, that may not be a very good idea. Four other employees expressed an interest in going to the festival, when we advertised the free tickets."

"Who?"

"Brock Hudson, Peter Pipistrello, Tony Olsen and Dakota Longshadow."

"Zack, are Peter, Tony, and Dakota the same people, who helped me with my first raid in the subbasements?"

"Yeah, and Tony and Dakota helped us with the second raid. Because they usually work the graveyard shift at the hotel together, they have become very close friends. If weird things are the subject of this group, you might actually consider including them. Peter and Dakota especially are interested in really strange things; it's probably why the three of them wanted to go to the festival tonight."

"Ashleigh, find Greg, Iris and Brock and then shepherd them here discretely. Zack, do the same with Peter, Tony and Dakota. Marcy... Clemente, start calling everybody else; tell them I am feeling much better; but I still want to rest today and tomorrow; but I will see them all on Sunday. When Ashleigh, Zack and Iris return, they can help you with those phone calls."

"What are you going to do, Paul?"

The question came from Ashleigh.

"First, I'm calling Nan and Pop, then I'm calling my family in Puerto Rico, and then I'll go get the last member of our little party. When I return, I'll fix us all a spaghetti dinner, before we go down to Scarsdale."

Ashleigh and Zack left, but returned with six others. Marcy and Clemente were able to call everyone rather quickly; and when they were finished, nobody suspected anything unusual had happened to Paul. As for Paul, he called Nan and Pop and then his Mom in Puerto Rico. After the phone calls, they too did not suspect anything particularly strange.

Having made his phone calls, Paul left his apartment, walked down three flights of stairs, and looked for Apartment 4213. The door was nothing out of the ordinary; there was no clue that an inter-dimensional traveler lived there. Paul knocked at the door. For a moment, Paul thought that John was not home, that he had the wrong apartment, or that he had imagined everything; but eventually, John Dorman opened his door; and for a moment, the two men simply stood there looking at each other.

"You're awake."

"Yeah."

"Again, I'm sorry we started on the wrong foot."

John Dorman offered his hand; and Paul noticed the crystal ring.

"I've thought about what you said. Can we be friends?"

Paul cautiously took John's hand. This time nothing happened, or rather nothing bad happened like last time. Instead, Paul could sense that John genuinely wanted to be his friend. Paul's ring started glowing, as a strong bond was forged between two new friends.

Paul led John back to his apartment and introduced him to everyone before starting to cook a spaghetti dinner of Caesar salad, spaghetti carbonara, garlic toast, sweet tea and for desert, chocolate ice cream. As they ate, the newcomers were briefed on the strange events, which had happened.

"Dude…speaking professionally…this…spaghetti carbonara…rocks! I know we're supposed to be talking about magic rings and demonic clowns and assorted other spooky stuff; but it just had to be said. "

There were nods around the table.

"Thank you, Zack. I really missed being in a kitchen and cooking for my friends; and it was the first thing I wanted to do when I woke up. Peter, did you get any garlic toast."

"I am…uh…allergic to garlic."

"Oh! I'm sorry. I should have asked everyone about food allergies. Let me make you some regular toast."

"No, Paul, really, it's okay; I have enough here; and as Zack said, it's very good. Even my Italian grandmother would approve."

"Thank you, Peter. Let me know if you change your mind about the toast."

They finished their meal and their discussion about matters fantastic then left for the festival. With only thirteen people, they were able to all go in the van, which Paul had recently purchased to transport Los Guardianes to work sites. Brock volunteered to drive.

CHAPTER FORTY-ONE

Although they arrived at the Hayne Family Scream Park early, the lot was already filling quickly. Brock let his passengers out and found a spot in the back of the lot. When he rejoined the group, the queue had moved enough that Paul was now at the attendant's booth. Paul introduced himself and handed the attendant thirteen passes. The attendant raised her eyebrows and picked up a telephone receiver.

"Mr. Gray, I just spoke with Mr. Hayne; and he will be here in a few minutes; if you and your party will wait just inside the turnstiles."

Paul and the others did as was requested and found a nook near the entrance but out of the traffic. They had not waited long, when a tram pulled up next to them. John Hayne was driving and Sam Hayne, in all his eccentric glory, was riding in the front passenger seat.

"Dear Cousin Paul! You're here! I'm so glad you came."

Sam Hayne disembarked the tram and gave Paul Gray a hug and several air kisses near both cheeks. The exuberant entrance caused some in the group to giggle, which did not escape Sam's attention.

"And you've brought guests! Splendid!"

"Sam, allow me to introduce everyone."

"Oh, there's no need for that, I already know everyone!"

Paul wondered how he could know everyone, when he himself had not even met Peter until a few hours ago; in fact, Paul did not even know he would be coming along. As Sam worked though the group, he greeted each person by name and with a hug and air kisses.

"You must be Marcella Green. It's so nice to finally meet you. With the phone calls and correspondence, I feel as though I already know you. We're going to be dear friends.

"You're Clemente Morales. Buenos noches, mi amigo! I'm so glad you came. I know that you and Paul are as close as brothers are; and since Paul is family, I consider you family too.

"And you must be Ashleigh Lovett, Clemente's lovely girlfriend. Enchanté!"

Sam Hayne added a kiss to Ashleigh's hand.

"You and Clemente make a most fetching couple; and I wish you many years of happiness together."

Both Clemente and Ashleigh blushed. Before Sam moved to the next person, he placed Ashleigh's hand in Clemente's and held their hands together.

"You're Zachariah Armstrong; and a strong arm it is."

"My friends just call me Zack."

Sam paid no attention to Zack's interjection; instead, he was grabbing Zack's bicep with his free hand.

"I simply can't wait to tell you all the family stories that you've been dying to hear. But there is so much to do first."

"Just tell me if the story of Mordecai Hayne is true."

"Sadly, no!"

"I didn't think the truth would be as incredible as the tale."

"I'm sorry if I've misled you, Zachariah; but in this case, the truth is actually much more incredible than the tale. Over the years, parents have watered it down so as not to terrify the kiddies."

Zack raised his eyebrows.

"And this is Iris Weber. Your reputation as a marketing expert precedes you. If you ever leave Paul's company, I'm sure I could find a job for you here. Plus, you're as beautiful as the flower for which you're named."

"Thank you."

Sam Hayne stopped and eyed Iris and Zack.

"How is it that you two beautiful people are not a couple yet?"

It was their turn to blush.

"Now, don't try to deny it. Zack, you've spent the last two weeks thinking of a way to ask her out; and Iris, you've spent the same time thinking of way to get him to ask you. Neither of you have any plans tomorrow, so spend the whole day together getting to know each other better."

Sam placed Iris' hand in Zack's and held them together. Paul was wondering if Sam had a magic ring of his own, because he just witnessed two of his employees fall hard for each other. He looked back at Clemente and Ashleigh and their previous handholding had been traded for arms around each other's waist.

"And this is Anton Olsen, a fine Norwegian name. Det er så hyggelig å møte deg."

Tony, who did not understand Norwegian, did not know how to respond.

"My friends call me Tony…"

Embarrassed that he could be the next victim of Sam's matchmaking, Tony felt the need to addend his statement.

"…and I don't have a girlfriend here."

"Yet!"

Sam's last word made Tony even more nervous.

"And this is Dakota Longshadow I believe. Sioux?"

Dakota nodded.

"You have enormous potential—untapped potential. Cousin Paul, if I were you, I would promote this one sooner rather than later."

Sam moved on without a response from either Paul or Dakota.

"You're Peter Pipistrello."

Sam raised his eyebrows and laughed.

"Oh, don't worry Peter. You're little secret's safe with me."

Sam composed himself before moving on, while everyone else wondered what had transpired between Sam and Peter. Peter looked confused and a little embarrassed.

"And this is Christmas Snow. Miss Christy, I am most honored."

Sam got down on one knee and touched the back of Miss Christy's hand to his forehead.

"I am always in your service."

Sam stood up and moved to the next person.

"And this must be your second great nephew, Gregory Washington."

Miss Christy interrupted.

"Mr. Sam, you feel free to work your love voodoo on this one. The family has been tryin' to get him a girlfriend for years; and ain't nothin' worked yet."

"Auntie Christy!"

"Well, it's true."

Everyone was laughing at Greg's expense; but Sam just smiled.

"Miss Christy, I tell you this. Before the moon sets next Halloween, Gregory will stand here hand in hand with his one true love...as will Anton...and Dakota...and several others.

"And this must be Brock Hudson."

As he did with Zack, Sam grabbed Brock's bicep as he shook his hand.

"My, but you're a solidly built one; aren't you. You could be Zachariah's brother; you could. But this just won't do."

Sam led Brock to the other end of the receiving line and placed him between Paul and Marcy. Then he placed Marcy's hand in Brock's and held them together. As Zack and Iris before them, the chemistry between Brock and Marcy was then apparent to everyone present.

"Brock, you have spent the last two weeks making excuses to be around Marcella, because you love her; but you thought she was interested in Paul, which she was. Marcella, you have been interested in both Paul and Brock; but you have been waiting on Paul to make a move. You now know that there can never be a romantic relationship between you and Paul. Marcella, neither you nor Brock have any plans for tomorrow, so like Zack and Iris, spend the day together and get to know each other a little better."

"Sam, I don't know what magic spell you've cast; but you can't just make my friends fall in love with each other."

Sam dropped his usual flamboyant behavior; his words now were serious.

"Dear Cousin Paul, I have performed no magic here today. These people are genuinely in love or would have been very soon. I simply accelerated the process. As you yourself recently said, how genuine is the love if one or more of the parties are forced.

"As you know, it is not on your life path to have a mate; your calling leads you elsewhere; and there is nothing wrong with that. But, that is not their path; their callings include each other; however, they also include strong friendships with you. That they are couples and that you are a single diminishes nothing and only strengthens everything.

"We face a great evil that magic trinkets have no hope against. The only hope is found in the only true magic—love. Whether it's romantic love…"

Sam looked at Clemente and Ashleigh holding hands.

"Whether it's family…"

Sam looked at Miss Christy and Greg.

"Or whether it's friendship…"

Sam looked at Tony, Dakota and Peter.

"Our love for each other is what will conquer this evil."

"Amen! Hallelujah!"

Everyone erupted with laughter at Miss Christy's response.

"Group hug! Bring it in!"

At Zack's suggestion, the fifteen of them formed a tight sphere of humanity. After everyone let go, Sam continued.

"There is one more introduction that I missed; and it's the one to which I've most looked forward. John Dorman, I presume."

Sam and John shook hands; and everyone sensed the importance of this moment in time.

"I insist that you stay the weekend as my guest; we have so much to discuss."

"Thank you, Mr. Hayne. I would be honored."

"It's Sam. And now, my friends, before I give you the grand tour and we enjoy the festival together, I sense that you have come here to tell me something of great importance, so let's retire to the dining room of my home, where we can talk privately."

They all boarded the tram; and John Hayne drove them off the parking lot of Hayne's Family Scream Park and a few blocks down the road to Sam Hayne's house, where they disembarked, and once inside, gathered around Sam's dining room table.

CHAPTER FORTY-ONE

With frequent interjections from the others, Paul related the stranger happenings of the last few weeks to Sam Hayne, who was enthralled by every detail. When everything Paul knew about his ring, his disappearance, evil clowns, and tattoos of winged demons had been shared with Sam Hayne, he sat back in his chair and silently ruminated over the trove of news.

"Sam, why didn't you tell me about the ring?"

"What's that?"

Paul's question had startled him.

"Why didn't you tell me about the ring's powers?"

"Because I didn't know about them."

"After all of the mysterious correspondence you've sent me, after all the strange things you've said, you actually expect me to believe that."

"My dear cousin, I pride myself in using all of my resources to keep abreast of matters that either concern or interest me; that obviously includes you and the members of your organization. Moreover, I admit to being insightful, perhaps eerily so. However, I can assure you that I'm not psychic. Yes, I was sure the ring had special properties; but I didn't know exactly what they were. And, even if I did know, I wouldn't have told you. You needed to prove that you would use the ring's power responsibly; and I'm proud to say that you've done exactly that."

As the conversation progressed, there were fewer interruptions from the others. In the end, the conversation was solely between Paul and Sam. This gave the others the time to enjoy Sam's hospitality. Marcy and Clemente silently questioned Paul's earlier experience, because this time, the refreshments, which Sam Hayne offered, were quite good.

When the discussion ended, Sam and John took the entire party back to the park and gave them the grand tour. Hayne's Family Scream Park was quite impressive. It was clean and well maintained. The employees were helpful and friendly. The attractions were well conceived and produced; and Sam prided himself on his parks impeccable safety record. In short,

Hayne's was everything Zumboland was not. Sam even remarked during the tour that Zumbini gave amusement park operators a bad image.

Paul and his group sampled some of the attractions at the park and enjoyed some of the special events of the festival before returning home to River City late that evening.

Chapter Forty-Two

Saturday, Paul stayed in the apartment and rested. However, love was in the air at the Canterbury. Zack and Iris spent the day together as did Marcy and Brock. And, Clemente and Ashleigh finally went on their date to the Stratosphere Room. Paul was happy for his friends. Although he knew it was never for him to have a mate, he was glad to see his friends find happiness together.

Noodles jumped on Paul's lap and started licking his face.

"You don't have a date tonight too; do you, Noodles?"

The dog stopped licking Paul and looked him eye to eye with the most serious expression.

"Well, the weather is unseasonably warm today. How about I take you for a walk along the river? And, when we come home, I'll make us some Salisbury steak and macaroni and cheese; and then we can watch some old movie on television. Would you like that, boy?"

"Yes, I would love that, Paul."

Paul looked around the great room. There was nobody except him and the dog.

"Noodles, was that you?"

The dog simply barked. With John's help, Paul had discovered that the ring helped him communicate with others. But, could that possibly include communication with animals? Where else could that disembodied voice have come from?

Chapter Forty-Three

Sunday morning, Paul dressed, exercised, and had a brief devotion before leaving the apartment. He took the elevator down to the first floor; and from there, he made his way to the River City Diner. Even for a Sunday morning, the city seemed deserted; he had not seen a single soul. Save for the Hoppers, even the diner was empty. Paul ate his breakfast in silence and then made his way to St. Anthony's for mass.

He found Marcy, Brock, Jose Fernandez and the members of Los Guardianes fully occupying one pew. Paul took a seat in front of them. As the services started, Officer O'Connell took a seat next to Paul. After mass, Officer O'Connell followed him out of the church, pulled him aside and spoke in a whisper.

"I've been thinking…actually, Baldo and I have both been thinking…and having some serious conversations."

The police officer looked nervously around him.

"We don't like what we're hearing around the department. Zumbini has something planned for your Parade of Steeples event; and he's asked Chief Conley for help."

Paul allowed Officer O'Connell to speak without interruption.

"He's ordering us not to attend the event, not to even be in the area. When whatever he has planned happens, there won't be police to respond."

The policeman looked genuinely concerned.

"I just thought you should know, Paul."

"Thank you for warning me."

"This development has really shaken several of the guys in the department. It turns out that there are more guys, who are upset with Zumbini and his control over the chief, than I thought. They don't like being told to not do their job when the public safety is at risk. I guess what I'm saying is Baldo and I may want to join your group soon; and there are other guys in the department, who might join too. It all depends on what happens at your event."

"Officer…Kevin, you and the others are welcome to join whenever you feel comfortable; and we will appreciate the valuable contribution your membership would bring; but please, don't jeopardize your careers. You've already helped us so much."

The officer nodded his head and started to walk away; but Paul called him back.

"May I ask you two questions?"

"Sure."

"Approximately what percentage of officers has…the tattoo?"

"I don't know, probably a third."

Paul considered this.

"And does Chief Conley have it."

O'Connell could not bring himself to vocalize his answer; he merely nodded his head before walking away from Paul.

Marcy, Brock, Jose and Los Guardianes had already walked back to the Canterbury, so Paul walked to his truck in the parking garage and then drove to his grandparent's farm. When he exited the cab, Noodles was excited to see him; and Paul spent a few minutes sitting on the front porch step scratching the dog behind the ears. Eventually, he walked to the church to discover his regular pew was already full; and so was the pew in front of and behind that.

In his usual pew, there was Pop Gray, Tomás, Clemente, Ashleigh, Iris, Zack, Zeph and Officer Havens. In the pew in front, was ten Armstrong siblings. In the pew behind were Zared Armstrong and his family and Tiny Smith and his family, who were getting along quite well. The pew behind that contained Chaplain Warner, Pastor Tim, Edith Sheppard and Elizabeth and Jack Bancroft and members of Covenant Baptist, who Paul only barely recognized. Paul squeezed into the pew behind that.

After the music portion of the service, Pastor Tom approached the pulpit.

"Before I start this morning, I would like to make one very important announcement. We will be dedicating the Forrest Baptist Mission in River City this afternoon. Pastor Tim will be leading that mission and officiating the services this afternoon. Please pray for that mission; and if you can, support them with your attendance too."

With everything that had happened, Paul had totally forgotten about the completion of work on the Forrest Chapel and the dedication of the Forrest Baptist Mission. He made a quick note in his notebook to regularly attend services there too.

"We continue with the fourth part in my series of sermons entitled 'God's Formula for Success.' You'll remember that the first three points are 'View the Situation Correctly,' 'Issue a Proper Solution,' and 'Challenge the Critics.' This week we examine the fourth point, which is 'Take Only What Is Necessary.' We remain in the seventeenth chapter of the book of First Samuel.

"Here, we see Saul attempt to prepare David for his encounter with Goliath. Saul dresses David in his own armor, a helmet of brass and a coat of mail; and he gives him his own sword. The coat of mail was a metal breastplate covering only the wearer's chest and abdomen.

"The armor mentioned was probably a linen undershirt with a dual purpose. First, it protected the wearer's skin from direct contact with the metal shielding worn over it. The other reason was for identification; with their heads covered by helmets, this article of clothing, which would have been personally distinctive and visible on the arms and below the chain mail, allowed combatants to identify each other quickly on the battlefield.

"David quickly and wisely removes these articles, because he is not accustomed to them; however, there is another more symbolic reason why David returned these items, particularly the armor and the sword. By wearing Saul's armor and using his sword, he would have been fighting on Saul's behalf; and Saul would have received both the spoils and the credit. As we will see in verse fifty-four, David takes the spoils himself; and in First Samuel 18:6-7, the women give David credit over Saul.

> 6 And it came to pass as they came, when David was returned from the slaughter of the Philistine, that the women came out of all cities of Israel, singing and dancing, to meet king Saul, with tabrets with joy, and with instruments of musick.
> 7 And the women answered one another as they played, and said, Saul hath slain his thousands, and David his ten thousand.

"Free of the more traditional tools of war, David prepares himself with items, which he already had and was familiar: his shepherd staff and his sling. He also takes five smooth stones, items provided by God, from a nearby brook; and puts them in his shepherd's bag.

"While incredible, David's use of a sling against one large Philistine pales against other miraculous battles. Consider Judges 3:31: And after him was Shamgar the son of Anath, which slew of the Philistines six hundred men with an ox goad: and he also delivered Israel. Or, remember the famous fight, which is mentioned in Judges 15:15: And he [Samson] found a new jawbone of an ass, and put forth his hand, and took it, and slew a thousand men [Philistines] therewith. Shamgar defeated six hundred Philistines with an ox goad, which was possibly a plowshare; and Samson killed one thousand Philistines with the jawbone of an ass. Through Scripture, God worked through His faithful people and used seemingly insignificant items to accomplish great works.

"David was also well prepared spiritually. In the preceding chapter, I Samuel 16, God, through Samuel, anoints David as the next king of Israel. As such, he is equipped with the best armor of all—'the whole armour of God,' which the Apostle Paul describes in Ephesians 6:10-17.

10Finally, my breathern, be strong in the Lord, and in the power of his might.

11Put on the whole armour of God, that ye may be able to stand against the wiles of the devil.

12 For we wrestle not against flesh and blood, but against principalities, against powers, against the rulers of the darkness of this world, against spiritual wickedness in high places.

13 Wherefore take unto you the whole armour of God, that ye may be able to withstand in the evil day, and having done all, to stand.

14 Stand therefore, having your loins girt about with truth, and having on the breastplate of righteousness;

15 And your feet shod with the preparation of the gospel of peace;

16 Above all, taking the shield of faith, wherewith ye shall be able to quench all the fiery darts of the wicked.

17 And take the helmet of salvation, and the sword of the Spirit, which is the word of God;

Paul wondered about his ring and how that figured into the whole armor of God. He was prepared to fight Claude Zumbini, Gilbert Gillenwater, Carlos Rivera and the other members of L'Ombra without it; but how could his ring defeat such people anyway. If he did not shake hands with them, there was not much it could do. Or, was there? Still, Paul held his traits of generosity and compassion, his ability to communicate with others, his friends and his faith in God as more valuable tools than his ring; and he supposed that was more in keeping with the Scripture too.

After the sermon, Pastor Tom gave an invitation; and it was almost as memorable as the one three weeks ago had been, when Clemente joined the church. In all, twenty-two people came forward; sixteen of them alone were the Armstrong family. However, Chaplain Warner, Ashleigh, Tomás, Iris, Elizabeth and Jack joined too. But, it was not so many people joining that made it memorable, it was what happened next.

Clemente came forward and expressed his and Ashleigh's desire to dedicate their relationship to God; and they asked that the church pray for them. Before he had finished, Zack and Iris interrupted and expressed a similar sentiment. Paul could not withhold his tears of joy for his friends; he would not have wanted to even if he could.

After the service, Elizabeth and Jack Bancroft approached Paul.

"How is George doing, Elizabeth?"

"He's okay. Thank you for asking, Paul. We're so sorry that he went to Claude Zumbini. We hope he didn't cause you any problems."

"It's not your fault. As far as telling Zumbini our secrets, I try to operate in transparency."

"Well, after he was released, he immediately went right back to him. Jack and I think that he might be working for him now. We don't know for sure."

"Elizabeth, is there a possibility that George got a tattoo in the last few days?"

"It's funny you would mention that. He did get a tattoo of a winged demon on his right forearm a few days ago."

Elizabeth and Jack looked puzzled at Paul's insight; but Paul looked concerned.

"Would you mind keeping me informed of any other developments?"

"Not at all. Again, we're sorry for any grief he caused you."

Elizabeth and Jack left; but Officer Havens replaced them.

"Paul, I wanted to talk to you."

"Okay."

"O'Connell and I have been talking."

"I know; he caught me after mass at St. Anthony's earlier this morning."

"Oh."

This caught the officer off guard.

"Paul, I've been a police officer for thirty years; and I don't mind telling you that I'm scared. Something is about to happen; I can feel it; and that—"

Officer Havens caught himself before swearing inside a church.

"—clown is behind it all."

Paul placed a reassuring hand on the officer's shoulder.

"As I told Officer O'Connell, don't do anything that will jeopardize your careers. You've helped so much already. Keep us as informed as you can. Quietly gather any similarly minded officers that you may find and keep their spirits up. We'll all get through this together."

The police officer nodded and walked away and was replaced by Zack and Iris.

"Dude, I told you I'd bring the whole family."

"You certainly did, Zack. If this church keeps growing, we'll need to build a bigger one with a couple pews just for the Armstrong family."

Paul, Zack and Iris laughed. Tiny Smith interrupted by bear hugging Paul.

"You had us all a mite worried down here disappearin' off like you did."

"Well, it turns out that I'm a hard guy to kill."

"That's for darn sure!"

Paul grimaced that he may have said too much; but Tiny just laughed and led his family out of the church. Several other members, most Paul did not even recognize, echoed similar sentiments of concern for Paul, as they passed.

"Paul!"

Nan was running up to him.

"Oh, Paul, I'm so glad you're okay."

Nan hugged him for a very long time and never did quite let go until their usual group had walked back to Nan and Pop's house. Paul noticed that Marcy and the others were not there and that Noodles was still on the porch.

"I wonder where the others are."

"Paul, they're waiting for us at Forrest Chapel; after the dedication ceremony, we're having a large potluck dinner in the Sunset Room at the Canterbury."

"Oh. Okay."

For once, Paul was out of the loop; but that was actually a good thing. He discovered that the wheels he had set in motion continued to turn even when he himself was out of commission. That epiphany alone was heart-warming. He helped load several dishes from Nan's kitchen and then joined the caravan back to River City. After unloading the food in the Sunset Room and putting Noodles in the apartment, they all made their way to the Forrest Chapel, where it was already standing room only.

Except for the two officers and the Bancroft's, everyone from Paul's St. Anthony group and Covenant group was there, as well as every staff member at Foster Gray Holdings and every member of the Forrest Council on Faith. There were also a small group from each constituent church, some members from the public and a newspaper reporter.

This was the third religious service, which Paul had attended today. Breakfast had been a long time ago; and he was getting hungry. Thankfully, the dedication service was short. After the service, Paul learned where some of his other employees attended church, as various introductions were made. Greg Washington and his great aunt, Miss Christy, attended Twelfth Street Baptist Church where the Reverend Kiango Jackson was the pastor; Paul also met Shaniqua, who in addition to being a laundry attendant at the Imperial was Reverend Jackson's daughter.

Although their attendance had become lax, Matthew Bailey and the Edwards twins were all members at St. George's Episcopal Church where Reverend William Vickers was rector; and they had, without encouragement or insistence from Paul or anyone else, recently resumed active membership.

Anthony Limin and Adam Miller were members of Maranatha Community Church, where Brother Harvey Morris was the associate pastor; and Frank Rhinehardt was the pastor at St. Boniface Lutheran Church where Tony Olsen and Dakota Longshadow attended.

After the dedication service, everyone made their way back to the Sunset Room, where Nan supervised a late potluck dinner. It was perhaps the largest social gathering Paul had attended since arriving in River City; and it flowed seamlessly into the Sunday evening fellowship, which he had recently instituted.

Paul, Zack and their kitchen crew did not need to prepare any more food as there was already so much food left over from the potluck dinner. Alex Ragman and Tsunami arrived and set up their instruments. They eagerly located Clemente and re-assimilated him into their band. Since the dinner had been potluck, the musical theme was a grab bag of styles and genres too. Matthew Bailey drew a couple of pictures, one of Alex Ragman playing the keyboard and one of Miss Christy. He promised to frame these, last week's and all future pictures and hang them in the penthouse hallway.

Towards the end of the evening as some people were starting to leave, Pastor Aaron found Paul and asked to speak with him privately.

"Saturday night after services, I overheard a conversation I wasn't meant to hear."

Paul waited for him to continue.

"I think our senior pastor is in league with Claude Zumbini."

"What makes you say that?"

"I heard them in the pastor's office. They were talking about the Parade of Steeples. They're going to sabotage it."

"Did they say how?"

"I'm sorry; I didn't hear that part. Paul, I need to make a confession. Lucas sent me here to spy on you."

Pastor Aaron was looking for some reaction from Paul upon this revelation but found nothing.

"I was already hesitant about it; but during that first council meeting, when I heard what you were trying to do for this city; and after I met you, I couldn't bring myself to give him any information he could use. I'm not even sure I can be associated with him or that church anymore."

"Why don't you build your own church?"

"The thought had crossed my mind."

"Perhaps a purple church?"

Pastor Aaron's jaw dropped.

"You…you had the dream too?"

Paul nodded his head and then explained everything concerning his ring and Zumbini. Pastor Aaron was stunned.

"Have you seen a tattoo like that on Lucas?"

The question shocked Pastor Aaron back into reality.

"No; but I've never seen him in a state of undress. He's always wearing a long sleeve shirt and usually a suit coat."

"And you have no idea how they plan to sabotage the Parade of Steeples?"

"I really wish I knew; but I didn't hear that part of the conversation."

"If you were to guess."

"I know that Lucas has always been obsessed with St. George's; but I don't know why."

Paul considered all of the intelligence he had gathered today from Officers Havens and O'Connell from Elizabeth Bancroft and now from Pastor Aaron. Zumbini was obviously marshalling his forces and planning something big for the Parade of Steeples; but what was it; and how could he prepare for it if he did not know the exact nature of the threat.

Chapter Forty-Four

Monday morning's staff meeting at Foster Gray Holdings was running efficiently under Marcy's direction. Paul received a progress report from every department. Everything had run smoothly during his absence and continued to run smoothly since his return. Some businessmen may have been insulted that their company could operate without their presence; but Paul was actually delighted. There would come a day, when he would be gone not just for a few days but forever; and he wanted assurance that his legacy was in place.

If anything, the meeting was quite dull, nothing like some past staff meetings had been. After all of the other staff members had given their report, Clemente went to the war room door and summoned a person, who was not visible from Paul's vantage but who had been patiently waiting in Foster Gray Holding's bullpen near Clemente's office for this exact moment. A young man wheeled a cart into the room. Although the contents of the cart were covered, the aroma betrayed the presence of food; and it smelled wonderful.

"Guys, this is Panny Provenza; he's the future proprietor of Panny's Pizza Palace."

Panny was greeted by polite applause.

"Dude, that's a mouthful!"

Zack's comment drew a few giggles and an explanation from Iris.

"Actually, Zack, you've stumbled onto my marketing idea for him. For his slogan, I'm developing a tongue twister followed simply by 'That's a mouthful!'"

"Ooh, she's sexy and smart too!"

Zack and Iris' conversation was quickly becoming more about them and their newfound love for each other and less about Panny and his pizza. Without Paul's interference, Clemente regained order of the meeting and brought the discussion back on topic.

"Marketing campaigns only get customers in the door. If the food isn't any good, then the advertising has been for nothing. That's why I wanted to introduce you to the man and most importantly, his pizza. Panny, you're up."

Panny, who had been serving during Clemente's introduction, now described his food as everyone sampled it.

"I brought two pizzas for you to try. The first is my take on a supreme pizza. It starts with a traditional pizza crust, tomato sauce and shredded mozzarella cheese; and it's generously topped with pepperonis, sausage, mushrooms, onions, green peppers and black olives.

"I'll also offer several specialty pizzas; and I wanted to bring one of them for you today; and since it's morning, I decided to bring my take on a breakfast pizza, which is the second pizza on your plate. It starts with a non-traditional crust based on doughnut dough, a citrus maple sauce and cheddar cheese; and it's topped with shredded potatoes, sausage, and scrambled eggs. The ingredients are cooked separately and the entire dish is only heated long enough to melt the cheese and to bind the ingredients together."

"Dude, this breakfast pizza is amazing! I could eat it every morning."

Both Panny and Clemente were beaming with pride. Paul, who had been silent thus far, offered his opinion.

"I agree with Zack; this is excellent pizza; and I know I speak for everybody here, when I say that we look forward to working with you in the future, Panny."

"Thank you, sir."

Panny was still in the war room gathering plates, when Paul took the floor.

"I have listened to each of you give a progress report; and I want to tell you how pleased I am with your accomplishments in such a short time and how proud I am of each of you. You perform your services admirably even when I'm not here; and that is more than I could have ever expected. I only have two issues to discuss with you.

"First, Zack, are we ready for Gillenwater's return tomorrow?"

"Yes, all departments are ready."

"Great. And secondly, I have learned of a serious threat to the Parade of Steeples."

There were gasps and murmurs around the room.

"Obviously, Claude Zumbini and his people are behind it; but exactly where and how they'll strike is unknown. I'll entertain your best guesses."

Clemente, Brock, Ashleigh, and Zack all answered Paul's question in rapid succession.

"We're not sure whether Carlos is a voting member of Zumbini's organization yet; but I know if he can, he'll campaign for some type of assault on the Canterbury."

"I agree with Clemente; it has to be the Canterbury. Carlos is not the only one, who hates you, Paul, and equates you with the Canterbury, so does George Bancroft; and he's already threatened you twice."

"My vote is for the Canterbury too. The reception and contract signing in the lobby that evening serves as the big finale for the whole event. Plus, targeting the Canterbury would include the diner."

"When we can ole Fishface tomorrow, Zumbini might retaliate by adding the Imperial to his hit list; but it's probably not even on his radar right now."

"Paul, we must consider that the Parade of Steeples is a religious event. One of the churches is a far more likely target. Lucas is infatuated with St. George's for some reason; and you attend St. Anthony's. We should concentrate on those locations."

This final offering had come from Chaplain Warner. Paul nodded as each suggestion was given; and then he took a few minutes to formulate his strategy.

"Ashleigh, I'll call Reverend Vickers at St. George's; you call all of the other churches and warn them.

"Clemente, you call all of the other Order of the Lamp members and associates and any of our other friends like Sam Hayne, John Dorman and Dan Tuley and warn them too. We can't assume Zumbini will operate logically.

"Zack, I know it's a lot with everything else going on over there; but make sure the employees at the Imperial are disaster ready.

"Marcy and Brock, I concur that the Canterbury is the most likely target, so we need to prepare to live and work elsewhere if necessary. There is no reason to call every resident and scare them unnecessarily. Have all Order of the Lamp members, associates and friends, who live in the Canterbury, pack a couple bags, each containing clothes and any valuable or irreplaceable items. We'll place those bags on the box truck a couple days before the Parade of Steeples and drive it outside the city. If nothing happens, that's great; but if something does happen to the Canterbury, we can at least start living at one of my other properties, possibly the York, without having lost everything we own.

"Oh…and Marcy…any important papers from Foster Gray Holdings needs to be on that truck too. We may need to work temporarily from the York as well."

"Paul!"

It was Pedro, who hardly ever spoke during staff meetings.

"What if the target isn't a location but a person—you? I would like the guys to serve as your personal bodyguards. Two of us will stay with you at all times until the Parade of Steeples; and then during the Parade of Steeples, all eleven of us will guard you."

"Thank you, Pedro; I'm flattered; but I don't need a bodyguard."

This was met by vehement disagreements from everyone in the room.

"Okay, okay. I'll accept your kind offer, Pedro."

"I want to be one of the guards."

"Absolutely not! Clemente, if something were to happen to me, I would need you to lead this company; and I want Tomás down in Cricksburg looking after Pop and Nan."

The matter of bodyguards for Paul was settled with everyone's agreement, so Paul dismissed the meeting. As everyone was dispersing, Paul made one final announcement.

"We have a couple new employees starting tomorrow, so if things get a little crazy over at the Imperial and I forget, please make them feel welcome."

Everyone nodded while exiting the war room. When the last employee left, Paul called Reverend Vickers on his cell phone and explained the new threat to him.

"Reverend Vickers, what does Stanley Lucas have against St. George's?"

The elderly minister laughed to himself.

"I'm sorry; I shouldn't laugh, it's not funny; actually, it's quite tragic. Lucas was a member here many years ago. He wanted us to ordain him as a minister; but we wisely refused. He swore vengeance, left the church and formed Zoara."

"May I ask why you didn't ordain him?"

Reverend Vickers paused for a moment.

"We discovered he had a record…larceny, fraud, assault…most of it while he was a juvenile. However, one matter really concerned us; he's a serial arsonist."

"Stanley Lucas is a firebug?"

"Yes, and his targets were all churches."

Chapter Forty-Five

Despite his two-week vacation ending, Gilbert Gillenwater was in a wonderful mood; he was almost skipping through the Imperial's lobby to the elevator. His time in Puerto Rico had been pure bliss; and the possibility of a promotion, based on his management of the hotel to date, had only emboldened him to make further, more draconian changes to his administration of the hotel. He was so mesmerized by his delusions that he failed to notice that Becky, his secretary, did not greet him as he walked to his office door. He attempted to unlock the door; but his key did not work.

"Becky, why does my key not unlock the door? Call for a maintenance man immediately."

"You're to report to the board room."

Becky gave the instructions without even making eye contact with him.

"What? What is the meaning of this?"

Becky remained silent trying to concentrate on her work, so Gilbert stormed down the hall to the boardroom. Outside the boardroom, lined up in attention, were ten young Latinos dressed in dark suits and wearing dark sunglasses. As Gilbert Gillenwater approached, one of the men opened the boardroom door for him; and as he entered the room, they followed closely behind.

Paul Gray sat at the head of the long conference table facing the door. To his right, sat Clemente Morales and Greg Washington; to his left, sat Zack Armstrong and Matthew Bailey. Gilbert only recognized Paul, Zack and Greg.

"Why is my office door locked?"

"Sit down, Gilbert."

"You will address me as Mr. Gillenwater, you worthless little rat. I'm still your boss; and I demand your respect. Just wait until I call your grandfather in Puerto Rico."

Two of the young men forcibly pushed Gillenwater into the chair at the opposite end of the conference table.

"First, I will address you any way I see fit, because you are not my boss nor have you ever been. Secondly, you do not demand respect; you earn it; and you have done nothing to earn it. Thirdly, please feel free to call my grandfather in Puerto Rico; I'll even dial the number if you'd like."

"I don't understand."

"My grandfather purchased this hotel for me and operated it in my stead until a few weeks ago. During those five years, he and I gave you carte blanche to manage the hotel as you saw fit; but I wasn't totally disinterested, an employee continuously briefed me on your actions; and I must say that I am very disappointed in what I learned. By the way, these are her reports; I saved each one of them."

Paul placed a large stack of papers on the desk.

"Who was it? Was it Snow? When I get my hands on that worthless old n—"

"Gilbert, I would consider my choice of words very carefully, if I were you."

Gilbert silently slumped down in his chair.

"As I was saying before you rudely interrupted me, when I returned to River City to assume a more hands-on operation of this hotel, I wanted to witness your management style first hand before I took any action. So I wouldn't tip you off with my presence, I had my grandfather contact you about giving me a job; and I must say that how you treated me that first day was abhorrent."

"That's entrapment!"

"Excuse me; but did I give you some indication that I wanted your input."

"But—"

"Shut up!"

Paul's exclamation scared Gilbert Gillenwater back into a seated position. Although he was now silent, he glared at Paul indignantly.

"I started my own private investigation. I inspected the property. I interviewed employees. I examined the hotel's records. In short, I built a solid case against you; and it wasn't difficult either. When I first discovered you had been sexually assaulting female employees, I asked my grandfather to bring you to Puerto Rico, so I could finish my investigation without you on the property. So, feel free to call my grandfather, he'll tell you there is no promotion or raise in your future."

Gilbert's face was turning dark red with rage.

"In fact, effective immediately, you're services are no longer needed here."

Gilbert Gillenwater slammed his fists on the table, which cracked under the force.

"You can't do this to me."

"The Imperial Hotel is owned and operated by Foster Gray Holdings, Inc, of which I'm the founder, sole owner, Chairman of the Board and Chief Executive Officer. I dare say that I can do this to you if I want. However, if you wish I will consult with Clemente Morales here, who is the President and Chief Operating Officer or Zack Armstrong, who is the Executive Vice President of Hospitality Operations. Together, we form the chain of command above the general manager of the Imperial Hotel. Gentlemen, what say you?"

"Fire him."

Their response was eerily in unison.

"I'll sue you for termination without cause."

"Oh, you don't want to do that."

"And why not?"

"Because if you do that, then we will submit evidence, which will destroy your case. For example, we didn't just discover one female employee that you had sexually assaulted; we found dozens; and we have their affidavits right here."

Paul placed a small stack of papers on the desk.

"We gathered correspondence, where past guests had complained about their stay, and coupled that with written requests from department heads asking to resolve those problems, all of which you denied. This corroborates my recent inspection of the shoddy state of the hotel and recent financial reports showing a decline in hotel revenues."

Zack placed a large stack of letters on the desk.

"We examined employment records and discovered almost forty employees, who you terminated without cause, we have their affidavits here."

Clemente placed a small stack of papers on the desk.

"When we audited the books, we discovered how you have embezzled hundreds of thousands of dollars over the years."

Greg Washington held up a folder.

"So, Gilbert, I don't think filing a lawsuit is in your best interests, because your hands are filthy. Gentleman, take this garbage out of my hotel."

The ten members of Los Guardianes forcibly escorted Gilbert Gillenwater out of the boardroom, down to the first floor, through the lobby and out the hotel. Along the way, dozens of employees witnessed his unceremonious exit; and they applauded and cheered as he passed them. Paul, Clemente, Zack, Greg, and Matthew followed behind; Zack and Clemente were carrying two large boxes. Outside the hotel, Paul spoke again.

"Gilbert, we took the liberty of boxing your belongings."

Gillenwater charged at Paul but collided with Zack's fist instead, knocking him unconscious for a couple minutes. Zack massaged his right hand.

"Man! That felt good!"

Gilbert was now upright but mumbling incoherently.

"I'll tell Zumbini about this; and then you'll really be sorry."

Paul got face to face with Gilbert Gillenwater, close enough to feel and smell his hot, putrid breath.

"Never…ever…threaten me. Understand?"

The look in Paul's eyes terrified Gilbert more than Paul's words had. He fumbled with the boxes of possessions and hurried away. When he was out of sight, Paul turned to the others.

"Gather the employees in the Mayan Room."

Except for one person to staff the front desk, all of the employees of the Imperial Hotel were shepherded into the Mayan Room. Employees from Foster Gray Holdings had joined them. Paul entered the room to thunderous applause. He had always tried to remain humble; but he was having difficulty not basking in this moment. He made his way to the front of the room, shaking hands as he went, receiving pats on the back the entire way, and hearing constant cheers from the crowd. It took several minutes after he reached the front to quiet everyone down. There was a brief pause and Paul was able to speak one sentence before the applause re-erupted.

"The nightmare is finally over."

The noise was deafening; and several guests had come into the meeting room just to see what was happening.

"I'm not going to make a long speech. You have my guarantee. You have Clemente's guarantee. You have Zack's guarantee. You have everyone at Foster Gray Holding's guarantee that the work environment at the Imperial Hotel will be much better starting today."

The crowd attempted to reignite their cheers; but Paul extinguished it before it could restart.

"Relations between the Imperial Hotel and Foster Gray Holdings are no longer a covert matter. This hotel shall be the prize jewel in Foster Gray Holdings' crown as it should be. And here to lead you towards those better times, my good friend and the new general manager of the Imperial Hotel, Jay Butler."

A man, not much older than Paul, stepped to the front of the room, shook Paul's hand and then briefly addressed the assembly, although the din made it difficult to hear exactly what he said.

When the meeting was over, Zack and Jay returned to the general manager's office, Matthew returned to his law office, and Paul, Clemente, and Greg went to the diner for lunch. It was crowded, the most crowded Paul had ever seen it. They could not find an empty table; but they did find Marcy and Brock sitting in a large corner table with Foster Gray Holdings' newest employee, Robert Papier. There was just enough room for three extra people, so they scooted in.

Ashleigh approached, ready to take orders.

"I thought you were working for us today,"

"I was; but when we got here, they were slammed and shorthanded, so I grabbed my apron and order book and just jumped right in."

When Ashleigh left to take their orders to the kitchen, Paul asked the obvious question.

"Marcy, obviously I'm thrilled for Ed and Georgia; but do we know why the diner is so busy."

"Iris' marketing campaign started yesterday."

"Oh! Well, it's effective."

The six of them ate their lunch with little conversation, because the noise prohibited it; but once they were back in the quiet of Canterbury's lobby and heading to the office, the friendly banter resumed.

"Robert, how is your first day going?"

"Great, I love it here."

"And, Paul, he has some terrific ideas for networking all of our computers and phones. We'll even be connected to the Imperial."

"I was more interested in the surveillance cameras, which I discussed with you several weeks ago."

Marcy was still so excited that she again answered for Robert.

"That's the best part! The cameras are part of the network too."

"I look forward to seeing the final product. Oh, Robert…"

Paul made stern eye contact with Marcy, who blushed.

"…is everyone making you feel welcome?"

"Very much so."

"Including the guys from Los Guardianes?"

"After the staff meeting, Pedro apologized on behalf of the entire group. They want to take me out for dinner tonight and make me an honorary member of their group; and they even want me to live in the Northwest Suite with them."

Paul considered this. He had not given Pedro or the others any special instructions. They had done this on their own. Innocent moments like this let Paul know he was doing something right.

Chapter Forty-Six

Late Wednesday night, as Paul and Clemente were watching an old movie on television, Noodles hopped out of Clemente's lap, where he had spent most of the evening, and ran towards the door. First, he barked; but the barking soon turned into a growl and then a whimper. Paul muted the television and studied the dog's behavior.

"That's odd. He's never acted like that."

There was a knock at the door; and Noodles ran behind the couch.

Paul whispered to Clemente.

"I'm going to open the door and see who or what this is. Be prepared for anything."

Clemente nodded as the knock repeated itself only harder and longer. Paul cautiously opened the door to reveal an elderly man dressed in a business suit and a lab coat standing in the threshold.

"Can I help you?"

"Uh…yes…my name is Heinrich…Dr. Heinrich Vanderstein. I'm here regarding the dog you found."

"The poster gave a phone number to call not an address; and this is a very late hour to be knocking on strange doors."

"Well…I…uh…meant to call that number; but I didn't have a pen or paper with me at the time; and later, when I looked for one of the posters, they were gone, so I asked around; and someone told me to come here."

Paul had a very bad feeling about this man; and he did not believe a single word of the man's story. He quickly glanced towards Clemente. His facial expression betrayed his attitude towards the man and his story; and his balled fists betrayed his intentions if the situation escalated.

"I'm sorry that you came here for nothing; but after a few days, when we didn't hear from the rightful owner, we decided to keep him. Good night, sir."

Paul started to close the door; but the elderly man showed surprising strength and determination and braced the door open.

"So, the dog is here?"

Paul was having great difficulty restraining his anger.

"Clemente, bring Noodles here."

"Oh, you named him Noodles. That's cute."

"Yes, we did. What do you call him?"

"Uh…I call him…uh…"

Clemente could not coax Noodles to leave his hiding place behind the couch, so he picked the dog up and carried him towards the door.

"Yes, that's my dog; I'd recognize him anywhere."

Dr. Vanderstein held his hands out to take the dog; but Paul kept him from moving any closer. Noodles was trembling with fear in Clemente's arms.

"Clemente, how many of our friends has Noodles been around since he started living with us?"

"Dozens."

"I agree. And how many of them have produced this reaction from him."

"None. Noodles loves everybody."

"Again, I agree."

Paul placed a calming hand on Noodles head and established a psychic connection with the animal.

"Noodles, is Dr. Vanderstein your owner?"

"Yes, Paul, he was; but I ran away from him, because he hurts dogs."

"Do you want to go with him or stay here with us?"

"I want to stay here with you and Clemente. Please, don't let him take me."

Paul silently studied the man standing in his doorway.

"Dr. Vanderstein, I believe you, when you say that this is your dog."

"Paul, no!"

Paul held a hand up to silence Clemente.

"However, I think you've mistreated this dog in some way, because he's obviously terrified of you. We will be keeping the dog. Good night, Doctor."

Paul started to close the door again; and again, Vanderstein held it open.

"Be careful, Paul. He's dangerous and hurts people too."

"I'll call the police."

"And when they come, I'll report you for animal cruelty. Clemente, take Noodles in my office and close the door."

Clemente followed Paul's instructions.

"Dr. Vanderstein, I've exhausted my patience. I demand that you leave immediately and never return here."

Vanderstein attempted to say something else; but Paul did not give him the chance.

"I said, 'Leave.'"

"This isn't over."

Dr. Vanderstein stormed towards the elevator; and Paul closed and locked the door behind him.

"He's gone."

Clemente and Noodles slowly exited Paul's office; and they all sat down on the couch.

"Noodles, what did he do to you?"

Noodles did not respond immediately; but it was not a refusal to answer. It was as though he did not have the vocabulary to answer.

"He has a machine that makes things disappear and then reappear later."

"Did he ever use it on you?"

"Yes, many times."

"What would happen to you when he made you disappear? Where did you go?"

"I went nowhere."

"Where is his laboratory? At the university?"

"Yes."

Paul grabbed his notebook and a pen and made a quick sketch. Unaware of the psychic dialogue between Paul and Noodles, Clemente looked on in amazement.

CHAPTER FORTY-SIX

"Noodles, did you ever see this picture on the doctor's arm?"

Noodles studied the picture.

"Yes."

Paul broke his connection with the dog and considered this revelation.

"What is it, Paul?"

Paul hesitated.

"I've been communicating psychically with Noodles."

"I guessed that part. What did he say?"

"Dr. Vanderstein is a professor at WURC. He experimented on Noodles. And, most importantly, he has the tattoo. Noodles saw it."

"Did noodles say what the experiments were?"

"He tried; but he couldn't accurately describe what he didn't understand."

"What does it sound like?"

"It sounds like Dr. Vanderstein has invented a machine that disintegrates and reintegrates living tissue."

Chapter Forty-Seven

Later that night, Clemente woke Paul from a deep sleep.

"Wake up, Paul. Wake up; we have a problem."

Clemente was shaking Paul, who was still very groggy.

"A problem?"

"Ashleigh just called me. Ed Hopper is in the hospital; he's at Integrity."

This news managed to fully rouse Paul. He leapt out of bed and started dressing hastily.

"What happened?"

"At closing time, Carlos, Vicente, and Ignacio attacked him and stole the money from the till. He's in serious condition."

"What about Georgia? Is she okay?"

"She's shaken up but no injuries."

As Paul and Clemente exited the apartment and hurried to the parking garage, Clemente asked Paul a question.

"Are you going to use your ring…you know…to heal him."

"Just enough to ensure an eventual and full recovery but not enough to fully heal him or else the doctors will get suspicious; and I don't want everyone knowing what the ring can do; or I'd have a nonstop line at the door of people looking for a miracle cure. Plus, I'm not sure leaving the hospital is the safest thing for him right now. It appears Zumbini has started his attack on us a little early."

Chapter Forty-Eight

As it happened, the healing properties of Paul's ring were not needed; Ed's injuries were not as serious as originally thought; however, he remained in the hospital for observation; and Paul insisted that Georgia remain with him. With little sleep, Paul took it upon himself to operate the diner for the Hoppers with himself as cook. Clemente and Ashleigh, who were no more rested than Paul, had had similar notions and met him at the diner as Paul was opening.

"Paul, obviously, I've never worked in a restaurant like you guys; but I'm a quick learner."

"Thanks, Clemente."

Ashleigh called the employees, who were scheduled to work that day; and then she called all of the other employees.

"Paul, it looks like it's just the three of us. After they heard about the attack on Ed, they were too afraid to work here anymore...so they quit...every single one of them. It's probably what Zumbini was hoping would happen."

"Well, somehow we'll manage; won't we?"

Early morning traffic was heavy and steady but not too hectic.

"Dude, why didn't you call me?"

It was Zack. He had bolted into the diner and headed straight to the kitchen.

"Marcy just told us about Ed. I didn't stay for the rest of the staff meeting I came down here immediately. I didn't even wait for the elevator."

Zack's heavy breathing confirmed that fact. He looked visibly upset. Clemente came into the kitchen with an order; and Zack glared at him.

"I'm upset with you too, Clemente."

"Me? What did I do?"

"When you heard about Ed last night, you didn't call me; and when you opened the diner this morning, you still hadn't called me. I thought we were all in this together...you know...the three musketeers."

Zack started crying. He took Clemente in his left arm and Paul in his right; and he squeezed them hard.

"Don't you know that I think of you two as brothers?"

"Don't you have eleven brothers already?"

Clemente was trying to interject some humor into the situation.

"Well, that just shows how much you know, because I have thirteen."

He squeezed them again to punctuate his last sentence; and then he let go and wiped his eyes. He turned his back to them and fumbled with an apron; and when he turned back around, his eyes were red.

"No matter what it is, the next time something happens, you better call me. Now, let's do this."

Zack started helping Paul in the kitchen; and Clemente went back to waiting tables. Business was starting to pick up now. After the staff meeting, Marcy, Greg, Iris and Pedro entered the diner.

"Paul, I feel responsible for all of this. The diner wouldn't be this busy if I hadn't started that marketing campaign."

"Iris, this is not your fault; you didn't put Ed Hopper in the hospital; and

I told you to start the marketing campaign. It was supposed to generate business; and it did. None of us could have predicted this would happen."

"Well, I can't cook; and the klutz in me would probably break too many plates; but I feel that I need to help out in some way."

"You can. All of the employees quit except for Ashleigh; and when Ed and Georgia return on Monday, I don't want them to come back to a staff-less restaurant, so would you place an ad and hire some cooks, servers and busers as soon as possible?"

"I can do that."

"How can I help?"

"Greg, Ashleigh is the only person here, who knows how to operate that cash register; and we need her waiting tables. Would you mind being the cashier?"

"I'm on it."

Greg quickly inspected the cash register and then reported to Paul.

"Piece of cake! I've actually used this model, when I was back in college."

"What can I do?"

"Marcy, I need you to make sure everything else is running smoothly upstairs. Oh…and order a basket of flowers to Ed Hopper from Foster Gray Holdings."

"Okay, Paul, let me know if there is anything else I can do."

Paul nodded as Marcy went back to the office and Pedro stepped forward.

"Paul, is there anything the guys can do?"

"Just continue helping Zared at the churches as we planned, so we can be ready for the Parade of Steeples."

"I still think two of us should stay here with you. Marcy told us about the guy, who came to your apartment looking for Noodles last night. What if he comes back?"

"Pedro, the diner's busy; and Clemente and Zack are here with me if there's any trouble. Besides, I don't think Vanderstein or Zumbini will try anything for a few days now."

"Will you promise to call us if there's trouble?"

Zack raised his eyebrows at this question; and Paul noticed.

"I promise."

As Pedro left the diner, Zack took the opportunity to expand on his earlier comments.

"Dude, you don't have to fight this battle alone; you have an army that believes in you. You just have to lead us."

Paul said nothing; and Zack said nothing else about it. He simply placed a reassuring hand on Paul's shoulder.

Jay Butler was the next interruption in the diner's busy day.

"How can I help, Paul?"

"Jay, we need you back at the hotel."

"Okay, but I should tell you that news of what happened has already traveled through the hotel; and there are eight employees, who are insisting that they help in some way."

Paul noted the recent uptick in business.

"Tell them that before or after their shifts at the hotel, if they want to help, come on over."

"I'll tell them."

That was not the last offer of help. There were two others. One was from Panny Provenza; the other was from Zhang Wei with Forbidden City. Both men had heard the news about Ed Hopper; and both men wanted very much to help.

Every regular customer of the diner, every member of the Order of the Lamp and every employee of the Imperial as well as a large turnout from the general community ate either breakfast, lunch or dinner at the diner to show their support for the Hoppers; some ate more than just one meal. One of the regulars brought a huge "Get Well" card for everyone to sign; another regular started a donation jar, which soon filled with money.

At one point, they had run out of the ingredients necessary for pecan pie, so Paul created a new pie to replace it on the menu; the new item quickly became popular with the customers and was christened Forrest Pie.

Tuesday's presidential election had been a close race. At noon on Wednesday, the race was still too close to call; but today during lunch hour, they finally declared Senator Henderson the winner. The only quiet moment the diner experienced that day is when employees and customers gathered around the television to hear the results. Paul wondered if Brenda Henderson would approve of the diner's food, especially his newly created Forrest Pie.

Near closing time, as things were finally getting quiet, Marcy came into the diner.

"We just adjourned."

Paul looked confused.

"Adjourned what?"

"The meeting. Of the Order of the Lamp. It's Thursday night."

"With everything that's happened, I completely forgot."

Clemente overheard and interjected.

"Oh man, so did I!"

CHAPTER FORTY-EIGHT

"Don't worry. I knew you all had your hands full down here, so I chaired the meeting; and of course, everyone in attendance totally understood why you weren't there. In fact, that's all we talked about tonight. Everyone's scared and mad. We had eighteen people join."

"Eighteen?"

Marcy nodded tiredly.

"Who?"

"John Dorman…Dakota Longshadow…Tony Olsen…Peter Pipistrello… Sam Hayne…John Hayne…who else was there…uh…oh yeah…Pastor Rhinehardt…Jay Butler…Robert Papier…and the last nine members of Los Guardianes."

"You can just go ahead and add me to that list too."

It was Panny. As everyone in the diner turned to face him, he offered an explanation.

"You've already welcomed me so warmly and done so much for me and my future pizzeria; helping you fight this clown, is the least I can do."

Zhang Wei was nodding his head vigorously.

"Me too!"

Then he started saying something that only Paul was able to understand; and Paul responded back to him before translating for the others.

"He said, next time, Zumbini might hit Forbidden City or Panny's Pizza Palace."

"Dude, I didn't know you could speak Mandarin."

"That wasn't Mandarin, Zack; it was Cantonese…but I can speak Mandarin too."

Zack's raised eyebrows betrayed the fact that he was impressed with Paul's language skills.

Paul addressed Marcy with instructions.

"Well, it looks like you need to add two more names to the list."

Marcy nodded and made notes on her notepad.

"Did anything else happen?"

"We added three more names to known L'Ombra members: Chief Conley, George Bancroft and your Dr. Vanderstein. And, we added Stanley Lucas, Ignatio Torres and Vicente Flores as possible members."

Eight of them had just put in an eighteen-hour day. Paul and Zack worked in the kitchen. Ashleigh and Clemente waited tables as Wei bussed. Greg manned the register and answered the phone; and Panny worked wherever he was needed, sometimes on the floor and sometimes in the kitchen. Iris put a "Help Wanted" sign in the window and interviewed applicants; but also spoke with Tricia Robertson from WRCI, who had heard about what had happened to Ed and wanted to do a story on it.

As Jay had stated, there were food and beverage employees from the hotel, who wanted to help; and as their schedule at the hotel allowed, Jose, Lisa, Rutger, Kevin, and Zeph all waited tables; and Tim and Kenny both helped in the kitchen. Rick switched shifts with another bartender, so he could volunteer more of his time; and he stationed himself at the counter as the soda jerk.

As it happened, they needed all of these extra hands, because the diner remained unusually busy Thursday, Friday and Saturday; there was never a lull in the traffic. The sixteen of them kept up this frantic pace for three days; and on Sunday, despite the stated hours, they closed the diner and rested.

Chapter Forty-Nine

When Paul woke Sunday morning, he was exhausted and briefly entertained the notion to remain in bed all day. However, Paul knew he could never do that and still honestly claim the example that he wanted to set for the others, so he forced himself out of bed, exercised, showered, dressed and had a brief devotion before leaving the apartment for the first leg of his well-established Sunday routine.

Because the diner was temporarily closed, Paul walked across the street to the Imperial Hotel and Tradewinds located inside. Marcy, Brock and the others had had the same idea; and Paul joined their party. Everyone looked as tired as Paul felt, because everyone had worked very hard that week either at the diner to keep it open during Ed's convalescence, at Foster Gray Holdings to pick up the slack of the missing employees, or at the churches trying to finish repairs before the Parade of Steeples. It was exhaustion; but it was a satisfying exhaustion. As the group walked from the Imperial Hotel to St. Anthony's Catholic Church, they were joined by Jose, Officer O'Connell, and their newest member, Panny.

"Paul, have you heard anything about Ed?"

The question had come from Officer O'Connell upon their egression from the church.

"Ashleigh called them last night before we left the diner. He's doing much better; and he plans to return to the diner tomorrow."

"That's good to hear."

"I suppose Carlos and his boys won't be arrested for it."

The question, more a comment, was rhetorical; and Officer O'Connell answered it with derisive laughter.

"Are you kidding? There won't even be a slap on his wrist."

Still drowsy, Paul made his way to Covenant Baptist Church and took a seat near the others, who were no more alert than the group at St. Anthony's was. Paul noticed that some of them fell asleep during the sermon.

"We continue our study of 'God's Formula for Success;' and we remain in the seventeenth chapter of the book of First Samuel. You will remember that the first four ingredients in the formula are 'View the Situation Correctly,' 'Issue a Proper Solution,' 'Challenge the Critics,' and 'Take Only What Is Necessary.' This morning we examine the fifth point, which is 'Offer the Proper Credit and Glory.' However, before we begin, I would like us to stand in prayer."

The congregation slowly rose from their pews as Pastor Tom provided an explanation to this deviation in the service.

"As many of you have no doubt heard by now, there was an incident in River City at the River City Diner this week. As the restaurant was closing for the night, three thugs physically assaulted the owner, Ed Hopper, and stole the money in the cash register. This was not some random act of violence. No! It was a premeditated act of revenge against not only the diner but against Paul Gray and his organization.

"I called the Hoppers this morning before services; and Ed is doing much better since being released from the hospital. Let's pray not only for the Hoppers and their diner but for Paul and his employees that God's guiding hand be with them through this difficult time."

Pastor Tom led the church in a brief yet sincere prayer covering these petitions; and when he finished praying, the congregation returned to their seats as he started his sermon.

"President Truman once said 'It's amazing what you can accomplish if you do not care who gets the credit.' Sadly, he's right. All too often, some politician or powerful businessman receives all the credit for something they didn't even do. However, this is nothing new; it happened back in Bible times. In the seventeenth chapter of the book of First Samuel, we see where Goliath boasts of how he would defeat David; but David states how God would instead be triumphant through him. Goliath is not offering the proper credit; but David is.

"This vanity is not isolated to just Goliath or even to other biblical heavies. Samson himself was guilty of this as we see in Judges, chapter fifteen, verses fourteen through nineteen.

> *14 And when he came unto Lehi, the Philistines shouted against him: and the Spirit of the Lord came mightily upon him, and the cords that were upon his arms became as flax that was burnt with fire, and his bands loosed from off his hands.*
> *15 And he found a new jawbone of an ass, and put forth his hand, and took it, and slew a thousand men therewith.*
> *16 And Samson said, With the jawbone of an ass, heaps, upon heaps, with the jaw of an ass have I slain a thousand men.*
> *17 And it came to pass, when he had made an end of speaking, that he cast away the jawbone out of his hand, and called the place Ramathlehi.*
> *18 And he was sore athirst, and called on the Lord, and said, Thou hast given this great deliverance into the hand of thy servant: and now shall I die for thirst, and fall into the hand of the uncircumcised?*
> *19 But God clave an hollow place that was in the jaw, and there came water thereout; and when he had drunk, his spirit came again, and he revived: wherefore he called the name thereof Enhakkore, which is in Lehi unto this day.*

"God freed Samson from his bonds and empowered him to defeat the Philistines under the most unusual circumstances imaginable; but after it was over, Samson bragged about his own accomplishments. He bragged so much that he dried his mouth. It was only then that he realized God was responsible for the victory and would make provisions for him.

"No man is an island; and I ask you this morning. Are you sharing the credit for your accomplishments with those, who have made it possible? Are you giving God the credit and the glory for the successes?"

After services, Paul and his two beloved church groups merged in the same place and in the usual fashion. But, with tired bodies from a week of hard and honest work and with stomachs full from Nan's delicious Sunday banquet, there were more than a few, who fell asleep during the Hornets game.

With Pastor Tom's words still ringing in his ears, Paul quietly asked Clemente and Ashleigh to do a favor for him; and as they all traveled back to the Canterbury, Clemente and Ashleigh's car broke from the caravan to complete the special task, which Paul had assigned to them. Everyone else re-assembled with other friends in Paul's apartment and set up for their usual Sunday night fellowship. They were just starting, when Clemente and Ashleigh arrived; they had brought Ed and Georgia with them.

"Ed…Georgia…every Sunday night we assemble here to enjoy food, music, and each other's company. I know many times, the two of you are either working or resting; but tonight is very special; and we wanted you to join us."

Paul called Zack, Ashleigh, Clemente, Wei, Greg, Panny, Iris, Jose, Lisa, Rutger, Kevin, Zeph, Tim, Kenny and Rick to stand in front with him and the Hoppers. Then he described the last three days in detail.

"I don't want you to think that I operated the diner by myself in your absence. I had great help; and I wanted the privilege of introducing you to the people, who helped me keep the diner open. But you should know that others were willing to help and even volunteered."

Paul motioned towards Marcy, Jay and Pedro.

"In fact, everyone here either worked at the diner, volunteered to work, or ate several of their meals at the diner during those three days. It really has been a group effort."

Georgia had broken down and was crying.

"I'm sorry that all of your employees quit on you in your moment of need; but Iris has hired some new employees; and we'll all stay on for the next couple of days to train them and get them started for you."

Now, even Ed was starting to get a little misty-eyed.

"We're not sure exactly who; but one of your regular customers purchased a huge 'Get Well' card for you, which everyone has been signing."

Ashleigh presented the card; and the Hoppers admired it for several minutes. The card contained hundreds of signatures, some attached to personal messages.

"Another customer brought this large glass jar and placed it near the cash register to collect donations for you; we deposited its contents every night; but you should know it was full every day."

The group started applauding, which only coaxed more tears from Ed and Georgia.

"Finally, this is the part that fills my heart with pride. At some point, each of the other fifteen people, who worked at the diner with me during those three days, asked to speak with me privately. And, each of them, without suggestion from me, asked that I remit whatever wages they would have been paid plus whatever tips they collected during that time to that glass jar. Between what your regular customers collected, and what the volunteers received in tips, and what some local businessmen donated after hearing your story on the news, you received over eighty-four thousand dollars."

The crowd's applause re-erupted. This was more than Georgia could take; and she hugged Paul for several minutes all the time with tears streaming down her face. Then she made her way down the receiving line hugging each person as Ed followed behind her shaking everyone's hand.

When both Georgia and Ed had passed him, Paul thought to himself. Was it necessary to tell them that half of that money was from him, because he had decided privately to match whatever was collected? In the end, he decided to omit that point from the record. Paul did not need or want the credit or glory. That his employees and friends were following his example of kindness and generosity was enough reward.

Chapter Fifty

Although Sunday is a day of rest, Paul did not get much of it. Sure, he was not working; but he was not sleeping either; and his workload was catching up with him. He could not ask others for help, because his employees were now as busy as he was. Monday would provide no relief. Between demands on his time at Foster Gray Holdings, the Imperial Hotel, the River City Diner, and St. George's, Paul had no free minute to spare. He was even eating his meals on the run. Later that afternoon, he finally met with the Forrest Council on Faith for the first time since its inception; and he was spent.

He forced himself to participate though, to listen to the clergy's concerns, and to patiently answer their various questions. Many times Marcy or Clemente came to his rescue by addressing a particular issue; but Paul could see it in their faces; they were tired too! When all normal business had been conducted, Paul asked Bishop Prescott for the floor and approached the lectern.

"The last time I stood before this group, I presented a list of faith-related goals for myself and for the community. I'm proud to report that although I have yet to publicly sign the contract binding myself to those goals, I have already completed them.

"I founded this body, the Forrest Council on Faith. I hired Chaplain Harry Warner, who, as you know is Foster Gray Holding's Executive Chaplain and Faith Community Liaison. I built Forrest Chapel. Although it wasn't on the list of goals, I founded Forrest Baptist Mission, which is tenanted at the Forrest Chapel and led by Pastor Tim Alexopoulus.

"And when I say 'I,' I mean God, because God done these things through me; but I also mean my staff, because God has placed amazing people around me to help me accomplish these wonderful things."

As he remembered Sunday's sermon, Paul found Pastor Tom sitting in the audience; he was grinning.

"I have also upheld my personal goals of faith, to regularly attend church, which now includes services at two churches and a mission; to regularly engage in personal daily devotion, to which Marcy has held me accountable; to tithe to my own churches; and to volunteer my time and resources to area churches.

"There are two new employees whom I need to ask about their faith; but otherwise, I am proud to report that the entire staff at Foster Gray Holdings and all former members of Las Ratas are regularly attending church somewhere. In fact, I have learned that many of the employees at the Imperial Hotel, which is not even covered by my promise, also attend church regularly. And, may I add that besides Las Ratas, or Los Guardianes as we call them now, I never issued an order concerning church attendance. They were either attending already or followed my example."

This was met by generous applause from the assembled clergy.

"The only other goals left to accomplish are organizing the Parade of Steeples, which is slightly ahead of schedule, and signing the contract, which Marcy has already typed."

Again, there was applause. Bishop Prescott was not able to fully quell it, when he adjourned the meeting. Paul lingered long enough to briefly greet everyone who attended before retiring to his bed. He was asleep before his head hit the pillow.

Chapter Fifty-One

A full night's sleep went a long way towards renewing his physical energy; but it did nothing to quell his mounting anxiety. For everyone else's benefit, he tried to mask it; but those close to Paul, like Clemente and Zack, could sense it in him, because they shared his fears. How do you prepare for something, when you do not even know what that something is? The anticipation was far more damaging than the actual incident could ever be.

The days passed in a blur; and Paul ambled through his schedule like a mindless zombie. Sunday came; and he was not attentive during breakfast at the diner, Father Andrew's message at St. Anthony's and most of the service at Covenant Baptist. Only when Pastor Tom gave the last point in "God's Formula for Success," did he finally snap out of it.

"The last ingredient is 'Run to the Problem.' Turn to the book of Jonah, chapter one, verses one through three.

> *1 Now the word of the Lord came unto Jonah the son of Amittai, Saying,*
> *2 Arise, go to Nineveh, that great city, and cry against it; for their wickedness is come up before me.*
> *3 But Jonah rose up to flee unto Tarshish from the presence of the Lord, and went down to Joppa; and he found a ship going to Tarshish: so he paid the fare thereof, and went down into it, to go with them unto Tarshish from the presence of the Lord.*

"God had told him to go to and preach in Nineveh; and Jonah refused. Jonah, instead, went quickly in the opposite direction. True, David did not immediately fight Goliath; without some preparation, that would have been extremely foolish. He followed each step, which we have already discussed; but when he was ready to fight, he did not hesitate or turn away as Jonah did. In fact, the Bible says several times that he ran towards the problem. Are you running from your problems like Jonah; or are you running towards the possibilities like David?"

Pastor Tom's words were haunting him during the Sunday dinner at Pop's and Nan's house. While the others were watching the Hornets game on television, Paul asked Pastor Tom if he could speak with him outside. Clemente started to follow them; and Ashleigh tightened her grip on his hand and shook her head.

"Actually, Pastor Tom, could we talk in the church?"

"Sure."

The two men walked back to Covenant Baptist in silence. Pastor Tom unlocked the doors and turned on the lights. Paul entered the sanctuary and sat down in his usual pew. Pastor Tom followed behind and sat down next to him. And, for several minutes, the two men sat there in the quiet and empty church.

"I'm scared."

"That's understandable."

"I'm not running away though."

Pastor Tom realized his sermon had struck a tender spot.

"Those words were not aimed at you, Paul."

"The others are looking to me for courage; and I just don't have it."

"That's not what I'm hearing."

"What are you hearing?"

"Clemente and Zack have both told me that they have only managed to stay brave during this impending crisis, because they see your bravery. I'm sure the others feel the same way."

"But what about running to the problem?"

"You're already at the problem. You just need to wait."

"I don't want to wait; I want to fight Zumbini now and prevent…whatever he's planning…before he hurts someone."

"Let me ask you something. What is the worst thing that he could do?"

"I don't know. I suppose he could have Carlos burn down the Canterbury or St. Anthony's."

"And what would you do, if that happened."

"Get everyone to safety and then rebuild."

"There. You see. You've already solved the problem."

"I don't want anyone to suffer because of him, especially when I should be doing something to prevent it. Why should I allow him to cause suffering?"

Pastor Tom was quiet for several minutes.

"What would a doctor do, if a broken arm mended wrong?"

"He would re-break it so he could set it correctly."

"Yes, and what would a gardener do to a tree that had a dead branch?"

"He would prune it so a new branch could grow in its place."

"Yes, and why does a smith put metal in a fire?"

"To remove the impurities and make the metal stronger."

"I think you've answered your own question, Paul."

Chapter Fifty-Two

Paul's conversation with Pastor Tom had been helpful. It had quelled his doubts and fears, clarified his purpose and steeled his resolve. While neither he nor Pastor Tom ever divulged the content of the conversation, it was obvious to everyone that whatever had been said had been significant. In the days that followed, whenever someone felt stressed or anxious over what Zumbini might do, a few minutes of being around Paul would put them at ease. Paul had always had that effect on people anyway; but it was more profound now; and some, including Clemente wondered if the ring was somehow responsible.

Everyone, in their own way, had prepared for the Parade of Steeples, either for the event itself or in preparations for what Zumbini might be planning. Thursday night, less than thirty-six hours until the event was to start, everything was ready; and the Order of the Lamp meeting that night was consumed by the one topic, which was on everyone's mind. All Order members were present as well as many other people like Imperial Hotel employees and Canterbury residents, who were curious about the many rumors they had overheard. Paul addressed the assembly.

"First, let me thank everyone for their hard work, these last few weeks. Through your efforts, every church in the Forrest is ready for the Parade of Steeples on Saturday."

This was met with applause.

"And, the Canterbury is ready for the reception later that evening."

Again, there was applause.

"Next, let me thank those of you, who have assisted in the counter-preparations for whatever sabotage Zumbini has planned for us."

This time, there was applause; but it was much weaker and accompanied by nervous chatter throughout the crowd.

"However, not knowing his exact plans, we can never be totally prepared. Everyone here has moved their valuables and irreplaceables outside the city and prepared bug-out bags if necessary. Also, we have temporarily transported the business records for Foster Gray Holdings, Imperial Hotel and other local businesses to secure locations outside the city. That is all we can do; but one thing we will not do is run. Whatever happens, we stand our ground, because this is our city, not his."

This was met with wild applause.

"When it happens, take cover and protect yourselves as best you can. As soon as possible, rescue any injured, then report in so we can reassemble. Whatever Zumbini destroys, we'll rebuild it. Now, who's with me?"

The ovation from this final comment almost brought the roof down.

Chapter Fifty-Three

The day of the Parade of Steeples finally arrived. After Paul's usual morning regimen, he met Marcy, Clemente, Ashleigh, Zack, Iris and Brock at the diner for breakfast. The weather was cooperating; although it was quite cold, the sky was clear.

Paul made an effort to visit every house of worship on the parade route. Every church offered several things to do. Most of the churches held organ recitals or choral presentations throughout the day. All of the churches conducted guided tours of their buildings; and some had interesting religious art on display. There were activities for the children at each location; and the pastoral staff at each church was available to answer any questions about their services and ministries.

Event attendance was impressive, certainly more than Paul's staff and local clergy had projected; and most importantly, everyone seemed to be enjoying themselves. Several area restaurants were offering lunch specials and displaying "Welcome Paraders" signs in their windows.

When Paul had visited each church and eaten both lunch and an early dinner, he returned to the Canterbury to prepare for the reception. Despite all warnings and many fears, nothing had happened; and when the parade officially ended, there had not been one report of the slightest problem. From this, Paul surmised that the Canterbury or the Imperial was Zumbini's target and that the incident, whatever it was, was yet to occur; and he mentally prepared himself for such an emergency.

"How's everything here?"

"We're ready, Paul."

Marcy mimed a swipe of her forehead with an exaggerated sigh.

"Good! Any problems?"

"The water pressure in the building is very low for some reason; and I haven't seen anybody I know all day; but otherwise, everything is running smoothly."

Paul grimaced from a sudden realization.

"That's strange. Since breakfast, I haven't seen anybody I know either... well...except for the clergy at each church and you just now."

Paul tried calling Clemente, Zack and Pedro; but nobody was answering. Paul wondered if they simply could not hear their phones ringing or if there was something more sinister afoot. He chastised himself for jumping to conclusions and embracing such negativity on a day intended for joyous celebration. Canterbury's residents were arriving early for the reception so Paul started greeting them; but nagging suspicions about the fate of his friends kept gnawing at the back of his mind.

"Mr. Gray!"

A distinguished man in his thirties approached Paul with an outstretched hand.

"I've been looking forward to meeting you, since I learned that you were the new owner of the building. My name's Daniel Garfield; I'm a professor at WURC."

"Oh, really! What do you teach?"

"Foreign languages...Russian mostly...but Arabic and Mandarin occasionally. I'm a polyglot; and I understand that you are too."

"I speak a few languages."

"Come now, Mr. Gray. I understand that you speak over forty languages fluently...including Navaho. Is that true? How many languages do you speak?"

Paul thought that Daniel Garfield was probably a nice enough guy but that he was a language snob. Paul had known several just like him over the years. Language snobs were multilinguals, who looked down on those, who spoke only one language. They liked you based on how many languages you could speak, how relatively difficult those languages were, and how fluently you could speak them.

On the other end of the spectrum were people, who thought foreign languages were simply a party trick. These people would ask him to say something in Spanish or German and then laugh hysterically. For these reasons, Paul did not like discussing his language skills with many people. To him, knowing how to speak a foreign language was the means to communicate and by extension, to help more people. When pressed, Paul would admit to knowing only forty-two languages; and he would never fully list them; but he was actually fluent in almost two hundred languages.

He mumbled a response to the professor's question.

"I know several."

Professor Garfield was pleasantly annoyed.

"Well, I would be very interested in knowing which languages you speak and how proficient you are in each of them."

"Perhaps some other time, Professor."

As Paul freed himself from Daniel Garfield and mingled with some of the other guests, he wondered if the professor would be interested in knowing that he could speak to dogs too!

A dressy older lady introduced herself to Paul.

"Mr. Gray, I'm Darlene Kallen, the Calendar Girl for *The River City Register*. I cover special events in the city; and I also happen to be one of your tenants."

"It's very nice to meet you, Ms. Kallen. I hope you were able to enjoy the

Parade of Steeples today."

"I did; and I'll be submitting my story to the paper later tonight."

"All good I hope."

"All good; but next year, I want a heads up, so I can give it more coverage, possibly a whole series of articles. An event such as this deserves more exposure."

"You shall have it."

Paul and Darlene shared a laugh as Marcy interrupted their conversation.

"Paul, I've gathered most of the ministers, if you'd like to sign the contract now."

Paul nodded his head.

"You'll excuse me, Ms. Kallen."

He made his way to a table, which Marcy had prepared for the occasion. Bishop Prescott, Father Andrews, Reverend Vickers and several others were already standing behind the table. Paul made a few prefatory comments before signing the contract; and he was treated to gracious applause from the assembly afterwards. It bothered him a little that Clemente and his other friends were not present to witness this.

After the signing ceremony, Paul heard a cell phone ringing and noticed Reverend Vickers answering it. There was something unsettling in that brief moment after the rector answered his phone and before he related the news to Paul; time seemed to move in super slow motion.

"Paul, St. George's just exploded."

That was just the first one. Moments later, everyone's cell phone started ringing as reports from across the city poured in. Zumbini had not targeted just St. George's; he had targeted all of the churches. Paul realized what was about to happen in enough time to save everyone assembled.

"Get out of this building. Make your way west to the river bank."

Paul ushered everyone out of the building as quickly as possible and pulled the fire alarm. He stopped at the diner's door and banged on the door.

"Get out of the diner!"

"What should I do, Paul?"

It was Father Andrews.

"Is there anyone inside St. Anthony's or the monastery?"

Father Andrews shook his head.

"Then drive these people towards the river bank; and don't let anyone stop."

Paul ran inside the hotel, pulled the fire alarm and shouted at the desk clerk.

"Get everyone out of this hotel now."

Hotel guests and employees ran out of the hotel; and Paul directed them towards the riverbank. Officer O'Connell ran towards Paul; he was out of breath.

"I can't find my partner."

The young officer was almost in tears.

"I'm sure he's okay. Are firefighters on the way?"

"No, the department has blocked off Forrest Township…nothing in or out. Any firefighters or ambulances that try to cross the line are arrested by Conley's men. He's even keeping Kenton Energies out."

"But if they don't shut off the gas lines…"

"This whole area is going to explode. Yeah, I know."

Officer O'Connell and Paul continued to herd people out of the city and towards the river. They were crossing West Avenue as simultaneous explosions rocked the Canterbury, the Imperial Hotel, St. Anthony's, and Forrest Library. Paul was barely able to hear his cell phone ring; it was Tiny Smith; and his voice was filled with terror.

"Paul…there's been an explosion down here…Covenant Baptist is gone… your grandparent's house is gone."

"Tiny, are my grandparents okay?"

"The ambulance just took them to the hospital; but it's bad."

"What about Tomás?"

"I can't find him; and I can't find Noodles either."

Paul had taken Noodles and Marcy's cat, Smoke, to Pop and Nan's house earlier in the week in case something did happen at the Canterbury. Apparently, Paul had not moved them far enough out of harm's way.

"The Sheppard's?"

"Miss Edith is okay; but they're shorthanded down here at the hospital; and she's helping out. Pastor Tom's injured; but I don't think it's serious."

"Are you okay, Tiny?"

"A bomb went off behind my shop; it's totally gone. I'm bleeding real bad. Something hit me on the head; I'm not sure if I have a concussion or not."

"Get yourself to a hospital, Tiny. When I can, I'll get down there; but I'm not sure when that'll be."

"What happened, Paul?"

"Apparently Zumbini has blown up the entire Forrest. There are too many explosions right now to assess the damages."

Tiny was silent for a very long time.

　　　　　　　　　　　　　　　　　CHAPTER FIFTY-THREE

"There is one more thing, Paul. They're saying there was a huge explosion over in Scarsdale at Hayne's too."

"Thanks for telling me, Tiny. Take care of yourself."

In his preparations for this day, Paul had contacted the Brown family of Nashville, Tennessee, and asked them if they would assist with communication, transportation and relief efforts if there were a disaster. Paul had stayed with them for several weeks during his five-year road trip. He had grown particularly fond of them; and they with him. Paul called them now to put his contingency plan in effect.

"Hello."

"Lois, it's Paul."

"Oh, Paul! We're watching it on the news right now. Are you okay?"

"Yes; but I have dozens of my people missing; and several more are in the hospital. It looks like I'll need your help."

"Nobody's checked in yet; but we're already set up; and we'll start making the calls for you."

"Thanks, guys."

"Take care of yourself, Paul."

Paul hung up and dialed Clemente's number; but network congestion, due to the widespread disaster, had made any further phone calls impossible.

Down the street, there was a group of people, who were having difficulty navigating the fires, rubble and downed lines. Officer O'Connell ran to their assistance with Paul following close behind him. When they reached the group, Paul led them back through the obstacles to the relative safety of the riverbank as O'Connell brought up the rear.

The closer Paul got to the riverbank, the clearer the faces of the people already standing there became. The pall of smoke from all of the fires had highlighted their masks of frozen terror. They were looking at something behind him; and when Paul rejoined them and followed their gaze, he discovered that a large stone from St. Anthony's steeple had fallen on Officer Kevin O'Connell crushing him to death.

Paul did not have enough time to fully process this horrific scene, before he heard Marcy Green scream. She and Father Andrews were being dragged away by Ignatio Torres and Vicente Flores. Paul ran to help them; but Carlos Rivera accosted him.

The three of them were wrestling with their captors, when Father Andrews managed to take Paul's hand and sate him with fury; Paul's ring glowed brightly in the haze. Charged with an irresistible mission, Paul turned loose of Father Andrew's hand and grabbed Carlos' hand instead. The ring started glowing again; and as it glowed, Carlos' life force was painfully drained from him. Carlos was aging quickly; his hair was graying and thinning. For a robust man in his twenties, he now looked to be ninety years old.

If it had continued much longer, Carlos would have been dead; but Father Andrew's rage, which had so fueled Paul's action, was now dissipating; and Paul was regaining control. Repulsed by what he was made to do, Paul tried to reverse the damage but was only able to do so much. When he finally let go of Carlos' hand, Carlos looked like a forty-year-old man with snow-white hair.

"What did you do to me?"

Before Paul could answer, he was hit on the back of the head by Ignatio and lost consciousness. When he awoke, he learned from Marcy and Father Andrews that they had been taken to an empty warehouse on the far east side of the Forrest. There, a group of sinister men, including Claude Zumbini, had gathered.

"So...Paul Gray...we finally meet."

Paul did not answer him.

"I have brought you here to discuss a small business matter; but first, I have a scientific demonstration, which might interest you."

Zumbini motioned to someone outside of Paul's field of vision; and moments later, a man in a lab coat pushed a small cart into view. On the cart was a strange machine. The man was, Dr. Vanderstein, the same man, who came to Paul's apartment looking for Noodles.

"Mr. Gray, you remember me, yes?"

Paul nodded; and the scientist cackled.

"Mr. Zumbini, to show your guests the power of this machine, I will require a couple of volunteers."

Zumbini snapped his fingers; and two young Latinos were pushed into the middle of the room. It was Ignatio and Vicente; and they looked terrified.

"Mr. Gray, I have invented a machine that can disintegrate living matter, store it indefinitely and then reintegrate it again. Behold!"

The scientist aimed the machine at Ignatio and pressed a button. A beam of light engulfed Ignatio; and a second later, he was gone. Vanderstein repeated the process with Vicente; and he too disappeared.

"They are safe in here."

Vanderstein patted his machine.

"And they will remain in here, until I decide to reverse the process."

He pressed a button and Vicente reappeared; but he was naked. Realizing his immodesty, he ran to the far side of the room as Zumbini, Vanderstein and the others laughed at his expense.

"I'm afraid the machine is not able to reintegrate a clothed body. Clothing and possessions are collected in the trap."

"Enough science, Vanderstein. Use the machine on the girl."

"No!"

Paul and Marcy said it at once; but it was all that either of them could say or do. The machine was pointed at Marcy; and a second later, she was gone.

"Now that I have your attention, Mr. Gray, we can discuss business. I want you to sign over everything you own to me, all of your money, all of your property, including everything you were to inherit from Silas Foster."

"Is that all?"

"No, and then, I want you to voluntarily stand in front of Vanderstein's machine and let him disintegrate you."

"What's my incentive to do this?"

"If you don't, then Ms. Green and all of your other little friends become permanent residents of Vanderstein's machine."

Paul gasped.

"That's right! We've been collecting them all day, while you were celebrating your Parade of Steeples. Morales...all twelve Armstrong brothers...every single one of your employees...all of your little gang members...even a few employees from the Imperial. They're all in there. Sixty of them by last count, I believe. If you don't give me what I want, I'll leave them in there forever or better yet, I'll have them erased permanently."

Paul wanted to vomit.

"So if I give you everything I own and allow you to disintegrate me, then you'll restore all of my friends unharmed."

"Yes, yes, whatever."

"Don't say whatever. Either agree or don't agree. You wanted to discuss business, so discuss business."

"Okay! Fine! I'll restore your friends. All of them! Are you happy now?"

"Almost. We haven't discussed what you'll do if you should breach the contract."

"I assure you that you won't be in any condition to know whether I breach it or not."

Paul looked at him sternly.

"Oh, very well! What did you have in mind?"

"If you fail to immediately restore all of my friends or if you use that machine on Father Andrews or any of my other friends, you will have breached the contract. You will immediately restore me and return all my possessions."

"Fine. Now will you sign over your fortune?"

"Wait! I'm not done. You'll also give me any property you own in Forrest Township…one hundred million dollars…Vanderstein's machine…two people from your organization…and…"

Paul was purposely mounting the tension of the moment.

"…you must obey any and every command I give you."

Zumbini was overly confident and spoke before thinking.

"Sure. Whatever."

"Then put all of that in an addendum to the contract you've already prepared; and I'll sign it."

Although perturbed by Paul's many stipulations, Zumbini handwrote an addendum to Paul's specifications and then signed it.

"Now, sign before I lose my patience."

Paul signed the contract and felt his ring grow hot. He had no more than set the pen down on the table, when Vanderstein pointed his machine at him. A second later, Paul was gone.

Chapter Fifty-Four

Paul woke up on the beach. John Dorman was sitting next to him.

"I don't know how I got here this time."

"Did Zumbini use that machine on you?"

"Yeah."

"Having been here before, your mind automatically returned here when your body was disintegrated."

"How do you know about the machine?"

"He used it on me earlier."

"What happened to the others?"

"What do you mean?"

"I'm here; and you're here; but where are Clemente and the others."

"They're suspended Paul; they aren't anywhere. I'm here, because I'm a traveler. You're here, because your ring brought you back here. However, they have nowhere to go. While they're trapped in that machine, reality no longer exists and time no longer passes for them."

"Oh…well…I may not be here very long. I tricked Zumbini into signing a contract. I'm not sure if it was intuition or not; but I had this strong feeling that the ring, being a signet ring, was capable of enforcing contracts, whether I touched the other person's hand or not. I guess we'll soon find out."

They sat quietly on the beach watching the waves for what seemed like hours. Paul was not sure how many real world minutes had passed. His ring started growing hot; and then it started glowing.

"I think we just did."

Chapter Fifty-Five

Paul's ring glowed so brightly, it whited out everything. When the ring's glow subsided and his vision returned, Paul was standing naked in the warehouse. Father Andrews was gone. Claude Zumbini was holding a sheet of paper, which was on fire. He dropped it on the ground so it could finish burning; and when it was totally consumed, it reappeared unscorched in Paul's hand. It was the contract, which Zumbini and Paul had signed earlier that evening.

"What are you doing back here? I thought I got rid of you."

Paul was able to commune with his ring and to glean the details of events, which had transpired while he was disintegrated.

"You didn't restore my friends as we agreed; and you just disintegrated Father Andrews. Your flagrant breach of our contract allowed me to return."

"Hit him again."

Vanderstein pointed the machine at Paul and pressed the button; but this time, the beam engulfed the machine and its operator and Vanderstein disappeared.

"What is happening?"

"You should've been more careful when entering into a contract with me, Zumbini, because, like it or not, I have the means to bind you to your word. I'm taking immediate possession of that machine and its contents; and Monday morning, I'll expect you to surrender all of your Forrest Township real estate and remit one hundred million dollars in liquid assets to Fifth National Bank. Now, which two of your people will you be handing over to me."

"You already have Torres and Vanderstein; they're in the machine."

"They don't count. Ignatio Torres was already in the machine, when we signed the contract; and Dr. Vanderstein is in there, because he tried to fire on me. Name two others; or the machine will take you instead."

"Never!"

The machine started glowing; and in fear and desperation, Claude Zumbini called out two names.

"Flores and Lucas."

As soon as the names were mentioned, the machine, unattended, shot beams at both men; and they disappeared.

"Now, I'm going to give you some orders; and you're going to follow them. First, starting tomorrow, you will use your influence to have Forrest Township seceded from River City. If local politicians and businessmen view the Forrest with disdain, then they shouldn't be allowed to influence it at all.

"Secondly, you and all present and future members of L'Ombra are never to enter the Forrest ever again. You are never to interfere with life in the Forrest. You are never to have contact with my family, my employees, or any member of the Order of the Lamp."

"I won't do it."

"Oh, I certainly hope you don't, because I'll enjoy watching this machine disintegrate you and then storing you on my shelf out of harm's way forever. Now, get out of my Forrest. Do not use a car or any vehicle. You are to run as fast as you possibly can, until you're out of Forrest Township. If you stop or slow down, this machine will gobble you up."

Claude Zumbini refused to move until he saw the machine start glowing;

and then he and his men ran out of the warehouse as fast as they could; but he was screaming at Paul during his exit.

"Gray, you may have won this battle; but I'll find a way of making you suffer for this."

Paul was now alone in the warehouse. He examined the machine to deduce its controls. There was a digital counter, which read "70;" and there was what looked like a file directory. Almost every item in the directory bore the name of someone Paul knew. There were several buttons; one was marked "Disintegrate;" another was marked "Reverse." There was also a sliding pointer, which could move along the directory.

Paul moved the pointer to "Fergus Andrews;" mouthed a quick prayer while crossing himself; and hit the reverse button. The machine emitted a beam; and Father Andrew reappeared naked but otherwise unharmed.

"I'm sorry, Father. I'll figure out how to get our clothes back as soon as I've rescued everyone."

Paul worked the controls and reintegrated Clemente, Zack and Brock.

"Gentlemen, this is an empty warehouse without any partitions. Until I can figure out how to rematerialize our clothes, we will need to arrange our bodies to form a wall, behind which the ladies can hide themselves."

The five men stood shoulder to shoulder and closed their eyes as Zack brought back Marcy, Ashleigh, Iris and Vicky. As each reappeared, they followed Paul's instructions and hid themselves behind the curtain of men. Paul then started reintegrating his male friends; and as each of them reappeared, he instructed them to line up along the far wall with their backs to him.

The last name in the directory, which Paul recognized, was Tommy Citrino. It was bad enough that Zumbini and Vanderstein had used this foul machine on women; but to use it on children, Paul thought, was especially caddish. Paul reintegrated Tommy and directed him to stand along the far wall with the other males.

The counter now read "11."

"I have no intentions of restoring these four; and I don't recognize the other seven. Nothing in the directory mentions clothing."

Father Andrews provided a helpful suggestion.

"Paul, as you've been operating the machine, I've been watching that directory; and it seems that the names are listed in reverse chronological order. The names towards the bottom have probably been there the longest. Perhaps, you should restore the oldest one first."

Paul had no other strategy on which to act, so he quietly nodded at the priest's proposal. The last entry on the directory read "Caleb;" there was no surname. Paul slid the selector and pressed the reverse button. A golden retriever appeared; and Paul realized that Noodles was not the only test subject Vanderstein had used. He wondered if these other names were his human tests. The dog, now free from his virtual prison, happily joined the group of men along the far wall.

Again, Paul selected the oldest entry in the directory; it read "Dayton Dewberry." Paul pressed the reverse button and a distinguished middle-aged man appeared. He looked startled at his surroundings, the immodest state of the people looking at him, and his own immodest state.

"What's the date?"

Paul answered him.

"It's Saturday, November 22, 2008."

"I've been trapped in that machine over eleven years."

"Who put you in there? Vanderstein?"

The man nodded before providing a detailed explanation.

"Vanderstein and I were research partners; we co-invented the disintegration machine. While I wanted to run more tests and establish a strict code of ethics regarding the machine's use, he wanted to use the machine immediately to exact revenge on his enemies and to extort money.

During our last argument, he used the machine on me."

Dr. Dewberry noticed the golden retriever, which was now standing near Zack Armstrong.

"I see you've already restored Caleb; he was one our earliest test subjects."

"Pardon me, Doctor; but do you recognize these five names?"

Dewberry looked at the screen where Paul was pointing.

"Yes, they're the other members of our research team. He must have used the machine on them after disintegrating me."

Paul restored the five scientists. As they reappeared, he instructed the female to stand behind him, while directing the four men towards the wall.

"Dr. Dewberry, do you know how to use this machine to bring our clothes back? It's getting really cold in here."

Dewberry brushed in front of Paul.

"There are still four people in there."

"Can we simply leave them in there? They're partly responsible for the predicament we're in."

"Not and empty the clothing buffer."

After giving special instructions to the members of Los Guardianes, Paul directed Vanderstein's former research partner to proceed. One at a time, Dewberry restored Stanley Lucas, Vicente Flores, Heinrich Vanderstein and Ignatio Torres; and as each man reappeared, he was tackled to the floor and restrained by three young Latinos. Next, Dewberry adjusted the controls on the machine; and a large pile of clothes materialized in the middle of the floor.

"This is not *Lord of the Flies*; and we will not act like savages. We men will turn our backs and allow the ladies to locate their clothes and get dressed first, and then they will sort the remaining clothes to make it quicker and easier for the rest of us."

"Why do they get to go first?"

"One, because I said so, and two, because it's chivalrous. It may be a quaint virtue; but I'm trying to resurrect it."

The five women quickly recovered their belongings and got dressed; and then as Paul had requested they sorted the men's clothes into piles.

"Okay, Paul, we're decent; and your clothes are sorted. You can turn around now."

"Thank you, Marcy."

Dr. Vanderstein managed to wrestle free and run towards the clothes. He grabbed his lab coat and ran out of the warehouse before anyone could catch him. Stanley Lucas, Vicente Flores, and Ignacio Torres attempted to follow suit; however, they were quickly apprehended.

"As I said, we will not act like savages nor cower like sissies; we will form an orderly line and wait our turn."

"But we're naked and there are women staring at us. Tell them to avert their eyes."

"Lucas, you are not ashamed, because you're unclothed and in the presence of the opposite sex; you're ashamed, and rightfully so, because that tattoo on your forearm is finally visible; and everyone here sees you for what you really are. And, you call yourself a pastor! You're no man of God; you're not even a man."

Paul had called out their sin; and Lucas, Flores, and Torres writhed their bodies in such a way as to cover their modesty and their tattoos all while inching towards the piles of clothes.

"We don't have time for this nonsense; we have more pressing matters, so I'm going to put the three of you back in this machine. I'll decide what to do with you later; but don't expect to return anytime soon, because my vote will be to leave you in there forever."

"No!"

They voiced their protests and attempted to escape; but Paul quickly aimed the machine in their direction and pressed the button three times in rapid succession. The three L'Ombra members disintegrated back into Vanderstein's machine.

"Now, let's try this one more time."

Paul emphasized the words, which he was repeating, some for the second time.

"We will not act like savages nor cower like sissies. We will form an orderly line and wait our turns in a civilized fashion. Does everyone understand?"

There were silent nods from the assembled men.

"Good! The boy goes first."

As Tommy Citrino gathered his clothes from the piles, Paul arranged the rest of the men in a line allowing the clergy and older men to go through the line first. Although each man felt a tinge of embarrassment about being on such grand display in front of the ladies as they were, they withheld any complaints and toughed it out. Paul waited for everyone else before finally getting dressed himself; and once attired, he found his cell phone and called Lois Brown.

"Oh, Paul, I'm so glad you finally called. When you didn't answer, I thought something may have happened to you."

"Something did happen; but I'm okay now. Were you able to determine at which of my properties we can re-assemble?"

"I'm sorry, Paul. According to the news, at least ninety-five percent of the buildings in Forrest Township are either on fire or in ruins. Your only remaining apartment building is the Peel in Cricksburg."

"The Peel? Well, it's unfurnished and not in the best condition; but at least it's empty and available, so it will have to do."

"I haven't been able to reach most of your people. I hope their okay."

"I just rescued sixty-three of them; but I left another huge group including local clergy, Canterbury residents, and guests and employees of the Imperial Hotel on the southwest side of the city."

"Before you called, I was talking to Reverend Vickers; he's in that group They're slowly making their way east along South Street towards the Audubon Memorial Bridge. Fires have cut off any other means of escape."

"Good! We're not far from the bridge here; and we'll head that way. Call Reverend Vickers back and tell him that we're all okay and that we'll rendezvous with them on the West Kentucky side of the bridge. Can you send some buses to pick us all up?"

"Four school buses are already there waiting for you."

"Lois, you're an angel. If you have a way of contacting the drivers, let them know that there are seventy in my group, who are very anxious for a ride. Oh yeah, before I hang up, would you call Beverly Citrino and tell her that her son, Tommy, is safe and with me? She'll want to meet us at the Peel to pick him up."

Paul had just given her the number of Beverly Citrino's cell phone when Pastor Aaron interrupted him.

"Ask her if Integrity was hit."

"Lois, what's the status on Integrity Medical?"

"The news said that it was destroyed but that the patients had already been evacuated. If they were not in critical condition, they were transferred to Cricksville."

"It's probably chaos down there by now; but could you see if Dougie Bishop was transferred there, if he's okay, and if his family is with him."

"I'll do my best."

Paul hung up with Lois and addressed Pastor Aaron.

"They've evacuated Integrity's patients to Cricksburg, so you're coming with us."

Chapter Fifty-Six

Everyone was now converging on the Peel in Cricksburg not far from Pop and Nan's farm. For guests of the Imperial Hotel and some displaced area residents of both Wabash and West Kentucky, it was a way station on their long way back home. For employees of Foster Gray Holdings and the Imperial Hotel, residents of the Canterbury, many area ministers, and several others, it was now their home for the near future. Everyone that Paul knew in the River City metropolitan area now lived under one very large roof.

The Browns had brought an entire warehouse of supplies in addition to the bags, which everybody had packed earlier in the week. Stations were set up to deal with people's needs: medical, communication, transportation. For those staying at the Peel, room assignments were made. People were doubling, tripling and quadrupling up to maximize the Peel's space; Paul, Clemente, Zack, Brock, and Caleb all shared one room.

Chapter Fifty-Seven

In lieu of the worship services, which were normally held at buildings that no longer existed, Bishop Prescott led an inter-denominational memorial service. There was religious and inspirational music. Area ministers representing several faiths and dozens of denominations gave prayers; some of the prayers were in other languages. The keynote speaker of the day was of course, Paul.

"Yesterday…Forrest Township…Cricksburg…and Scarsdale were viciously attacked by Claude Zumbini with the acquiescence of local politicians and law enforcement. Ninety-five percent of Forrest Township now lies in ruins. Hundreds of thousands of Riverites have been affected, whether homeless or unemployed or both. Thousands, including my grandparents, have been injured, some critically so. Dozens are still missing. Sadly, twenty-nine people died in this senseless tragedy, including Officer Kevin O'Connell, who gave his life to save others. Nevertheless, in the wake of this heartbreak, there is much for us to be thankful; the death toll could have been much, much higher. Zumbini certainly intended it to be so.

"Forty-five days ago, I came to River City to repair the damage my evil great grandfather caused. That objective has not changed; but the scope is now much larger. I will rebuild the Canterbury, the Imperial Hotel and every other building in the Forrest, until it's not just the city it once was but exceedingly better in every measurable way.

"The accommodations may not be regal at the Peel; and for a while the food might not be first class; but I won't let any of us go homeless or hungry. If you worked at Foster Gray Holdings, the Imperial or one of my other companies, you still have a job; but for a while, that job may be one drastically different from what you originally had. With your help and patience, I will get us, all of us, through this. Thank you."

The crowd cheered wildly, as Paul stepped away from the podium; he was replaced by Bishop Prescott.

"I regret to report that St. Anthony's Catholic Church will not be rebuilt."

There were gasps throughout the audience.

"Instead, St. Anthony's Cathedral will be erected in its place."

The bishop had emphasized the future church's status; and the cheers resumed.

"St. John's Abbey will be rebuilt; as will the convent. I want everyone here to know that not only do I personally support Paul Gray and his efforts to rebuild the Forrest; but he has the full support of the diocese too. We will take this unique opportunity to enlarge our presence in Forrest Township and not retreat from it as some may have hoped we would."

Bishop Prescott quelled the crowd's enthusiasm long enough to offer a brief closing prayer and benediction.

The time immediately after the memorial service was a jumble of hellos and goodbyes and necessary promotions. Marcy Green resigned, explaining that the job was far more than she had bargained for and that she couldn't cope with magic rings that toyed with her feelings, or psychotic clowns, who were bent on causing her harm, or bizarre contraptions that disintegrated her body only to reintegrate it naked and in front of a group of men. She did not allow Paul to offer a counterargument or say anything; she simply collected her few remaining belongings and stormed away.

Noodles returned. He was scared and hungry; and after eating, it was several hours before he would leave either Paul's or Clemente's side; but he was okay; and after a few minutes of interacting with Caleb, who Zack had unofficially adopted, he was back to his old self again, mindless of his recent trauma.

Shortly before the Parade of Steeples, Paul had discovered that Dakota

Longshadow was a trained and gifted architect, so Paul offered him a promotion to Chief Architect, explaining that the Forrest was now an empty canvas waiting for someone to build something on it. Dakota happily accepted the job.

Paul also hired Baldo Havens as Director of Security. After the loss of his partner, Baldo simply did not have the will to return to the RCPD especially after the Chief's cooperation in the disaster. He vowed that security at Foster Gray Holdings, the Imperial Hotel and throughout the Forrest would be much different under his watch.

That evening, Paul spent some time looking at his father's scrapbook, which was among the items recovered from the rubble of what was once Pop's and Nan's house. Paul wished very much that his dad were still alive, so he could offer Paul badly needed guidance.

During this time of reflection, three ministers visited him. The first was Reverend Vickers, who informed Paul that the diocese had decided to rebuild St. George's. They found the increased church attendance leading up to the Parade of Steeples as well as the community interest generated by the Parade itself as justification for the time and resources necessary for the church's reconstruction. The second was Pastor Bishop, who informed him that he had resigned from Zoara that morning and would be founding a new church in Nilesville. The third clergyman to visit Paul was Father Andrews.

"I've come to make a confession."

"Isn't it supposed to be the other way around?"

Paul tried to laugh to lighten the mood.

"I'm serious. I've sinned; and I've come to ask forgiveness."

Paul stopped looking at his father's scrapbook and gave the priest his full attention.

"I used you to hurt Carlos Rivera."

Although Paul knew very well to what Father Andrews was referring, in the interest of secrecy, he played dumb.

"Oh, drop the act, Paul; I know all about the ring."

"Since when?"

"Since the first meeting of the Forrest Council of Faith, when I saw it glow. In addition, Marcy came to me after the near sexual encounter the two of you had. She was more than a little upset about that by the way."

Paul shrugged his shoulders in resignation.

"Obviously, you've discovered that the ring has powers and even what some of those powers are; but I doubt that you know the history of the ring. I thought I could share my knowledge of it with you as a part of my penance. But first, allow me to make one final confirmation. Does the ring have an inscription inside?"

Paul removed the ring and checked for an inscription. He nodded his head.

"Does it read 'Servite Domino in laetitia?'"

Again, Paul nodded his head.

"You understand it?"

"Of course. It's Latin for 'Serve the Lord with gladness.' From Psalms 100:2 I believe."

"Very good."

Father Andrews cleared his throat as if to prepare for a lecture.

"One gold signet ring depicting a bee volant inscribed inside a regular hexagonal cell on the seal. Interior inscription reads, 'Servite Domino in laetitia.'"

Father Andrews paused for dramatic effect.

"Paul Gray, you possess one of the ten greatest relics of Christendom: The Melissa Ring of St. Ambrose. It was given to him by Theodosius the Great."

"Is that the reason for the bee?"

"Yes, even during his lifetime, Ambrose was closely associated with beekeepers and candle makers? And it is also the origin of the name; as you probably know, Melissa is the Greek word for 'bee.'"

Paul nodded his head in agreement.

"This is very interesting; please continue, Father."

"After his death, Ambrose's many rings were scattered. One was buried with him. One was melted down to fashion a ring for his successor, Simplician. One was given to Pope Siricius another to Emperor Honorius. But one, the Melissa Ring, was simply lost to time; most religious authorities don't believe it ever existed."

"Why does it have special powers?"

"Theodosius and Ambrose were responsible for supplanting paganism with Christianity; and the ring was a token of the emperor's appreciation to Ambrose for his help in that cause. The gold used to forge it came from pagan temples that had been recently pillaged, so legend says, the gold, which was magically charged during its use in pagan service, merely adapted its powers to the personality of its next and most famous wearer."

"I don't see how."

Paul then started ticking off the rings attributes as Father Andrews provided explanations for them.

"The ring allows me to communicate with others."

"Ambrose was a polyglot and a gifted orator."

"Including dogs?"

"Ambrose is the patron saint of domestic animals."

"The ring protects me from injury and disease."

"Ambrose lived a long life for a man of his time; he miraculously escaped death on numerous occasions; and his corpse to this day seems not to decay at the usual rate."

"The ring protects my wealth from depletion."

"Ambrose was quite wealthy before becoming bishop and famous for donating huge amounts of money to the poor; yet his coffers were never empty."

"Most importantly, it allows me to give someone anything they want."

"Throughout his reign, the people, who lived in his diocese, would line up to ask for his help with all manner of things; and he would help them as best he could. On numerous occasions, Ambrose was asked by Theodosius to negotiate treaties with bordering armies; many of those treaties were lopsided in favor of the Roman Empire. Paul, I think it is worth noting that Ambrose, like you, was also celibate and reluctant to accept ordination. In fact, your lives are eerily similar in so many ways."

There was a long silence before Father Andrews spoke again.

"I'm sorry that I filled you with my hate and nearly forced you to kill him, Paul. I was just so mad that he had destroyed St. Anthony's, a church I love so much."

"If the truth were told, Father, I was plenty angry with him too, which made it difficult not to act on your desire; but fortunately, I didn't kill him. I would like to think that a higher power is responsible for that."

A period of silence followed during which Paul was formulating a plan.

"Father Andrews, I think I know a way that we can both do penance for this…that is…if you're interested."

Father Andrews raised his eyebrows.

Chapter Fifty-Eight

Early Thanksgiving morning, the Brown family of Nashville, Tennessee, had a huge surprise for the temporary residents of the Peel. Twenty buses were lined up outside to take them to a Thanksgiving dinner at a large hotel banquet hall in Nashville.

However, that was not the only surprise. Paul's entire family from Puerto Rico was there too, as well as scores of people from around the country, who Paul had befriended during his five-year road trip. In fact, there were only a few people from Paul's life, who were not there. Although large, the banquet hall was packed full of family and friends.

"Paul, after everything that's happened recently, we just wanted to remind you of how many blessings you still have in your life."

"Thank you, Lois. Yes, I have much to be thankful for."

Paul's eyes were wet. As peculiar as it was, this was possibly the best Thanksgiving he ever had.

Chapter Fifty-Nine

Nine days after the tragedy, there was a special meeting at a hotel in Cricksburg. Paul and Clemente had been specially invited to attend by Brendan Kenton of Kenton Energies, who also chaired the meeting.

"Mr. Gray...Mr. Morales...I've called this meeting of interested parties to discuss the rebirth of Forrest Township. As you know, there was a press conference on Friday. The governor, the commissioner, the mayor, along with Claude Zumbini and prominent area businesspersons declared Forrest Township an unincorporated city. Although it is still in the state of Wabash, it is no longer a part of River City or Adams County.

"Furthermore, Governor Strickland has ordered all state services removed from the township; and he's seeking assistance from Washington in removing all federal services too. We still have to pay taxes obviously; but with the exception of the post office and the two interstates, which already run through the township, we will be without any government assistance in our reconstruction efforts or afterwards. I, as well as many here, am confident that they are doing this to break our spirit, so we will beg them to return even if it means living under an authoritative and increasingly draconian bureaucracy."

Paul did not bother to correct him. This had actually been a stipulation of his contract with Zumbini; but he did agree with the sentiment behind Kenton's words; and he agreed that Zumbini and the local government leaders, who lived in his pocket, were hoping this political exercise in autonomy would backfire gloriously as to assuage any future murmurings against the state or local government.

"Mr. Gray, I understand that you returned to River City to repair damage caused by your great grandfather; but I ask if you're willing to not simply rebuild your company but the entire township as well, because we would like you to lead us in that endeavor."

The assembly contained many businesspeople, representing both big business and small business. They hailed not just from the Forrest either, but from Riverside, the Nilesville neighborhood directly across the Wabash River from the Forrest; Stembridge, the unincorporated Cricksburg community directly across the Ohio River, where Grays Farm, the Keel and Tiny's Army and Navy Surplus Store were all located; and of course, Scarsdale, where Sam Hayne held court. Paul could see that Dan Tuley, Wayne Carter, Tiny Smith, and even Sam Hayne were all present.

In addition to business leaders, every member of the Forrest Council on Faith was in attendance as well as the chancellors of WURC and River City College and the hospital administrator from Integrity Medical. Paul correctly estimated that the people in the room either owned or administrated nearly all of the land and commerce in the Forrest and the three other communities.

"At this time, I would like to apologize for Kenton Energies' unwilling contribution to the disaster; by not being able to shut off the gas lines, deliberately set fires and explosions were allowed to escalate into a full-scale urban conflagration that decimated the area.

"Chard Paulsen, who was not able to attend this meeting, has asked me to extend his apologies as well."

Chard Paulsen was an eccentric and reclusive billionaire, who owned several businesses in the River City area including WRCI, *The River City Register*, and Margins bookstore among several others. It was unusual for him to concern himself with community matters such as this.

"Mr. Paulsen regrets that his newspaper and television station were manipulated by Zumbini and local leaders to spin news coverage of the disaster to their political and commercial benefit. Both he and I would like to join you in your efforts to rebuild Forrest Township and later to relocate our corporate headquarters and our primary operations to the Forrest."

This was met with applause.

"So, Mr. Gray, will you lead us?"

Paul nodded; and the room erupted with more applause.

Chapter Sixty

On the morning of Monday, January 26, 2009, Paul signed the legal papers necessary to claim his inheritance from his great grandfather's estate effectively increasing his wealth a thousandfold. It was also his thirtieth birthday. After the very public ceremony of the Parade of Steeples, he wanted something more subdued for this special and rather personal occasion.

Crookston Tower, the former location of Avery Law Office, had been destroyed in the disaster, so Paul met Pop and Nan in Matthew Bailey's temporary law office; and he brought Clemente and Zack as witnesses. There was no pomp and circumstance this time; Paul and Nan simply signed a few papers; and it was over in minutes. When they exited the building, Zack asked the question Paul had been somewhat dreading.

"Dude, it's your thirtieth birthday. How do you want to celebrate?"

Paul thought about it for several minutes.

"I would like to drive down to Columbus, Georgia, where my dad is buried, and visit his grave. There's this great little barbecue shack down there out in the middle of nowhere; and I would like to take you guys there. After everything that's happened, I need a day where I'm not the head of some company, or rebuilding a city, or fighting an annoying clown, just a normal day with my two best friends and the two dogs."

Zack looked at Clemente, who nodded.

"Then let's grab Noodles and Caleb and do this."

"Zack, drive slow; I want to savor it."

Zack grinned from ear to ear.

Chapter Sixty-One

As Pastor Aaron Bishop was meeting with a couple dozen people in an empty warehouse on the east side of Nilesville and founding the Amethyst Cathedral, Paul was standing at the intersection of Fourth Street and Oak Avenue surveying the reconstruction of his city. Foundations had been laid and walls were already erected; but there was still a long way to go before this patch of earth was his home again.

"I thought I might find you here."

It was Marcy Green.

"You shouldn't be here without a helmet."

Paul turned his back to her and faced the lot where the Imperial Hotel had once stood and would very soon stand again.

"I…I would like to come back."

Paul ignored her.

"I said—"

"I heard you."

There was a long and awkward silence.

"Well?"

"Well what?"

"Can I come back?"

"Why? Why do you want to come back now, Marcy? Do you think that working at Foster Gray Holdings will get any easier when we move back into these buildings? Huh? Do you think you'll be any less of a target for Zumbini? He may not blow up the whole city or disintegrate all of my employees the next time; but he's not finished with me. In fact, he's just getting started."

"You're mad."

"You're right."

There was another long and awkward silence.

"I'm sorry; I shouldn't have come here."

Marcy Green started to walk away; but Paul stopped her.

"Wait! You can come back."

Paul turned around to face her.

"I don't want anyone to ever say that I didn't forgive someone or offer them a second, third or fourth chance, especially when it was painful for me to do so. You can come back to Foster Gray Holdings; and you can come back as if you never resigned. However, know this; you hurt me. Leaving like you did hurt me."

Marcy Green started to respond but changed her mind and slowly walked away. Paul returned to his new truck and drove back to Cricksburg.

Since the disaster and while the new building was under construction, Covenant Baptist Church had been meeting in an abandoned shopping center near the Peel. Services had already started; and there was a large crowd, when Paul snuck in and found a seat in the back near the door. The congregation was singing "Blessed Assurance," the same song they were singing when he entered the church on his first Sunday back in River City; and Paul thought how fitting that song was to his life at that moment.

EPILOGUE

In the early hours of February 2, as every person, who was awake, was watching a certain Pennsylvania groundhog make his annual prediction, Paul Gray and Father Andrews quietly entered Dougie Bishop's room at Cricksburg General. It was well before visiting hours; but this was important; this was penance for what they had done to Carlos Rivera three months ago. There was an overcast outside, which portended better weather ahead; and Paul wondered if it heralded better times ahead too.

The two men took a moment to look at the young boy; he seemed sweetly angelic lying there in his bed. Paul took Dougie's right hand in his left; Father Andrews took Dougie's left hand in his right; and then Paul and Father Andrews completed the halo around and over Dougie's bed. Paul's ring shone brightly; and when it faded, Dougie awoke. He looked around the room; and when his eyes met Paul's, there was a moment of realization.

"Listen to the gargoyle's chant, Paul. Listen to the gargoyles."

THE END

Acknowledgments and Closing Thoughts

This book is a work of Christian fantasy, so it is important for you to know that I have been a Christian since the age of five; however, I did not truly make Jesus Christ the Lord of my life until I was thirty-four. That final act of submission had a profound effect on every aspect of my life including my writing. When I dreamed of being an author, I never imagined I would be writing novels with Christian themes and symbols; and yet, this novel has much of that and in the strangest of places. Sometimes, I inserted the themes and symbols intentionally, while other occasions, their manifestation has been quite serendipitous.

Authoring is not an island occupation; it is only sustainable through a supportive network of family and friends, of which I have one of the very best. Starting with my parents, James and Anna Bee, my entire family has encouraged my literary career long before I ever started seriously pursuing it. I have been blessed to have aunts and uncles like Doris Stahl, Bertha Cooper and Charles and Peggy Bee; cousins like Van and Marilyn Bee, Richard and Porcia Bee, Carol Reed, Donna Allen, Karen and Trafton Ellis, Charlie and Jonni Bee, Ancil and Trinity Goodman, and Rex and Sandy Goodman; and extended family like Butch Cooper, Tyonne Crabtree, Tonia and Dennis Hill, Jerry and Cindy Stembridge, Carol and Jimmie Milan, Pat Hape, Vance Bee, Stephanie Bee, Tracy Bee, Tim Bee, Stacy Yandles, Susan Tallant, Jim Allen, Robin Hancock, Chris Mulzer, Candy Ellis, Chad Ellis, Craig Bee, Heather Bee-Lucke, Cassie Bee, Ashlynn Goodman, Bobby Crabtree, Craig Crabtree, Mark Hape, Maylan Bond, Ira and Phyllis Harris, Matt Harris, Luke Harris, David Fleeger, Laura and Aaron Wining, and Julie Huff, who have all provided me with a lifetime of love and understanding.

At this time, allow me to add a special note regarding my cousin, Rex

Goodman, who is a clown affiliated with the Hadi Funsters. I, in no way, based the antagonist of this novel, Claude "Zumbo the Clown" Zumbini, on my cousin, Rex. I first envisioned the character many years ago, when Rex was still a very young boy and had not yet taken up clowning. Rex is aware of this; and we often joke about it. During the writing of this book, he has even given me insights into the clown community to better develop the character for future books; but before rumors start flying, I wanted to state that none of my characters, including and especially Zumbini, are based on any real person. Any similarities are purely coincidental. Besides, Rex is a nice guy and a good clown, nothing at all like Zumbo!

Few people can say that they have even one true friend. I happen to have two. Jeff Reine has been my best friend for over thirty-five years; his unwavering support and constant encouragement has carried me through the darkest moments of my life. Ryan Maglinger, who is also this book's cover artist, is a new friend; but I feel like I have known him for years, because we mutually admire each other's talents and share a unique creative vision. Many times, Ryan has had faith in this project even when I did not. I could not ask for a better creative partner than Ryan; and I could not ask for two better friends than he and Jeff.

In addition to my regular family, I have also been blessed with a phenomenal church family. Rev. David Cullison and the entire congregation of the First South Baptist Church in Evansville, Indiana, including but certainly not limited to Kim Cullison, Reggie and Alice Haire, Christine Maglinger, Jackson and Megan Van Dyke, Hala Bachynsky, Jeff and Michelle Brasher, Jamie Cage, Dorothy Cash, Marcus and Jennifer Church, Donald Davids, Mike Devine, Reba Devine, Randall and Ruth Drake, Jim and Catherine Ellard, Jon and Cheryl Evans, Bob and Belle Green, Brenda Gruelich, Carolyn Gulick, Kathy Hammond, Charles and Nancy Hawkins, Larry and Nancy Hazelwood, Verma Dell Hensley, Bill and Aileen Hupp, Landon Maglinger, Coleman and Martha Mason, Brenda Martin, Rick and Mary Mayes, Ricky and Kelly Mayes, Drew McCall, Larry and Janis McLaughlin, Ed Miller, Charles and Sharon Riley, Kim and Keith Sallee, Beth Sumner, Ray and Catherine Sullivan, Ron and Becky Wiandt, John and Janet Worth, and Brent and Regina Zerby have showered me with emotional support and spiritual guidance, which have been beyond comparison.

Although they may have moved away, I have stayed in contact with many rmer church members like Fred and June Alcott, Mark Alcott, Todd lcott, Debbie Behme, Louise Blackburn, Dennis and Barb Cash, Jerry nd Ellen Cunningham, Bill Cusic, Joe and Allison Mayes, Linda and Dan liver, Steve and Sue Payton, Glen and Jamie Spradlin and my former astor Rev. Don Moore and his wife, Edie Moore. Distance has not faded ny relationship with any of them nor their concern for my career and me.

he Spirit convicts me to call out Dawn Oneal, who, outside my family and hurch, is my single greatest prayer warrior. I remember one very trying lay during the development of this book, when I messaged her asking ner to pray for me. I know she did, because she sent me back a touching mail prayer that I will never forget. Thank you, Dawn; I have felt your continuous prayers on my career.

i am honored to have a very talented writer-friend in D. A. Kreilein, who approached me several years ago seeking career advice. Her own literary successes with the delightful *Culverton Kids Mystery Stories* has since eclipsed my own accomplishments and motivated me to work even harder towards my literary goals. I am so proud to call her friend and wish her continued success.

I would beg each person reading this to support independent authors like Kreilein and me. Large publishers and bookstores have conspired to create an environment hostile towards our very existence; and many thanks goes to Lulu, one the wonderful organizations out there, which makes it possible for us little guys to publish and sell our work.

There were several times during the production of this novel, when I was frustrated with where the storyline was going; and my good friend, Carmen Dill would always keep my spirits lifted; she also served as a sounding board for character and plot developments, although sometimes she was not always aware of this! Thank you so much for your support and contribution, Carmen.

I would also like to pay a special tribute to two authors, who had major influences on my work. The legendary Ray Bradbury is the author, who I have most wanted to emulate since I first decided to become a writer; and John Reynolds Gardiner, author of *Stone Fox*, took time out of his busy schedule to give me valuable advice at the beginning of my literary career. During the writing of this novel, both of these literary heroes of mine passed away; they will be greatly missed.

When I published my first book ten years ago, I had not reconnected with many of my schoolmates, because for me, school did not hold many fond memories. However, with water under the bridge and maturity gained with age by all parties, I have become re-acquainted with many of them through social media. Sitting at my desk at Stringtown School, Washington School and Bosse High School, I would never have predicted that people like Dane Dennis, Wendy Johnson, Scott Foster, Raymond Akin, Rhonda Fowler, Shaun Madding, Pat Pawlowski, Barry Alder, Tim Anslinger, John Baus, Michelle Beck, John Bullock, Chris Cantwell, Walter Caswell, Shauna Cavins, Art Clark, Darla Crawford, Brian Crook, Veronica Embry, Judy Forgy, Mike France, Lori Goodloe, James Hale, Lisa Holder, Ken Howell, Thomas Keenan, Charleen King, Joanie Merson, Rob Mills, Cathy Mitchell, Lynn Mitchell, Anita Morris, Yvonne Orth, Susan Phillips, Bobby Ramsey, Anthony Rango, Orlanda Roth, Sheryl Samm, Bambi Schu, Cindy Skelton, Tim Skinner, Carmen Sutton, Andrew Thomas III, Sonja Thomas, Tina Wade, Robin Weller, Melissa Williams, Lance Willis, Andy Yarber, Kyle Ritter and Jamie Utley would become some of my dearest friends and staunchest supporters of my literary career. And, to Pat Sutton, school librarian and my favorite teacher, I owe you so much; you helped me cultivate my love of books.

I was once told that the hospitality industry was infective and that after working in a hotel, you could never completely leave. I have found that to be absolutely true; and this novel is evidence of that. My time working in hotels, a condominium, a travel agency and a bookstore has manifested itself in my story in the form of the Canterbury, the Imperial Hotel and Margins Bookstore among many others. I would like to thank all of my coworkers over the years at Belle Manor East, International Tours, Bookland, Ramada Inn, Super 8, Hampton Inn, and A. B. White & Son; you have either given me beautiful memories, which I cherish, or incredible stories, which I'll eventually adapt in future books. I would especially like to thank the following people for making those jobs so unforgettable: Jeff Grammer, Kathy Tretter, Dottie Browne, Aaron Bittner, John Jagielski, Ellen Powell, Tella Payne, Lana Murphy, Jon Hudson, Jeff Jordan, and Allan Scales.

God has also blessed my life with dear friends discovered outside the usual social institutions of family, church, school, and work. Finding wonderful

ACKNOWLEDGMENTS & CLOSING THOUGHTS

riends like Karen Dollison, Dr. Stacey Embry, Carol Grace, Kim Harper, .yn Hayden, Jennifer Holmes, Tom Morris, Thea O'Bryan, Karen Samuel, Randy Smith, Bill Springer, Timm Wallis, Dr. Christopher Woods, and Carolyn Yancey has been a real treat.

I will not apologize for the length of these acknowledgments. No other profession relies so heavily on a dedicated support network as writing does; and since I "retired" to focus my time on writing, I have gained one of the best support networks imaginable. If there is something you especially like about my writing or me, you can thank the individuals listed here on this page. In a way, this book is as much theirs as it is mine. They, along with dozens of people, who are not listed here simply because they have passed away, have left their positive and indelible marks on my life and craft in some way, even if they did not realize it. They are my greatest treasure. I will only apologize that I did not include more, equally deserving individuals in my life; and perhaps, I will rectify that oversight in future books.

Evansville, Indiana, my home for the last forty-seven years, exists merely as a passing reference in this novel. In its place, I created the much larger and more sinister River City, Wabash. Yes, if you are reading these acknowledgments before reading the story, I seceded the southern third of Indiana away from the rest of the state. I did these things not out of political spite but to create a unique and engaging yet vaguely familiar setting, where I was free from the limitations a real world location would impose on the story. I love my hometown; and as an author, I hope I represent mine honorably. Careful readers, who are familiar with Evansville, will still recognize Evansville in the descriptions of various locations, as it was and will always be my primary inspiration.

As I conclude these acknowledgments, I would like to proudly declare that I am a citizen of the greatest country on earth, the United States of America. I said it in the acknowledgments of my first book, *40 Days*; and I say it again here in the acknowledgments of my first novel: The words I write are not in ink but in the blood of those brave service personnel, who fought for my freedom. Thank you for your service.